THE BLADE OF THE COURTESANS

VERTICAL.

THE BLADE OF THE COURTESANS

KEIICHIRO RYU

TRANSLATED BY JAMES M. VARDAMAN

VERTICAL.

Published by Vertical, Inc., New York

Originally serialized in Japanese in *Shukan Shincho*, 1984-85, and published as *Yoshiwara Gomenjo* by Shinchosha, 1986, Tokyo.

ISBN 978-1-934287-01-9

Manufactured in the United States of America

First Edition

Vertical, Inc.
1185 Avenue of the Americas 32nd Floor
New York, NY 10036
www.vertical-inc.com

THE BLADE OF THE COURTESANS

Nihon Embankment

Early in the evening of the fourteenth day of the eighth month, by the old calendar, in the third year of the Meireki era (1657), Matsunaga Seiichiro stood on the top of the Nihon Embankment, along the moat at Asakusa.

As far as the eye could see, the rice plant stalks left standing after the harvest quivered gently in the faint breeze. It was an entirely rural scene, one that gave Seiichiro a sense of relief.

Having spent the previous night at an inn in Kawasaki, he had set out early in the morning and traversed the entire city of Edo with hardly a moment's rest. It was his first view of the burgeoning metropolis, and somehow he didn't think much of it.

"Is this all there is to the great city of Edo?" he wondered.

There was a great clamor, a crushing throng. Tradesmen addressed one another as if cursing, and street peddlers raised their high-pitched voices. He sensed a vague atmosphere of bloodthirstiness. There was a sharpness in the way people looked at one another. Altogether, it left him in low spirits.

"Mountain creatures," he thought to himself, "possess a lot more tranquility and grace." He really did think so.

Until he had turned twenty-six, Seiichiro had lived in the mountains of Higo, in the far-off southern island of Kyushu. There, the beasts did not violate one another's domains, but lived peacefully, proudly. Among them he had never sensed unnecessary malice nor received harsh glares.

"Why did the master will on his deathbed that I should come to such a vulgar city?" he wondered.

The master was none other than Miyamoto Musashi. Seiichiro had been abandoned as a child, and for as long as he could remember, he had been raised by Musashi in the mountains of Higo. Musashi was simultaneously master and father to him. Some twelve years prior, in the second year of the Shoho era, Musashi had departed from the present world, but on his deathbed he entrusted Seiichiro to the care of his most trustworthy disciple, a retainer of the daimyo of Higo domain named Terao Magonojo.

"Do not allow him to leave these mountains until he turns twenty-six. When he reaches that age, send him to Edo, and have him call upon Shoji Jin'emon in Yoshiwara."

Musashi passed to Terao a letter of introduction to be used on that occasion. Seiichiro was still fourteen at the time, but he still vividly recalled the affection in Musashi's face at that moment, and knew that Shoji must have been dear to him.

Toho shinan issai muyo—absolutely no need for tutelage in swordship.

Musashi had thereby enjoined Magonojo to give no further instruction to Seiichiro, and Magonojo had obeyed. Seiichiro, whose swordsmanship skills had until the age of fourteen been beaten into him under Musashi's direct tutelage, was forced to perfect those skills entirely on his own.

In Seiichiro's mind, Musashi always stood commandingly in front of him, blocking Seiichiro's way, eagle-like eyes fixed upon him. Seiichiro could strike again and again, but Musashi remained before him. The master's tenacity, his physical presence was stunning. And then last winter, Musashi's figure disappeared. Musashi's stare, which had never left him, was suddenly gone. Seiichiro had attained absolute freedom with his sword.

As if waiting for this moment to arrive, Terao Magonojo visited Seiichiro and announced that the time had arrived for him to descend from the mountains. After a half-year's instruction on the conventions of the everyday world, Seiichiro had set out on his journey to the capital.

"I wish I had never turned twenty-six," he thought to himself, then smiled wryly when it dawned on him that he sounded like a peevish child.

A sharp bird cry roused him from his thoughts.
(Sounds like a cuckoo)
He was suddenly assaulted by a sense of foreboding. Having grown up in the mountains, Seiichiro was acutely sensitive to such sensations.

It was a variety of foresight. Slowly breathing in and out, he consciously relaxed his whole body from head to toe. This was the stance with which he faced danger. In this way he set off in the direction of some houses where the occupants were beginning to light their evening lamps. Seiichiro was unaware that the wobbling, helpless step he had assumed was the *uho* gait. The same is used even today by the priests during the Mizutori ceremony at Todaiji Temple's Nigatsudo, though it originated in China as one of the forms of tonko military technique. Tonko was the Chinese equivalent of *ninjutsu*, the art of the ninja. Completely unconscious of what he was doing, Seiichiro had come to employ ninjutsu techniques.

As an aside, the figure of Yoroboshi in the Noh play is a dancing monk at Shitennoji, and it is his role at the temple to chant magical incantations. The *uho* style of walking appears as a wobbling, faltering stagger, and it is precisely this that Seiichiro's gait resembled.

Although he was entirely unaware of it, that day—the fourteenth day of the eighth month of 1657, the third year of Meireki—was an epoch-making day for Yoshiwara. It was the opening day of Shin-Yoshiwara, the new Yoshiwara pleasure quarters.

The original Yoshiwara had been opened by Shoji Jin'emon in the Fukiyacho neighborhood of Nihonbashi, later to become Horidomecho Itchome. The quarter had been in business for four decades when, on the ninth day of the tenth month of the year before, the city magistrate suddenly issued an order that the district be relocated. A choice of locations was offered: either Honjo or Asakusa Nihon Embankment. Honjo was on the other side of the Sumida River, and at the time there was not a single bridge over the river. The elders of Yoshiwara put their heads together and decided that although the Nihon Embankment location was in the middle of rice paddies, it was the wiser choice.

In response to their decision, the Kitamachi Magistrate Ishiya Shogen granted five special privileges to Yoshiwara.

I.   Instead of just the current land of the Nicho neighborhood, they would be granted both Nicho and Sancho, which would increase the total area by fifty percent.

II. For the first time in 15 years, since the prohibition had gone into effect in the 17th year of the Kan'ei era, night-time business would be permitted, in compensation for moving to a distant location. (During this 15-year period, Yoshiwara had been a place for daytime pleasures only. Samurai of the time were not permitted to leave their residences at night unless they had business of considerable importance. That such a prohibition was put into effect indicates that these samurai composed the majority of the clientele of the Yoshiwara in the early period.)

III. The more than two hundred bathhouses within the city of Edo would be put out of business. (Needless to say, these bathhouses had female attendants who worked as prostitutes. In comparison with Yoshiwara, which was bound by various codes and regulations and where prices were exorbitant, these bathhouses, where one could accomplish one's aim at less expense, were very popular and therefore had made the Yoshiwara operators highly anxious.)

IV. The new area would be exempt from fire-fighting duties during the Sanno and Kanda festivals and when fires broke out nearby within the city.

V. The sum of 10,500 *ryo* would be provided for relocation. (This amounted to some fourteen *ryo* for every *ken*, about six feet, of frontage. The dimensions used in Yoshiwara, however, were not those of Edo, but rather those of Kyoto. In accordance with the regulations of the Tokugawa shogunate, the residences of the city of Edo were built using the country measure of six *shaku* to one *ken*. But Yoshiwara had been constructed by using the larger Kyoto measurements in which six *shaku* three *sun* equaled one *ken*. It was the measure that Toyotomi Hideyoshi used in the land survey of the Bunroku era. It was singular proof that Yoshiwara had been constructed in imitation of the old capital's Shimabara pleasure quarters.)

Yoshiwara received this sum on the twenty-seventh day of the eleventh month of the second year of Meireki. Those in charge of the quarter had been promised that construction would begin the following spring, but on the eighteenth day of the first month of the third year of Meireki, a devastating fire broke out in Edo. The enormous conflagration would come to be known as the Great Meireki Fire, or as the Furisode Fire.

The flames were thought to have started after noon on the eighteenth, at Hongo Maruyama Honmyoji Temple, and the fire continued through the nineteenth until it was finally extinguished on the twentieth. The city of Edo was burnt to the ground, and estimates of the numbers who perished ranged from 35,000 to 100,000. The actual number of those who died in the inferno or froze to death was some 50,000 to 60,000. Fire and freezing may seem an odd combination, but on the twentieth after the fire was extinguished, in the dead of night a great snowfall began to accumulate, and large numbers of those who had survived the fire but had no means of warming themselves actually perished from the cold.

The writer Asai Ryoi describes the wretched spectacle in *Musashi abumi*: "It was destined that they would die, if not from the fire, then by drowning, by starving, by freezing to death. No matter what, their lives would be taken, mercilessly and without meaning."

Needless to say, Yoshiwara was completely burnt to the ground. For a short while, business resumed in temporary structures in the old quarter, but on the fifteenth and sixteenth of the sixth month all of the *yujo*, courtesans, were loaded onboard houseboats and transported to Asakusa Nihon Embankment. Borrowing several farmhouses, they carried on business while the construction was continuing. Finally in the middle of the eighth month, the construction was completed. The move was completed on the tenth day of the eighth month and a few days later, the new pleasure quarter was open for full-scale business. (With this move as a turning point, the previous quarter became known as Old Yoshiwara, and the new district as New Yoshiwara.) The very day Seiichiro reached Edo was the actual opening day of New Yoshiwara. Naturally enough, the people of the licensed quarter, the inns of Nihon Embankment and the teahouses were in high spirits as they awaited customers that first day.

No one could have taken Seiichiro, as he wavered along, as anything other than another of the distracted pleasure-seekers heading to the newly opening quarter.

"Excuse me, sir."

When he reached the midpoint of the embankment, he heard someone calling to him. In front of one of the newly completed teahouses, a man with an ingratiating smile stood rubbing his hands together. The teahouse would before long prosper as Doromachi-no-Nakashuku, a sort of intermediary area for Yoshiwara. The town's actual name was

Tamachi, but it became known as Doromachi, "mud town," because it was here that customers heading for Yoshiwara were provided with washbasins in which to wash their feet before continuing on.

Sidling up to him and speaking in an overly familiar tone, the man said to Seiichiro, "Hey now, I understand how impatient you must be, but if you go in with feet looking like that, you know, the *oiran*, you know, they'll just…"

The man theatrically turned his head aside.

Seiichiro understood less than half of what the man was chattering on about. What did he mean by being impatient? What was an *oiran* anyway? All he understood was that his feet were covered with mud, and without doubt it would be far too discourteous to go as he was to meet anyone for the first time.

"Thank you. I'll go wash my feet." Giving a slight bow, Seiichiro started down the embankment to the Sanya moat.

"Hey, wait!" the man stammered in confusion. "Come to our shop! Please come there to have your feet washed, and your hair, too! You don't want to go looking like that now, do you? Put on a bit of fragrant oil and you'll get a nice warm reception from the *oiran*."

"What do you mean by '*oiran*'?"

"Huh?"

As if absolutely astounded, the man responded shrilly, but he quickly regained his composure and laughed.

"Ha, ha, ha! You're a real tease, aren't you?"

"Really, what is an *oiran*?"

Seiichiro asked with a straight face.

"You…you're headed for the *cho*?"

"What's the *cho*?"

"Come on now, you're not being funny at all."

The man shook his head in disapproval.

"The *cho* is the *cho*. Yoshiwara Go-*cho*."

"I see. If that is what it is, then it's true I'm headed that way."

"You're going to the *cho* but you don't know what an *oiran* is?"

The man seemed to think he was being made fun of, and he looked miffed.

"I'm not going to meet someone called *Oiran*. I simply have business with a man named Shoji Jin'emon."

Suddenly the atmosphere chilled. From within the body of the odd fellow radiated a tremendous unexpected murderous air. With a slight averting of his eyes, Seiichiro dodged it. And in a split second, the bloodthirst disappeared. It happened in such a flash that someone other than Seiichiro would hardly have sensed the change at all.

"If it's Master Shoji's shop, you'll find it on the corner of Edocho Itchome. The shop's name is Nishidaya."

The man offered his directions with utmost politeness.

MISESUGAGAKI

As he washed his face and feet in the cool water of the Sanya moat and slapped the dust of the road off his clothing, Seiichiro was perplexed. He had felt menace aimed at him from all directions. It was not the free-floating malice that he had felt in the regular neighborhoods of Edo. It was a piercing sort of bloodthirst, aimed at a specific target. That target was himself. But he had no recollection that might tell him why.

"What have I done?" he asked himself.

All he had said was that he was headed for Yoshiwara Gochomachi and that he had come to see Shoji Jin'emon. Only those two things. Could it be that the name Shoji Jin'emon could arouse great malice? Did a large number of men bear bitter feelings toward Jin'emon? He could hardly believe it. He recalled that the man who had given him directions to Nishidaya had suddenly begun to speak so politely as to be almost humble.

(I don't understand.)

Shaking his head, Seiichiro progressed along the embankment, still sensing upon his back the menace and gazes of large numbers of people. He continued as before, walking with the *yoroboshi* gait.

From behind him, there approached a clatter of hoofbeats. A beautiful white horse, taking the bit firmly in his mouth, was overtaking Seiichiro. Riding the steed was a large-nosed *bushi* in the prime of life. Whether he was a *hatamoto* of some rank, or a samurai in charge of the Edo residence of a major daimyo in his lord's absence, he made a splendid appearance.

Whoosh!

On horseback, as he closed in on Seiichiro, the man drew his sword. There was no malice involved. It was a rough prank but a prank nevertheless. Seiichiro didn't so much as bat an eye.

Having undergone direct instruction from Musashi on "The Art of Seeing," Seiichiro knew that the tip of the sword would just barely miss its target. Letting out a loud, boisterous laugh, the samurai descended the broad sloping and curving road known as the Fifty-Ken Road. The first of the downward slopes was called Emonzaka and at the top of the slope, on the right, on a stone foundation, was a roofed board for the display of official notices. To the left, on the opposite side of the road, grew a willow tree known as *mikaeri yanagi*, so called because those who departed the quarter after a night of pleasure stood at the willow and "gazed back reluctantly."

As Seiichiro descended Emonzaka, he saw, at a distance and for the first time, the Yoshiwara quarter. It was just the time of day when lamps are first lit. In contrast to the darkness along the embankment, the brightness was dazzling. Seiichiro had come to a complete halt. In his entire life, he had never beheld such a scintillating vision at nighttime.

(What is this?!)

He was at a complete loss, but more than that, he was disoriented. Gradually his confusion turned to astonishment.

"Now this, this is the capital!"

Seiichiro was unable to move. Gazing upon the flood of lights, he stood motionless.

Abruptly the sound of shamisen rose up. It was not just one or two instruments, but easily more than a hundred, all joining in producing the same timbre. It was mixed with a song, but he did not recognize the words.

And yet...

"Ah!!"

Seiichiro heaved a sigh. He was in turmoil inside, unable to do a single thing. His heart was flustered. In the mountains of Higo in early spring, he had experienced the same sort of inexplicable pounding of the heart any number of times. It was as if his body and soul were somehow floating interminably through thin air. Before he realized it, his cheeks were wet.

"Why these tears?" he wondered.

Beneath the utterly light and heart-lifting tones of the shamisen, there was an undercurrent of utter sadness. That was what brought the tears to Seiichiro's eyes.

"What have I been doing with my life, all these years?"

The shamisen were performing *Misesugagaki* to proclaim the raising of the curtain on Yoshiwara's night world. "Suga" derived from "suutai" meaning Noh passages sung without accompaniment, and kaki referred originally to the strumming of the biwa, but later the term "sugagaki" came to mean any music performed on a stringed instrument without vocal accompaniment. At dusk, when the *yujo* had finished preparing themselves for the evening, someone in each shop would clap hands together before the small Shinto altar, and strike the bell on the altar over the lintel of the entrance. After this, the young apprentices would bring their shamisen, line up before the shrine and begin to play. To this music, the *yujo* would come down from the second floor and line up at the showing area, a latticed veranda towards the street. This was *harimise*, "the showing," when the women lined up to await customers. In later years when geisha performers came into existence at Yoshiwara, they themselves played the *sugagaki*. Until the close of the evening's business at twelve midnight, the unaccompanied music would continue without pause.

This *Misesugagaki* would dramatically change the life of Matsunaga Seiichiro.

Immediately to the right after passing through the enormous black-lacquered *Omon*, the Great Gate, whose tiled roof resembled some daimyo's grand residence, was Nishidaya.

Seiichiro was kept waiting for some time. Presently a fortyish looking heavy-set man appeared and announced with considerable regret, "Shoji Jin'emon passed away in the first year of Shoho (1644). The one who stands before you is his son, Jinnojo." The first year of the Shoho era was thirteen years ago. That was the year before his master Miyamoto Musashi had died.

NAKANOCHO

"Regrettably, the women of the shop have already taken their baths, and it would be most improper of me to have an honorable up-and-coming samurai like yourself follow them in the bath. Please allow me therefore to introduce you to a *yuya*, a bathhouse."

Jinnojo, second-generation master of Nishidaya, rose nimbly, apparently to guide Seiichiro to the bathhouse himself.

Seiichiro had been stunned to discover that the anticipated Jin'emon had been dead for thirteen years. Jinnojo had said gently that for the sake of his deceased father, Seiichiro was cordially welcome to stay there for as many months or years as he liked. And after that, Jinnojo's first words were about the bath.

Seiichiro declined being guided to the bathhouse and instead merely asked for directions then left the Nishidaya.

How kindhearted, he thought. Here anything and everything was different from the city of Edo itself. Everything here was bright, gentle and filled with grace, like some entirely different capital.

The shamisen continued playing *Misesugagaki*. Buoyed by its timbre, the enormous crowds of men passed along the road at a leisurely pace.

Nakanocho was the road that ran straight from the Great Gate all the way to Suidojiri. It was the main street of the new Yoshiwara. On both sides of the street were pleasure houses fronted with lattice-work behind which sat the resplendently attired *yujo*, whispering and laughing through the lattice with the men outside. The men themselves were almost all stylishly dressed. The samurai invariably wore broad woven hats that covered both head and face, to conceal their identity. Among the townsmen were some who wrapped a cloth over their head and tied it under the chin in order to achieve a similar anonymity. Almost all of the men hummed a tune, restlessly opening and closing a fan and looking upon the women with eyes ablaze.

"So, we meet again."

From the boisterous crowd, someone spoke to him unexpectedly. It was the large-nosed samurai who had a while ago suddenly drawn his sword and thrust at Seiichiro back along the embankment. With him were four or five companions, all samurai, but not one was wearing the concealing woven hat. Each appeared equally ferocious and they all came to a complete halt, glaring at Seiichiro.

With a smile on his face, Seiichiro nodded a greeting. The passing sword-thrust had been rather rough usage, but the robust laughter that followed indicated a sense of mischief. Moreover, Seiichiro found the man's easygoing manner to his liking.

"What is this man?" said a man with a broad forehead like a crab, who stood next to the nose man.

The Nose replied, "Back there on the embankment I feigned a swipe at this guy and he didn't so much as blink an eye. He seems to me a man of ability beyond his years." The Nose apparently found Seiichiro to his liking as well.

"So what?" replied the Crab. Letting out a yell, he pulled his sword and in the same gesture struck at Seiichiro. This attack was different from that of the Nose. In terms of timing and bloodthirst, it was sufficient to be lethal.

Turning slightly, Seiichiro evaded the strike. This was the *gobu-no-mikiri*, a one-half evasion. Through strict training Seiichiro had mastered even the one-tenth evasion, that is, the ability to evade a blow by the absolute minimal space. If one mastered *mikiri*, then it was unnecessary to make the slightest excess movement, and one could move that much more effectively. Had Seiichiro moved, the Crab would be dead. But Seiichiro simply evaded the strikes and made no other movement. He could not feel like drawing his sword over a matter so foolish.

"Fight! Fight!"

At the sudden outcry, the men in the street gathered round. It appeared that the residents of Edo loved to fight and were also used to the role of spectator. They gathered in a half circle around Seiichiro and the Crab, leaving sufficient room for the two men to move about. It was like a ring for sumo wrestlers.

Seiichiro's expression had tightened. That was because he sensed bloodthirst again, aimed at him from all directions. This was what he had sensed along Doromachi earlier. It was troublesome. If he happened to show any opening, some sort of weapon might suddenly come hurtling toward him.

(Why am I having to deal with this?)

In total bewilderment, Seiichiro grew disheartened. Crab, perhaps conscious of the spectators who had gathered, took a showy *hasso-no-kamae* stance. From there he unleashed a downward strike aiming from the shoulder with appalling speed.

At that moment, Seiichiro vanished.

"Ugh!" groaned Crab.

"Behind you, Kai!" yelled the Nose.

Whirling around, Crab stared in wonder. Diagonally to his left, in the shadow of a paper-covered lamp, stood Seiichiro. It was the only place where there were no spectators, and it was also a place from which he could use the light of the lantern to his own advantage. Standing beside the lantern, he placed himself in the shadows while the light shone entirely on his opponent. It was a unique *fuhai-no-chi*, an invincible position.

"You! What did you do? My sword suddenly became heavy!"

Seiichiro became aware that Crab was no ordinary swordsman. In fact, after Crab had struck downward, Seiichiro had ridden the back of the sword on the upswing as Crab raised it over his head again, leaping high over Crab's head. Having heard from Musashi that there was such a move in the Kuramahachi-ryu school of swordsmanship, he had trained secretly, going through a steady toughening regimen in order to master it.

"He jumped on the back of your sword and rode it!" said the Nose. Crab widened his eyes in a glare.

"So, Kai! Are you going to risk your life on this fight?"

"Hah! You must be kidding! Why would I die before my 'battle' with the beautiful Komurasaki?"

And with a resounding laugh he sheathed his sword until it clicked. But there was sweat glistening on his enormous forehead.

The Nose laughed.

"It takes real swordsmanship to bring out a sweat in Kagazume Kai. What's your name? I'm Mizuno Jurozaemon, and all of this bunch are members of the Jingi-gumi."

A hatamoto—direct vassal of the shogun—with an annual stipend of 3,000 *koku* of rice, Mizuno Jurozaemon was the leader of the Jingi-gumi, a band of ruffian samurai known for making trouble in the streets of Edo. Kagazume Kai was one of his subordinates.

Who is it that passes in the dead of night
Could it be Kagazume Kai or some thief
Or then again, could it be Sakabe no Sanju

Kagazume was notorious enough an outlaw to be included in such a satirical poem, but Seiichiro had no way of knowing that.

"I am Matsunaga Seiichiro."

"What school of swordsmanship?"

"Niten'ichi-ryu."

"Aah, so you're a disciple of Miyamoto Musashi?"

"Yes."

Abruptly an enormous emanation of malice that had poured upon him came to complete halt. The change was instantaneous. In its place, Seiichiro felt himself enveloped in a curious warmth.

(What is going on here?)

Inadvertently Seiichiro tilted his head slightly to one side.

"You must have had a long trip."

A voice spoke to Seiichiro from the darkness of the narrow opening that led to the bath. The lighting was poor due to the boarding that hung down from the ceiling and on top of that, the air was thick with steam. One had to have stupendous powers of perception to perceive in that environment that someone had had a long journey. Seiichiro peered through the steam to see who had spoken. Thanks to having grown up in the mountains, Seiichiro could see even at night, so he quickly perceived the figure of the man who had spoken to him. He was startled. The voice belonged to an old man somewhat past sixty. On the top of his gray head rested a small topknot. The man rose up, moved forward right in front of Seiichiro and squatted back down.

The public bathhouses of the day were steam baths. It would probably be more precise to say that they were semi-steam baths. Originally the *furoya* baths were entirely different. The *furoya* were steam baths and at the *yuya* bathhouses one lowered oneself into a tub of hot water. The latter were the precursors of the present-day public bathhouses. Due both to the unique construction of the pure steam bath and to the fact that the steam escaped easily, *furoya* had the shortcoming of not allowing a large number of bathers. Commercially it simply was not profitable. It was altogether natural that the *yuya* bathhouses grew more numerous than the *furoya*. Nevertheless, the *yuya* sought to claim the advantages of the steam baths by introducing half-steam baths. These half-steam combinations made use of planking to trap steam, either in the form of a closeted bath or a "pomegranate" bath. The closeted bath, as one might surmise, was enclosed like a closet with a door, which one closed upon entering the tub itself. The "pomegranate" bath was enclosed with boarding that descended from the ceiling. There was a narrow opening between the bottom of the paneling and the floor, so one had to stoop in order to duck under it. According to one theory, *kagami-iru*, to duck in, was homonymous with *kagami-iru*, to polish a mirror, and since pomegranate vinegar was used to polish mirrors, these steam-bath entrances were called pomegranate baths. In any case, a minimum of hot water was used in the tub and the steam it generated would induce perspiration. In those days, it was the custom to bathe wearing a loincloth.

The old man was unusual-looking in that his face was exceedingly broad. His eyes, nose and mouth were all large and seemed almost arbitrarily attached to his face. Judging from his face alone, he appeared to be a giant of a man, but in actuality he was just over five feet tall. He was short, but his physique was impressive. His muscles were like steel plates fastened to his frame, and he carried not a single scrap of fat anywhere. From his build, one would assume that when he was young he must have undergone rigorous training.

"I came from Higo," Seiichiro answered simply.

"Higo, huh? Once knew a guy named Miyamoto Musashi from Higo. A real filthy character. Didn't bathe even once a month."

The old man laughed to himself. When it resounded off the ceiling, his voice seemed strangely loud.

"Did you know my master, Miyamoto Musashi?"

Seiichiro found himself growing somewhat cautious.

"Indeed I did."

The old man wiped the sweat from his face in one swipe.

"It must have been the fifteenth year of Kanei (1638). Master Musashi was setting out to join the fray at the Battle of Shimabara, and he left from Yoshiwara. Of course that wasn't the present Yoshiwara but the old one."

"Musashi? From Yoshiwara?"

At first, Seiichiro found it hard to believe.

"Over in the house run by Kawai Gon'emon in Shinmachi there used to be a woman named Kumonoi. Musashi had been a patron and frequent visitor of hers. When he went off to fight, he wore a battle surcoat lined with part of her white-spotted red kimono. He walked through a crowd of courtesans who came to see him off as far as the Great Gate, and after saying a word of farewell to those who had gathered, he leaped on his horse, whipped his mount once and rushed off. It was a glorious departure, just like a picture."

As he was speaking, the old man became filled with deep emotion. That emotion filled Seiichiro with a potent nostalgia.

(So that's why! That's why the master sent me here. He wanted me to experience what he himself had experienced.)

Seiichiro felt Musashi's affection for him.

But Seiichiro was mistaken. Musashi's reason for having Seiichiro sent all the way to Yoshiwara was concealed in a far deeper, far more dreadful secret. It was a secret of which at the moment Seiichiro was still unaware.

The old man said that his name was Gensai. He laughed as he said, rather as if presenting a riddle, that the characters of his name meant that he was an old man like a phantom in broad daylight.

Old man Gensai was terribly kind. When they rose to go to the washing area, without so much as asking permission, Gensai caused Seiichiro some consternation by insisting on washing Seiichiro's hair for him. As he washed, the old man—apparently inquisitive by nature— asked one question after another about Seiichiro's long journey.

Did he visit the Shinmachi pleasure quarters when he was in Osaka? Did he go to the Shimabara quarters when he passed through Kyoto? When Seiichiro responded negatively, the old man heaved a sigh.

"Do you mean to say you went through Kyoto and didn't even enjoy the company of a *kottaisan*?"

"A *kottaisan*? What's that?"

Gensai heaved another sigh.

"Here in this part of the country we call them *oiran*."

There was that word again: *oiran*. When Seiichiro asked exactly what an *oiran* was, the old man was indignant.

"An *oiran* is a top-notch courtesan. *Oira no neisan*, my older sister, is what it means. In Yoshiwara the *tayu* and the *koshi* have child-attendants called *kamuro*. Those *kamuro* used to refer to the older courtesans as *oiran*, so now, it's become the general name for them all."

"So what are the *kottaisan*?"

"That's just a shortened form of the name for the *tayu* here."

Seiichiro suddenly recalled the exchange that he had had with the man at Doromachi in front of Nakashuku. Realizing how foolish he must have appeared, even he had to laugh at himself.

"Could it possibly be that you've never slept with a woman?"

Seiichiro turned red.

"Up there in the mountains, I was all alone."

"I see. All by yourself, eh?" Gensai had become deeply serious. "So Master Musashi was that pitiless."

"That's not true."

Seiichiro unconsciously became argumentative.

"There was so much to do. Even if there had been people around, there would have been no time to pay them any attention. Besides, wolves, bears and foxes came to visit so often, they practically gave us no peace."

Gensai finished washing Seiichiro's hair and tied it in a bundle at the back.

"So, you're going to be here a while?"

"I hope to."

"In that case, I'll show you around. Yoshiwara is a difficult district. You could walk around here for ten years by yourself, and you still wouldn't figure it out. Go around with me, and you'll have it figured out in three months. Whatever it takes, I'll teach you all about it."

Gensai seemed inexplicably determined.

On his skin, fresh from the bath, the early autumn breeze was refreshing.

Led by old man Gensai, Seiichiro came to a place right at the entrance to the Great Gate. Sitting on a row of low narrow felt-covered benches were several *yujo* smoking tobacco in long slender pipes. Gensai plopped himself down and motioned for Seiichiro to do the same.

"This is *machiai-no-tsuji*," he explained, "the place where women wait for their regular customers. It's the best place of all to have a look at Yoshiwara."

It seemed just as Gensai said. From here, you could observe those who passed through the great gate, the *tayu* walking along Nakanocho, the *ageya* with their bamboo screens through which were partially visible the banquets going on inside—all of this visible with one sweep of the eyes.

"Do you see? This…is paradise. I'm not talking about paradise for men. It's paradise for women, for these *yujo*."

Gensai's words exuded a definite gravity.

"What does that mean?"

"By and by, you'll understand."

With that, Gensai clammed up.

The sound of *Misesugagaki* continued. Once again Seiichiro felt as if he were drifting buoyantly in the air.

(Paradise? Not for men, but for women did he say?)

As Seiichiro was vacantly immersing himself in such thoughts, Gensai abruptly rose to his feet. "Now then, shall we go look at hell?"

SUIDOJIRI

At the entrance to an alley was a door and next to it dangled an elongated red paper lantern. On it was painted the oddly long drawn-out character *tsubone*—chambers.

The *tsubone-mise* was also called an *ichimei-kirimise*.

"It's called *kirimise* or 'one slice' because in about ten minutes you can tend to your business."

The alley had been covered with wood flooring, which creaked under their feet. The meandering walkway was so narrow that the two could not walk side by side. On the left, the Ohaguro ditch side, were rowhouses, each of which were divided into several dozen small rooms, each containing a single woman. Women calling out to customers while seated before a folded futon with two pillows on top. Women standing in the doorway clutching a customer's arm or waist and dragging him inside. In all cases, the woman was invariably of mature years and heavily made up. For a moment, Seiichiro almost choked on the heavy odor of cosmetics that hung in the air.

These *kirimise* were also known as *hyakumongashi* and *teppo-mise*. The former term referred to the low 50 or 100 *mon* that was the price for a ten-minute dalliance. The latter referred to the chance of being "poisoned" with the same probability as being poisoned from eating blowfish. The frontage of each of these small rooms was about six feet, half of which was a sliding wooden door and half of which was wainscot. On the post by each door was a small square paper lantern with the name of the house written on it. The woman's room was two mats in size, and in the back was a similar room, often for the mistress of the house. "Extension please," would call out the women at the right moment, so that a customer never got away with just the initial 50 to 100 *mon*. Of the east-west riverfront houses, the eastern side was dreadful enough to earn the name Rashomon Riverfront. Needless to say, the name came from the folktale about a demon who was said to grab hold of a human's arm and never let go.

Gensai laughed.

"These shops, now, are where women who have finished their terms of service in the smaller shops fall, if fate says that they still have to earn money. For their parents, a man, or loans that have to be paid back. There are all kinds of reasons. But when all is said and done, every one here knows all about the hardships of a woman's life."

When the women looked at Gensai, they uniformly showed a sense of awe and refrained from talking. Perhaps because he was viewed as a companion of Gensai, no hands reached out to tug at Seiichiro.

"How old do you think that one is?"

The woman sat inside her doorway, twisted seductively at the waist, puffing on a long narrow *kiseru*. Plump and almost translucently white, her skin was firm. Perhaps because she had been drinking, her skin was flushed pink.

"I don't know."

"Come on, take a guess." Gensai was smiling.

Seiichiro summoned up his courage. "Thirty, maybe not even that."

"Hey, Oren!" Gensai called to the plump woman. He spoke amiably, as if he were talking to a member of his family. "Just how old are you now?"

"You're awful to ask that!" The woman twisted her body in embarrassment. "Absolutely wicked."

"Come on, I want this young man to know, for his own edification.

I'm not asking in order to be mean."

Seiichiro was startled by the gentleness of Gensai's tone. There was a softness in his voice, like a feather gently stroking the skin. The woman's eyes turned unbelievably sensual and faintly misty.

"I've turned 52."

"What? Fifty-two?"

Gensai's teasing tone turned even more gentle.

"Actually, I'm fifty-three. My, how embarrassing."

Seiichiro was stunned. Here was a fifty-three-year-old woman contorting her body like a young girl, covering her face coyly with the sleeve of her kimono.

"That's terrible of you. I grew moist, just at the sound of your voice."

The reproachful look she gave Gensai was distracted now and a more tearful expression came to her face.

"Forgive me." Gensai put the palms of his hands together and bowed to her, then walked on, as she placed a hand on her breast as if to still her fluttering heart.

"I can't believe it," Seiichiro said dejectedly.

"That's an apparition. In this hell, she's unusual because she's not in business for the money. She just loves men. She can't help it. The truth is, the more men she has, the more of a sheen she gets and the whiter she becomes. Men are her only medicine for rejuvenation."

Gensai's tone was changing. There was fatigue in it now, a sense of pain.

"It's said of course that it's women who eat men alive, but…."

Seiichiro felt a chill run down his spine. He felt in Gensai's voice something that could be called truth.

(That's nonsense!)

On the one hand, one wanted to call it utter foolishness, but on the other hand he couldn't shake off the feeling that he had caught a glimpse of the sordid relationship existing between the sexes.

"Want to go for a drink?"

Gensai's tone had returned to its original carefree brightness.

Perhaps four hours later, they settled in the second floor of a shop in a back alley of Kyomachi which displayed a lantern with the characters for sake, side dishes and rice served in tea.

Seiichiro had been trained in the imbibing of sake by Musashi from the age of ten. It was perhaps rather a rough method of child-rearing, but as a result, Seiichiro had learned to drink sake as if it were water. Regardless of how much he drank, he might brighten up but never got drunk. Sake had no impact on either his reflexes or his movements.

But Seiichiro found drinking with Gensai disconcerting. More than anything else, the problem was the unpleasantness of the place, a *kirimise* woman's room. In the odd-smelling room facing the alley and separated from it by wooden planking on a pounded dirt floor, they sat filling each other's cups over and over. The woman talked on about her parents and family, her distant relatives, her former lovers and even companions who had gotten married. Rather naturally, Seiichiro had not a single clue about anything she said. From moment to moment the woman would laugh and then suddenly break wholeheartedly into tears. Surprisingly, at the latter moments, Gensai would also break into tears.

Moreover, Gensai did the same in shop after shop. It appeared that all the women knew Gensai quite well. It seemed as if he were the master of the *kirimise*. The women, for their part, were opening their hearts to the old man with absolutely no compunction and telling him everything. For the most part, those confessions ended in "weeping."

Gensai was brought to tears so often that Seiichiro began to wonder whether the old man needed women's tears as a relish for his sake. But Seiichiro eventually realized that after giving vent to their tears, when they saw Gensai and Seiichiro to the door, each and every one of the women seemed refreshed and more cheerful, as if they had been relieved of some inner bitterness.

Finally Seiichiro began to conclude that the old man was a genius when it came to handling women.

Every single one of the women suffered the hardships particular to women, and their characters had perhaps been warped by those hardships. Yet they became docile as young girls in Gensai's hands. In admiration, Seiichiro stood by and watched how each began by talking about the hardheartedness of her husband, the meanness of the proprietress or the miserable food that was provided and ended up inevitably with sighs and tears over how unfortunate they were. Yet through this commonplace recitation of tribulations, gradually the malice and consuming hatred vanished into thin air and an entirely different, good woman made an appearance.

Gensai had told Seiichiro how good a hot one-pot meal could be, even in the heat of summer. As they sat enjoying the lightly flavored melt-in-your-mouth white fish on the second floor of a cheap restaurant, Seiichiro asked, "Could that be hell? It seemed to me that everyone was pretty much enjoying life after all."

"That's true of course," Gensai nodded, tasting the sake in his cup. "Women are easygoing. In Gocho, it's only in the *kirimise* that the women get paid directly. They get to keep between a tenth and three-tenths of what they take in. And their term of service is short, usually just three to five years." ·

"In that case, why is it hell?"

"It's hell from the men's point of view. The men who are playing around cheaply in such places—they're truly in hell," asserted Gensai.

"And yet, they don't have a clue that they are in hell. That's what makes it worse."

"I don't get it," Seiichiro sighed.

"Of course you don't! How could anyone understand that so easily?" Perhaps it was the sake, but Gensai's manner of speaking was growing spirited.

"The more deeply you go into the ways of men and women, the more difficult it gets. Even with our thousand years of tradition, it's not at all easy." He shook his head.

"Thousand years of tradition?"

Gensai raised his head deliberately.

"Did I say that?"

"Yes, you did."

"What an impossible old man I am."

He grabbed his own lips and gave them a twist as if to reprove them.

"Some day I'll tell you about that, too."

He said it cheerfully, almost singing the words.

All of a sudden, the *Misesugagaki* came to an end.

Bells were ringing.

"That's Sensoji's bell."

"It's midnight."

Seiichiro had counted the strokes of the bell.

"No, it's only ten o'clock."

"How could that be?"

Seiichiro took offense. Could Gensai be thinking that because Seiichiro was from the countryside he was unable to count?

"Listen. That's the night watchman beating his wooden clappers."

Sure enough, the wooden clappers, announcing the time, were passing around the quarter. Seiichiro counted. Clap-clap, clap-clap. Didn't he hear the four claps that announced ten o'clock?

Suddenly Gensai laughed.

"In Gocho, that's called *hike-yottsu!*"

"What's that?"

"According to the regulations in the quarter, the women can serve customers just until ten o'clock. But if they actually quit at ten, they wouldn't be able to stay in business."

Gradually Seiichiro began to understand.

"So, when they hear the bell for midnight, the watchman makes his rounds clapping the announcement for ten o'clock. And then, shortly afterward, he makes the announcement for midnight. See?"

It was true. The clappers had changed their rhythm. Now they were letting people know that it was midnight.

"Before, it was *hike-yotsu*, and now it's *kane-yotsu,* or *obike.*"

"Hmm."

"As they say, in Yoshiwara even the wooden clappers announcing the time of day don't tell the truth."

Seiichiro began to laugh despite himself.

But in the very next second—"…!"

Seiichiro put down his chopsticks and grabbed his sword. He had heard a faint scream. He immediately knew it as the shriek let out by someone who has just been cut down and is on the verge of death.

"What's wrong?" Gensai again filled the cup with sake.

"Excuse me."

Seiichiro opened the window and looked in the direction of the scream. He couldn't see who had been cut down, but he could see two or three dark shadows running along the rooftops of the shops along Kyomachi Itchome.

"I'm going to have a look."

Taking his leave, Seiichiro in his leather split-toed socks went out the window onto the roof. He ran. When he reached the edge of the roof he leaped to the next. He made no more sound than a cat would as he crossed the roof.

Gensai watched his graceful figure from the window.

"Ah, to be young." His tone was filled with admiration. The master of the shop came up behind him.

"The Yagyu?"

"It has to be. Better tell Sannojo."

Without a word, the master of the shop nodded and ran down the stairs.

Gensai slowly climbed out of the window down onto the roof.

"Who are you?" Seiichiro's voice echoed around the Suidojiri neighborhood.

Gensai chuckled.

Suidojiri was the southernmost part of Nakanocho, the dead end opposite from the Great Gate. There were several ways to write the name of the place, but whatever the characters, the name was read Suidojiri. There were various theories about the name, but the one recorded in *Jisekigoko* is apparently the accurate one. It says that Suidojiri was constructed to enclose the area of Yoshiwara and drain the so-called Ohaguro ditch.

Seiichiro was standing at Suidojiri with his back to the Akihasan Jotomyo lantern. About a dozen men dressed entirely in black stood before him like black shadows. At their feet lay sprawled the body of a young man. It appeared he had been cut down when he came to bring oil for the lamp. The death cry Seiichiro had heard a moment earlier had come from the young man.

The Nakanocho boulevard was already entirely devoid of other people. All one could see was the dim light from the street lanterns. Fog suddenly enveloped everything.

One of the shadows spoke curtly. "Interference not advised." He appeared to be the leader of the group.

"A person has been cut down. I can't help but get involved."

Seiichiro replied with composure. He had already adopted the *yoroboshi* position of readiness, and his attitude appeared to draw the disdain of the shadowy figures.

"Troublemaker!" At the exact moment the leader spoke, two shadows, one from the left and one from the right, simultaneously unleashed a furious attack. The terrific speed made it obvious just how formidable they were.

The usual evasion would be to drop back or leap forward, but Seiichiro slipped under the sword coming from the right and drew right up to that shadow. In that instant, the short sword in his right hand stabbed the opponent's chest, and the long sword in his left hand cleaved the other attacker straight in two, from top to bottom. For Seiichiro, the movement was absolutely natural, a virtually unconscious wielding of the sword. But to the shadows, such swordsmanship seemed alarming. They were left absolutely dumbfounded. Without a sound, they formed a half-circle around him. He stood rocking back and forth slightly. Both of his swords hung loosely downward, pointed at the ground. *Click!* He switched swords left and right. It was a come-on.

Sha! Three more attacked all at once. It was no ordinary method of attack. Two attackers were one thing, but with three there was a high probability that at least one of the three would be cut by one of his own allies. They were obviously aware of how dangerous such a strategy was; they intended to cut down their opponent even if it meant sacrificing one of their own members. It was a sure-fire method of attack. But Seiichiro wasn't to be seen. He had somersaulted, and as he rotated, with his long sword he had struck the legs of the two from the left and the right. Springing back to his feet, he stabbed the third opponent, standing right in front of him, with his short sword. In a single breath, he had dispatched all three. His breathing was not the least irregular. As before, he resumed the *yoroboshi* stance, his back to the offertory lamp.

"Clear out!" ordered the leader. In a flash, he had lost half of his subordinates.

The remaining shadows ran to the west riverfront. They slipped between a gap in the shops. To Seiichiro, it seemed there should have been a black wooden fence there, facing Ohaguro ditch, but...

"Oh!"

The fence seemed to collapse outward. It wasn't a fence at all. It was a drawbridge, crossing over Ohaguro ditch. Beyond were the so-called Yoshiwara rice fields. But the shadows suddenly seemed to fling themselves backwards. As Seiichiro came up, he saw that they each had a short arrow in his chest. Out in the rice fields lurked a considerable number of archers. Two of the shadows were still alive and they came back to launch a desperate attack on Seiichiro. In no time, they were struck by arrows from behind and collapsed. There was not a single survivor. To Seiichiro it all seemed so merciless.

(What futile deaths)

Without knowing why, he was angered. There might be someone alive among those he had cut down, he thought, so he headed back to Suidojiri.

(What?)

Back at Suidojiri, however, there was no one to be seen. Nor were there any dead or wounded—everyone had completely vanished. He looked closely at the ground...and there was not a single drop of blood.

Suddenly he turned and ran back toward the west riverfront.

(Just as I expected!)

Here, too, the dead had disappeared. Not only that, the drawbridge had been raised, and the black wooden fence had returned to its original place. Only a stray dog sniffed around at the ground.

Seiichiro stood stupefied. The brilliant moonlight transformed the surroundings into a world of pale blue.

MACHIAI-NO-TSUJI

Early afternoon in the quarter weighs down with a peculiar listlessness. The sunlight of early autumn tends to stagnate there, and one has the illusion that the people who come and go, the stray dogs and cats, everything, ceases movement. Everything possesses a transparent brilliance and everything wavers in indolence.

Seated on the bench at *machiai-no-tsuji* near the Great Gate, Matsunaga Seiichiro immersed himself in that languor. He enjoyed such laziness. On a rocky ledge in the mountains of Higo, he had frequently spent half a day just like this. Thoughts would come to mind and then just as easily drift away, come and then drift away. In the end, the thoughts would merge with nature and sentiment, and his mind would drift unfettered interminably...an indescribable pleasure.

Nakanocho was lined not just with pleasure houses and teahouses but many other kinds of shops, selling straw mats, rice and wheat bran. At the corner of Edocho Nichome were the vegetable shops, and the shops selling side dishes for sake were clustered at the corner of Sumicho. The errand runners and child attendants of the *oiran* came out of the confectionery shops carrying things in bowls back to the houses. Water drawers shouldered poles on which they balanced water pails, carrying their loads in a rhythmical gait through the Great Gate. It was said that they hauled the water all the way from a well in the precincts of Asakusa Kannon. There were also hawkers selling fan paper and lamp wicks.

What was different from the mountains of Higo was that these people all moved about in different ways, so he never grew tired of watching them. Seiichiro leaned forward, cupping his chin in his palms, intently observing the spectacle.

(How sad human beings are)

The feeling suddenly came home to him. There was no cause for the thought. He simply felt it deep down inside. Was it not precisely because they were such pathetic living creatures that they were engrossed in the absolutely useless pursuit of pleasure? Wasn't it because it served no purpose at all that this place for amusement could be made so resplendent and spectacular? Was this not the reason that the nighttime in Yoshiwara Gochomachi was so colorful and bright, and so elegant? Seiichiro felt his heart fill to overflowing with an indescribable melancholy.

Two days had passed since he had arrived in Yoshiwara. He had spent the first day steeped in a dizzy succession of feelings. For the very first time in his life, he had seen the capital known as Edo. He had heard *Misesugagaki* for the first time. He had seen Yoshiwara's heaven and hell for the first time.

And for the first time, he had taken someone's life.

The feeling of sorrow that now filled his heart was not unrelated to his having killed someone.

He felt no regret. Would it not be inconsistent to learn the art of the sword in order to cut someone down and then to feel remorse for having actually done so? The single act of gripping the handle of a sword had to be thought of as dedicated to cutting that enemy down. Musashi had taught him that. One could even say that the hallmark of Musashi's teachings of the sword was just this kind of rationality and practical application. Therefore, he felt no regret. But a thought remained lodged in Seiichiro's heart: human beings easily died.

Two nights earlier. After the crossing of swords at Suidojiri, Seiichiro had returned to the eatery of the alleyway back of Kyomachi. He found the shop dark and closed up tight, and however long he called out, no one replied. Needless to say, old man Gensai was gone. When Seiichiro returned to Nishidaya, the master, Jinnojo, was still up, calculating on his abacus. Over a cup of tea, Seiichiro slowly talked about the sword fight. Although he had been raised deep in the mountains, even Seiichiro realized that a person could not cut down five men without expecting some repercussions. But the fact that his opponents were masked and dressed entirely in black would surely work in Seiichiro's favor. The death of the one who offered oil to burn in the lamp at Akibayama was the same. Having told this much, Seiichiro fell silent. For the very first time, he realized the significance of the fact that all the bodies had completely disappeared. The essential evidence that would prove his story simply did not exist. But on reconsideration, there was nothing to prove his guilt, either. Going a step further, there was no proof that anything at all had occurred. As one might expect, when Jinnojou had heard the tale, he gave a broad grin saying, "The drink of the gods seems to cause us to see a variety of dreams... How much did you have?"

Seiichiro countered that he had not been drunk.

"I fully understand," responded Jinnojo. "Still, they do say that on a moonlit night, specters work all kinds of mischief."

In short, Jinnojo did not believe any of what Seiichiro had told him, and Seiichiro lost all desire to speak further. However, he pressed on, and asked whether he should go to the authorities, just in case. This was because he was worried about ultimately causing trouble for the Nishidaya. On the left side of the Great Gate was the Menbansho, the police office, where two agents of the Edo city magistrates took turns staking out the quarter. Seiichiro had also learned from Gensai that there were a large number of ex-ruffian commoners hired by police officials to stay on the watch. But Jinnojo claimed that the Menbansho was there merely to monitor the customers coming in and that everything that happened within the quarter was dealt with within the quarter. With an air of nonchalance, Jinnojo added that there was absolutely no reason to be concerned.

The next morning, Seiichiro woke early and went to take a look at Suidojiri, but there was no commotion at all. All that was to be seen were several pairs of *oiran* and customer bidding one another their sensuous morning farewells. He felt as if he had been bewitched by a fox, and found the situation vaguely disagreeable.

There was a fragrance in the air. Turning, Seiichiro noticed another *oiran* with her hair done up in an unusual chignon. Katsuyama tied her hair at the back near the top, made a large loop frontward, and fixed it with a kougai pin and then a broad white ribbon. This was the "Katsuyama topknot" that had taken the quarter by storm, and the woman he saw was none other than the originator of the style, the courtesan Katsuyama. Seiichiro, of course, was unaware of that fact. He thought only that the woman's eyes were full of life, and how attractive that was.

Katsuyama had originally been a *yuna*, or bathhouse woman, at the Kinokuniya bath, situated in Kanda Kijicho in front of the residence of Hori Tango no Kami, and she became widely celebrated under the name "Tanzen Katsuyama." It was said that she was born of a noble family but because she was disowned by her father, she became a *yuna*. Whether that was the case or not, she preferred the male dress of the Kabuki theater, which consisted of a woven hat, lined hakama pantaloons, with a short and a long sword stuck in the waistband. In this attire, she strutted the streets singing the ballad *Tanzen bushi*. Four years earlier, in the second year of Shoho (1653), when the Kinokuniya bathhouse had gone under, Katsuyama had reinvented herself as a *yujo* in Yoshiwara. She was hired by the prestigious Yoshiwara house of Yamamoto Hojun, with the highest of all statuses: *tayu*.

The first time Katsuyama paraded through the Yoshiwara quarter to the *ageya*, in the ostentatious procession called *dochu*, all of the ranking courtesans of Gochomachi, whether *tayu* or *koshi*, lined both sides of Nakanocho to watch. Through the throng, Katsuyama strode, entirely undaunted, in the unique *hachi moji* step of the courtesans, so-called as the footprints were in the shape of the Chinese character for the number eight. Her performance was not only flawless, but she reversed the eight by pointing her toes outward in the *soto hachi moji* style. Courtesans until that time had used the *uchi hachi moji* style, toes pointing inward, but her procession was so majestic that from that day forward all of the *tayu* of the quarter adopted her style. She was that impressive a woman.

"...?"

Something horribly soft pressed against Seiichiro's back. Katsuyama had sat down on the other side of the bench and was leaning against him. Perplexed, Seiichiro attempted to slip away, when a low but sweet voice whispered, "You've killed someone, haven't you."

It was not a question. Rather it was a straightforward statement of an established fact.

"It was a dream," replied Seiichiro, surprised at the speed with which the rumor had traveled. Katsuyama's supple body became animated.

"How many did you kill in that dream?"

"Five," he answered, as if she were drawing this out of him.

"You must be very strong. I like strong men best of all."

Her extremely cold hand was placed on top of his.

"Your hand's so cold."

Seiichiro the man was completely astonished at how cold the hand was.

"The more passionate a woman is, the colder her hands are."

His body trembled. She ran her fingers lightly up the back of his hand. She was smiling. Then her fingers inched their way from the back of his hand to his wrist. The sensation was so delicate that he could barely tell whether she was actually touching him or not, but it was arousing his masculinity. Seiichiro lost his composure.

"That simply will not do!"

The voice was clear. As if he had been rescued, Seiichiro turned to the one who had spoken. Her skin white as snow and her hair clipped the same length all the way around, a girl stood near the bench. Seiichiro knew that she was nine years old because the girl was Shoji Jinnojo's only daughter. Her nickname was Oshabu.

She was a curious little girl. Her skin was extremely pale, but not even out of courtesy would one call her beautiful. She was a plain-looking child, plump and with full cheeks. Around the house, she almost never spoke. On the other hand, her silence wasn't gloomy either. Just by being present, she uncannily brightened a room. It may well have been because she was always smiling.

Today was only the second time Seiichiro had heard her speak. The first time was on the day after Seiichiro arrived in Yoshiwara. It was at their first encounter. With eyes that sparkled, she looked fixedly at Seiichiro for a moment, then abruptly stood up and came to sit down right next to him. Her behavior was peculiarly charming and amusing, and Jinnojo laughed.

"Now this is an unusual occurrence," Jinnojo had commented. "It's not every day that Oshabu sits next to a gentleman."

He explained to Seiichiro that she was usually almost prickly about keeping her distance from men.

Oshabu spoke distinctly. "Well, it's only natural if you are man and wife."

Seiichiro laughed at the precociousness of what she had said, but Jinnojo unexpectedly fell silent. His eyes tensed, as if he suddenly frightened of something, and he stared at his daughter, finally letting slip a curious comment.

"I see. Well, in that case, we'll have to let him know."

But that was the end of it. She had not appeared before Seiichiro since then. Until today, that is, when her second comment was that something would not be acceptable. Owing to what she had said, Seiichiro's arousal disappeared, as did his general consternation. Katsuyama too automatically moved away.

"Is that so?" replied Seiichiro with latitude.

"The woman will bring harm to Sei-sama," the girl continued.

At that moment, Oshabu was looking at neither Seiichiro nor Katsuyama. Her posture suggested that her eyes were fixed on some corner of the sky and that she was listening to someone's voice.

(This child is listening to the voice of heaven!)

It was intuition—a sixth sense. Suddenly Seiichiro unraveled the meaning of that first encounter with Oshabu. If Oshabu were a *miko*, a spiritual medium who conveyed the voice of heaven, then that would mean that one day Seiichiro and Oshabu would become husband and wife. Seiichiro disconcertingly looked at the little girl who was currently only nine years old.

"Even at her age, she's filled with jealousy, such a suffering woman already," Katsuyama mocked.

Oshabu's eyes returned to Katsuyama. Her gaze was vacant, as if misted over.

"You will be killed by someone you believe in."

Katsuyama turned white. As she sprang to her feet, her fingertips lightly touched Seiichiro's cheek.

"I hope we shall meet again," she whispered, before turning away. She walked off with an elegant gait, her back perfectly straight. Enchanted, Seiichiro's eyes followed her, and when he returned his gaze to Oshabu, the little girl had vanished.

THE GREAT MIURA HOUSE

O-Miuraya, the great Miura House, stood at the corner of Kyomachi Itchome. It was the largest pleasure house in Yoshiwara at that time. Its master, Shirozaemon, had served as the headman of Yoshiwara Gocho ever since the death of Shoji Jin'emon.

It was early afternoon of the day that Seiichiro had met Katsuyama, on the second-floor drawing room of the O-Miura House.

Five elders had gathered together. In front was old man Gensai. As usual, a smile spread across his unusual face, and he alone sat with his legs crossed drinking sake in little sips. Compared to his four companions, who sat formally in a square, he seemed either arrogant or, if seen in a more favorable light, naturally rugged. Considering his age, the vitality emanating from his entire being was astonishing.

Seated to his right was Shirozaemon. Shirozaemon's appearance could also have been called somewhat peculiar but more than anything else he was large. He was fat. Perhaps twice the size of Gensai, he was all flab. With even the slightest movement, his prodigious flesh quivered like jelly. Furthermore he perspired so profusely that he had to constantly wipe away sweat with a cotton *tenugui*. It seemed as if the movement of wiping away sweat caused his corpulence to quiver even more, causing even more sweat to pour down his face. There was not a single wrinkle on his huge round face, and his extremely narrow eyes drooped.

The rest were Nomura Gen'i from Shinmachi, Yamadaya Sannojo from Edocho Nichome and Namikiya Genzaemon from Kakucho. All were masters of houses with women of peerless beauty.

Gen'i had studied the Rokuji-ryu style of swordsmanship under Hitotsubashi Nyokensai and was himself known as a consummate master. Sannojo and Genzaemon were both senior disciples of the master Miyamoto Musashi. Surprisingly enough, these three wore exactly identical clothing and had their hair styled exactly the same. They imitated the style of Gensai perfectly. Seated together here, their differences were obvious, but if one moved back slightly, they all seemed exactly like one another. At a distance, one would hardly be able to distinguish between them at all. In short, the three were "shadow warriors," doubles for Gensai.

Shirozaemon opened his mouth to speak, setting in motion his superfluous flesh.

"A truly troublesome incident has occurred."

"It's not troublesome in the least." Gensai's response was clear and crisp.

"There you go again. In the first place, you shouldn't have done what you did—to insist on involving someone who has absolutely no connection with the Yoshiwara."

"I didn't insist. That is simply how things worked out. Even I hadn't anticipated that the Yagyu would make a move the instant we opened for business."

"Oh really?" Shirozaemon said doubtfully, wiping away sweat.

"Anyway, what's done is done, and there's no point in complaining about it," Nomura Gen'i commented with some displeasure.

"The important thing is, how are we going to handle young Matsunaga Seiichiro? Knowing the Yagyu, they are certainly going to track him down. If we leave things as they are, he will certainly be cut down."

Namikiya Genzaemon nodded emphatically.

"Well, I'm not so sure that's true." Gensai's tone sounded as if he were enjoying himself. Yamadaya Sannojo cleared his throat. The previous evening Gensai had told the owner of the eatery to notify Sannojo, and this was the man to whom he had referred.

"He should be sent back to his home province immediately. He may well be a master of Niten'ichi-ryu, but if he were surrounded by that pack of Ura Yagyu...well I'm not so sure..."

"That is not how things are. That Gisen of the Ura Yagyu, however much of an Ashura demon he is, once he finds out who this young man really is, do you think he'll really dare to kill him?"

"What do you mean about 'who this young man really is'? What's that all about?"

Gensai whispered something into Shirozaemon's plump ear.

"What?!" Shirozaemon's large body bent backward. At that moment, a young man came running in, kneeling on one knee in the hallway just outside the door.

"I have urgent news! Master Matsunaga has just gone out toward the center of Edo, and several of the Yagyu are following him!"

"What?" Gensai raised one knee.

"This is serious. This is very serious, indeed." Shirozaemon groaned, setting his flesh quivering.

Seiichiro had become aware that he was being followed, just as he passed through the gate of Shotoji Temple.

Planning to go into the city, he had gone out of the Great Gate, but when he reached the Nihon Embankment, he changed his mind. Had he turned to the right, he would have gone toward Okawa in the direction of Sensoji, but instead he had turned to the left. It was because he recalled the clamor and the congestion of the city he had passed through three days earlier.

Turning left along Nihon Embankment, passing Jokanji, he would have come to Senju-machi, but well before that, Seiichiro turned left again, passing along Ohaguro ditch coming out to Daionji-dori, and looking at Otori Jinja on his left, he came to Shotoji Temple.

Toyozan Shotoji was a branch temple of a Zen temple in Kyoto named Myoshinji. Throughout Edo, it was celebrated for its autumn foliage, but once the New Yoshiwara was founded nearby, visiting the temple came to be used as a pretext for visiting a place of ill repute.

The Zen temple has autumn colors in the right direction,
Going to see them is an annual observance,
And yet, the foliage remains unseen

This is how it happened, and the wives of the world responded,

Hearing about going to see the foliage,
The wife has him take the children

In other words, having the children along would act as a constraint. The wives felt employing such a sad form of wisdom was essential.

The temple foliage lies not far from the home of demons

This was how the wives of the city viewed Shotoji and the quarter.

As he sat sipping a cup of tea within the precincts of the temple, Seiichiro frowned. At first, the party that was tailing him had been composed of only five men, but it was rapidly growing in number. At present, it was fourteen or fifteen members strong. They were each plainly attired, with carefully selected footwear, and each wore a long sword with a steel sword guard—suited for practical use—and without exception, each wore a wicker hat to hide his identity. However one viewed them, they did not seem to be merely dressed up to walk around looking for a fight like some bands of ruffians did. One could see in them traces of a disciplined, trained combat group. The face under each concealing hat was invariably young, but entirely devoid of natural youthful cheer.

A slightly older samurai, who seemed to be the leader, walked up to Seiichiro and spoke abruptly.

"Where is the *gomenjo*?"

"*Gomenjo*? A permit? Do you mean my travel permit?"

"Are you trying to play dumb?"

In a moment, there were four *bushi* encircling the bench where Seiichiro sat.

"I left my travel papers in the inn when I went out. It's at the Nishidaya in Edocho…"

"Are you saying the travel permit is at the Nishidaya?"

"If that is what you are referring to, yes."

"No. I'm talking about the *Shinkun gomenjo*, from the shogun!"

The man gave Seiichiro a piercing look. He had spoken softly, but he had definitely said, "*Shinkun gomenjo*."

Seiichiro responded, "*Shinkun…?*" The characters for *shinkun* didn't immediately connect with the sound of the word in his mind. He somehow guessed what *shinkun* might mean, but he hadn't the faintest idea how that connected with his travel papers. The combination simply did not fit together.

"I'm no good at riddles, so you'll have to tell me exactly what you mean."

"You're really obstinate," the man replied derisively. "It also sounds like you have certain skills. That is…if what they say about your killing those five is really true."

The man raised his chin ever so slightly. Apparently that was the signal. The four warriors surrounding the bench simultaneously drew their swords in a flash and came at Seiichiro. In that same instant, Seiichiro stood the bench on end, employing the technique of "folding back." By lightly applying the palm of his hand, he could make a tatami

mat stand on end. It was a technique designed for defense when attacked
by multiple opponents in a large matted room. One stood the mats up
one after another and moved along behind them to make one's escape.
In such a case, the large room would be transformed into a swelling sea
of tatami mats, and the enemy would not be able to grasp exactly where
he was. Unfortunately here in the temple grounds, there was only the
single bench in front of the tea shop and Seiichiro was unable to stir up
a billowing sea of benches. Yet, the upright bench did absorb the sword
strikes coming from behind and from both sides, and the opponent
attacking him from the front collapsed when Seiichiro struck him with
a fist to the pit of the stomach.

For the first time, anger rose within Seiichiro. He swiftly glided
across the ground toward a nearby camphor tree. However, three of his
attackers had anticipated this move and were already standing in front
of the tree with swords drawn. Seiichiro halted, quickly registering the
current situation. He was at a disadvantage. Seven men now formed a
complete circle around him. Another seven were forming a second outer
circle. Seiichiro had unconsciously unsheathed his two swords, the long
one in his right hand, and the short one in his left. He dangled them
artlessly in front of him, spread slightly outward.

The circular formations slowly began to move. The inner circle
moved to the left; the outer circle, to the right.

(A deception?)

Seiichiro fearlessly looked up into the sky. In the corners of his field
of vision, he could see that the inner circle of men, slowly rotating around
him, had now taken on a diagonal position with their right shoulders
towards him.

(It's a one-handed strike!)

The speed of the rotation of the two circles was increasing. At the
same time, they were closing in. Seiichiro guessed that in due course
the inner circle would commence a consecutive attack of one-handed
strikes.

(But what will the outer circle do?)

Seiichiro could not divine their action at all. They still maintained
their *seigan-no-kamae*, each facing Seiichiro. How they intended to
attack remained a mystery. To try to guess how they might come at
him was of no use at all. Thought merely delayed the movement of the
sword. Seiichiro calmed his mind. He still kept his eyes wide open and

focused upward into the sky. If he continued this way, might he not be completely sucked up into the sky? The figure he presented was one of such pure detachment that his opponents might well be deluded into thinking he might just rise upward.

"Sha!" At a voiced signal from the apparent leader, the inner circle began a simultaneous attack of one-handed sword strikes. At almost a run, they whirled to the left, raining ferocious strikes on him. Any ordinary man would have been sliced to pieces after a single rotation. With the technique of *mikiri*—knowledge of the other sword's reach— Seiichiro altogether escaped the strikes of the seven swords. His was the suppleness of pampas grass bending without resistance in the wind. What was astonishing was that he had not moved his feet from his original stance.

For the first time, the face of the leader showed signs of concern. The man suddenly raised his hand. The circle abruptly stopped, and the outer circle expanded slightly.

(Here they come!)

Seiichiro spread his two swords wide apart, like two great wings. If he were to flap those wings, a number of people would die, and he too might be wounded.

But at that very moment a voice rang out.

"Well, if it isn't Sagawa Shinza! It's quite unusual for a member of the celebrated Yagyu school to be involved in a sword fight, isn't it?"

It was Mizuno Jurozaemon who had spoken. Behind him, as before, were a dozen or more of his henchmen, the Jingi-gumi.

"Hmpf."

The boss of the band that had been referred to as Sagawa Shinza clicked his tongue, then flashed a signal with his hand, and in the next instant, the fifteen samurai had vanished from sight, including those who had been wounded by Seiichiro. Theirs was the quickness of the wind. Seiichiro saw once more the beast-like quickness exhibited that night by the black-clad men who had raced from Suidojiri toward the drawbridge.

"You're a man who seems to get involved in fights on a frequent basis. What did you do this time?" Mizuno asked, breaking into a broad smile.

"I'm not sure."

At the instant Seiichiro replied, intense anger welled up within him.

How much longer would he have to make such asinine replies? He had looked for someone to explain that to him.

"Master Mizuno, do you know Lord Yagyu Munefuyu?"

"Wonderful, wonderful. So, even that abominable Jingi-gumi serves a purpose on occasion. From now on, I won't say a word against them."

"I don't know, Old Man. I wouldn't start celebrating so soon."

"Why?"

"I don't know how things will come out in the end, but Matsunaga went out to the Lion Gate with that Jingi-gumi bunch…"

"Damn! To the city residence of the Yagyu clan?"

"Right. From the scraps of information I've gathered, sounds like Matsunaga insists he has to meet Munefuyu. Seems like Master Mizuno was going to serve as a go-between in setting up a meeting."

"*Go-Inkyo*! What should we do? If he goes into the Yagyu's lair, the chances of his coming out alive are almost…"

"Master Yagyu Naizen-no-sho Munefuyu, sword instructor to the shogun himself, is surely not a personage to do anything imprudent. But that rabid dog Sagawa—it's hard to know what he might start."

"That's what I mean. That guy Sagawa Shinza is a direct disciple of the Ura Yagyu leader Gizen, and they say that Sagawa only listens to orders from Gizen. Master Munefuyu is such an amicable person that it's even more difficult to keep them under control."

"Miuraya-san, it seems that it's your turn to go into action. You're the only one who can bring things to a successful conclusion here."

"That's too harsh. How can you do that to me? You know I'm twice as timid as other men."

"If the people of Yoshiwara stand by and let him be murdered, it will be a blot on our reputation that won't disappear for generations to come."

"…"

"You'll go, Master Shiroza?"

"Okay, okay, I'll go. At any rate, Matsunaga has sure set out on an unexpected journey."

The journey he was referring to was of course a play on the courtesan's *dochu* promenade. Someone in the gathering snickered at the reference, but it fell short of a full laugh and turned into a heavy sigh. There were five other sighs.

BOHACHI: KEEPERS OF THE PLEASURE HOUSES

Together with Mizuno Jurozaemon, Seiichiro had proceeded to the
main residence of the Yagyu clan. Two hours had passed since they had
been shown to a waiting room. Mizuno sat nervously jiggling his knee,
but Seiichiro sat self-possessed, not stirring an inch. His posture made it
clear that he had determined to wait however long it took.

Originally, it was Seiichiro who had raised the issue. By all means,
he had hoped to meet Master Yagyu, so he asked Mizuno if he were
acquainted and could write a letter of introduction for him. When
Mizuno asked why he was so eager to meet the leader of the clan,
Seiichiro told him about the fight that night at the lamp at Suidojiri and
about the odd phrase that had escaped the lips of his assailant: *Shinkun
gomenjo*. Mizuno had never heard of the *Shinkun gomenjo* but exhibited
an almost excessive curiosity about it, and he proposed to accompany
Seiichiro to the Yagyu residence himself. On top of that, he nonchalantly
explained the purpose of their visit to the retainer who received them
when they arrived at the Yagyu mansion.

"I am *hatamoto* Mizuno Jurozaemon, accompanied by the *ronin*
Matsunaga Seiichiro, and we have come to request a direct audience
with Master Munefuyu regarding the matter of *Shinkun gomenjo*."

Seven years later—in the fourth year of Kanbun—Mizuno
Jurozaemon would tragically be executed, precisely as the result of
that sentence uttered by him on this occasion, but at the time, neither
Mizuno nor Seiichiro had any inkling of that fate.

In a back room of the Yagyu clan's Edo residence, three samurai
sat looking at each other gravely: the current head of the clan, Yagyu
Munefuyu; chief retainer of the Yagyu domain, Notori Takumi; and
Sagawa Shinzaemon.

"Shinza, what was your motivation for so casually mentioning the
gomenjo? Are you saying that was an order from Gizen as well?"

Out of anger, Munefuyu's voice was extremely low. It was a rasping
voice, hardly more than a whisper.

"It was my own personal decision to do that. To find out whether a
man is connected with the Yoshiwara or not, hitting him with that phrase
is the most effective means. The answer inevitably shows in his face."

In other words, it served as a touchstone. Judging from external appearances, Sagawa Shinzaemon was merely a dull country samurai, but in reality, he was both cunning and tenacious. No matter what anyone said to him, it appeared to run off him like water off a duck's back. But when it came to grudges, he never forgot, and he would settle old scores with savagery when the other person least expected it. That was the kind of man he was. And at this very moment, he had the expression of a man who has done nothing wrong.

"So, how did this Matsunaga respond?"

"Well…"

For the first time, he showed a certain hesitation.

"He simply played dumb."

"You're saying he didn't respond at all?"

Muneyuki's voice turned even more caustic.

"Just what do you intend to do, once you know he isn't connected with the Yoshiwara?"

"The same thing—kill him. It was a stroke of bad luck for him, to be suspected by us."

Muneyuki averted his glare, as if he had been looking at some detestable worm. What he hated more than anything was just this sort of man who came out with such violently irresponsible statements.

"But now Mizuno knows about the *Shinkun gomenjo*, too. Are you planning on cutting him down as well?"

"Of course. Before we ever had this discussion, they should have been wrapped up together and killed."

"You idiot!" Muneyuki exploded. Simultaneously Sagawa jumped back several feet.

"My lord! Do you intend to kill me? You've got the wrong party!"

"Mizuno is related to the Tokugawa clan by marriage. Do you honestly think that the Yagyu clan could, with no pretext whatsoever, murder a bannerman, a *hatamoto* of 3,000 *koku* stipend, and get away with it? You damn fool! Without the Omote Yagyu, the Ura Yagyu wouldn't exist either. Don't you forget that! From now on, I forbid you to act on your own discretion on the streets of Edo—regarding anything. Everyone in the Ura Yagyu is ordered to clear out of the Yagyu villa residence!"

The villa residence, outside the city proper, was at Shimo-Meguro, and it was where the well-known Yagyu dojo was located. Every member of the Ura Yagyu who came from the private estates of the Yagyu lodged in the training hall there.

"Your intention is to cut us off from our means of living?"

"I'm telling you to go back to the Yagyu valley."

"We Ura Yagyu only obey the commands of Master Rendo. Even if it is the Lord's command, we will not act on the orders of the Omote Yagyu." Sagawa Shinza smiled callously.

Yagyu Rendo was Munefuyu's youngest brother. His name was Rokuro, but he had taken Buddhist orders and assumed the name Gisen. He had established the Hotokuji temple in the Yagyu estate and as temple head received 200 *koku* per year from the bakufu. He was the commander-in-chief of the Ura Yagyu.

"That being the case, the Ura Yagyu shall go into concealment. I shall excuse myself now."

Having watched Shinza throw out his chest and withdraw, Notori Takumi commented quietly, "It's like setting a wolf loose."

"You, now. I imagine you have one or two of the Ura Yanagi under your wing."

Notori Takumi was the Yagyu clan's best tactician.

"As a matter of fact, I do," Takumi replied coolly.

"Report to me on where Sagawa lives, what he does, everything, every minute of the day."

"At your service, my lord."

"And now, what about those two in the waiting room?"

"The only means available is to feign illness."

But Muneyuki could not use illness as an excuse for not meeting the two. The reason was that a member of his household staff came to announce that Miuraya Shirozaemon, a *bohachi* from Yoshiwara, had appeared at the back entrance.

A *bohachi* was the proprietor of a house of beautiful courtesans, the superb kind referred to as "castle topplers." The term *bohachi*, meaning "forgetting the eight," suggested that one could hardly carry on such a business unless he forgot the eight principal virtues of filial piety, respect for elders, loyalty, faithfulness, politeness, righteousness, modesty and a sense of shame. But another view held that this was a mere distortion and that the term was actually a Japanese reading of the Chinese word *wang-pa*, snapping turtle, which was a term of abuse.

Miuraya Shirozaemon had entrusted the retainer with a letter to Muneyuki requesting, with respect, that it be opened and read immediately. Upon reading it, Muneyuki's face lost its color.

It read: "I hasten to inform you of important information. The Matsunaga Seiichiro who is at this moment on the premises is the concealed son of Go-Mizuno-in. Should there be any doubts regarding this, please examine the sword which he wears at his side. It is without doubt the long sword known as *Oni-kiri*, the Demon Cutter."

That was all the missive contained.

Go-Mizuno-in was none other than the retired Emperor Go-Mizuno-o. The Demon Cutter was a famous sword that once belonged to several generations of the Genji clan and which had been sent to the imperial prince by the second shogun, Hidetada.

The letter fell from Munefuyu's hands. From his lips came a mysterious remark: "What karma!"

At that very moment, Matsunaga Seiichiro, the concealed son of the tonsured ex-emperor Go-Mizuno-in, with the Demon Cutter sword laying at his knees, remained seated upright, peacefully asleep.

Suddenly his eyes opened wide.

"Is this it?"

Mizuno Jurozaemon tensed, straining to hear something, but he detected nothing. He was about to grumble about something, when instead, his mouth gaped wide open. Without a sound, a sliding door opened, and there stood Yagyu Munefuyu. For one instant, Munefuyu fixed his eyes on Seiichiro, then, gliding forward, he took the seat of honor in the room. He paid no attention at all to Mizuno. He wore everyday clothing, with only a short sword at his belt.

"I am Yagyu Munefuyu."

Munefuyu's eyes remained fixed on Seiichiro.

"Are you Matsunaga?"

"Indeed, I am Matsunaga Seiichiro, masterless samurai from Higo province."

There was no hesitation whatsoever in Seiichiro's reply. It flowed like water in an even tone, with no strain, no affectation at all.

"Excuse my abruptness, but I would like to have the honor of inspecting your sword."

Startled, Mizuno tensed up. One of the names for Yagyu sword technique was "the sword of intrigue." It indicated a willingness to use any strategy whatsoever in order to sustain the Yagyu reputation for having the most superior swordsmanship in the land. The Yagyu school would think nothing of pretending to ask to inspect the other party's sword and then, in the instant the person leaned forward to hand it over, slashing him from the head downward.

But before Mizuno could get out a single word of caution, Seiichiro replied, "As you request," and readily pushed the sword forward, the grip toward Munefuyu. His movement was entirely natural, and his posture changed not a whit. He provided no opening at all. Mizuno unconsciously emitted a groan of awe.

Without a word, Munefuyu removed a piece of paper from the fold of his kimono and placed it between his lips. He then unsheathed the sword, held it vertically and gazed at it intently. To be sure, it was the Demon Cutter, the famous long sword which Minamoto Mitsunaka was said to have used to cut down a demon in the mountains of Togakushi. When he was young, he had seen this very same sword in the weapon storehouse of Edo Castle together with his father, Tajima-no-kami Munenori, and his elder brother, Yagyu Mitsuyoshi Jubei. The distinctive markings along the blade were so remarkable that he had desired the weapon intensely at that first moment. The ardor he had felt at that time returned vividly to him as he gazed at the weapon in his hand. Sheathing the sword with a click, he pushed it back toward Seiichiro, hilt facing its possessor.

"It has a truly excellent tempering. Could it be a memento from someone?"

The casual inquiry was a probe to find out whether Seiichiro knew his own lineage or not.

"I have heard that it was a memento from my father."

"And what sort of person was your father?"

It was a hazardous question. If the name Go-Mizuno-in came forward, Munefuyu would have to kill both Seiichiro and Mizuno Jurozaemon. Even if he had to gamble the Yagyu clan's 10,000 *koku* stipend and his own life, he would have to slay both of them. He had entered the room with that resolve. Munefuyu had already mobilized all of the swordsmen in the residence, and additional ones as well, and all of its vital points were secured. Now he waited with bated breath for Seiichiro's reply.

"I don't know."

The response that came was, as before, entirely unaffected.

A sigh passed Munefuyu's lips. The tension was broken.

"You don't know?"

"I was abandoned. Master Miyamoto told me strictly: never seek to know those who abandoned you."

"Your master was Miyamoto Musashi?"

(So that was Musashi after all.)

In Munefuyu's mind rose up vividly the event twenty-five years earlier that shook the foundations of the entire Yagyu clan.

(And the one and only child who escaped the deadly Yagyu blades is standing here before me!)

ASSASSINATION OF THE IMPERIAL PRINCE

In order to tell the story of that incident twenty-five years earlier which terrified the entire clan—the Omote Yagyu, the Ura Yagyu and the Owari Yagyu—it is necessary to first tell about Emperor Go-Mizuno-o.

Go-Mizuno-o took a daughter of the Tokugawa as his wife, and he was the first to be called Mikado. It was the second shogun Hidetada's strong desire to have the daughter of a Tokugawa enter the court as imperial consort. From the time that Minamoto Yoritomo established the Kamakura bakufu, even though the governance of the land was in the hands of the military houses, no one from a warrior household had ever become emperor. At least, a woman of the samurai class might become an empress, and if her son became emperor then Hidetada could gain the status of a relative of the emperor. This was Hidetada's dearest desire. On the eighteenth day of the sixth month of Gen'na 6 (1620), just as he had wished, Hidetada's youngest daughter Masako completed her bridal procession and entered the imperial court along with an enormous number of large oblong clothing chests bearing her trousseau. The bride's entry to the court was rumored to have cost an amazing 70,000 koku. In that year, the emperor was twenty-five years old and Masako was fourteen years old.

Nine years later, on the eighth day of the eleventh month of the sixth year of Kan'ei (1629), Emperor Go-Mizuno-o suddenly abdicated in favor of Masako's daughter, the child who became Empress Meisho. This child became the first female Emperor in 860 years. Furthermore, the child was only seven years old, while Go-Mizuno-o, at age thirty-four, was still in the prime of life when he abdicated.

There are said to be two causes for this abrupt abdication: the Purple Robe Incident and the *Kasuga no tsubone santai* Incident, both famous historically. The first of these involved the procedure for granting a particularly meaningful robe. The highest-ranking Buddhist priest in the land was granted a purple robe, and that was granted directly by the imperial family. However, the bakufu decided that the request for the robe should be passed though the imperial official in charge of communications between the samurai and the court, to obtain the sanction of the bakufu. That is, if the emperor granted such a robe without going through this official and without obtaining the bakufu's permission, then that priest would be divested of his position.

The second incident involved Tokugawa Iemitsu's wet nurse, the daughter of a samurai of no official rank or position, who visited the imperial palace and requested an audience with the emperor. For the imperial court, this was entirely unprecedented. Needless to say, for Emperor Go-Mizuno-o, said to be the most hot-tempered emperor of the entire Tokugawa period, both of these incidents were absolutely infuriating.

But the actual reason for his decision to abdicate was not anger; it was fear. In a letter written one month after the abdication, on the twenty-seventh day of the twelfth month of Kan'ei 6 (1629), Hosokawa Sansai wrote to his son Hosokawa Tadatoshi that the imperial princes born of minor court ladies—anyone other than Masako—were being smothered to death and that court ladies with unborn children were by one means or another being forced to miscarry. These unbelievably cruel measures had been implemented by the cold-blooded Hidetada even before Masako had entered the court.

There was the earlier Kamonomiya Incident, for instance. Two years prior to Masako's arrival at court, a woman beloved of the emperor and known as Oyotsu Goryonin gave birth to an imperial prince. The child was named Kamonomiya. However, in the most authoritative genealogy of the imperial house, the *Honcho koin shounroku*, this particular prince's name does not appear. Yasui Santetsu, at the time a frequent visitor to both the Court and the bakufu, writes that everything related to this prince was kept completely secret. His existence was consigned to oblivion and nothing at all about him was passed to later generations. All that is known is that in the eighth year of the Gen'na reign, two years after Masako became the imperial consort, this particular prince died at the age of five. Could the cold-blooded Hidetada have possibly refrained from staining Masako's accession to court with the blood of an imperial prince?

Those who carried out the appalling series of assassinations were none other the Yagyu clan. The elite corps of Yagyu ninja, led by Tajima-no-kami Munenori, stole into the imperial palace and gang-raped any court woman bearing a child of the emperor, causing miscarriage. Any child who had escaped their notice and managed to be born healthy was mercilessly murdered. Every woman who mothered an imperial child met the same fate. It is entirely understandable that Emperor Go-Mizuno-o was seized with fear and concluded that it was best to abdicate.

On the fifth day of the first month of Kan'ei 9, during the third year after Go-Mizuno-o abdicated and became the cloistered ex-emperor, a certain lady of the court gave birth to an imperial prince. That child was Seiichiro. Due to the fact that he had already abdicated and, further, that the all-powerful Hidetada had fallen ill toward the end of the previous year and was expected not to survive, Go-Mizuno-o must have assumed that this time around there was no reason for alarm over the birth of his child. Emblematic of his lack of misgivings was the fact that he sent to the lady the Demon Cutter sword, which had been given by Hidetada to Masako's son Takahito Shinno, who died two years afterwards. But Hidetada was hardly as weakened or as indulgent as Go-Mizuno o supposed. Hearing the news during his illness, Hidetada immediately summoned Tajima-no-kami Munenori. The result was the grisly affair on the night of the seventeenth day of the new year in Kan'ei 9.

That night, snow fell on the capital. There was a figure who walked through that snow, protected only by a battered straw hat that came down over his face. The man was forty-nine-year-old Miyamoto Musashi. Suffering physically from the severe wounds of more than sixty duels and mentally from being blocked from entering government service in both Edo and Owari province by the Yagyu clan, he was despondent. To Musashi, this street in the illustrious capital was no more than one leg of a journey he had to complete. His thoughts were already of Higo. Surely the warm sunlight and secluded hot springs there would alleviate the pains that afflicted his body. He had already given up all hopes of a government position, as well as hopes of fortune and making a name for himself. All he could hope for now was personal ease and freedom. He lengthened his stride, for he hoped, during that evening, to clear the capital city. There were remnants of the Yoshioka band scattered in the capital, rendering it unsafe.

Musashi abruptly halted. The hair on the back of his neck bristled. Musashi's ability to perceive danger had become keener in the latter part of his life. He was passing outside the roofed mud wall of what seemed to be the residence of some court noble. A sense of murder issued ominously from within the walls. Musashi vaulted. In the same instant that he landed in a pile of snow inside the wall, he unsheathed his two swords. With a dull splish, blood spurted out onto the snow. Two bodies collapsed upon one another without a sound. The two were black-masked, black-clothed ninja. Musashi ran across the garden.

Inside the residence was a grisly scene. A lady of the court stripped completely naked was being raped from front and back by two black-garbed men. The man underneath was violently penetrating her vulva, while another on top penetrated her anus. Both entrances were already bathed in blood. Three other black-clad men crowded around watching indifferently. In the adjoining room lay the corpses of a middle-aged noble and his wife, evidently the woman's parents. Neither had been cut with a mere single slash of a sword. Instead they had been hacked to death. It was clear that they had died after being brutally tortured.

"Where is the prince?"

The man whispered in her ear as he goaded her violently from below, raising a spray of blood.

"The prince! Where is he?"

The other figure repeated the same question, as he penetrated her anus, which was by now split open like a pomegranate.

The men were tools of the Yagyu, under orders from Hidetada, but they were so used to such work that they were caught off-guard. They had forced their way into the residence, skillfully dispatched the servants, the low-ranking samurai guards and the wet nurse, and then had entered the lady's private quarters. Once inside, however, they were astonished to discover that the baby prince was nowhere to be seen. The lady had been raised in the imperial palace and was, as a result, extremely cautious, so each night she hid the child, together with the *Oni-kiri* sword, in a storage closet behind some bedding. The only two people who were aware of this were herself and the wet nurse. Her parents, though savagely tortured, could not be forced to tell something that they were entirely unaware of in the first place. The lady herself, having the tenacity of a birth mother, remained rock silent, not uttering a word. For the Yagyu, it was a major blunder. From the relentless attack, the lady had lost a good deal of blood and was on the verge of death.

There was a howl—one that could hardly have come from a human being. Rather, it seemed like a growl from a wild beast. Musashi stood in the hallway.

"You inhuman scum!"

Both swords flashed, and in an instant three Yagyu henchmen lay dead. The two on the floor had pushed the woman aside in a hurry and risen to their feet. Still naked from the waist down, they were decapitated. Their heads struck the ceiling and fell to the floor with a dull thud.

The court lady stopped Musashi when he tried to tend to her wounds, telling him where the imperial prince lay hidden, and identifying her assailants. Asking him to raise the emperor's son in some hidden, unobtrusive place, where no one could lay hands on him, the noblewoman breathed her last.

Placing the thirteen-day-old Seiichiro inside the top of his kimono and the *Oni-kiri* sword, wrapped in a straw mat, upon his back, Musashi left the capital, where the snow continued to pile up. That was what happened on gruesome night of the seventeenth day of the first month of Kan'ei 9.

Via the noble in the neighboring household, word of the grisly affair reached the imperial palace, and the ear of the retired-emperor Go-Mizuno-o, even before it reached the shogunate's military government stationed within the city. The retired emperor flew into a rage. Bitter remorse for having been so lacking in caution further fueled his rage. Immediately crossing over into the quarters of the retired empress, he severely abused Masako. Until that very moment, however, Masako had absolutely no knowledge of her father Hidetada's actions. She was naturally tremendously shocked. When she heard the lurid details of the sexual assault on the noble mother who had just given birth, she virtually lost consciousness. At the same time, such anger welled up inside her that her body shook. That the shogunate's governor Itakura Suonokami Shigemune was ordered to deal harshly with all of the rogues involved in the incident was one result of her intense fury. Naturally enough, Shigemune was aware that the scoundrels belonged to the Yagyu stable. It was also clear, however, that their orders came from the powerful Hidetada. If there was anything to fault the Yagyu with, it was on the poor execution of their mission, and the indiscretion of allowing seven samurai to be executed by some unknown swordsman and left for all to see.

An express messenger was dispatched to Edo, and the core of the shogunate was shaken. Yagyu Munenori was put in an extremely awkward position. More than anything else, the problem was that the image of the Yagyu—the most renowned warriors in the realm—had been shattered. The Yagyu had been deprived of their reputation as dependable assassins. Fortunately or not, seven days after the incident, in the late evening of the twenty-fourth day of the first month, Hidetada died. It could be said that his death saved the Yagyu. But the loss of confidence in the Yagyu as warriors was to have a lasting impact.

The same thing was occurring in Kyoto. Masako's distrust of the military government would last all her life. In the third month of the following year, a court lady named Kyogoku gave birth to a prince, son of Go-Mizuno-in, and Masako swiftly took the child to raise as her own. This was Suganomiya, later to become Emperor Gokome. Further, Go-Mizuno-in had twenty-one other children, all imperial princes and princesses, with mothers other than Masako—and not a single one fell victim to the bakufu's swords. This was all due to the protection of Masako. Her almost insane fondness for clothing in her later years was quite possibly a means of spiting the central leaders of the military government. Hayashi Razan noted that every year the retired-empress Masako required some 200,000 *koku* for her expenses. She died on the twentieth day of the sixth month of Empo 6 (1678), at the age of seventy-two, but in the half year preceding her death, she is said to have ordered from Kariganeya, purveyor of clothing to the imperial court, over 340 items, amounting to as much as one hundred fifty *kan* of silver. As the cost of clothing for a seventy-two-year-old woman, over a mere half year, the amount defies the imagination. In that figure can be read the depth of Masako's suspicion of and anger toward the bakufu.

Thereafter, the Yagyu clan frantically attempted to determine the "perpetrator" of the murder of the seven assailants. The barbarity had been committed by the seven henchmen, so it was inappropriate to refer to the person who cut them down as the perpetrator of a crime, but from the point of view of the Yagyu, that was precisely the case.

More than anything else, the culprit's swordsmanship was completely out of the ordinary. Each of the seven who were cut down had been very carefully selected swordsmen, yet, to a man, they had been dispatched by a single long sword. There was not a nick on any of their sword blades to indicate that there had been some sort of struggle. This evidence indicated that they had all been defeated without so much as an exchange of blows. Was it possible that such a master swordsman actually existed? This was what was foremost in the minds of the Yagyu. They considered every noted swordsman with any reputation at all, but they could not believe any of those who came to mind actually possessed the incredible skill that had been exhibited that night. Further, all of the names that were raised were accounted for in some other location on that particular night. Ultimately, none of the candidates seemed to meet the relevant conditions. Naturally enough, Miyamoto Musashi's name was raised, but the leader of a group of mountain nomads reported that Musashi had been in the mountains of Kumano on the night in question. That report, however, was baseless. The Yagyu ignorance of the make-up of the mountain nomads—and their relationship with Musashi—blinded them to the ultimate truth.

And now, the truth of what had occurred twenty-five years earlier stood right in front of Munefuyu, in the figure of this composed young man. Munefuyu was thrown into turmoil.

EXPIATION

"What is the *Shinkun gomenjo*?"

Seiichiro's question woke Munefuyu from the depths of his private thoughts.

"Yes, what about that? And we'd like to know why it is that this young man has had to undergo attacks by Yagyu men on two separate occasions." Mizuno Jurozaemon spoke the words in a rush.

Munefuyu remained silent. His consciousness had not yet fully returned from that day twenty-five years in the past.

"Lord Yagyu!" Mizuno pressed impatiently.

Munefuyu gave him a sharp glance. It was the first time he had looked in Mizuno's direction. His eyes were like glass. As if doused by cold water, Mizuno suddenly recovered his senses. He awoke to the fact that out of idle curiosity he had inadvertently ventured into extremely dangerous territory.

(Looks like I'm going to die)

Even Mizuno had his own variety of sixth sense. It was just that his next thought was different from that of normal people.

(Oh well, bring it on then)

What would happen would happen. The thought that he might wind up dead, to the contrary, stirred him up. His was a mode of thought that was shared by the strange new young dandies of the age who were known as *kabukimono*. They possessed the sensibilities of young men who arrived too late. During the civil wars between the mid-15th to mid-16th century, a samurai could snatch a castle and a province with a single spear. Now, in a world where samurai no longer served a purpose but were forced to listen to sermons on the virtues of peace and order throughout the land, what would be the purpose in living out a life?

Having lived too long, now twenty and three
I swear to Hachiman, I'll never back down

These were the lines inscribed on a vermilion-lacquered sword sheath carried by one of the dandies depicted in the folded screen called *Hokokudaimyojin rinjisai reizu*. It expressed the heartfelt feelings of those young men "who arrived too late," precisely the temperament of the members of the Jingi-gumi who would in no way regret risking their lives in some trivial fight.

"Lord Yagyu, I would like to inquire as to the nature of this matter." Mizuno for the first time spoke with determination.

In a low voice, Munefuyu replied, "There are things in this world of ours that are best left unknown."

Once Mizuno made up his mind, however, he could be hard to shake.

"But there does not come to mind anything that could be best left unknown that might account for the attempts to cut down this man."

"That was a mistake on Sagawa's part. You could call it an accident."

"Was what happened in Yoshiwara also an 'accident'?"

As always, Seiichiro spoke in a level tone.

"I'm afraid I'm unaware of what you are referring to."

Munefuyu feigned ignorance. In fact, when it came to that particular incident, Munefuyu could under no circumstances tell him the truth. After listening to Seiichiro's story with patience, he replied.

"This household was in no way involved in that affair," he said, raising the tone of his voice.

Seiichiro smiled. It was a charming, likeable smile.

"Is there something?" Munefuyu inquired.

"I was just recalling something that the Master once told me. He said that when a person tells a lie, the voice grows tense."

Munefuyu unconsciously gave a wry smile. Not bad, not bad at all. The young man possessed the means to slip into the mind of other people, and what's more, to do so without leaving the other person feeling any discomfort. Munefuyu realized that he was beginning to take a liking to Seiichiro.

Thirty minutes later, Seiichiro was in a small dojo inside the precincts of the Yagyu residence. Ultimately Munefuyu had breathed not a single word regarding the *Shinkun gomenjo*.

"At least allow me to offer some compensation," Munefuyu had said.

With these words, he had brought Seiichiro to this training hall. Mizuno Jurozaemon had attempted to accompany them, but he had been flatly turned away. Upon entering the dojo, Munefuyu had asked Seiichiro for the details of the style of swordsmanship Sagawa Shinzaemon had employed.

"He should not have used *Ranken no jin*..."

With this comment, Munefuyu had slipped out, not to return.

From the window of the dojo, Seiichiro could see the rays of the sun as it began to set. Somewhere a cicada shrilled.

The wooden door slid open and Munefuyu entered the training hall. He was followed by six samurai in training gear. Each carried a leather-covered mock sword in his hand. This *fukuro shinai* was split bamboo wrapped in leather, and it was a practice weapon particular to the Yagyu school. Munefuyu placed an identical mock sword in front of Seiichiro.

"We shall show you the Yagyu-style *Ranken no jin*," Munefuyu announced seriously.

"It is also called *Koran no jin*. This is not among the formal set of *kata*. It is our school's secret technique, used only when one absolutely must deliver a deathblow to an opponent. I hope you will consider the fact that this is being shown to you as a sincere expression of apology from me, the leader of the Yagyu clan."

Three warriors surrounded Seiichiro, and three others formed a second circle outside of them. True enough, the numbers were different, but it was precisely the same attack formation that Sagawa had directed at Shotoji. Seiichiro took up the mock sword and slowly stood up. The circular formation was beginning to rotate. The inner circle moved to the left; the outer circle, to the right. The men in the inner circle shifted so that their right shoulders faced Seiichiro—the staqnce for a one-handed stroke. At the same time, the circle was drawing inward. The outer circle moved slightly away from the inner circle. Its members took the *seigan-no-kamae,* facing Seiichiro directly. At Shotoji, Seiichiro had seen the movement up to this point, and he had dodged the attack without difficulty. But not this time.

"Ah!" Seiichiro made a sound of admiration. Suddenly the three in the inner circle dropped to one knee, striking a one-handed blow, aiming at his legs. The three on the outside then sprang inward, each stepping on the shoulder of a man in front, and from there leaping up. These three struck simultaneously from above, cutting straight down the middle, from the crown of the head to the ground. It was a full-blown offensive from above and below at the same instant. An entirely cold-blooded attack, it was carried out with no hesitation whatsoever, despite the risk of cutting one of their own men.

Seiichiro was unaware of exactly how he eluded the sure-fire assassination technique. It was a purely instinctive move, like that of an untamed beast, which transcended any learned form. To be precise, with his bare hand, he seized one of the leather-covered mock swords that was aimed at his legs, and he used the energy of the assailant, who tried to pull back on his sword, to leap outside of the ring. When he did so, he also unconsciously struck the bushi beside him with his own mock sword. The struck warrior fell in agony.

"Hmm." This time it was Munefuyu who let out a sound, impressed. The five bushi left standing were disquieted.

"No." Seiichiro smiled with embarrassment. "That was no good. It seems that I grabbed and pulled on a sword."

Had the mock sword been a live blade, he would have lost his fingers. Like a child who has been caught cheating, Seiichiro was embarrassed. It was only a split-second movement, but he was completely covered with sweat. Had Mizuno not happened along at Shotoji, Seiichiro would have been killed. He truly thought so.

For his own part, Munefuyu was thunderstruck.

(Here's a once-in-a-hundred-years prodigy)

Seiichiro was unaware of it, but since the founding of the Yagyu Ryu, this *Ranken no jin* had never before been defeated.

(Musashi's Niten'ichi-ryu is truly astonishing! Matsunaga Seiichiro is a man to fear.)

Once again, deep inside, Munefuyu groaned.

His enormous mass of flesh trembled like rippling waves, and he incessantly wiped away the sweat that poured forth from him. Miuraya Shirozaemon was finally able to lower his enormous behind onto a gargantuan folding stool, one which a young man in his employ had purposely brought all the way from Yoshiwara. Unless this specially made stool accompanied him, Shirozaemon could go nowhere. He was so overweight that simply standing up was a hardship. Another young man stood nearby sending a constant breeze his way with a large round fan.

They were in front of the Yagyu residence.

Surrounding Shirozaemon, there were ten young men altogether. One man stood apart holding the reins of an abnormally large black horse, which Shirozaemon had ridden from the Yoshiwara. There were also two white horses tethered to a tree.

Each of these men appeared to be both wiry and agile, and each wore a deep-blue cotton kimono with the bottom tucked up, dark-blue underclothing and leather sandals. Each also wore a livery coat with the characters "O-Miuraya" dyed on it. Underneath this short coat, each carried a short, broad straight sword along his spine, and four of them also carried a black foot-long blow tube. The latter was an arrow blowpipe, and each carried in a hidden tobacco pouch ten or so darts tipped with the poison of tiger beetles. From the saddle of the black horse casually hung a leather bag holding three unstrung small bows and twenty odd short arrows. The group was fully armed.

Each of the ten, under Shirozaemon's direct command, was a master of sword, bow and Chinese martial arts and was capable of traveling 120 miles in a single day.

Not a word was spoken. It was like the hush of a forest.

In reality, with this group as the spearhead, fifty men were positioned on all sides of the Yagyu residence, ready to fight at a moment's notice. These *kubidai*, named for the money that one paid to escape execution, were usually to be found wandering aimlessly around the Yoshiwara quarter. Once some kind of trouble arose, they would instantly transform into combatants. Once the conflict was quelled, several of these men would take on the guilt of the whole group and turn themselves in to the local magistrate. Even if they were sentenced to beheading and to having their heads exposed to public view, the expression on their faces wouldn't change in the slightest. These fearsome characters, disguised as masterless *ronin*, craftsmen and farmers, surrounded the residence, waiting for a signal.

And that wasn't all.

Out of nowhere, a group of some thirty ascetics had assembled at the back gate of the Yagyu residence. They wore white robes, white hoods, white leggings and rugged sandals. With prayer beads wrapped around their hands, they held hand drums shaped like round fans, which they pounded as they chanted the Nichiren prayer, *Namu myoho renge kyo*. In appearance, they were Fujufuse sect ascetics, whose practitioners refused to accept offerings from anyone besides fellow believers in the Lotus Sutra, but in the center of the group was none other than Gensai. Surrounding him were Nomura Gen'i, Yamadaya Sannojo, and Namikiya Genzaemon. With all its might and main, Yoshiwara had prepared for an all-out assault on the Yagyu residence.

Namu myoho renge kyo! Namu myoho renge kyo!
The prayer, chanted as if it were a threat, reverberated throughout the entire Yagyu residence. The faces of everyone within the residence were drained of color. As one might expect of disciplined warriors, they were not thrown into confusion, but they automatically congregated at the main and back entrances. Some moistened the rivets of their sword-hilts and the more impetuous tied their sleeves back with leather bands.

Munefuyu smiled wryly. Having returned from the dojo to a room in the main residence, he was drinking tea with Seiichiro and Mizuno.

"Master Matsunaga," Munefuyu said as he set his tea bowl down with a click, "it might be best if you were to leave now. If you don't depart rather quickly, it's possible that things might become rather troublesome."

Seiichiro nodded. He had sufficiently sensed the signs. He had even detected Gensai's voice among those chanting outside the gate.

(Just who is that old man?)

It was the first time Seiichiro had paused to wonder about Gensai's true identity.

The chanting of the name of the sutra and the sound of the drums abruptly ended. Seiichiro and Mizuno had walked out of the gate of the residence in one piece.

Munefuyu stood on the verandah gazing at the garden in the dimming light of evening. Notori Takumi, one of the highest ranking counselors to the shogun, came in and silently sat behind Munefuyu.

"How many were there?" Munefuyu asked without turning around.

"About a hundred."

"A hundred? It appears they were in earnest."

"They even came with gunpowder and lighting devices."

"Mutual death." There was bitterness in Munefuyu's voice. "Mutual death" or *shinju*, the word for sincerity used among lovers, was later widely used to signify lovers' double suicide.

"No, not exactly mutual death. As long as the *Shinkun gomenjo* exists, Yoshiwara is secure. It would simply mean the end of the Yagyu clan."

There was a slight tremor in Takumi's voice.

"At the end of the fight, Miuraya would be gone. All that would remain would be the corpses of the nameless fighting men. On our side, the residence that was bestowed on us would be burned to the ground, and we would have a large number of dead followers on our hands. That is, if any of them at all were left alive."

"You have so little courage, Takumi."

"It is only natural that those with the most to protect are the ones who are weaker."

The weakness of the Yagyu clan was its lineage as the instructors of swordsmanship to the Tokugawa shoguns. If the Yagyu were to be attacked by a group of warrior vagabonds and end up suffering casualties and losing their base, the Yagyu clan would be completely ruined.

"Tell me. Just who is that young man, the one who has led the Yoshiwara to become so earnest?" Takumi spoke boldly.

"Send a fast courier to Yagyu Valley. I want to talk with Gisen immediately."

"Lord!"

"Until I talk with Gisen, I can say nothing about who that young man is. I'm not sure it's wise even to speak to Gisen…"

Munefuyu was vacillating. There was a possibility that there might be an adverse reaction from Gisen. The bitterness of twenty-five years ago might well stir Gisen's bloodthirsty spirit. Gisen was by nature given to bitter resentment, and Munefuyu could not abide that characteristic. But when he began to think of what might happen if Sagawa and the Ura Yagyu grasped through their own lines of communication exactly who Seiichiro was, it seemed necessary to take strong measures immediately. There was little doubt that a spontaneous outburst by the Ura Yagyu would lead to the ruin of the Omote Yagyu. The earnestness of the Yoshiwara people earlier that day was an advance notice of that possibility, an unmistakable show of how determined they could be.

"If Gisen says that he will not comply with my wishes…"

"He must comply."

Takumi's color changed. "If it's my Lord and Gisen who…" However, even he did not dare continue. Munefuyu gave a sour smile.

"Are you saying that I might lose?"

Though the founder had been of another class altogether, his father Muneyoshi and his brother Jubei had been master swordsmen. It was the accepted view among all of the Yagyu School that Gisen had inherited rather more of that talent than Munefuyu.

"But might that be the result?" Munefuyu gave a cold, unpleasant smile. Not even the master strategist Notori Takumi was able to decipher what it implied. And in that instant, Munefuyu made a firm decision that even he had not foreseen having to make.

BOAR-TUSK BOATS

Under an evening sky in which the sun was loath to set, one black horse and two white horses ran at full tilt. Surprisingly, Shirozaemon held the reins of his mount rather adeptly. On both sides of the horses, the young men wearing O-Miuraya *happi* ran in neat formation without the slightest heaving of breath. Riding on one of the white horses, Seiichiro marveled at the stamina with which they ran.

"Where are we going? If we're headed for the Yoshiwara, we're going in the wrong direction!" shouted Mizuno from his horse.

"From Yanagi Bridge, we're taking a boat," responded Shiro-zaemon.

"A boat?" At the time there were no boats yet going to the new Yoshiwara, and even palanquins were not allowed, so the only way to get there was on foot or on horseback.

"From Asakusa River to the Sanya Moat. If we go that way, any pursuers will give up."

If a battle were to break out in town, the Yagyu would suffer no injuries. It would be a mere fight. The Yoshiwara party would naturally end up at a disadvantage. Shirozaemon was thinking that far ahead.

"On board what's called a 'boar-tusk boat.'"

These boats were just beginning to appear, and one day they would become the main type of vessel used by visitors to Yoshiwara. The name came from the narrowness of the boat, said to resemble the tusk of a wild boar, although some said it came from the snipping sounds of the sculls that pulled the boat along. Originally, sails were attached to the narrow boats and they were used by the fishermen off the coast of Choshi to bring fish from the offing to the better restaurants in town. In Choshi, sails were attached as well. During the Bunka period (1804-18), an amazing 700-plus Yoshiwara tusk boats were in use. The fee was 148-mon one way. Since a fishing boat went for 100-mon per day, it can be seen that the Yoshiwara boats charged quite a sum.

They were also known as "disinheritance boats." By the time a prodigal son had taken these boats to Yoshiwara with sufficient frequency that he was accustomed enough to it to be able to stand up in one of them and piss into the river, he would be disinherited, it was said.

These boar-tusk boats had a shallow draft, so they were unsteady, and therefore hard to board. As he boarded from the boathouse at Yanagibashi, Shirozaemon let out an incessant stream of faint shrieks. Shirozaemon was seated facing in the direction of the boat's progress, with Seiichiro and Mizuno seated side by side facing each other. There were three oarsmen, one in the bow and two in the stern. It was usual to have only two, and in Shotoku 4 (1714), even the two-oarsmen boat was outlawed.

The boat glided along the water. The moon was finally beginning to rise in the sky. The famous Kubio pine tree did not yet exist, and after passing the ferry crossing at Takemachi, on the left side, one could dimly see Matsuchiyama come into view.

For your sake, crossing at evening the Matsuchi hill

That poem expresses the longing of a man in love as he approaches the quarter, but even Seiichiro, who did not yet know a woman, looked upon the Matsuchiyama hill with feelings of sadness. Mixed in with the sound of the oars, from across the surface of the river came the delicate sound of *Misesugagaki*. Just as he had that first time, when he heard it the sound stirred his spirits. It seemed he had lost his heart to the quarter.

Gensai, who had come to meet him at *machiai-no-tsuji*, spoke sternly, with not the hint of a smile.

"Sei, it's about time you got to know a woman."

SENDAI TAKAO

It was the Hour of the Tiger, about five in the morning. The sun was already rising, but there was still a morning mist and the sky was a milky white.

Seiichiro was involved in a peculiar task. He was thrusting seven bamboo staves into the ground in the form of a circle. He was in the pampas grass field near the gravel pit in Tamachi. The bamboo staves he had obtained from one of the menservants at Nishidaya, where they were used as kindling for heating the bath. He stuck them into the ground without concern for their thickness or length. Naturally, they formed a bamboo circle of varying heights.

Having completed the figure, Seiichiro stood right in its center. He let his arms hang limp, in the *yoroboshi-kamae*. For half an hour, he simply stood there, motionless. Eyes closed, he concentrated his thoughts.

It was an attempt to devise a means of defeating the *Ranken no jin*, which Yagyu Munefuyu had demonstrated to him. Every morning, beginning the very next day, Seiichiro had come to this spot and worked to find a way to escape such an onslaught. When he closed his eyes, the bamboo staves were in no time transformed into Yagyu swordsmen, who began to stream to the left. Suddenly the inner group knelt, and the one-handed sword attack converged upon his legs. At the same moment, seven swords rained down upon his skull and shoulders. The outer ring of swordsmen had stepped on the shoulders of the men in the inner ring and were leaping inward.

(The only way is for me to jump an instant faster)

This was Seiichiro's conclusion. Caught between an attack from above and below, there was simply no way to evade such an offensive.

(Whether to jump high, or jump low)

If he jumped high, it would take time to touch ground again. While he was in the air, his defense would be weak, so the longer he was in the air, the greater the probability of his being wounded. If he jumped low, the landing would be quicker, but there was the chance of colliding with the swordsmen from the outer ring as they came over the top.

(Collide, send him flying)

He had to jump with the knowledge that he and another man would collide. If it was he who would be sent flying by the force of the collision, he would fall backward into the midst of the striking blades coming from above and below, to be cut to shreds.

(Take them by surprise—that's the thing to do)

Use an entirely unexpected tactic.

(Jump directly backward)

The opponent directly behind him would surely not expect Seiichiro to come in his direction. He ought to be unprepared for someone to come slamming against him. If there were a single blind spot to be taken advantage of, this would be it. But it would require not looking over his shoulder at all, and just jumping backward. In other words, while facing forward, he would have to see behind himself. Seeing behind oneself—to achieve this mental capability was the ultimate form of swordsmanship that every master aimed for. Seiichiro was deep in thought, striving to achieve just that.

Another thirty minutes passed. The Hour of the Rabbit, six o'clock. Morning in the great city of Edo began early. The thirty-six guarded accesses to the gates of Edo Castle were opening, and the merchants were opening their shops.

Suddenly Seiichiro let out a piercing shout, channeling all of his spirit, as he jumped six feet upward and directly backward. His feet landed precisely on one of the short bamboo staves, and in his hands were the two swords he had unsheathed. In his mind's eye, Seiichiro had indisputably seen the stave directly behind him, and his swords would have without doubt cut down the two swordsmen who should have been about to jump. He was about to jump diagonally forward, but abruptly stopped and instead landed outside the configuration.

"Good morning."

As he sheathed his swords, he turned around. His backward vision had detected the image of Gensai emerging from the thicket.

"Morning."

Gensai came out of the woods wearing a self-conscious smile.

"Practicing acrobatics so early in the morning?"

"Well, something like that."

Smiling, Seiichiro pulled up the bamboo sticks.

Gensai nonchalantly touched the end of the bamboo stave that Seiichiro had jumped upon a moment earlier.

(Incredible!)

The bamboo was completely shredded. Had it been a human being, the man's skull would have been shattered.

(Not just two would have been dispatched. There would have been a third as well.)

Gensai trembled slightly.

Carrying the bundle of bamboo staves bound with straw rope, Seiichiro walked alongside Gensai along the Nihon Embankment toward the Great Gate.

"Your companion has been selected," Gensai said.

"Companion?" Seiichiro seemed perplexed.

"The *oiran* who will be your companion."

"Oh." His response was half-hearted. This business had been an annoyance to Seiichiro from the outset. The first time Gensai had brought up the suggestion that it was about time he experienced being with a woman, Seiichiro had flatly refused. It was Seiichiro's view that he wasn't entirely ignorant regarding matters between the sexes and that when the time came, just as when fruit on a tree ripened and fell in the natural course of events, it just happened. He wouldn't stand for having some woman simply forced upon him. However, Gensai trotted out a curious reasoning that left Seiichiro bewildered.

"You do want to learn about the *Shinkun gomenjo*, don't you?"

Seiichiro was truly taken aback. He was shocked that the old man knew about the *Shinkun gomenjo*, but to be more precise, he was more amazed that the old man knew that Seiichiro had heard about it. What Seiichiro had not noticed was that at Shotoji, when Sagawa Shinzaemon of the Yagyu had flung those words at him, someone from the Yoshiwara was crouched near the grand gate of the temple. Seiichiro had even less of a chance of knowing that this young man was a *mimisuke*, a master at hearing sounds far in the distance. In the past, there had been a spy known as *Nabari no mimi*, the ears of Nabari, and it was said that he had once heard the sound of a pin dropping some fifty feet away. This particular *mimisuke* had a full half of that capability, so it was no trouble at all for him to catch the give-and-take that took place between Sagawa and Seiichiro.

"How about it? Do you want to find out about it, or not? If you do want to know what it's all about, then you'll have to know a woman."

"Why? What's the connection between the *Shinkun gomenjo* and a woman?"

"The *gomenjo* is a Yoshiwara secret. That secret is only revealed to people who are born in the quarter, or people who have become well acquainted with the quarter."

"But…"

"There's no way you can really understand Yoshiwara without spending time with a woman there. After all, Yoshiwara is a woman's capital."

This was Gensai's reasoning. Seiichiro gave up. He agreed to leave the matter in Gensai's hands.

"Since the matter was entrusted to me and I'm responsible, I thought it over a lot and discussed things with certain people before reaching a decision. It will be O-Miuraya's *tayu* Takao, a courtesan among courtesans. There is no other woman like her in all of Japan. You won't find her equal among the wives of the great feudal lords, nor among the princesses of the noble families…you couldn't possibly…"

Gensai shook his head as if to show profound emotion.

The image of Katsuyama briefly flitted through Seiichiro's mind, but he felt it best to say nothing.

Takao was the most famous of Yoshiwara's *tayu*, the highest-ranked courtesans. In actuality, there were more than one *tayu* bearing that name, for the name was passed down from one generation to the next among the *oiran* in the employ of O-Miuraya. There were several theories regarding how many generations passed the name along, but the exact number is unclear. It could have been anywhere from six to eleven generations. Among the most prominent were Myoshin Takao, who was said to have made her elaborate procession through the streets accompanied by a nursemaid who carried the courtesan's child. There was Sendai Takao, who was redeemed by the feudal lord of Sendai domain, Date Tsunamune, by paying her weight in gold *koban* coins. Her letter to him appears in Shokusanjin's Ichigon Ichiwa, along with the following poem:

(Leaving Yoshiwara) Perhaps you are around Komagata/ I hear a cuckoo

It was this Sendai Takao whom Seiichiro had selected for Seiichiro.

It should be noted that in this particular period, *tayu* were by no means mere prostitutes. They were, in a manner of speaking, "women who did not exist anywhere." Among the wives of the various powerful daimyo and the young women of the nobility, there were simply no women who could compare with the *tayu* in learning or artistic accomplishments. They were superior in playing the koto, hand drums and shamisen; they were well versed in tea ceremony, incense and flower-arranging; they excelled in calligraphy, waka poetry, linked verse and painting. Among the *tayu* were some who were said to always have at hand the first eight imperial collections of waka and *The Tale of Genji*. In short, they were superwomen who had received the finest education of their day.

One would be mistaken to conclude that it was a matter of buying and selling such a woman. The *tayu*'s right to turn down a guest was absolute. According to one anecdote, when the wealthy Osaka merchant Konoike Zen'uemon visited the Yoshiwara, he behaved with the arrogance of his home city and informally held out a cup of sake to a certain *tayu*. Not only that *tayu*, but every other woman in the room immediately stood up and left. Zen'uemon lost face as a result and was allegedly shoved out of the Great Gate. This anecdote illustrates the spirit and pride of the *tayu*. The fee for the appearance of a *tayu* for one evening was between one *ryo* and one *ryo* three *bu*. This was well beyond what a laborer could earn in an entire month, and it was during a period when a shop assistant in a large merchant household might not earn as much as five *ryo* in an entire year. One might pay such a large sum of money for the presence of a *tayu* and still be rejected by her. The guest could hardly afford to behave shamelessly with such expenses at stake.

A little girl passed along the broad Nakanocho boulevard through the quarter. She hopped along the boards in the middle of the street and kicked along pebbles as she passed Edocho in the direction of Kyomachi. It was Oshabu from Nishidaya.

Oshabu's mother Nabe, only daughter of the first generation, Shoji Jin'emon, had died five years earlier in Jo'o 1 (1652). Oshabu was only four at the time. Her father Jinnojo was an adopted son, so at present the direct blood line of the Shoji family ran through Oshabu. Since she had an extraordinary ability to foresee the future, the *oiran* and *kamuro*— and even her own father—were somewhat intimidated by her and kept their distance from her.

Oshabu was used to solitude. How could such a child not be isolated, one who, from her earliest recollection, possessed exceptional powers to foresee the future and—although she had not allowed even her father to know of this—also possessed the ability to read the minds of other people. Oshabu had read the name "Takao" in her father's mind; it was the name of Seiichiro's "companion." Oshabu was drawn to Seiichiro, and at least one reason was that she could not read his mind. It might be more accurate to say that although she could read his mind, it seemed like an infinitely luminous, translucent white void, with none of the murky shadows one invariably found in ordinary people. It was rather as if all she could feel was a faint sorrowful breeze blowing through it. It was a mental state that Seiichiro had achieved as a result of twenty-five years of training in swordsmanship, but Oshabu had no way of knowing that. She had simply never before encountered such a pure, serene man. She could not hear the name of the woman to whom Seiichiro would pledge his love and still remain composed. She was sad that she herself was not yet a woman. It was the usual course of things that a woman with psychic powers is prematurely developed mentally but rather slow to blossom physically. Oshabu was no exception to the general rule.

Before she was aware of it, Oshabu was standing in front of O-Miuraya. She stood staring at the shop curtain dyed with the characters "O" and "Miura," as if she could see straight through it into the center of the shop.

Drip. A single drop of black ink dropped from the paintbrush in Takao's hand. It ran in the paper right before her eyes. Takao looked curiously at her brush. This had never happened to her before. She could not have mistaken the amount of ink she had absorbed into the brush. Anyway, the painting itself was ruined. It was something that a guest had requested, but since she felt that making such a mistake was inauspicious, she was not inclined to start over again. Just as she was about to have a *kamuro* put everything away, the *banto shinzo*—the courtesan's personal secretary—came to her door and knelt before the entrance to her room.

"The Old Man is asking to see you."

In the old Yoshiwara, at least until the middle era of that quarter, the title "Old Man" had been bestowed on Shoji Jin'emon, and after his demise, O-Miuraya's Shirozaemon had succeeded to the name. Takao frowned and stood up.

In a private room, Shirozaemon, as always oscillating his surplus fat and constantly wiping sweat from his face, sat facing Oshabu. He found her an awkward presence. Under her detached gaze, he felt as if all of his deepest thoughts were exposed to the light of day. Shirozaemon was felt to be a man of good judgment, and he believed that himself. Rather naturally, in his heart of hearts there whirled around any number of ambitions and motivations, and it was a bit too much to have every single one of them detected. A year earlier, thanks to Oshabu, he had had occasion to shudder to his very core.

It was shortly after the end of the New Year celebrations. There was a gathering at Nishidaya, and during a drinking party, Oshabu had suddenly spoken up.

"Uncle Shiroza, you want to become shogun some day, don't you?"

Because it was such a fantastic notion, everyone had a big laugh and that was the end of the matter, but Shirozaemon had felt his entire body break out in sweat. It was because his secret, never spoken to a soul, had been pointed out so clearly. In fact, he did want to become shogun. Of course, he would never be able to become the shogun, but he ardently embraced the hope to put his own grandson or even a great-grandson in that position of power. This ambition had slowly grown within him, and he was just about to take concrete measures to approach that goal.

(What a frightening child!)

From that evening onward, Shirozaemon had endeavored to avoid being near the girl whenever possible.

To move the story some 101 years later to the eighth year of the Horeki era (1758), Shirozaemon's dream would be only one step away from realization. An O-Miuraya descendent, Miura Gorozaemon, gave his daughter Oitsu in adoption to Matsudaira Matajuro, and sent her to serve the Shogun Yoshimune's heir Ieshige. This Oitsu gave birth to Ieshige's second son Manjiro Shigeyoshi. Oitsu's father Miura Gorozaemon therefore duly became a bannerman of 500-*pyo*. In Horeki 8, Horeki Manjiro Shigeyoshi founded the Shimizu branch, one of the three Tokugawa branch families next in succession to the shogunate. At that point, the O-Miuraya House disappeared from Yoshiwara. They must have judged that, in case a shogun did come into being from the Shimizu household, there would be a problem if his relatives were Yoshiwara proprietors. This, indeed, was the fruit of the numbingly far-sighted plans laid by that old bag of tricks Miuraya Shirozaemon.

"You asked to see me?"

Takao entered the room. Shirozaemon drew a deep breath. Until that very moment, Shirozaemon had been concentrating his thoughts on the trivial business of balancing accounts in his head, thereby narrowly escaping having Oshabu read what was in his mind. Even for a man like Shirozaemon, it had definitely been a major expenditure of energy.

"This young girl says she wants to speak with you. You recognize her, don't you? This is Oshabu from the Nishidaya."

Takao gave Oshabu a puzzled look.

(She has such beautiful skin.)

Oshabu was about the age of a *kamuro*. Takao couldn't help considering her in that light. The training of a *kamuro* was entirely the responsibility of the *oiran* who acted as her older sister.

(Once she turns into a woman, she'll become a loving *oiran*, one with a pleasing personality.)

Takao knew well how a child's face would change. But…

"Thank you, but I can't become an *oiran*."

Without blinking an eyelash, Oshabu looked at Takao and smiled. Takao drew back in alarm.

(This child reads people's minds…)

In spite of herself, Takao looked at Shirozaemon. Still turned away, he made a slight nod.

"And what was it that you wanted to see me about?" Takao asked curtly. Certainly no one could enjoy having their thoughts read, and that was Oshabu's misfortune.

"Actually it was nothing," Oshabu replied in a small voice. But she quickly added, looking directly at Takao, "Please take good care of Sei-sama." Her eyes glistened with tears. Takao was greatly shocked.

(This child is thinking of Master Matsunaga as her sweetheart.)

But Oshabu shook her head slightly. Takao was mistaken. Oshabu's tears were not for Seiichiro. They were directed toward the fate that awaited Takao. Oshabu's eyes could see that two years in the future, Takao would be suspended from a boat, mercilessly murdered. The person who would, would be none other than the great daimyo Date Tsunamune.

(Any woman who gets involved with Sei-sama comes to a violent end)

To Oshabu, this was unbearably sad.

That evening, the sound of *Misesugagaki* seemed to descend from above, and at the same moment that Seiichiro was approaching the *ageya* Seiroku, a shadow appeared before the gate of the Yagyu clan's Edo residence. It was that of a priest, over six feet tall. In a voice so murderous that the gatekeeper turned for a moment white, he spoke. "I am Gisen from Yagyu Valley! Tell my older brother that I am incensed!"

SHOKAI—THE FIRST VISIT

The sound of the shamisen playing the now familiar *Misesugagaki* continued on without interruption. From a second-floor room of the Owariya Seiroku *ageya* house of assignation, through the green-bamboo screen that was pushed outward by a pole, one could see the radiant lights of Kyomachi. Boisterous crowds of people. Squeals of *oiran* coming from inside the lattice-work houses. Against the light blue of the sky, which seemed like the backdrop of a theater stage, shone a thin moon. A cool, refreshing breeze played in the hair at his temples.

(Only because you're alive can you experience such an evening.)

He was feeling so good, and it was this mood that drew such thoughts from him.

Perhaps it was the fact that he had entrusted both his short and long swords to the proprietor, and his hips were therefore bare, that Seiichiro, contrary to expectations, felt a sense of freedom. It was a feeling of buoyant exhilaration.

"Here, how about having one?"

Seiroku, proprietor of the shop, offered him some sake.

"Thank you."

He lightheartedly accepted the sake that was poured for him and drained the cup. He was handsome, in an irresistible way, and everyone in the room gazed at him with rapt attention.

The party was made up of six men. In addition to Seiichiro and Gensai, there were Miuraya Shirozaemon, Nomura Gen'i, Yamadaya Sannojo, Namikiya Genzaemon and serving them were Owariya Seiroku, the proprietor, and his wife. Perhaps because each one of these guests was a master of houses with courtesans of peerless beauty—castle-topplers, in the parlance of the quarter—both Seiroku and his wife appeared to be considerably strained.

With the exception of Gensai and Shirozaemon, all of the others were new to Seiichiro. Each appeared physically hardened and wore an expression of fearlessness, and there was no wasted movement in anything they did. Why these three were masters of *keiseiya* houses was incomprehensible to Seiichiro.

(These are no common samurai)

Were they to put on armor, one would take them for military commanders. Their skill in martial arts appeared to be beyond the ordinary. Evidence for this conjecture was supplied by their arms, which were as hard as knotty wood. In particular, Gen'i's hand seemed to have hardened in the shape it would take to grip a sword. Curiously enough, these old men, all of whom seemed like difficult men to deal with, were all smiles as they gazed at Seiichiro, and they were delightedly draining cup after cup of sake. It was almost as if they had returned home to the Yoshiwara with a favorite grandson. Seiichiro began to feel depressed.

Ever since he had become old enough to understand things, he couldn't remember ever being taken care of. From the time he was a mere toddler, Musashi had left him on his own. Musashi had given him only a short, heavy forester's hatchet, the kind used by the nomadic mountain people called *sanka*, and simply turned him loose. Musashi looked the other way, thereafter, even if the young Seiichiro lost his way or fell into a mountain stream. When Seiichiro was four years old, he had fallen down a precipice into a ravine, and because he had sustained bruises to his entire body, he had been unable to move for three days. Fortunately, he had not broken any bones, but half-submerged in water, he had been unable to move at all. Naturally enough, he became hungry, and during those three days, he had learned how to use the forester's hatchet. He caught trout in the river and killed a wild hare. That was also when he had learned to start a fire. When he was cooking the hare meat on the fire he had finally managed to start, Musashi suddenly turned up.

"Mmm, that smells good."

That was all that Musashi said. But even now, Seiichiro recalled how proud that one comment had made him feel. In silence they had stuffed their mouths with the succulent meat and drunk water from the mountain stream, and then they returned to the cavern the two normally inhabited. It was a strain for him to walk, given the pains all over his body, but Musashi neither lent him a hand nor even slowed his pace. Seiichiro gritted his teeth and did his best to race after Musashi.

Gensai bombarded Seiichiro with questions about his life in the mountains. When it came to such a subject, Seiichiro had plenty to talk about. He spoke without reflection just as the memories were revived in him, and the old men listened intently, nodding their heads. Their reactions indicated a peculiar sense of nostalgia. They appeared deeply affected, almost as if they were listening to stories of a land where they had once lived. They seemed so pleased with his tales that by the end he was almost expecting them to break down in tears. In actual fact, Nomura Gen'i took a folded piece of paper from his kimono and loudly blew his nose.

They're just like old mountain people, Seiichiro thought, recalling the legends Musashi had told him of mountain folks. At that moment, Seiichiro was unaware of just how accurate his intuition was, for that was exactly what they were: five old men from the mountains.

Nakanocho became a degree more lively.
"It's Takao!"
"Takao Tayu!"
One could hear the shouts of the customers in the streets. It seemed that the courtesan that would be Seiichiro's companion was making her elaborate *dochu* down the central boulevard of the quarter.

As was true in the days of the old Yoshiwara, in the early days of the new Yoshiwara, until to be precise Horeki 10 (1740), it was the custom for a customer who wished to be entertained by a high-class courtesan, whether a *tayu* or a *koshi*, to visit one of the *ageya* houses of assignation and to call for the courtesan to come there. One would be entertained as well as sleep there. In the New Yoshiwara they were all located in one neighborhood, called Ageyacho, but in the old Yoshiwara, these houses were scattered here and there. As a consequence, the courtesans from their Edocho houses of residence went to the Kyomachi *ageya*, and those in Kyomachi houses went to the Edocho ageya. These comings and goings were likened to the journey between Edo, the new capital, and the old capital of Kyoto, and were therefore called *dochu*, "journeys."

The *dochu* was an opportunity for the courtesan to make a glorious display of herself, and it also served as an advertisement for the house in which she resided. Therefore, the *oiran* made every effort not only to dress in spectacular attire with an elaborate hairstyle, but to create her own distinctive style through details such as her way of holding the hem of her kimono and of stepping during her procession.

This procession varied from generation to generation. In the days of the old Yoshiwara, it was more sedate, and even in the early Meireki years of the new Yoshiwara, the women wore not geta with high supports but ordinary flat sandals. High geta were first used during the Kyoho years, by a *yujo* named Fuyo from Kakucho Hishiya. I will write here how a *dochu* looked in the glory years of the Bunka era. At the head of the procession was a manservant carrying a *hako-chochin* imprinted with the crest of the house to which the *tayu* belonged. Then followed two *kamuro* wearing triple-layered, wide-sleeved kimono. There was no particular rule regarding what they carried, but one might carry a doll and the other a dagger, or a tobacco tray with smoking utensils and a long, thin *kiseru* pipe. Following the *kamuro* came the *tayu*. She held the hem of her four-layered kimono in her right hand, and wore the black-lacquered *tatami*-covered geta that measured some six to eight inches in height. Behind her came another manservant carrying a long-shafted umbrella (about nine feet high) with the name of the house painted on it. Following him came two *shinzo*, each wearing a three-layered kimono, and a stylishly-dressed *yarite*. Then came another manservant wearing a leather haori. Any number of these processions made their way along Nakanocho through the heart of the quarter.

"The first time a *tayu* appears is called *shokai*, the first meeting. During the first encounter there is a ceremony called *hikitsuke*, 'drawing close.' Where we are now is a *hikitsuke yashiki*, a place designed for such occasions," explained Gensai.

Once again, Seiichiro looked around the spacious twenty-mat room. It was a room directly up the stairs from the front entrance. Even with a large 100-*momme* candle, there was not enough light, so the four corners of the room were dark. In the middle of the room were placed a *haidai* stand for drinking cups, with an earthenware vessel for serving sake, and a stand for serving food.

"In the Shimabara quarter in Kyoto, there is a *tayu kashi no shiki,* a ceremony for entrusting a courtesan to a customer. The ceremony here in Yoshiwara is a simple version of that."

"So it's an imitation of Kyoto?" Seiichiro commented, with disappointment.

"The history of Kyoto's pleasure quarters is longer. It started at Yanaginobaba, then moved to Rokujo-Misujimachi and finally to Shimabara. It's only natural that Yoshiwara mimicked it. But look at it this way—even Shimabara and the older Yanaginobaba were imitators."

"…!"

"They imitated the Pingkangli licensed quarters in Chang'an during the T'ang period. The Yanaginobaba quarter was established by the Taiko's footman Hara Saburozaemon and the *ronin* Hayashi Mataichiro. Supporting those two were none other than Gozan priests. These Buddhist priests traveled all the way across the seas to China to study and when they came back, they remembered what they had studied and also the pleasure they had taken in the gay quarters of the Chinese city. They made use of the latter experience in Yanaginobaba. As a matter of fact, the *Tayu kashi no shiki* was an imitation of a similar Chinese ceremony, *Jian ke*, 'seeing the guest.'"

Seiichiro was taken aback. It was due to the fact that old man Gensai had so fluently pronounced the Chinese words. On his way to Edo, Seiichiro had detoured to Nagasaki, and had from there boarded a boat for Osaka. In Nagasaki he had stayed two nights and had seen both Europeans from the Iberian peninsula and some Chinese. The pronunciation of the latter seemed perfectly reflected in Gensai's words. Given that among the Japanese at that time only Gozan priests and the interpreters at Nagasaki could pronounce Chinese words, Seiichiro was naturally impressed.

"Were you ever in Nagasaki?" Seiichiro asked.

Gensai laughed mischievously. "There's no place in this country that I haven't been. Of course, I didn't exactly travel around with official documentation."

"Ahem!"

Shirozaemon cleared his throat as a warning. And almost as if on cue, the door opening onto the hallway smoothly slid open. Six *tayu*, led by Takao, gracefully entered the room and took the seats of honor. As one might expect, they presented a grand spectacle, as if flowers had suddenly burst into bloom. Not a single one of the courtesans betrayed even a slight glimpse of a smile. Judging from their completely indifferent attitude, they might not have even noticed the guests in the room. Even when they sat down, they did not face the guests, but rather sat at an oblique angle to the men. All six courtesans sat at the same angle, giving them the appearance of a formation of wild geese. They each sat with the right leg folded under and the left knee slightly raised, the right arm slightly angular and the left hand holding the right arm near the opening of the sleeve. This was the formal style of sitting.

The proprietress of the Owariya took sake cups from the stand, offered it to Takao addressing her as *"Anata-sama,"* and then to Seiichiro with, *"Konata-sama."* After three formal exchanges of sake cups, she returned the cup to its original place on the stand. After the same ritual was repeated with the other five *tayu*, Takao once again nimbly stood up and led the others out of the room. The ceremony had come to an end.

Seiichiro was open-mouthed with astonishment. Ceremony though it was, it had happened all too hastily, and he had not even had time to take a good look at Takao.

"Is that the end?" he whispered to Gensai.

"We're going to change rooms," responded Gensai with a wry smile.

But even in the second room, with the *shinzo* and *kamuro* and the banquet, Takao's attitude changed not a whit. She ate absolutely nothing of the food that was brought out. When offered a cup of sake, she would accept it, but she would put it down without drinking from it. She exchanged not a word with Seiichiro.

In actual fact, although Seiichiro was unaware of it, this was exactly how a *tayu* was expected to behave during the first encounter.

At the first meeting, sitting as if stuck to the wall
Even if delicacies are served, eating none of them
Nothing is supposed to take place, at the first meeting

As conveyed by each of these comic senryu verses, it was the generally accepted view that nothing was supposed to happen during the *shokai* gathering. Least of all could one expect to sleep together with the *tayu*. Still, why was it that the people of Yoshiwara, who were so attuned to the subtleties of the human psyche, went to such extremes to disappoint their customers? There was, of course, a good reason for doing so.

It is said that men prefer a lusty relationship with a higher-class woman, while women prefer a licentious relation with a lower-class man. It is virtually impossible to exhaust the list of instances of this notion, beginning with Hideyoshi and Yodogimi. It was precisely this propensity that the Yoshiwara people aimed to exploit.

The *tayu*, accomplished in learning and the arts and attired with elegance, was a complete noblewoman. She was therefore a flower out of reach. How could such an unattainable woman possibly stoop to ingratiate herself with a customer? It was instead the man who had to flatter, use money, and make every effort to get the woman to turn in his direction.

The long-shafted umbrella that protected the *tayu* during her formal procession through the streets was formally known as an *ogasa*. In ancient times, the only women who were allowed to use such a formal umbrella when they walked were the high-ranking ladies of the court and the official wives of the Grand Minister, the Minister of the Left and the Minister of the Right.

The courtesans also followed the ladies of the imperial court in wearing a lined, pure white kimono on the first day of the eighth month. The single reason in the official pretext for the confiscation of the property and land of Yodoya Tatsugoro was that he wore just such a lined pure white kimono and rode in a palanquin—an outrageous act for a merchant. This was permitted only to the *yujo* because it was clear that by such dress they were emulating women of high rank. In fact *joro*, as they were called, a word that came to mean "prostitute," was a variation of a term for "court lady."

Most unfortunately, the intention of these people of Yoshiwara was entirely lost on Seiichiro. There was no distortion in Seiichiro's own mind, so for such a man, there could be no "higher-class" or "lower-class." To him, Takao was simply a beautiful woman. She seemed just like a peony. She was not like some graceful flower that blooms in an open field; she was a large peony, thick and velvety to the touch. With upturned eyes and a shapely nose, there was only the finest of lines between her beauty and arrogance. Arrogance was one thing that Seiichiro could not abide. He left his seat quietly.

In the Yoshiwara, the urinal for customers was in a corner of the second floor. In a traditional townhouse, one never saw such a place, so a boorish customer would not be aware that it even existed. There was no door or enclosure whatsoever. One simply put on low clogs, stepped up to the highest place and did one's business. It was broad enough for three or four men to stand side by side. The woman of the houses tended to their business downstairs in a room adjacent to the bath.

Whenever a customer stood up and left the room for that purpose, a *furisode shinzo* always accompanied him. It was said that this was done to prevent a guest from sobering up, during the instant that he was pissing, and having thoughts of home. This being Seiichiro's first such experience, he was understandably somewhat embarrassed. As, self-conscious, he let loose his stream, a man came to stand next to him. It was Mizuno Jurozaemon.

"Well, hello," Seiichiro said with a broad smile. Upon seeing Mizuno, he breathed easier.

"A little while ago, I happened to peek into your room," Mizuno replied. "It seems that Takao is to be your companion."

Mizuno unceremoniously wiggled his hips as he spoke.

"That's right."

Detecting in Seiichiro's reply a note of weariness, Mizuno grinned.

"You seem bored."

"Not really," Seiichiro hesitated to say anything in front of the girl behind him.

"The first encounter is always that way," Mizuno said with amusement. "Still, any ordinary man would be so enchanted by Takao that time would just fly by. You must be a real grumbler at heart."

Seiichiro smiled wryly.

"How about it? Let's go out on the rooftop," Mizuno suddenly suggested.

"The roof?"

"Yeah, this roof right here. It's really entertaining."

The roofs of the Yoshiwara were required to be shingled. Each was dominated by a rain barrel, which was used in case of fire, and there were two fire brushes, for use in beating out flames.

Seiichiro followed Mizuno out from the platform for drying clothes onto the roof. Nakanocho lay right below them.

Men walked down the street below as if carried on the sound of *Misesugagaki*. Those who wore hoods and woven hats to conceal their identity were, in all likelihood, samurai, physicians, priests or merchants.

Those who were "just looking" were mostly craftsmen. Mizuno explained that these artisans and gamblers of the Yoshiwara neighborhood were referred to as "local hoodlums," and those who were just looking at the goods were called "roaches."

A woman in one of the *harimise* was rolling up a piece of paper and pushing it through the latticework of the window to convey some kind of secret to a guest outside on the street. Matsunaga said that she might be arranging a rendezvous with a man who had no money to spend, or making a request for him to come on one of the *monbi*, a day when the courtesan's prices were doubled and she had to secure patrons in advance.

In general, the men's eyes were all bloodshot, and it was clear that the blood was pumping to their heads in anticipation of the pleasure that awaited them. They were looked at askance by those contemptuous men who hurried through the streets, but even the latter type, upon coming across a courtesan on her procession, would gaze in wonder, thus exposing his true feelings.

A single black cat yawned and slowly walked along the roof above the men's heads. Seiichiro detected in the cat a shadow of a sage. At the same time, he began to feel somewhat melancholy.

"All those men, what are they doing?"

"They've all come to lose their hearts to women, of course," replied Mizuno.

"No, that's not what I meant. I was wondering what they do when they aren't here."

Mizuno lapsed into silence. When he finally spoke, his tone had turned slightly grim.

"What are you trying to get at?"

"Nothing particular. I don't have anything to do myself, and I was just wondering."

It was half true and half a lie. When he attained perfect mastery over his sword, Seiichiro remembered how he had become aware that he had nothing more to strive for, and that sudden awareness had left him at a loss. But now the situation was different. The five older men in the room below very clearly wanted to take him somewhere. Regardless of where that would be, surely it was better to have a place to go than not to have one. Further down this particular path, what sort of trouble lay to engulf him? Seiichiro awaited that with a twinge of pain in this heart.

(What does Heaven have in store for me?)

He wanted to scream out to the void above. He felt that powerful an emotion welling up within him.

Mizuno finally spoke.

"Go to ruin."

"Go to ruin?"

"That's right. That's the only thing we can do. Destroy people, destroy homes, destroy yourself. That's it. I've had enough of continuing to survive covered with shit in this filthy world. Show up at the castle at the appointed time, leave at the appointed time. Work an abacus like a damned merchant, flatter your superiors, lay out your subordinates. All that for what? For status and money. It's a dirty way to live. Is that how a samurai is supposed to live? No—that's not what samurai are all about! I won't even say samurai, a human being can't do such sordid things. Living ought to be something more magnificent. It's so fantastic that just thinking about it makes you sigh, makes your blood rush. But if it's like this…if that's all it is, then I'll cast it all aside. Any time, I'm ready to die!"

Seiichiro felt deep sympathy with Mizuno's fire-breathing words. Something seemed to seethe up from deep inside. To relieve the frustration that seemed directed nowhere in particular, he lay down on the roof, looking up at the starry heaven which seemed to fall toward him.

(Where is Heaven leading me?)

Once again Seiichiro heaved a groan within himself.

At that very same moment, an extraordinary thing was taking place in the room below.

THE DRUM

Takao's eyes seemed to glisten. In an instant, a large transparent teardrop welled up and coursed down her cheek.

"*Oiran!*"

The first in the room to notice it was one of the *kamuro*, who in absolute astonishment reached out unconsciously towards Takao's knee, but then suddenly stopped her hand. Takao's pose had changed not a bit, and her face still retained its formal composure, but her eyes were wide open, and from them welled, then overflowed, a constant stream of tears. They fell to her cheeks, then down her chin, and finally dropped to the robe that covered her kimono. In the room, which had fallen perfectly silent, that sound of tears falling on cloth was oddly distinct.

Even the proprietress of Owariya, who had keen insight into the affairs of the quarter and who was well-versed in the psychology of the *oiran*, and the *banto shinzo* who accompanied Takao, turned pale and could not speak. The *shinzo* and *kamuro* were only trembling. None of the women had seen Takao cry before. With the possible exception of her bedchamber, regardless of what happened she had never allowed anyone to see her cry, even in her own rooms. Everyone considered her a hard-hearted woman, but here Takao was, in tears.

O-Miuraya Shirozaemon was bewildered. He could understand Takao's vexation. Seiichiro's treatment of her was outrageous. It was unheard of for a guest to abandon a *tayu* on the first visit and climb out onto the roof. He had never heard of such unjustifiable behavior. And yet, if that were the case, then Takao should simply stand up and walk out. It was her prerogative to leave, and not even he as proprietor or her house could do a thing to prevent her from doing so. In a way, in order for her to maintain her pride, he wished that she would do so.

But here she sat, in tears, like a girl of fifteen or sixteen. Her comportment was unsuitable. Had she been an ordinary courtesan, Shirozaemon would undoubtedly have taken her to task, but this was Takao. She was a woman who was very much aware of what she should do. That left Shirozaemon all the more bewildered as to what he himself should do next.

There was nothing complicated about Takao's emotions.

She had become a courtesan among courtesans as a result of her ability to empathize. She could easily and quickly feel the same feelings as her guests, and see things from the same point of view. That evening, she had read Seiichiro's inner feelings with the briefest look into his eyes. And she had seen herself through his eyes, and found that image repulsive. It was that which upset Takao from the outset.

It was entirely natural. She had never before encountered among her customers an uncultivated man who had literally emerged from the depths of the mountains. So when Seiichiro had left the reception room, she had seen what he did as entirely natural. When, at Mizuno's instigation, he had climbed out onto the roof, she had taken that, too, as a variety of refreshing behavior, but now for the second time she found herself at a loss. Almost without realizing it, she had begun to have feelings for Seiichiro. At the same time, as a *tayu*, she knew that she had to condemn such uncouth behavior on his part. However, it was obvious that if she were to stand up and walk out, she would never be able to see Seiichiro again. This was the first time since she had become a *yujo* that she had no idea what she should do. It was this perplexity that had produced the tears.

Amidst this oppressive silence, Shirozaemon waited as if in prayer for Gensai to return. Shirozaemon knew that he was no match at all for Gensai when it came to handling women. When Gensai had heard that Seiichiro had gone out onto the roof, he had immediately stood up and left the room.

Not a single person in the room spoke, and no one made the slightest movement. They seemed to think that if anyone inadvertently moved a single finger, something extraordinary might happen. Everyone could feel the tension heightening perilously.

"I'm back now," Gensai said breezily as he walked in.

Whew! Shirozaemon, Gen'i, and even Sannojo and Genzaemon unconsciously heaved a deep sigh of relief.

Gensai in a flash grasped the atmosphere within the room. He did not return to his own seat, but sat down directly in front of Takao. For a moment, he fixed his eyes on her teardrops, but then he began shaking his head and smiling, as if he was absolutely charmed by something. "*Tayu*, have you any idea what that boy was doing up there on the roof?"

Takao shook her head petulantly like a little girl.

"That boy was sprawled out on the roof, talking about his view of life, what the world is all about, how people should live their lives. He and Mizuno were totally absorbed in their discussion. The two of them up there, as if they had completely forgotten where they were."

Gensai spoke with pleasure. Takao stared fixedly at Gensai.

"You know, I went up planning to drag him back with me, but in the end, I couldn't even say anything to him. There they were, talking away about things that won't profit them in any way, questions that have no real answer—and as if their lives depended on it! People may say they're a pair of fools, but that's what it means to be a young man, don't you think? I guess that's the prerogative of young men. I'll have to admit, *Tayu*, that I'm envious of them. Just plain envious of those two."

Suddenly Gensai's voice choked. Memories of something he and the others had lost seemed to constrict his chest. In contrast, Takao's tears had at some point completely dried up. She was still staring fixedly at Gensai.

"Please be patient, *Tayu*. These things happen to men. And especially to young men. Any man in this world who hasn't had times like this... well, you can't trust them if they haven't had such an experience. That boy has a pure heart; he's the kind you can trust. *Tayu*, you must have heard the origin of the *nimaigushi*, haven't you? Any woman of pleasure who has been at a battle front is bound to know well what a man is really worth."

Long ago there was a work called *Gojinjoro*, which tells of a group of courtesans who lived in a forest of katsura trees along the banks of the Rakuseikatsura River during the Heian and Kamakura periods. It is said that they participated in battle with a group of samurai. They each wore two ornamental combs in their hair. One was to be used for her own grooming, and the other was to be used in the event of misfortune. The misfortune referred to here was when an enemy general was decapitated. They would then wash the head and smooth the hair with the other comb. All of the women in Yoshiwara wear two combs, and this *Gojinjoro* was where the tradition originated.

Gensai continued.

"For that young man's rudeness, I apologize, from the depths of my heart."

Gensai placed his hands on the tatami and bowed his head deeply. Every woman in the room was dumbfounded. And it was not just Gensai. Miuraya Shirozaemon, Nomura Gen'i, Yamadaya Sannojo, Namikiya Genzaemon—all four also placed the palms of their hands on the tatami and made a formal bow. In the entire Yoshiwara, could there be anyone other than Takao who could make these four great proprietors bow their heads so deeply? After all, they were the ones who ran Yoshiwara, and here they were doing almost more than necessary to save Takao's honor. At the same time, their actions betrayed just how great their expectations were for the young man Matsunaga Seiichiro.

"How ought a person to live..." Takao repeated. "And what does he think about that?"

"This world we lived in is so defiled as to be worthless, an entirely wearisome place altogether... Rather than to live a dreary existence in this corrupt world, it would be better to cast everything aside and bring ruin upon oneself..."

"Well!"

"That's Mizuno's view of things—but Matsunaga sees things differently. Precisely because the world is so tainted and corrupt, he says, a person ought to live in such a way that at least he himself is unsullied. Mizuno responded that trying to live that way is too lonely and difficult and that he just doesn't have the patience to endure it. But Matsunaga just remained silent. *Tayu*, what do you think?"

"Does Master Matsunaga perchance intend to enter seclusion in a monastery?"

"Perhaps, or he might intend to return to the mountains, and never set foot in this world again. But we will not allow him to do that. We will teach him roundly that there are many ways of withdrawing from the secular world. At the very least, the path we have chosen for him will be far from monotonous. That's the good thing about it."

Shirozaemon, rippling in giant waves, laughed without making any sound at all. The other three men smothered laughter as well.

"And, *Tayu*, he needs your help. We'd like you to help him understand just how enjoyable this world can be. *Tayu*, you are the only one who can do this. Please accept our request."

Takao's cheeks blushed shyly, like an unsophisticated young girl's. The face powder having been washed off by her tears in patches, the faint pink of her complexion now shone through.

(Oh, how beautiful!)

Everyone in the room saw her in this same way. Even the other *tayu* and the *furisode shinzo*—they all, with no envy whatsoever, felt the same emotion.

Shirozaemon was struck with admiration. But it was not for Takao's beauty. Rather, it was for Gensai's ability to delude a person, an ability that had brought out Takao's beauty.

(He's incomparable)

In his heart, Shirozaemon once again bowed in honor of their group's true leader.

Takao turned round to the *banto shinzo* seated behind her.

"A drum," she said.

"*Tayu!*" Shirozaemon spoke in spite of himself. He had never heard of any *tayu* performing at a first meeting.

Takao laughed slightly.

"If a guest climbs up on the roof during the first visit, surely there can be nothing wrong with a *tayu* playing a drum."

Shirozaemon fell silent.

"And what's more…" Takao's expression turned serious, "Isn't it my responsibility to make him want to come down from the rooftop?"

Kaang!

At the first, penetrating sound of the drum, Seiichiro unintentionally sat upright.

Kaang! Kaang!

(What was it?)

Some sort of sensation deep within his body stirred him.

Kaang! Kaang! Iyooo!

It was a memory of a time long, long ago. The leaves were translucent green. Through them spilled shafts of sunlight. The tree trunks were thicker than his own waist. The rich, black humus was soft beneath the feet.

(A forest. A thick, unpleasant forest covering a mountain.)

He was not sure exactly where the forest was. It must have been some place they had passed through before settling down in Kinbozan, during that long period of drifting from Bizen province to Higo province, somewhere along the way. A man with wild hair like a mountain man, and a boy. *My feet hurt!* The boy stumbled painfully over the stubble. *My feet hurt!* But the complaint was spoken only in the boy's heart. It did not pass his lips. *They hurt! They hurt!* With this unspoken protest as a beat, he moved his feet forward, as if with strings of a puppet, first one, then the other, relentlessly onward. His eyes were fixed on the ground, and the boy felt as if he had become some sort of insect. If he didn't keep his legs moving, he would be left behind. *You have been abandoned once before,* he told himself. He moved on frantically. *My feet hurt! They hurt really bad!*

At that moment, he heard the sound.

Thump!

The penetrating sound threw off the beat to which he was walking. The pain penetrated to the very crown of his head, and he sank to his knees.

"It's the Kugutsu."

The man with the unkempt hair looked down at the boy with no expression at all on his face when he spoke.

"Kugutsu?"

"A mountain tribe, puppeteers. If we find them, there'll be medicine. Food too."

The boy stood up. They hadn't eaten for a day.

Kaang! Kaang! Iyooo!

In the intervals between the penetrating sounds, there came rhythmical shouts. It was only after the unexpectedly refreshingly dressed women of the group had gently attended to his feet, and after he was filled with a warm meal, that the boy learned that the instrument that made that uncanny sound was called a hand drum. It was a woman who struck the hand drum, and it was also a woman who sang that mysterious song. The men were dancing. Several of the men danced as if they were drunk. The sound of the hand drum continued into the night. Half-asleep, the boy listened to the drum's beat. He felt the sound violently striking something within his heart.

Kaang! Kaang! Pon! Pon!

The sound continued, and before Seiichiro was aware of it, he was standing up on the roof. For some reason, tears were streaming down his cheeks. Seiichiro himself didn't know whether the tears were tears of apprehension that he might be left behind in the mountains, or tears of relief that he would be able to rest at ease this one night through. Mizuno said something to him, but he couldn't hear well enough for it to register. He had begun to step along the roof as if drawn along by a string.

(This isn't music for a reception room. It's music for the open air.)

Considering which, the sound oddly enough matched the

Misesugagaki. On second thought, with the addition of the small hand drums, the music of *Misesugagaki* had changed to a sound that could be heard in the broad outdoors. With no logical connection whatsoever, a great river appeared to flow before his eyes.

(Why a river?)

In an instant, the boisterous throng plying its way along Nakanocho boulevard appeared in Seiichiro's eyes like a sparkling river of light. The courtesans on parade, their young attendants, and the men clustered around them all appeared to wriggle along on the bottom of this river of life. And on the surface of this river moved a gigantic boat. On board this boat, a Kugutsu woman was striking the drum while Kugutsu men danced. It was an extraordinary overlap, an illusion.

(Why a river?)

Seiichiro asked himself once more, but there was no reply.

FIERCE WIND OF AUTUMN

Retsudo Gisen was a man of "spirit." An intensity of spirit always permeated his body and radiated fiercely from it. His Buddhist name, Retsudo, was highly appropriate for it conveyed his ardent, impassioned character very accurately. He concentrated that spirit in such a mass that it struck anyone who confronted him like an enormous stone. The person facing him at the moment was his older brother, Yagyu Munefuyu. The latter, like a dark, bottomless chasm, sought to submerge his own emotions entirely and to absorb Gisen's fierceness.

They were in an inner room of the Yagyu main residence in Edo.

It was well past three in the morning.

But Munefuyu knew that all of the Yagyu vassals, including the Chief Councilor to the Shogun, Notori Takumi, were wide awake, swords close at hand, paying close attention to what was happening in this very room.

Dusk. From the moment that Gisen arrived, the Yagyu residence had been in a veritable whirlwind. Gisen's undisguised spirit and ferocious roar reverberated throughout the residence, sending shivers up the spines of the retainers. The uproar could not have been greater had a hundred wandering samurai have suddenly invaded the premises with drawn swords.

Gisen had heard the news from Sagawa Shinzaemon even before Munefuyu's express messenger had reached him. The single matter of the Ura Yagyu men being driven from the main residence in town to the country residence was sufficient to send Gisen into a rage. Munefuyu attempted to assuage this anger by identifying Matsunaga Seiichiro's lineage and describing the demonstration of force by the Yoshiwara group. But precisely as Munefuyu had feared, such words backfired. It was like pouring oil on a flame, and Gisen simply became even more enraged.

"You should have killed him—without a second's hesitation. Not just let him walk away. You should have hacked him into small pieces! It was the absolute perfect opportunity to with a single stroke avenge the long-standing bitterness of the Yagyu clan."

"What? And destroy the entire Yagyu clan?"

"We would not have been destroyed. Through successive generations now our clan has served the shogun through shadow operations. If even a part of that were made public, the core of the shogunate would be shaken. If that were made known, neither the imperial family nor the daimyo would remain silent. If things were to go wrong, the entire Tokugawa clan would be toppled. There is no way that a mere suspicion could lead anyone to make a move against the Yagyu."

"Are you suggesting blackmailing the shogun?"

"If the situation required," Gisen replied boastfully.

Somberly and intently, Munefuyu watched his brother. This younger brother of mine, he thought, doesn't understand anything at all. The Tokugawa clan has ruled for four generations now, and the country is at peace. The third shogun, Iemitsu, had taken tough measures and defanged all the various daimyo, so that there was no longer a single trace of the ambitious spirit brandished by the warlords of the Warring States period. If it came to an actual battle, no one would be more terrified than those daimyo. It was even truer now that the Laws Governing the Imperial Court and Nobility had been enacted. Now the imperial house had no power to start a war of any kind. The Yagyu clan's repugnant covert activities were now both antiquated and useless, just a fragment of a terrible nightmare. If Gisen were to foolishly make an intimidating move, the central Bakufu leadership would launch an all-out offensive and move to annihilate the entire Yagyu clan, that much was absolutely obvious to Munefuyu.

(It might come to that after all)

Munefuyu made up his mind.

(It's the only thing to do)

He meant the secret plan: murder his own brother in order to save the Yagyu clan's very existence. It would have to be carried out at the earliest possible opportunity. His eyes darkened, like a chasm on a moonless night.

From the early hours of the previous evening, a strong wind had blown, and throughout the night, fire wardens had passed through the quarter knocking together wooden clappers to call on the residents to take precautions against fire. By dawn, the wind had weakened slightly, but here in the field near the gravel pit, the stems of the flowering pampas grass rubbed against one another intensely in the wind. It was a fierce autumn wind.

In the middle of the pampas field stood Seiichiro. The wind was pulling at the sleeves of his kimono and his loose-pleated *hakama*, but he stood as firm as a rock. His eyes were open slightly, but he wasn't looking at anything. Reflected in his eyes were his surroundings, with himself at the center; that is, he could see in every direction. He was practicing *kanso-no-ho*, the technique of seeing behind oneself. Seiichiro had mastered this technique in the mountains of Higo province, but now he felt the need to become even more skilled in the art in order to devise a means of defeating the *Ranken* attack strategy. That was why every morning he came to this pampas field to practice for two hours. There were no longer any bamboo staves stuck into the ground. He simply stood motionless, watching. Day by day, the distance he could "see" grew perceptively longer. It was said that a true master could observe things 25 miles in the distance, but Seiichiro was not that good yet. At the very most, he was aware of what was going on along both sides of the Nihon Embankment.

At that moment, Seiichiro was aware of the "spirit" of a particular man. That spirit had come from the Asakusa gate, along Umamichi and up onto Nihon Embankment. This spirit—or volition—would not have been called piercing. However, it was deeply embedded, and what spilled forth from it was a spirit that could only be called ghastly. The spirit finally took form. It took the form of a concealing basket-like straw hat, a dark-gray over-jacket and identical-colored *hakama*, one black-lacquered sheath each for a short and a long sword. The man wearing these was somewhat small of stature and plump. Seiichiro had encountered the man before. It was Yagyu Munefuyu. The man projected no intent to kill, but it was evident that he was tightly strung. Seiichiro felt that there must be considerable resolve inside him to bring him out to such a place. Munefuyu entered the thickly wooded area bordering the field, and it was clear that he was headed precisely to where Seiichiro stood—in the middle of that field. Munefuyu clearly knew where Seiichiro was at that moment. Seiichiro slowly turned so that he would face Munefuyu. The fierce wind struck him directly head on. In a fight, wind coming from this direction would be a disadvantage, but Seiichiro already sensed that Munefuyu was not intent on fighting.

When Munefuyu came out of the thicket, he stopped.

Seiichiro bowed slightly.

"I would like to thank you for instructing me the other day."

For a moment, Munefuyu stared fixedly at Seiichiro. He nodded ever so slightly, and as he slowly approached, he said, "It would seem that you have devised a way to counter the *Ranken* attack."

"I have a method, but am not yet sure."

There was, of course, no way of knowing whether he had found a way or not—without actually trying it out in actual combat. But he couldn't very well say so. Munefuyu once again nodded his head slightly. The pace with which he approached Seiichiro did not change. The distance between them rapidly narrowed, and in almost no time, they were within halberd range.

"Unh."

With an almost unvoiced *kiai*, Munefuyu's body sank into the pampas. As he bent one knee under himself, he drew one sword and struck straight upward like a flash of lightning. Seiichiro moved slightly to avoid the long sword's blade. In the next instant, Munefuyu leaped up, using his bent leg as a spring. From an overhead stance, his sword struck straight downward. With a minimal shift of his body, Seiichiro escaped this strike as well. He still had not drawn a sword. Munefuyu next turned the edge of his sword blade and struck diagonally from lower left upward. In reverse, this would cut from the shoulder down across to the opposite side of the body. The pace of the attack was ferocious. Seiichiro was barely escaping the blade at this point. Munefuyu was once again striking at him upward across the body through the shoulder. Unable to bear the attack any further, Seiichiro made a great leap. It was the only way to avoid the attack.

"Just where you landed, I have a sword concealed."

Munefuyu sheathed his sword with a resolute click. Seiichiro nodded.

"So I would be dead?"

"In theory," he answered with a slight smile.

"It is called *gyakufu no tachi*, the reverse sword attack."

Seiichiro looked at Munefuyu with amazement.

"Why?"

"Why what?"

"Why are you instructing me in the *gyakufu no tachi*?"

"That is not all. I will teach you the Yagyu clan's secret teachings of swordsmanship—all of it."

It was an astounding announcement.

"Every morning, at the same time. In this pampas field."

Munefuyu spoke in no uncertain terms. This was what he had resolved to do—to gamble on Seiichiro's prodigious abilities. By instructing Seiichiro in the entirety of the swordsmanship possessed by Gisen and the Ura Yagyu, Munefuyu intended to train Seiichiro to become an absolutely invulnerable warrior. It was a desperate strategy to save the Omote Yagyu from the recklessness of the Ura Yagyu.

"But…" Seiichiro remained puzzled.

Munefuyu answered so as to keep Seiichiro under control, "It would be inconvenient if you were to be killed."

"What?"

Munefuyu once again drew his sword. When he advanced with his left foot, he grasped the hilt of his sword with his right hand. With his left hand, he supported the back of the sword. At first glance, it appeared he was taking a throat-thrust position, but…

"This is called the *marubashi no tachi*."

In the instant that the right foot moved forward, the sword feinted a thrust but swiftly changed to a ferocious attack from the right. Seiichiro's sword rang.

URA: THE SECOND VISIT

"Today let me tell you about the *mikaeri yanagi*, 'the willow where one looks back longingly,'" said Gensai. It was Seiichiro's second visit to a brothel. In this world, the second visit was called *ura o kaesu*, "looking from a different angle." The location was the same as before, the second floor of the *ageya* Owariya Seiroku. Three days had passed since the evening of the first visit. Gensai said that this was exactly the appropriate interval. This evening, it was only Gensai and Seiichiro, and as before, Seiroku and his wife were doing the serving. Neither Takao nor Gensai's companion had arrived yet. It seemed that the room somewhat differed from the previous occasion, and Seiichiro realized it was because the location of the candlestand was different. The hundred-*momme* candle gave off the same dim light as it had before.

"What is this *mikaeri yanagi*?" asked Seiichiro.

Gensai breathed an exaggerated sigh. "Did you hear that? This young man has been in Yoshiwara a full ten days now and he still doesn't know about the willow."

Seiroku's wife suppressed a giggle behind the sleeve of her kimono.

"Perhaps it's because he is so open," said she, "that you find such significance in instructing him."

"I've been outwitted," Gensai replied, slapping his forehead in self-mockery.

"When you go out of the Great Gate and up the Fifty-Ken Road, when you get to Nihon Embankment, on the left-hand side is an official announcement board, right?"

"Yes."

"And just across from that board, on the right side of the road, there's a willow tree."

"Oh, that one."

"Yes. When a customer of the quarter leaves in the morning, he stands there and looks back at Yoshiwara with lingering affection...and that is why it's called *mikaeri yanagi*."

Gensai then took a sip of sake.

"Most people don't realize that the willow has a history of a thousand years."

"A thousand years?" Seiichiro was incredulous. He had no idea how

long the average willow tree lived, but the current tree certainly wasn't
that old.

"I'm not talking about the age of the tree. What I'm talking about is
the reason why the tree is there."

Gensai's tale concerned T'ang China, far across the seas.

It was said that the pleasure quarters of the T'ang and Sung dynasties
were always surrounded by willows. In fact, a willow-lined road became
symbolic of gay quarters everywhere in China. The pleasure quarters
also had flowers, which in China meant peonies. Therefore the pleasure
quarters were called willow havens, or flower streets. From these two
associations came the Japanese words *karyukai*, flower-willow world,
and *karyubyo*, the word for venereal disease.

The first pleasure quarter constructed in Japan was *Yanagi no
Baba*, "the willow riding ground," in Kyoto. It was an officially licensed
quarter, located south of Madenokoji Nijo. This quarter was lined with
willows, clearly in imitation of the Chinese quarters of the T'ang and
Sung dynasties. For that reason, the Kyoto quarter was also called
Yanagi-machi. In those days, the reign of the Emperor Tensho, the
vicinity was a burnt field, left as it was from the destruction caused
during the Onin Wars. That was why the area could be enclosed with
willow trees. Thirteen years later, however, the entire quarter was moved
to Rokujo-Muromachi. The new quarter came to be known as Rokujo-
Misujimachi, but the area was already densely populated, so it wasn't
possible to surround the new quarter with willow trees. Nevertheless,
out of nostalgia for the old days, the proprietors planted a single willow at
the entrance of the quarter. This single tree came to be known as *mikaeri
yanagi*. The name and the custom of planting a single tree continued
when the quarter was moved to Kyoto's Shimabara area. From there, the
custom continued in the original Yoshiwara in Edo, and then to the new
Yoshiwara.

Hence it was that Gensai traced the history of the current willow one
thousand years back into history, all the way to the pleasure quarters of
T'ang China.

Seiichiro was impressed—not with the origins of the willow
outside the gate, but with the way Gensai conveyed the story. As
Gensai continued his tale, Seiichiro began to feel as if he were growing

intoxicated. Right before his eyes arose a vivid image of the Chinese pleasure quarter, surrounded with green willows. The people of T'ang going back and forth, the courtesans beguilingly waving silk cloth to and fro...the atmosphere of Kyoto's *Yanaginobaba*...noblemen and armed samurai...the metal fittings of sharply curved battle swords flashing in the sunlight...the women's white hands lightly removing them...the dazzlingly ornate Shimabara *Kottaisan* courtesans making their promenade through the avenues. All of these were superimposed on the scene of Nakanocho in the new Yoshiwara, which he could see through the bamboo blinds. It was a fantastic threefold, fourfold overlap of images. It was safe to say that this new way of apprehending reality was entirely new to Seiichiro, and he had learned it from Gensai.

(A few days ago, up on the roof, when I heard Takao Tayu striking the drum...)

Seiichiro suddenly recalled the incident.

(Nakanocho boulevard turned into a river of lights. The *oiran* and the customers gleamed like jewels at the bottom of that river, and then, there was that large boat that seemed to float across the surface of the river...)

In that boat rode the men and women Kugutsu puppeteers that he had encountered in the mountains of Higo, who beat the drum, plucked the shamisen and danced so strangely.

(That was surely not an illusion.)

As he listened to Gensai's story, Seiichiro became convinced that it had been real.

(Was that not another "face" of this world?)

But why was it that the boat was crossing over the river of light? And why were the Kugutsu on board? That remained as much of an enigma to Seiichiro as before.

Takao made her grand procession down Nakanocho boulevard. The customers and hangers-on in the streets stopped in their tracks, watching the parade as if totally engrossed. For Takao, it was an entirely ordinary spectacle, so she should have been accustomed to it, but for some reason she felt under certain constraints that night. It was because this second meeting with Seiichiro had become a heavy pressure weighing down upon her heart.

Takao now felt strongly that Seiichiro was no ordinary man. It was neither because of his lineage nor because of his skills in the military arts. It was because of his extraordinarily deep sensitivity. The night of their first meeting, when he returned to the room where Takao sat striking her drum, he had spoken most clearly.

"That beating of the drum is not a skill for a room inside a house. It should be struck in wide open spaces, under the skies."

Takao almost shuddered at his perceptive comment, because she, too, had long felt the same way. In plain terms, that particular style of beating the drum was called *otokokaeshi-no-ho*, "the way to turn a man around," and she had learned the secret technique from the previous *tayu* who had borne the name Takao. She did not know exactly why it had that name. She had simply been told that it was a secretly transmitted method and that she was absolutely forbidden to teach it to anyone. Still, a young apprentice at the time, Takao had accepted the teaching with absolutely no doubts at all, and had single-mindedly endeavored to acquire the skill for herself. When her "older sister," the previous Takao, finally told her that she had acquired the skill, there rose in her mind a doubt as to whether what she had mastered was actually an accomplishment to be performed for entertainment inside a room. And now Seiichiro had, at a single encounter, perceived that. It was clear to her that he possessed an almost frightening sensibility. Takao had heard absolutely nothing from O-Miuraya's Shirozaemon about Seiichiro's lineage and origins.

"Until now, he's been living alone somewhere in the mountains."

That was all she had heard. She wondered whether that sensibility had been fostered as a result of a solitary mountain life. Or could it be explained by the rumor that he was an extraordinary swordsman? Regardless, to her, he was a difficult customer, and a highly agreeable one, possessed of an inexpressible dignity. He was the kind of man that a courtesan—or simply any woman—would want to keep all to herself.

"I can't explain the reasons, but for the new Yoshiwara, he is more important than any other single person on earth," Shirozaemon had added.

If she could get him to the *najimi*, the third encounter, where they would share a bedchamber, Takao knew that she had the art to bring the patron close to her and not let him go. This was something that every courtesan of her day was absolutely confident of being able to do.

A courtesan was confident that she possessed the skills for holding a man that no common woman dreamed of. By "common women," a courtesan meant a woman outside the quarter. It didn't matter whether the woman was beautiful or ugly, of high status or low, wealthy or poor, the common woman was an amateur, and she was to be looked down upon by the women of the quarter.

In the case of Seiichiro, however, Takao felt that third meeting at *najimi* would be too late. She somehow had to captivate him utterly at the second meeting, *ura*, on this very night. Takao knew this intuitively. Seiichiro was a man for whom the future was of little consequence. That did not mean that he didn't know what life would bring the following day, but rather that he did not live one day with any thought for the next. It would be foolish to talk about "tomorrow" with a man for whom everything was here and now. She simply had to enthrall him tonight during the *ura* encounter. For a change, Takao was desperate.

"It's Katsuyama!" came a shout from the midst of the throng.

"Tanzen Katsuyama!"

Takao saw Katsuyama making her procession from *machiai-no-tsuji*. As always, with her back ramrod straight, Katsuyama made a magnificent progress down the street.

However...

(Why is the expression in her eyes so fierce?)

When Katsuyama flashed a harsh glance in her direction, Takao was momentarily stunned.

(What could I possibly have done to warrant such a fierce stare?)

The look she gave her bordered on malevolence. But her impending rendezvous with Seiichiro caused her to forget whatever doubts she entertained.

Katsuyama, too, was aware that she had looked fiercely at Takao. She disliked herself for doing so. Her displeasure was certainly not the result of any malice she felt toward Takao. It was merely that all of her loathing of the affairs surrounding the man Seiichiro had naturally come forth in her eyes when she noticed Takao.

Loathing.

It was a feeling that, as far as Katsuyama was concerned, could even be called taboo. It was a feeling that violated both her position as *tayu* and her status as a female ninja of the Ura Yagyu.

In fact, Katsuyama was a ninja from Yagyu Valley. When she was a child, she had been trained by Yagyu Jubei himself, and after Jubei died, she became an agent of the Ura Yagyu under the command of Retsudo Gisen. When she became a woman of the baths at the Tanzen Bathhouse, her aim had been to reach Yoshiwara. But she was too old to be taken in as a *kamuro* and it was too risky to try to sell her as a *shinzo*. The people who controlled Yoshiwara were extremely cautious and assiduous in probing the background of any woman who was the least bit suspicious. The only means by which to circumvent such a probe was to have her make a name for herself outside of Yoshiwara as a courtesan, and then have herself introduced to Yoshiwara from there. The fact that from her first appearance at the Kinokuniya Bathhouse she had dressed as a male dandy and acted flamboyantly was a mere pose, a desperate strategy.

The previous night, Katsuyama had taken as a customer a tall, older physician with a white beard. It was Gisen in disguise. From the days when she worked at the Tanzen Bathhouse, he had paid regular visits to her as a customer. In their bed, while taking his pleasure with her, Gisen issued her a single order.

"Find out what day Matsunaga Seiichiro and Takao will make their pledge and let us know."

Their plan was to wait for Seiichiro to exhaust his masculine powers in bed with Takao, then attack him as he left the next morning and hack him to pieces. Imagining Seiichiro sliced to shreds, covered in blood and writhing in agony sent Katsuyama into ecstasy. She was fully aware that her ecstasy came from feelings of longing for Seiichiro.

As the saying went, "Upon the second meeting, they sit a few inches closer." At the first meeting the *oiran* virtually clings to the wall, as far away from her customer as possible, and then on the second meeting, she moves slightly closer to him. The difference between the first and second encounters was that minute. But the two occasions were virtually identical in that the *oiran* still drank no sake, ate none of the feast that was offered and said virtually nothing.

Another saying held that "the mark of the second meeting is the eating of a single loquat." But of course there was more to it than that. For the Yoshiwara community, which embraced a tradition reaching far back into the past, there were far more customs than that single loquat. The object of the second meeting was exhibited in manifold ways. As Seiichiro had perceptively noticed, the position of the candlestand was different. The result was a change in the lighting of the room, and when the courtesan entered and sat down, the guest would for the first time become aware of the change. With the shift in the position of the candle, the impression that the courtesan would make would be entirely different. Women are strange creatures and the slightest shift in her mood changes her face completely. Dress and cosmetics can make her a different person too. Lighting plays the role of emphasizing such changes. In other words, the guest will find in the courtesan "a different woman." That was precisely what Yoshiwara people aimed for on the occasion of the second meeting.

That was why, on this evening, Seiichiro felt an odd sense of difference when Takao took her seat. There was none of the haughtiness she had showed at their first encounter. In its place was another Takao, from whom wafted an air of helplessness and fragility. There was no change in her splendor, but one had the impression that if one so much as touched this wondrous blossom, the fragile petals would immediately fall to the floor. One felt like gently putting an arm around her shoulder but would be afraid that she might instantly shatter into pieces. She appeared just that delicate. Seiichiro felt that he was looking at the deeply sorrowful look of the true Takao, the expression hidden in the shadows of her previously exhibited haughtiness.

The sweet fragrance that emanated from her kimono was also entirely different from that of their first meeting. On the earlier occasion, she had used musk, which was said to be the most effective of all fragrances in arousing men to sexual excitement. But tonight Takao gave off a fainter scent. Her kimono had been perfumed with the incense called *jiyu*, "lord in waiting," which gave off a captivating, nostalgic fragrance. The pure, captivating fragrance had just the effect that Takao had sought. Seiichiro fell almost entirely under its spell.

The proprietress of the Owariya had a manservant bring in a gold lacquerware box about three feet long and place it in front of Takao. Takao then untied the cords that bound the box. She removed from the box a two-and-a-half-foot doll of an *oiran* dressed in exactly the same clothing as Takao herself. It would be more precise to say that it was a dancing doll, one of the ancient Japanese figures used by the Kugutsu puppeteers. It was manipulated by holding onto one of the legs. Some of the early puppets of this type were highly sophisticated—with some, even the fingers could be manipulated. This is clear from the fact that in Heian times, there was a puppeteer who could have his puppet shake a tube with dice in it to play a game called *sugoroku*. Takao possessed both the doll and the ability to adeptly bring it to life.

Gensai's own companion and the Owariya proprietress appeared absolutely astonished, for until that evening, they had never seen Takao manipulate a puppet. In actuality, it was an artifice that Takao had come up with after three full days of deliberation.

One of her youthful assistants beat the drum; another played the shamisen. While singing in a thin, subdued voice, Takao adroitly worked the puppet. Seiichiro was unable to grasp the words very well, but the song seemed to tell the sad, sorrowful tale of an *oiran* who has been misunderstood by the one she loves and abandoned. The song and the lyrics were heartbreaking and penetrated to the depths of a listener's heart. All listened with rapt attention. Gensai's companion removed a piece of folded paper from inside her kimono and dabbed at her eyes. The puppet twisted its fingers in tears and the heaving of its shoulders seemed to express Takao's own grief.

Seiichiro pliantly responded. He was moved not just by how well a puppet could portray human emotions but even more by the depth of the feelings of the puppeteer who used the puppet to express these emotions. For the first time, Seiichiro was drawn to Takao.

Suddenly the tone of the song changed. The sound of the shamisen became more spirited, and at the same moment, the movements of the puppet changed entirely and became all at once more animated. The movements almost seemed designed to dispel the previous sorrowful movements. The driving force of the movements seemed to arise from an intense desire to beat all of the sorrow into a dance in order to somehow forget it. The continuous manic motions of the dance were overflowing with both a tremendous vitality and an overwhelming grief.

And then it happened.

Unexpectedly, Gensai stood up. His movements were stiff and forced—he had not intended to, but against his own will, he was forced to stand. He didn't look at anyone in the room but began to dance awkwardly, as if his arms and legs were being manipulated by hidden strings. Before long, however, that jerky movement began to disappear and he began to dance more naturally. Amazingly enough, without the slightest effort, he seemed to be duplicating the movements of Takao's puppet. The way he danced was absolutely exquisite. He was at one with the puppet—but there was more to it than that. From his entire body,

Gensai projected a primordial life force. The dance was obviously not something performed for others to see. His eyes showed that. He was in a trance, absolutely oblivious to everything around him. Entirely absorbed in dancing, he knew neither who was around him nor who he himself actually was. Seiichiro suspected that Gensai was even unaware that he was dancing. Gensai merely moved his arms and legs in obedience to the commands of some life force deep within himself.

Seiichiro, the women, even Takao stared at Gensai in blank amazement. But presently Seiichiro felt a tightness seize his body.

(This old man!)

Here was Gensai absolutely beside himself in dancing...and yet entirely impervious to attack. He left not the slightest of openings. Even if Seiichiro were to ferociously attack Gensai, there was no doubt that the old man would be able to deflect the attack with ease, but not only that. Seiichiro had heard that accomplished dancers and Noh performers had such expertise, but in Gensai's case, it was different. There was, after all, the story of how Yagyu Munemori had said he could find no opening at all in the performance of the Noh actor Kanze Sakon. But in Gensai's case, if someone launched an attack, not only would there be no opening, the attack would result in an instantaneous counterattack that would fell its initiator. Gensai's dance was just that intimidating.

But then Gensai's expression began to change. It almost seemed as if he were going to cry. There were no differences in the movement of his arms, but somewhere in his expression was a sense of distress. He seemed to be mumbling something. Straining to hear what it was, Seiichiro heard him wailing.

"This is too much, *Tayu*. I can't bear this anymore. This is intolerable. Stop this, just stop this!"

Despite his expression and the words that spewed forth in snatches, his arms continued their movements and his legs continued their dance. It seemed as if as long as the music and the song continued, Gensai would dance for several nights on end, even until death took him. Was this perchance the dance of death?

YAMATO KASAGIYAMA

Alone on a bench at *machiai-no-tsuji* sat an old man. He wore a hood, so it was impossible to see the actual color of his hair, but his long, splendid beard was pure white and his eyebrows were long and white. He appeared to be a samurai. The short sword he carried was slightly longer than average, and the long sword that he had placed on the bench was also longer than usual. The old man was that much taller in stature than the ordinary man. His ramrod-straight upper body, entirely unsuited to an old man, was clearly that of someone younger than he appeared. That was only natural, because the man in actuality had just turned forty. It was Yagyu Gisen in disguise.

For some time now, he had been sitting on this bench appearing to be enjoying the festive mood along Nakanocho. Actually, Gisen's full attention was focused on a room on the second floor of Owariya. From where he sat, through the split-bamboo blind hung in the window, he had a full view of what was happening inside the room. He had been watching Gensai dance with such interest that he could almost reach out and touch him.

Gisen had watched at first with a bitter, contemptuous look in his eyes. But then...

('That figure—I've seen it before somewhere)

He half-closed his eyes as he searched his memory. Suddenly, his eyes opened wide.

(That's it! It was that night!)

In the instant that he remembered the occasion, he almost stood up. It was only with a supreme act of will that he refrained from doing so. With a purposeful air, he took out his tobacco pouch and began to fill his silver metal smoking pipe. His fingers trembled every so slightly.

(No doubt about it. I'm sure. It was that night.)

There was a reason for remembering the occasion so clearly. There had of course been one singularly adept dancer among the group.

(My brother. His face. Suddenly his face turned red and then...)

Gisen recalled vividly what had happened seven years earlier.

It was the night of the twentieth day of the third month of Keian 3 (1650). In the living quarters for the monks of Hotokuji Temple, in

Yagyu Village in Yamato province, Gisen was with great irritation changing into the black garb of a ninja. He was preparing to go out for his routine mountain walk. But in his case, it was more of a mountain run. He ran at full speed like a wild beast through the mountains. Whatever blocked his way he cut down. He cut brambles, trees, any living creature. Wherever he passed, he left behind a trail of dead bodies of small animals. Unless he did some such act bordering on insanity, he could not dispel the mood of depression that seemed to hang over him at all times.

Four years earlier than that—on the twenty-sixth day of the third month of the Shoho 4 (1646)—upon the death of his father, Tajima-no-kami Muneyori, Gisen had believed that it was his time to go out into the world. Until that time, his days had been filled with training, and he had not stepped outside Yagyu Valley for a moment. Gisen knew that his father's possessions would be divided among his brothers and himself. Sure enough, the Yagyu fief of 12,500 *koku* of rice was divided among the three brothers, but the oldest brother, Jubei, received 8,300 *koku*; the second oldest, Munefuyu, received 4,000 *koku*; and Gisen, the youngest, was left with a meager 200 *koku*. Even that small stipend he received in the form of a temple estate at Hotokuji. Gisen was consumed with anger. He could understand why Jubei had received the 8,300. After all, Jubei was the successor to the family name and tradition, and he was a highly gifted swordsman. But he could in no way accept the fact that Munefuyu had received 4,000 *koku*. However anyone looked at it, in terms of swordsmanship, Munefuyu was inferior to his younger brother, Gisen. Munefuyu was short, cut a sorry figure, and had an entirely submissive manner, which made him perfect for what he was up until their father's death, Goshoinban guard in a secretariat office at a stipend of somewhere around 300 *koku*. He had not a single ounce of ambition. He had the timid personality of a minor functionary, showed no ambition, and seemed embarrassed to be a member of the Yagyu clan. In actual fact, that was precisely why Munefuyu had received the 4,000 *koku* stipend, but Gisen, who had never served in the castle administration anywhere had no way of understanding that. He was single-mindedly dissatisfied and furious. In addition, despite the fact that Jubei had succeeded his father in the honored position of fencing master to the shogun, Jubei for some reason had immediately retreated to Yagyu Valley. As a result, the little freedom that Gisen had enjoyed in Yagyu Valley was also taken away. One might say that it was only natural that Gisen was left in low spirits.

A nocturnal beast ran. It belonged to the cat family. Gisen's movements were just that lithe. He bent his tall frame, racing like the wind with his head forward. A giant flying squirrel hurriedly tried to get out of his path, but without so much as a sound fell into the grass, cut in half. Before the two halves hit the ground, Gisen's sword was already back in its sheath. There was not a shadow of hesitation in his step, and moreover, there was hardly a sound.

Suddenly, he came to an abrupt halt, and instantly dropped flat on the ground. He had heard the faint sound of a drum. He pressed his ear to the ground, but could hear no footsteps. Listening very carefully, he heard not only a drum but also a flute mixed together with the sound of a shamisen.

(It's coming from Kasagiyama)

The instant he had ascertained where the sounds came from, he was off and running. The late spring was releasing night-time fragrances that stirred the blood, but deep in the mountains there was no one of refined taste who would enjoy the pleasures of song accompanied by shamisen music. It was not such a refined locale. Those who wandered the mountains—such as woodworkers and mountain nomads—were not the type to carry such instruments as a drum and a shamisen, so this was definitely unusual.

(I may be able to kill a human being for a change)

Such thoughts spurred Gisen to a faster pace. He turned into a veritable whirlwind.

Kasagiyama, in the upper reaches of the Totsu River, was not Yagyu territory. In a hollow at the top of the mountain were gathered together ten or more men. They had built a large bonfire and were seated in a circle around it. Those playing the flute, drum and shamisen were all men. They were neither woodcutters nor nomadic mountain people. Their clothing was somehow sophisticated, and although none of them appeared to be samurai, they did not give the impression of being traveling merchants either. They were men of unknown occupation. But their musical skills were outstanding—as were their dancing skills. Around the bonfire, three of the men were dancing as if possessed. Gisen could not see their facial features. Each of them wore a white cloth over his face and it was tied around the head with a white string. It was called *menbaku*, a custom followed in battles in T'ang China and on the Korean peninsula. When a defeated commander surrendered to his enemy, he wore such a cloth over his face. But Gisen had no knowledge of that. He simply thought it was an awkward disguise and he lay flat on the ground looking down over this odd assemblage. He lay watching them for half an hour and to his amazement, the dance continued the entire time. Among the three dancers, there was one of small stature who was an exceptional dancer. His rapid movements were superb and filled with such vitality that they would excite any onlooker.

(If I could dance like that, it might lift my spirits a little)

It was a dance that aroused a sudden envy in Gisen, whose only skills were killing and wounding people. This feeling of envy to some degree lessened Gisen's bloodthirst. He did not feel it would be particularly difficult to kill ten or so men, but he began to feel it was more enjoyable to lie as he was and watch the dance continue. He heaved himself over and rested his head comfortably on his elbow.

The next day, the twenty-first day of the third month, early in the morning. Returning to Hotokuji from Kasagiyama, Gisen was stunned to find his eldest brother Jubei seated on a bench outside the gate of his temple.

Jubei cast a sharp glance at Gisen, who was still wearing the attire of a ninja.

"There's a rumor going around Yagyu Valley these days that there's a big wildcat on the loose."

"…!"

"They say that wherever that wildcat appears, it leaves animal corpses lying around. Most of them are cut right in two. Sometimes it even goes after people."

Gisen's entire body broke out into a sweat.

"What's the meaning of all that? Did you feed on someone last night, too?"

"I…I didn't do anything last night. I was just watching some men dancing."

Gisen's voice was almost a wail.

"Dancing? Where?"

"Kasagiyama. Up near the peak. There were ten of them. Faces covered with a white cloth, tied around the head with strings."

That was when it happened. Blood suddenly rushed to Jubei's head and his face took on the look of a furious red ogre. His expression was so ferocious that Gisen, who was afraid of absolutely nothing, unconsciously took a step backward.

"You say they were wearing *menbaku*?!"

"*Menbaku*?"

"Yes. What exactly did they look like? Tell me what you saw and heard—everything!"

Jubei had reached out, grabbed Gisen's collar and pulled him up close. Gisen could hardly move. It had been that way ever since he was a child. He had never been a match for his oldest brother. He resigned himself and told exactly what he had observed. The drums, the flute, the timbre of the shamisen. The three men who danced. Especially about the short dancer who stood out so prominently. Jubei's eyes opened wide.

"A short man?!"

"Yes, but even though he was short, he was well built, and didn't give the impression of being short at all. And he was surprisingly light on his feet."

"It's him!" groaned Jubei. "But that's not possible...not that funeral..."

Having blurted out what seemed to Gisen absolute nonsense, Jubei in the next instant cast Gisen aside and sprinted off with an enormous burst of energy. It would be the last time that Gisen would see his oldest brother.

That same day, in the early afternoon, on the banks of the river by the Okawahara village in the foothills of Kasagiyama, farmers who lived nearby found Jubei's body, cut down with one stroke of a sword.

Jubei's wound was strange. His right carotid artery bore a cut barely an inch long. It was if it had been cut in two. His death had resulted from blood loss from that small wound. There was little doubt that Jubei's blood had spouted forth into the wind like a fountain. Near where he fell was a large rock stained by a prodigious spurt of blood from just one direction.

What was suspicious was the minuteness of the wound itself. To inflict such a small wound, and so accurately, with a Japanese sword would have been virtually impossible. There would have been no reason to purposely inflict such a delicate wound, for it would have been much easier and more reliable to cut deep into the neck. Some thought that the weapon was a hand weapon other than a Japanese sword, but if it was not a *katana*, what could it have been? The wound was like what was called a weasel slash, an extremely thin cut in the skin that results from exposure to extreme cold.

Reflecting on the course of events early that morning, Gisen became convinced that his brother had been killed by that group of men up on Kasagiyama. What was curious was that there was not a drop of clotted blood on Jubei's sword, nor was there any indication that his sword had struck against another weapon. His blade had definitely not done battle against ten men. It was clear that he had fallen at the hands of a single combatant. Gisen's intuition told him that it was that small man he had seen dancing, but just who the man was remained entirely unclear. There was no swordsman with a reputation who was that short of stature. Yet it was certainly inconceivable that an entirely unknown swordsman might have the skill to cut down Yagyu Jubei. Jubei may not have been invulnerable, but it was incredible that Jubei could be cut down by an unknown without returning a single stroke of the sword. In particular, he had a hard time believing that the man who danced as if transported could be the swordsman who had killed Jubei.

Jubei's death was officially recorded by the shogunate as an accident that had occurred while hawking. The position of leadership of the Omote Yagyu went to Munefuyu, while Gisen succeeded to the leadership of the Ura Yagyu. Munefuyu, in his petty bureaucrat manner, inquired about the death of their brother Jubei, but in the end Gisen told him nothing of what had happened on the mountain prior to that death. He refrained from saying anything because he knew that he himself would be reprimanded. Gisen's pride would simply not allow Munefuyu a chance to rebuke him. Seven years had passed. Until this moment, when the Yagyu mission against the Yoshiwara group had become clear and he was the one leading the Yagyu into battle, Gisen had not known the identity of the dancer on that mountainside long ago.

But now, right there on the second floor of that house danced that very man. True enough, the dancer was not wearing a white cloth to mask his face, but there was no doubt. He was the one Gisen had watched in the mountains. Just as on that earlier occasion, the man was frenetic in his movements. Gisen himself was in a virtual frenzy, sorely tempted to haphazardly rush in and launch a ferocious, vengeful attack. But seven years had bestowed upon him at the very least a certain degree of self-control. He slowly drew in smoke from his pipe and exhaled a ring of smoke. It was a signal for a henchman, one of the local ne'er-do-wells, to approach.

"Say, do you suppose I could have a light?" the man asked.

Gisen struck the burning remains of his pipe into the man's hand.

"How many men can you get ready right away?"

"Twenty."

Rolling the lit tobacco plug in the palm of his hand, the man skillfully lit his own pipe.

"Is Shinza around?"

"No."

Gisen hesitated. If they were really to do battle with the one who had murdered Jubei, then twenty wouldn't be enough. Tonight perhaps all they could do would be to tail the man, find out where he roosted, then some other day gather enough men, plot out a careful strategy and launch a full-scale attack. Yet Gisen had a premonition that if he let this opportunity slip, he might not ever have a second chance. What lay behind this ominous presentiment was the fact that after seven years of searching around Yoshiwara, Gisen had never so much as heard rumors of this character on the second floor. He made up his mind—it would be that night. No matter what, he would settle scores then and there. But just in case the man might escape, two of Gisen's men would be reserved from fighting and be ready to tail him. It did not occur to Gisen that his own camp might lose altogether.

"Second floor of the Owariya. Remember the face of that old man who's dancing. Don't forget it."

With this parting order, Gisen suddenly stood up and with long strides walked toward the Great Gate.

DOTETSU OF THE EMBANKMENT

The women of the gathering went down to the earthen-floor entrance of Owariya to see off Seiichiro and his group. From *najimi*, the third encounter, the courtesan and her young apprentices would animatedly accompany them as far as the Great Gate to see them off. But until that time, it was the custom in the Yoshiwara for the women to accompany their customers only to the entrance of the *ageya*.

As Seiichiro put on his leather sandals at the entrance and turned to face Takao, she abruptly drew close, knelt and, without a word, took his left hand in her own and gently brought it to her cheek. Her cheek was cool and smooth like elegant white porcelain. For the first time in his entire life, Seiichiro experienced what it was like to be absolutely helpless. The *shinzo* and *kamuro* gaped in astonishment, for what Takao was doing was simply not done at the second meeting. If Takao's other customers were to hear of this, they would in all likelihood collapse in envy. Seiichiro knew absolutely nothing about the intricate customs of the quarter's denizens, so as a result, he stood coolly, looked if anything a little worried, merely standing there letting her do as she wished. He was really an impossible man.

Takao released his hand. In terms of time, the act was over in an instant. Yet Takao was absolutely certain that in the brief moment she had conveyed to Seiichiro her feelings for him.

"Until next time..."

With those short words of farewell, she smiled sweetly. Her brilliance was like that of a flower that has suddenly come into bloom. That may have been the moment of the evening when Takao was at her most attractive. It was the first time since the first meeting that she had smiled. She had saved it all up for this very moment, to let her smile shine all at once. In fact, that was precisely Takao's aim. Everything she had done this evening—the sadness, the sorrow, the puppets, the dancing—everything was preparation for this sudden smile.

Seiichiro's mouth opened slightly. He had unconsciously drawn a step closer to Takao. Gensai slapped him resolutely on the shoulder.

"You are one extremely fortunate guy!"

Gensai spoke for everyone who happened to be present, but Seiichiro didn't know that. He walked off without a word, but embraced tightly in his heart was Takao's flower-like smile.

A cool breeze blew along Nakanocho. To Seiichiro, who was in an unusually excited mood, it was a particularly pleasant breeze. It was as if the breeze were blowing away the coarse feverishness of the pleasure-seeking crowds of men.

For some reason, Gensai, on the other hand, was in a foul mood. He looked here and there with a scowl on his face.

"Is anything wrong?" Seiichiro inquired.

"Not in particular."

There was none of the usual amiability in Gensai's response. That made the situation increasingly strange.

"That was really a wonderful dance."

It was not flattery. Seiichiro was entirely serious. Gensai shook his head sharply to negate the compliment.

"But why was it? That while you danced, you were constantly grumbling about something. "

"So you heard me, did you?" Gensai smiled grimly. "That was absolutely wrong of Takao to do that. To take me by surprise like that just wasn't the right thing to do. Absolutely inexcusable."

"Take you by surprise?"

"That puppet. That was truly regrettable. To use the puppet and sing that song—it was entirely uncalled for."

The comment sounded as if he were vexed from the very depths of his soul.

"Do you dislike such songs?"

Still, Gensai's dance had blended beautifully with the song.

"No, I do like it," Gensai answered simply. "That's the whole problem. Even if I try to refrain myself, my body just won't listen. It just starts to dance, all by itself. It's an illness we have. No one could be happy having their illness given big play like that."

It was an odd form of reasoning, one that Seiichiro couldn't really comprehend.

"An illness?"

"Yes, it's an unfortunate illness among our clan."

"Clan?"

"Some day I'll get around to telling you about our people. Some day rather soon."

Unnoticed, his mood had improved. He was smiling again as he usually did. Once again, he looked around.

"He's not here."

"Who?"

"A little while ago, an old man was sitting here on the bench. An unusually tall man."

Gensai too had been looking through the split-bamboo screen, and had seen Gisen.

"An old man with absolutely straight posture." Seiichiro had noticed him, too.

"Perhaps somebody came to receive him and they went into one of the houses."

"I wonder."

Gensai's tone indicated that he doubted it.

"*Go-inkyo*, where do you live?"

"What?"

Gensai looked fiercely in Seiichiro's direction.

"What I meant was that I might accompany you on your way home tonight."

On the night of the first meeting with Takao, Shirozaemon and the others had said they would see him off, and they had parted for Seiichiro in front of the Owariya.

"It's right near here. In the Kujaku row house in Tamachi Nichome."

It was right next to the quarter itself. The name *kujaku*, peacock, came from the Peacock Acala that was venerated at the Yanagi Inari Shrine in the neighborhood. The proprietor of the shrine, as a result, came to be known as Kujakuya no San'emon, San'emon of the House of the Peacock. When palanquins were later permitted for traveling to the Yoshiwara quarter, this row house would become the residence of a large number of people in the sedan chair trade.

"You don't need to go to all the trouble of seeing me home, but..."

Gensai looked up at the sky. It was a starry night, but the sky looked like it might rain.

"It is a nice night, and it would be good to walk a bit."

Seiichiro nodded. Gensai headed for the Great Gate. Seiichiro made as if to follow, but suddenly stopped in his tracks.

There was an air of menace, a fierce murderousness that exceeded anything he had ever encountered.

A tall, older samurai with a white beard had appeared in the middle of a group of loiterers.

"*Go-inkyo.*"

Without so much as turning around, Gensai replied, "So you noticed, eh?"

"This evening would seem to be ill-suited for a stroll. I must not put you to any trouble…"

"I believe you've miscalculated."

Gensai's tone was rather cheerful. They had stopped right in front of Shirobei Bansho, the gatekeeper's guard station.

"It's not you they're after. It's me," Gensai added.

Seiichiro was confounded. What could this old man have possibly done that would make anyone make an attempt on his life? And with such ferocity? Seiichiro suddenly recalled that first night after he arrived in Yoshiwara, when he had himself been surrounded by exactly the same sort of menace, a whirlpool of murderousness that seemed of unknown origin.

(There is too much of this feeling of menace here in Yoshiwara)

Cheek by jowl with magnificent beauty and boundless tenderness was an intense bloodthirst and the presentiment of death. What was so puzzling was that the juxtaposition did not seem to be the least bit surprising.

(How could this be?)

Perhaps it was precisely the sense that sudden death is near that gave birth to this gentleness and beauty.

(Setting all that aside, just who is this old man?)

Seiichiro wondered once again.

"Have you any idea why?"

"I have a pretty good idea."

It was the kind of casual reply that supplied no clue at all.

"When you get to be as old as I am, if there isn't someone somewhere who'd like to see you dead, then you wouldn't have much value as a man. Wouldn't you agree?"

There was really nothing Seiichiro could say in response. He noticed that there wasn't the slightest amount of distress in Gensai's voice.

(He's enjoying this)

That was the only way he could interpret Gensai's attitude. But could he really—at his age—be enjoying this give-and-take of life as some mischievous kid would?

(That may be the reason he seems so young)

In his last years, Miyamoto Musashi had made every possible effort to kill his own fighting spirit. He never let down his readiness to fight, and yet, he never of his own will sought out a fight. People said that he had achieved a state of enlightenment, but Seiichiro, who had been right at his side the whole time, knew without a doubt that Musashi was aging.

(This old man is far younger than the Master was)

He felt that he had suddenly awakened to something.

"Normally it would be time to take to my heels," Gensai commented, as if in apology. "But tonight, I'm itching to do something. It's all because of that dance. It's all because of that unforgivable Takao."

Seiichiro couldn't help smiling at Gensai for blaming anything and everything on Takao.

"What're you going to do? Change your mind about coming along with me?" Gensai spoke in a teasing voice.

"I hope you are not making fun of me."

"In that case, shall we head off?"

Beaming, he exited the Great Gate.

"It's been quite a while, I must say," he said loudly, in a tone that could only be called cheerful.

They went up the Mimigari Slope onto the Fifty-Ken Road toward the Nihon Embankment. Along the road on both sides were a dozen some *amigasa* teahouses, so called because they loaned out *amigasa*, the woven hats that allowed the wearer to conceal his face. Actually these *amigasa* teahouses and other types of teahouses along the embankment were part of the new Yoshiwara, and they were under the administration of Yoshiwara Gocho. So as soon as one climbed up onto the dike, one was in Yoshiwara. In that sense, these teahouses were the outer-quarter enclosure of the new Yoshiwara "castle."

If one went to the right, along Nihon Embankment, and then after passing the gravel pit, went down the slope to the right, one came to the road toward Asakusa Gomon, the Gate of Asakusa, and just at the foot of that slope was Saihoji, a Jodo sect temple formally called Koganzan Saihoji. It was well known for its priest, Dotei no Dotetsu, or Dotetsu of the Embankment.

Dotetsu had not founded the temple, nor was he even the head priest. In former times, there had been an execution ground nearby, and Dotetsu with his own money had constructed within the temple grounds a hall in which to offer prayers for the salvation of those who were executed, so that they might attain buddhahood. It was said that without fail he prayed both night and day for their souls. Anyone passing on the way to Yoshiwara could not help but hear Dotetsu's ceaseless prayers to Amitabha. Not just once, but twice—once going to Yoshiwara, and again returning from there. They could hardly help being profoundly impressed. In those days, he was considered to be without parallel in his devotion. Some sources say that he was actually Sendai Takao's lover, and that when the Lord of Sendai domain cut her down, that was when Dotetsu began his daylong chanting to Amitabha, but there is no truth to that story, because Dotetsu began his nonstop incantations long before Takao met her tragic end.

Gensai and Seiichiro were inside the precincts of Saihoji. Night had come, and the sound of the chanting had ceased for the day. Gensai stood at the entrance to the invocation hall and knocked on the wooden door.

"Dotetsu! Dotetsu! It's me—Gensai!"

The door opened, and a priest appeared, his face lit by the flame of a candle. The priest was small and slender and wore a kind expression. Given Dotetsu's delicate appearance, one could not help wondering how he possessed sufficient vitality to continue to intone Buddhist prayers day and night, 365 days a year.

"Good evening. It is certainly refreshing outside tonight."

His voice was calm and serene.

"On such an elegant evening, I hesitate to make such an insensitive request, but it seems that I am suddenly in need of that item you are keeping for me."

Gensai's voice was also tranquil. Seiichiro could sense that dark shadows, one after another, were already entering the temple precincts.

"That is most unfortunate."

Dotetsu's expression turned sorrowful, as if he had just been told that someone had fallen ill and was in need of medicine. Dotetsu retreated inside and returned quickly, holding out the heavy object that he had retrieved. Seiichiro's eyes opened wide.

(What is this?!)

What Gensai took so casually into his hands was a pair of swords, one long and one short. They were not, however, an ordinary pair of Japanese *katana*. Judging from the way they were made, they were Chinese swords. Once Gensai had thrust the swords in his sash with a skilled touch, he bowed most politely to Dotetsu.

"I'm very sorry to have imposed on you. Good night."

"Good night."

With that, Dotetsu withdrew inside the temple, and the light disappeared. But because it was a starlit night, the precincts were not entirely dark.

Gensai carefully selected a foothold, drew the swords, and for some reason raised them high overhead. They were straight swords, with no curve at all in the blades. They were longer and apparently more flexible than Japanese swords and seemed to bend easily. In the light of the stars, the blades shone brightly.

Gensai was mumbling something. It was some sort of incantation— and it was not in Japanese. The words were Chinese. His expression and everything about him was in dead earnest. When he had finished the incantation, he returned the swords with a metallic click into their respective sheaths.

"*Go-inkyo*, what was that?" Seiichiro allowed himself to ask.

"A prayer, asking the gods their permission to kill."

Gensai's reply was astoundingly composed.

"That will not do," Seiichiro said with sudden fervor, "Please stand to the side, and let me do whatever killing has to be done."

Quite a number of shadows now began to form a wide circle around the two of them. Seiichiro had counted nineteen in all. They varied in appearance from local troublemakers to masterless samurai, from physicians to priests. There were shop clerks among them, as well as artisans.

"I'm afraid they won't allow that."

Gensai gestured at the men with his chin. The previously mentioned older, tall samurai came forward and stood directly in front of Gensai. The man's long arms hung down loose, giving him an uncanny air.

"Old man," the man said.

When Seiichiro heard the raspy voice, he became aware of two things. First, the man wasn't old, but was, rather, in the prime of life. Second, it was indeed Gensai who was the target this time. The husky voice continued.

"There's something I want to know."

"All right. Ask away."

There wasn't the slightest tension in Gensai's voice. To the contrary, it was entirely calm.

"Where were you on the night of the twentieth day of the third month, seven years ago?"

"Don't ask the impossible," Gensai laughed in a happy-go-lucky manner. "How would I remember something that happened seven whole years ago? I'm getting on in years, you know."

"In Yamato province, in the Kasagiyama mountains." It was like an axe splitting something in two. "You were dancing there—you and nine others. It was you, old man, wasn't it?"

Gensai looked at Seiichiro.

"I told you—it's all Takao's fault. So unforgivable..."

"Don't try to talk your way out this, old man! Answer me!" The words were sharp, like a slap in the face. "Kasagiyama! Were you there?"

"Hmm, I don't seem to remember. But if I had been, then what?"

"I'll kill you!" The man spoke with the momentum of a sword cleaving bamboo from top to bottom.

"And if I say that I wasn't there?"

"It's a lie!"

Gensai burst into laughter.

"Either way you kill me, is that it? What nonsense. Is this any way to carry out an interrogation? Is that how the boss of the Ura Yagyu should work?"

"Nn!" Gisen had taken a step backward, and in a flash had taken a stance for drawing a sword.

"That's a pretty poor disguise you're wearing, Gisen. Or do you prefer to be called Rendo? In Edo, you know, not even a five-year-old would be fooled by that fake beard of yours."

"Who are you, you old bastard?"

"A ghost," Gensai laughed scornfully.

Gisen glided backward. The men with him had already formed two concentric rings of nine men each, with Gensai and Seiichiro together in the center. It was the *Ranken* or *Koran no jin*.

This is not good, Seiichiro thought to himself. If it were just me, I could try the strategy I've been pondering over as a means of defeating the *Koran no jin* attack, but with Gensai here I can't risk it. If I were to try it, Gensai would probably end up cut to shreds. There's only one choice—I'll simply have to leap at random and draw all of their swords in my direction.

But as he started to move, Gensai gently gripped his shoulder.

"Don't worry," Gensai said, "I'm good at acrobatics, too." Then he winked. "And one more thing. I've been dealing with these characters a lot longer than you have."

Could that be true? Seiichiro was puzzled. He knew that the old man had observed him trying to figure out a way to extricate himself from the *Koran no jin* circles of death, but there was a huge difference between watching and doing. Then Seiichiro remembered how Gensai had danced earlier in the evening, the overwhelming speed of his movements. And in particular, he recalled the ferocious spirit which seemed ready at any moment to launch a counterattack. Yes, the old man just might be able to pull it off. And as if to substantiate Seiichiro's intuition, Gensai whispered into Seiichiro's ear.

"I'll go front left. You go backward. Got it?"

Seiichiro gave the slightest nod and assumed the *yoroboshi* stance. Rocking back and forth ever so slightly, he began to employ the *kanso-no-ho* method of seeing.

Gensai crossed his arms like a Chinese warrior and stood firmly with his legs planted. The opponents in their two rings had begun to circulate, the inner ring to the left, the outer ring to the right. The rings closed in, and the nine in the outer ring took two steps backward. The inner nine bent their knees...

Here they come!

With his *kanso-no-ho* vision, Seiichiro clearly saw the henchman directly behind him place one foot up on the shoulder of the *ronin* in the inner circle. Together with an unvoiced *kiai* yell, Seiichiro leaped directly backward. At the same instant, he saw Gensai jump forward to his left. The strength with which Gensai sprang forward was sufficient to put a much younger man to shame.

As Seiichiro had anticipated, when he jumped straight backward, he crashed right into the ruffian coming forward, sending the man flying. The enemy had made no preparation for such a move, and was taken completely off guard.

As he leaped, with a double sword-drawing technique Seiichiro relieved the two Ura Yagyu in front of him who had started to leap—one dressed like a shopclerk and the other dressed as an artisan—of their heads. Like two living things, their heads danced in mid-air. In the next instant, he landed on top of the head of the local thug who had briefly offered his shoulder as a jumping platform. Seiichiro's heel smashed the man's skull to pieces. Having killed three men, his movement continued. Propelling himself off of the skull that he had fragmented, he jumped once again to his front right. He slashed two of the kneeling Yagyu through the shoulder and across the body. And smashing the face of a man in the inner circle who had just risen to his feet, Seiichiro at last landed on the ground again. In one breath, he had dispatched six opponents.

When Gensai leapt forward and to his left, he cut down two men as he flew past them, and upon landing he killed one more man in the inner ring with a backwards swipe of his long sword. The additional length of his Chinese sword had given him an advantage in that encounter.

In an instant, nine of the Yagyu henchmen had died. Gisen was dumbstruck. It was such a complete defeat that he could hardly believe his eyes. Until that night, the Ura Yagyu had prided themselves on the fact that their *Koran no jin* attack had never been defeated. But it was not only that. This supposedly inescapable formation had been defeated so simply by two men.

At the same time, Gisen had noticed the weapon that Gensai had used. It was a long, supple Chinese sword. Compared with a Japanese sword, the blade was flexible, so that when a strike was parried, the momentum of the sword caused it to bend inwardly. The point of the sword must have been what had caused that miniscule cut in the carotid artery of his brother Jubei!

"You're the bastard who killed my brother!" Gisen roared. "And with a Chinese sword on top of that! Who are you? A Chinaman?"

As he shouted, Gisen and the remaining nine attackers were retreating inch by inch. Even in the dark, the faces of the nine living Yagyu swordsmen were visibly pale with terror. Seiichiro and Gensai's skill with their swords could not possibly be human. The Yagyu men had never before in their lives run up against such prodigious swordsmanship. When his troops are in a state of fear, a commander cannot continue the battle. So while his shout was a question, it was simultaneously a camouflage for the fact that he and his men were pulling back. Gisen possessed at least that much toughness.

"It's not over yet, Gisen."

Gensai spoke in a restrained tone, but was all the while narrowing the interval between them. Seiichiro followed one step behind. With no pause at all, Gisen launched a ferocious strike at Gensai. It was swift and absolutely accurate in its aim. Gensai parried the blow with his long sword, and the tip of the sword bent inward, cutting Gisen's cheek. In that split second, Gisen remembered his brother's wound, with the result that he contracted his neck. Had he not done so, there was no doubt that his own carotid artery would have been sliced open. Gisen shuddered. He suddenly sprang back and shouted.

"Fire!"

It was now Gensai's turn to be thunderstruck. From the hands of the remaining Yagyu came a rapid succession of eggs. It was a strategy for distraction. Instantly both Seiichiro and Gensai bent almost to the ground to avoid the attack, dashing forward at full speed. A warrior who possessed any skill at all would not allow himself to be hit by such missiles and would not use a sword against them. As expected, when the eggs struck against a solid object and shattered, white powder exploded from inside—a powder that could be seen even at night. It was an irritant like powered red pepper designed to momentarily blind the opponent. But it appeared that the eggs contained other substances as well. Some of them caused small explosions and scattered fire. They seemed to contain some sort of oil, and the fire spread along the ground where the egg shattered.

Gensai responded with uncharacteristic panic.

"Oh no! This is trouble!"

As if he had forgotten Gisen and the Yagyu assassins, in a flurry he doubled back and began stomping out the fires. Had Gisen at that moment attacked, Gensai might have been cut down. As a matter of fact, two of the Yagyu, drawn in by Gensai's movements, charged forward. But Seiichiro drew himself up from his low stance and using one sword on each, cut them from the waist up through the opposite shoulder. His strike was like an eagle suddenly spreading its wings wide. The technique of the upward cut across the body was the Yagyu-style *gyakufu no tachi*, a technique with the long sword which Seiichiro had learned from

Munefuyu, and to which he had added a second sword.

Gisen was astonished. He had recognized it as a variation of a Yagyu-style strike. In spite of himself, he shouted, "That strike!"

"The secret Eagle Wings stroke!"

Just after Seiichiro shouted, he dealt Gisen a single side sweep with his sword. Gisen's long sword countered it, and their swords rang. It was a strike to be remembered, for from that moment on, there would be a long series of fierce battles between them. In the starlight, they for the first time crossed drawn swords and looked straight into one another's eyes. Yagyu Gisen, age forty; Matsunaga Seiichiro, age twenty-six. It was without doubt a clash between two natural enemies.

Gensai's voice broke the tension.

"Quit playing around and help me here. If we let the temple burn down, we won't know how to ask the Buddha for forgiveness."

Seiichiro and Gisen simultaneously leaped backward. Their first clash of sword guards had come to an end. Gisen and the remaining Yagyu swordsmen dashed out of the precincts with the speed of wild beasts.

"Hurry! Over here!" Hearing Gensai's urgent tone, Seiichiro smiled wryly and returned to stamp out the fires.

Unnoticed, Dotetsu had emerged from the Hall of Eternal Invocation of the Buddha and without a word handed a small pail to Seiichiro. Dotetsu then walked around to see whether all of the fallen men were dead, before gathering their bodies all together in one place. This chore completed, he then put his hands together in prayer to Amitabha. His chanting continued until all of the fires were out.

"Jin'nai-dono."

In Dotetsu's voice was a darkness of exhaustion. With no further words, he silently reached out his hands. Like a child who has been caught in the act of mischief, Gensai dejectedly handed the Chinese swords to Dotetsu. Turning on his heels, Dotetsu carried them toward the Invocation Hall. From behind, he appeared not to be blaming Gensai in any way. His posture simply revealed a deep, unbearable sadness.

"Go-inkyo, is Jin'nai your real name, then?"

Seiichiro asked casually. They had started back in the direction of the quarter.

"When I was young, that's what some people called me."

Gensai's response was vague.

"Master Dotetsu and I go way back. He doesn't find fault with anything wrong any of us does. He just prays to Buddha on our behalf, so that we will be forgiven for every wrongdoing and sin we commit. A long time ago, I used to laugh and call him 'Lamenting Dotetsu.' I was really impossible."

Come to think of it, there had been in Dotetsu's voice something of how a bullied child calls out the name of the bully.

"And what is your family name?"

For a moment there was silence.

"Shoji. Shoji Jin'nai. Later I also used the name Shoji Jin'emon."

Seiichiro caught his breath. Shoji Jin'emon? That was the name of the man he had been told by Musashi to meet once he turned twenty-six! It was the name of the man who was supposed to have died some thirteen years earlier in Shoho 1 (1644).

"That couldn't be!"

"But it is. I'm the Shoji Jin'emon who built the Yoshiwara. The same one who died thirteen years ago. My grave is over there in Unkoin, a temple in Bakuro-cho."

Gensai's expression was entirely nonchalant. Seiichiro, for his part was speechless.

"Mind you, there's not a single bone in that grave. However it is true that the bones of both my wife and daughter are there."

An indescribable sadness crossed Gensai's face.

Seiichiro was still bewildered.

(So that's it)

It suddenly occurred to him that he should have trusted Master Musashi's words more thoroughly.

Come to think of it, Musashi had died in Shoho 2, the year after Shoji Jin'emon was supposed to have died. If Jin'emon had actually passed away, by one means or another, word would have gotten to Musashi. And since Musashi had been completely alert until just before he died, he certainly would not have written an accompanying letter for Seiichiro to carry to a dead man. Seiichiro now regretted his lack of confidence in what Master Musashi had told him.

Be that as it may, the old man before him certainly had a youthful vigor. If Gensai actually was Shoji Jin'emon, then he would have to be eighty-two years old. No matter how you looked at him, he was a good twenty years younger. It was questionable whether he looked even sixty.

At the very oldest, that was what one would guess.

Appearing to guess Seiichiro's thoughts, Gensai commented, "With almost everyone in our clan, it's the same. The men are long-lived and the women are short-lived. It's just the way we are."

He sounded deeply lonely. Seiichiro saw this expression on Gensai's face for the first time.

"But...why...?"

"In this world, there are some people who are simply better off dead, so there is nothing for such people to do but up and die."

He suddenly guffawed.

"Anyway, I want to tell you, my funeral was really something. It was quite impressive, in fact so impressive that some inconvenience arose."

"Inconvenience?"

"Yes, every single woman with whom I had been close converged on the place where the ceremony was held and collapsed in tears before my coffin. In almost no time, the expression on my wife's face turned into that of a vengeful demon. That caused me real problems, I tell you. It was years before my wife would forgive me. Ha, ha, ha!"

From the sound of his laughter, his good mood had returned.

"But on the whole, it was a really good funeral. As I watched, I couldn't help crying and crying. I must be just about the only person who has ever cried at his own funeral."

"You actually attended the funeral?"

"Of course I did. How could I fail in my obligations to attend?"

Gensai squared his shoulders when he offered this peculiar rationalization. Despite himself, Seiichiro laughed. It was because Gensai had seemed so sincere in expressing his sense of duty.

Upon hearing an indistinct shriek, Seiichiro turned around. Two local hoodlums were falling down the dike into the water. Seiichiro instantly discerned something that flashed from the back of each man. They were the two men ordered by Gisen to shadow Seiichiro and Gensai, but that Seiichiro did not realize. Several men from the lodgings casually went down the embankment.

As if a curtain had suddenly been raised, the basic outline of everything that had confounded Seiichiro suddenly became clear.

Each of the men in the lodgings was actually a "soldier." They were soldiers in the Yoshiwara battle formation led by Shoji Jin'emon. Now

Seiichiro understood the meaning of that peculiar highly charged atmosphere that had enveloped him when he had first arrived in Yoshiwara. It was these Yoshiwara "troops" who had killed those escaping Yagyu who had attacked him at Suidojiri. And it was these same men who had in a flash disposed of the bodies of the fallen Yagyu. Seiichiro then recalled the battle formation of Yoshiwara soldiers who had surrounded the Yagyu mansion in order to rescue Seiichiro. They were no casual gathering of fighting men. He should have recognized that at the time, but he hadn't. He was disgusted with his own dullness.

But still certain doubts remained.

Why was it that Yoshiwara needed such a powerful collection of fighting men in the first place?

MINOWA

A dreary autumn rain was falling.

The veranda of the detached room at the back of Nishidaya was dripping wet.

Seiichiro sat on the veranda looking up at the misty sky, seeming somehow frail. It was chilly, and the rain left one feeling forlorn.

Before he was aware of it, a month had passed, and it was now the ninth month. Autumn was well advanced.

It had been raining since the previous evening, and this morning, despite getting soaking wet, Seiichiro had gone as usual to the pampas field near the gravel pit. He had gone to wait for the arrival of Yagyu Munefuyu. Since the morning following the fight at Saihoji, Munefuyu had failed to appear. Nonetheless, every morning promptly at six o'clock, Seiichiro stood in the field. This was not because he earnestly hoped to receive instruction from Munefuyu. However, being there despite the weather was only proper for one who received instruction. In actual fact, his initiation into the secret Yagyu style of the long sword was almost complete. There were two more days. Munefuyu had told him as much. Every morning Munefuyu had taught him three or four variations, so it was only natural that they were approaching the end. After all, there was a limit to the ways in which a sword could be utilized. All the rest consisted of showy, deceptive tactics. The Yagyu style of swordsmanship which Munefuyu was teaching was, in that sense, filled with deceptive techniques. Moreover, there were techniques involving large numbers of swordsmen that amounted to a variety of bloodbath. From time to time, even while he was receiving this unique instruction directly from the master of the school, Seiichiro experienced an intense loathing of it all. Apparently these moments of revulsion showed in his expression, and on one occasion Munefuyu forced a bitter smile.

"In a battle between good and evil, evil always wins. The same is true of a contest between purity and ugliness. The swordsman must not be afraid to use what is ugly and vicious. Consider survival to be the extreme right."

Musashi had said exactly the same thing. Even if there is a right way of living, a beautiful way of living, he had said, in combat there was no such thing as a right way of dying or a beautiful way to die. Anyone who judges death to be beautiful or noble, he said, has never participated in war. It is unbearable to allow one's own life and death to be judged by someone else. Seiichiro believed that from the bottom of his heart, as a man who had been in battle. That was why he had what could be called a visceral repulsion against Mizuno Jurozaemon's ideology of destruction.

To a man of Seiichiro's sensibilities, the Ura Yagyu sword techniques were overly malicious. The main reason why he felt this was that they used their swords in group formations, rather than as individuals. Theirs was not a boundlessly lonely attempt to protect one's own life with a single sword. Theirs was a school of swordsmanship whose aim was to mercilessly slaughter an individual through a group effort in order to achieve some specific purpose. One could call it "political swordsmanship." It was precisely for this reason that Tajima-no-kami Munenori had been appointed to serve as *sometsuke* within the bakufu leadership. More than anything else, this fact irritated Seiichiro. In spite of everything, he felt this was pure maliciousness. His own aspiration was to use the sword on behalf of the individual.

And this morning…

When Seiichiro reached the field of pampas grass, there stood Munefuyu, wrapped in a straw raincoat and wearing a sedge hat. Upon recognizing Seiichiro, Munefuyu flashed a quick smile, and laughed. It was a smile that exceeded Seiichiro's powers of comprehension. Just a few days earlier, together with Gensai, Seiichiro had killed eleven Yagyu men, and if one included the two tails, that figure rose to thirteen. While realizing that there was a difference between the Omote Yagyu and the Ura Yagyu, still, to lose that many members of your own school of martial skills could hardly leave one smiling, could it?

"My younger brother is half insane with frustration," Munefuyu said. "It would seem that the means of defeating the *Ranken no jin* attack formation was superb. I wish that I had been there to see it."

His serene tone remained unchanged. Seiichiro did not know quite how to respond, so he said nothing. Surely he could not say, thanks to you.

"I was told that an old man you call '*Go-inkyo*' who used a Chinese sword was with you... What is his real name?"

Seiichiro maintained his silence.

"So, you can't tell me. I suppose that is only natural. I won't insist on asking, but..."

There was a long silence. Only the sound of the dreary falling rain enveloped the two of them.

"I have just one request to make of you." Munefuyu's voice grew faintly huskier. Unusually for him, his emotion was visible.

"I await your request." Seiichiro's voice was clear. Seiichiro felt from the emotion he perceived in Munefuyu's voice that this was going to be one request that he would have to give ear to.

"From what my younger brother told me, it seems that the old man is the culprit who cut down my older brother Jubei. Or rather I should say..."

Munefuyu waved his hand in a preemptive denial. It was an entirely unusual movement for Munefuyu.

"I am not saying that doing so was good or bad. Only...how was my brother killed? I would like to know the details of what happened that day that he was cut down. Would you please ask the old man for me?"

"For...for what reason?"

Seiichiro was perplexed. It was because when he considered the character of the Yagyu school, he couldn't help wondering if there was some ulterior motive behind the request.

"It is because he was my older brother. Isn't it natural that a man would want to know how his brother met his end?"

There was an unmistakable tone of sadness in Munefuyu's voice. It was the same sadness that came forth from the autumnal rain that came down between the two of them.

(So what if I'm being deceived)

Immediately Seiichiro made up his mind.

(It makes no difference what is behind this. I simply have to respond to this request.)

If he did not respond, he was not a human being. He felt himself under the pressure of necessity to do that much.

"I understand. I promise you that I will inquire."

"Tomorrow morning your instruction comes to an end. If it is at all possible, could you do so by then?"

He had set a time limit.

Seiichiro silently nodded assent.

"I would be deeply grateful. Well then…"

Upon making a slight bow, Munefuyu removed his straw raincoat. His *hakama* were already tucked up in preparation for fighting. Perhaps to prevent himself from slipping, he was wearing straw sandals.

Whoosh!

A sword sliced through the autumn air.

Seiichiro lowered his center of gravity and fixed his eyes.

"The Yagyu-school secret attack—*Murakumo no tachi!*"

The tip of his long sword slowly rose upward…

(Difficult)

Seiichiro, still seated upright for meditation, pulled out a hair from his stubbly beard. Judging from what he could see from this detached room, there was no sign that the rain might soon stop. He was not distressed by the rain itself, but it was a question whether old man Gensai would show up in the Yoshiwara in this weather.

(He said he lived in the Renjaku row house)

Seiichiro decided he would go looking for Gensai. He returned to his room and just as he was reaching out toward the sword rack, he heard light footsteps in the connecting corridor. A smile came to his face. It must be Oshabu. The puzzlingly cheerful girl, several times a day, came to take a peek into this detached room. Sometimes she would speak and then come in; other times, she would merely look into the room and silently return to the main part of the house. Apparently she was just checking to see whether he was in, and if he was, that was enough to ease her mind. It was so sweet that just hearing her footsteps comforted Seiichiro.

The *fusuma* slid open an inch, and Oshabu peeked through the crack.

Seiichiro had put down his swords, and was seated formally.

"Don't just peek, come on in."

A smile naturally came to his face. He knew how she bent over whenever she came to have a peek. On one occasion he had chanced upon her peeping into her father Jinnojo's room, doubled over with her rear end stuck straight back, and her head lower than her rear end. It was a curious as well as cute pose.

"Hello."

Oshabu entered with short steps and sat down just inside the door. She very properly touched her fingertips to the tatami and bowed her short bobbed hair. As soon as she raised her head, she looked into the garden near the veranda.

"Oh! A bellflower!"

Seiichiro came close to the veranda, sat beside her and looked out into the garden.

Well, how about that? Virtually within arm's reach, there bloomed a single dark-purple bellflower. Perhaps the reason he had not noticed it earlier, when he was sitting on the veranda, was that it did not possess the characteristic commanding presence of the bellflower. Unable to stand up beneath the weight of the rain, it was leaning against a small garden stone.

"It's like Sei-sama," Oshabu said, looking radiantly at Seiichiro.

"Do I seem that lacking in energy?"

"It's because this rain is cold and sad."

"Well, if that's the case, then who is the stone?" Seiichiro asked wryly.

"Oshabu," she answered nonchalantly.

"I'm leaning on Oshabu?" he asked.

She blushed slightly and shook her head.

"No?"

"Not leaning, resting your head on my lap." She managed to say it while looking straight at him.

"Hmm, I see."

A mischievous streak came out in Seiichiro, and he suddenly stretched our sideways and made as if to lay his head in her lap.

"Like this?"

Initially, he was just mimicking the act and not one hair of his head actually touched her lap, but Oshabu pushed his cheek down so that it was actually touching.

"Don't you even know how to rest your head?"

She was smiling happily. Somehow Seiichiro felt guilty. He felt like he had led a nine-year-old girl into mischief, and had misgivings. Quickly he tried to raise his head, but Oshabu wouldn't let him move.

"If you don't stay still, I'll cry."

Her eyes showed that she was in earnest. Giving up, he relaxed. Her lap was so full and soft that it was hard to believe it was a child's. He could easily imagine falling asleep just as he was. He felt his inexpressible loneliness gradually fade away.

(There's serenity in this lap)

He had become filled with a sense of peace and contentment.

Oshabu's skin, seen from below, was absolutely beautiful. Hers was a pure beauty that neither Takao nor Katsuyama possessed. Her skin was bursting with freshness, and it was so thin that it seemed if that if you touched it, it would make a sound as it burst. Unconsciously, he stretched out a finger and stroked her cheek. It almost seemed as if her cheek would swallow the tip of his finger.

Something was making a light thumping sound. He soon realized it was the throbbing of Oshabu's heart. Startled, Seiichiro sat upright.

"Sorry, my head must have been heavy." His apology was sincere. He felt that he had done something terribly wrong.

"It wasn't heavy at all."

"No, I shouldn't have done that, not even in fun. It was inexcusable."

He bowed in earnest.

"Five years," Oshabu whispered softly. "Please wait five years."

"…?"

"Five years from now, I'll let you leave your head in my lap all day long."

She suddenly sprang up, and ran outside the sliding door. She slid it shut once, then opened it once again.

"Grandfather is at the O-Miuraya boarding house in Minowa."
She had regained her usual carefree voice.

When one departed from the Yoshiwara and turned left along Nihon Embankment, the road headed toward Senju. Another left turn would take one toward Minowa. That road passed Kanasugi and Sakamoto, and after passing Shinano Slope, Byobu Slope and Kuruma Slope, the Ueno Toeizan Kan'eiji would be reached. In contrast to the Asakusa-Sanya route, this road from Ueno to Yoshiwara gave one the feeling of being on a back road. There is therefore the following linked verse:

Minowa for its rear gate, Sanya-mote for the main gate—
Entering Yoshiwara from Minowa road is a "reverse route."

The first verse likens Yoshiwara to a castle, of which Sayna-bori is the front gate, Minowa the rear. The second answering verse likens Minowa street to the "reverse route" of ascetic monks' mine-iri pilgrimage, from Yoshino to Kumano, instead of the "ordinary route" from Kumano to Yoshino.

In Minowa, there were a number of dormitories for the large Yoshiwara houses. Seiichiro had heard that they were where the *oiran* who had fallen sick went in order to recuperate. But when Seiichiro followed the directions he had been given and was finally standing in the entranceway to the O-Miuraya dormitory, he was astonished to hear the sound of a baby crying. Actually, it was not just one. At the very least, there were three of them. In addition, a small boy about two years old came toddling out to the door, looked at Seiichiro and grinned. Seiichiro unconsciously smiled back, and as he stood there not entirely comprehending what was going on, a woman who appeared to be the mother came out looking for her son.

"Oh, you bad little thing! I'll have to spank you again." Both from the Yoshiwara manner of speaking and the flicker of charm that she briefly showed as she swept up the child and took him away, it was clear that she herself was an *oiran*.

(What is going on here?)

As he stood there bewildered, Gensai suddenly appeared with an amused expression on his face.

"For an *oiran*, having a baby is about the worst 'illness' imaginable."

Come to think of it, what he said was true. And yet, this dormitory was far more serene than Seiichiro had imagined it would be. Both the *oiran* whose stomachs were swelling outward and the *tayu* who were resting their bodies after giving birth seemed to feel no special embarrassment about their situations. To the contrary, they all seemed cheerful, comfortable and entirely at ease. The women who surrounded them seemed warm and loving, there was no sense at all of any faultfinding or chastising, and the *oiran* seemed not to feel any special worry about the children themselves. They seemed so candid and open that Seiichiro was somewhat overwhelmed by it all.

(I don't understand)

He let out a sigh. These living beings known as women were simply incomprehensible.

Gensai seemed to be teasing him when he asked, "Are you learning a little bit more about how frightening women can be?"

The statue of Jizo, guardian deity of travelers and children, was stained dark with the rain. Oddly enough, this Jizo stood with its back to the broad road, the Oshu Ura Kaido, a back road that provided an alternate route to the northern provinces.

"It's called the 'Backward-facing Jizo of Yakuoji,'" Gensai explained.

When Seiichiro explained what Munefuyu had asked him to find out, Gensai had silently pulled Seiichiro out into the rain.

"When you go along this road," Gensai pointed west, "you come to Kan'eiji. It's *our* escape route for emergencies. If such an event occurs, the Minowa dormitory would become a rearguard fortress where we could hole up."

"What does this mean?" Seiichiro was stumped. He simply could not understand what Gensai was talking about.

"Can't you understand?" Gensai said, heaving a sigh. "What exactly do you think the new Yoshiwara is? It's surrounded by a moat called *Ohagurodobu*, and although it doesn't exactly have a stone wall on the near side, it is closed off by small shops and a black wooden fence. Outside the moat, it is completely surrounded by the Yoshiwara rice fields that would hinder anyone approaching on foot. To make it convenient for surprise attacks and evacuations, there are nine drawbridges in the wooden fence.

The Great Gate, which is the equivalent of the main gate of a castle, is the only way in and out of the quarter, and that gate is solidly protected by the Shirobei gatehouse. Moreover, the *amigasa* teahouses on both sides of the Fifty-Ken Road and the houses along Nihon Embankment are like outlying castles for observing enemy movements. The waterway of Sanya Moat is only broadened halfway on purpose. No boats are able to come as far in as the front of the Great Gate. And then there is the dormitory at Minowa, which would protect a retreat."

Seiichiro was stunned. Come to think of it, everything was just as Gensai described it.

"So, that means the new Yoshiwara quarter is an independent castle?"

"Of course. The public, of course, thinks that the Ohaguro ditch and the gatehouse are simply devices for preventing the *oiran* from escaping, but that is just a rumor we purposely spread. Those who have eyes can see, and those who know can understand the reality."

"But…what is the castle for? Who is it protecting from whom?"

"Needless to say, this castle is to protect the people of Yoshiwara from the shogunate," Gensai answered in no uncertain terms.

"The military government? Do you mean that the shogun wants to conquer the people of Yoshiwara?"

"The reason for that lies in the *gomenjo*."

Due to a ghastly feeling that came over him, Gensai's voice quavered slightly.

THE LICENSED QUARTERS

"The shogun's *gomenjo*."

It was another way of referring to the *Shinkun gomenjo*, and it was these words that had gotten Seiichiro into so much trouble.

The first occasion he had heard the name was when Sagawa Shinzaemon had abruptly confronted him saying, "Where's the *gomenjo*?"

That single word had led Seiichiro to the swordfight at Shotoji, and had also led him to make that visit to the city residence of the Yagyu clan.

Then when he had asked what the *Shinkun gomenjo* was, Munefuyu had enigmatically replied, "There are things in this world that are best left unknown." That had to mean that it was a secret that harbored something of an exceptionally troublesome nature.

Shinkun meant Ieyasu, the founder of the Tokugawa regime and the first shogun. *Gomenjo* was a charter or license. So this *Shinkun gomenjo* surely meant a charter that Ieyasu had granted someone. From Sagawa's question, it could be inferred that the charter had been bestowed on Yoshiwara. Gensai had later told Seiichiro that if he became deeply acquainted with the Yoshiwara, then Gensai would tell him what the *gomenjo* really was. And now, he was being told that, because of this very same charter or whatever it was, the Yoshiwara quarter was exposed to a potential attack from the shogunate itself.

"Does the shogun now want to destroy Yoshiwara?"

Seiichiro had asked the question because it sounded as if the shogunate was for some reason attempting to retrieve the charter that Ieyasu had granted.

"No." Gensai categorically denied that was the case. "To begin with, the *gomenjo* was given by Lord Ieyasu directly to me, Shoji Jin'emon. It was a charter signed by him permitting the opening of a gay quarter, and that document was called *Shinkun gomenjo*. But the content of the document was nothing more than what is posted on the official notice board at the top of the Fifty-Ken Road."

The announcement board stood in front of the "gazing-back" willow tree and was covered by a small roof and surrounded by a stout stone wall. Upon it were written a number of prescriptions:

If *yujo* are discovered to be hiding outside the Yoshiwara quarter, the discoverer shall report the fact to the government. Should he fail to do so, the five-household neighborhood group to which he belongs shall share his punishment.

Persons other than doctors are prohibited from entering the quarter in a palanquin or on horseback. Long weapons may not be brought inside the gate.

It deserves special mention that these regulations were charter prerogatives granted to the Yoshiwara quarter. Especially the first prescription was of major significance—the one which prevented prostitutes from taking employment anywhere else other than in Yoshiwara. To underscore the regulation, anyone caught operating a house of prostitution *outside* the quarter would incur severe punishment from the government—along with anyone else connected with the operation. What this meant, in essence, was that the bakufu itself would protect this exclusive charter. In the medieval period, this kind of monopolistic association would have been called a *za*, or guild. Such guilds would be forced to pay a form of tribute to the licensing feudal lord for the charter, but on the other hand, the lord himself would bear the responsibility for preventing any non-guild enterprises from competing with them. This was an ironclad rule within medieval law. The Yoshiwara was, in effect, a guild of "castle topplers" and that was precisely the meaning of the term "licensed quarter."

The operators of the various classes of bordellos in the quarter were, in effect, shareholders in the Yoshiwara guild, and among the various forms of tribute they were required to provide was three *tayu* for certain official occasions and the labor of a certain number of their male employees when time came for changing the tatami mats and cleaning Edo Castle.

The second of the prescriptions was to make Yoshiwara unique. No matter how many spearmen a daimyo might bring along or how many warriors accompanied his palanquin to impress people with his prestige, all of that came to an abrupt halt outside the Great Gate. No one was allowed to continue into Yoshiwara with such an entourage. Even the Minami and Kita Machi Magistrates, men of no small consequence, had to alight from their palanquins and leave their entourages behind when they made their ceremonial rounds of the quarter. They may have walked about in formal *kamishimo* attire, but they walked with only a few assistants, leaving their subordinates outside the gate. In fact, in the early days of the Yoshiwara, there was even a regulation that if a samurai and a townsmen got into a quarrel and the samurai was killed, the death would be ruled a pointless death and the townsman would not be prosecuted. In other words, in the licensed quarter, there was no distinction at all between the high and low of society. Precisely for this reason, townsmen, artisans and peasants could play at ease here—unlike the world outside.

"So, is that what the shogun dislikes?"

"Not at all. The shogun isn't that narrow-minded. And after all, we are paying a considerable sum of money to the shogun every year," Gensai laughed scornfully. "Of course the shogunate, in public, acts as if they aren't taking in a single small coin. Look at it this way. It wouldn't look too good if it were known that the shogunate was taking a percentage off of the money made by selling sex, would it? That's the way government officials see things."

With that, Gensai roared with laughter.

True enough, no records would ever be found showing that the Tokugawa shogun received tax or tribute from the Yoshiwara quarter. Only much later when the Tokugawa shogunate collapsed would anyone become aware that such payments had been made. Only then would it become known that Yoshiwara in its day had taken in 1,000 *ryo* a day—an enormous sum—and that a full ten percent of that ended up in bakufu coffers. That amounted to 36,000 *ryo* in a single year.

"If that's the case, then why would the shogunate be so down on Yoshiwara?"

"To be more precise, it is not the shogunate. The senior councilors, the younger officials of the shogunal government, the inspector general, the inspectors…the core members of the bakufu don't care at all."

"…?"

"The only two parties who want to retrieve the *gomenjo*, by fair means or foul, are the shogun himself and his pawns, the Yagyu clan."

"But why would the shogun…?"

"It is said that the actual charter was written and signed just three days before Ieyasu died. The only two people who were right there with him were the priest Tenkai and Honda Masazumi. Konji'in Suden was also around somewhere, but at that exact moment, he had apparently withdrawn to take a nap."

It was apparently Tenkai who introduced the subject of the pleasure quarter. Ieyasu had reputedly broken into a smile and said, "Ah yes, you old womanizer. You were going to write up an agreement, weren't you?" he said in good humor.

Ieyasu stamped the charter with his official seal, added a short postscript to the document and handed it back to Tenkai.

"Give this to the Old Man as is, and let him put it to use."

When Masazumi took a sidelong glance at the short postscript, his jaw dropped.

"Masazumi," Ieyasu's voice grew suddenly sharp. "Keep this to yourself."

"As you wish, my lord," Masazumi said as he prostrated himself.

Gensai suddenly fell silent.

"What exactly did he write on the document?" Seiichiro asked impatiently.

"I can't tell you that."

"But..."

"Not yet, at least."

Gensai laughed.

"If what he wrote were made known to the public...the shogun himself might be overthrown. It is of that consequence."

"...!"

"In fact, it was of such importance that after turning it over and over in his mind—and despite the direct command from Ieyasu while he was alive—even Honda Masazumi could not keep it to himself. He divulged the secret to Lord Hidetada. Upon hearing the secret, Hidetada was so astounded, so furious, that in the end, Masazumi was destroyed."

"Are you referring to the Suspended-ceiling Incident?"

Honda Masazumi resided in the castle at Utsunomiya, and when Hidetada—who had become shogun—was returning from a visit to Nikko Toshogu, he was to have stayed overnight at Utsunomiya. Hidetada, however, suddenly changed plans and returned directly to Edo. Shortly thereafter, a rumor was floated that Honda had hatched a plot to murder Hidetada during his planned stay at Utsunomiya. The plot involved a suspended false ceiling in the room in which Hidetada was to sleep. The ceiling was concealing a massive piece of stone that was to collapse and crush Hidetada to death. The rumors, of course, were entirely baseless. A retainer of the shogun himself investigated Utsunomiya Castle and concluded in his formal report that there was no evidence that supported the claims of such a conspiracy.

"It was pure fabrication," Gensai sniffed. "The whole thing was a frame-up to incriminate Masazumi."

According to Gensai, when the Utsunomiya fief of 155,000 *koku* was confiscated for this ridiculous reason and Masazumi was instead given a fief far off in Dewa Yuri which came with a stipend of a mere 55,000 *koku*, Masazumi awoke to Hidetada's intentions. Saying in response that he did not need a fief of 55,000 *koku* but that a mere 1,000 *koku* would do nicely, Masazumi brought Hidetada's full fury upon himself, and was exiled to Yokote, far to the north. It was a magnificent act of sulking by a man who could read his own fate.

"But wasn't Tenkai censured in any way?"

"Of course not. There wasn't a single person within the shogunate who could touch him. Tenkai was a ghost. Once someone is dead, you can't kill him a second time."

"Tenkai, a ghost?!"

"He was. Just like me," Gensai laughed.

"Of course, you probably won't tell me Tenkai's actual name either." Seiichiro said, somewhat peeved.

"I'll tell you, but you probably won't believe me anyway," Gensai replied.

"It's not possible that I wouldn't believe you."

It was unthinkable. Gensai glanced at Seiichiro's earnest expression.

"While he was still in the secular world, Tenkai was known throughout the entire land…as a military commander." His voice dropped even lower. "He was none other than the general Akechi Mitsuhide, Hyuga-no-kami."

It was a whisper that seemed to fade entirely in the falling autumn rain.

Seiichiro was speechless. The shock would have been the same if he had been punched directly in the face.

(How could that possibly be true?)

And yet—Gensai's own face had taken on an unusual pallor.

In the tenth year of the Tensei era (1584), in the dark night of the thirteenth day of the sixth month, in the village of Ogurusu, Akechi Mitsuhide, notorious for betraying and assassinating the great Oda Nobunaga, having been defeated in the battle of Yamazaki and having been stabbed in the side by the local warrior Nakamura Chobei, committed seppuku with his loyal vassal Mizoo Shobei as his second. At least that is what the historical records say. But even in those days, it seemed like some sort of cock-and-bull story. Some sixty years later, an investigator went to Ogurusu village to find out what he could about the events.

First of all, the investigator could find not a single soul who knew anything about a man named Nakamura Chobei. A document titled *Daigo zuihitsu* even questioned whether such a person had ever existed. In the second place, it is peculiar that Mitsuhide was escorted and protected by twelve loyal retainers, and that one of these stabbed him with a spear, while none of the others knew anything about it. Mizoo Shobei, who supposedly served as Mitsuhide's second, is alleged to have not severed Mitsuhide's head—as was required in ritual suicide— and there is even doubt as to whether he followed his lord in death. Furthermore, at Shozenji Temple on Mt. Hiei, north of Kyoto, there is a stone lantern that bears an inscription saying that it was donated by Mitsuhide in Keicho 20 (1615), which would have been thirty-four years after Akechi Mitsuhide is thought to have died. Considering these and a number of other enigmatic facts, several other records contend that Mitsuhide's vassals helped him to seek haven on Mt. Hiei, while they placed his personal armor on a headless corpse to make it look like the body was his and buried the head of the unknown person somewhere else. All of this was covered up by allowing some of Akechi's loyal vassals to "follow him" in death.

Of the first half of Nankobo Tenkai's life, absolutely nothing is known. The first time he appears in history is when he meets Ieyasu, and by that time he was already sixty-five years old. But from that point onward, his activity was mind-boggling. He immediately became Ieyasu's confidante, and together with Konji'in Suden and the Confucian scholar Hayashi Razan, they hammered out a strategy for the complete annihilation of the archrival Toyotomi clan. When Ieyasu died, he ran roughshod over Suden as he grasped power and became literally "prime minister in black robes." By this time, he was eighty-one years old. Thereafter, he founded Higashi Hiei-san Kan'eiji and promoted the publication of his edited *Okura-kyo* sutra, while simultaneously manipulating the government from behind the scenes, and living to the astounding age of 108. That a man of such vitality could have lived the first 65 years of his life hidden away in the priests' living quarters of some obscure temple on Mt. Hiei without doing anything worthy of note is simply beyond comprehension.

A sage whom Ieyasu treated with the utmost respect upon their first encounter. A military tactician who devoted himself to the destruction of the entire Toyotomi clan with abnormal intensity, working out both a political and a military strategy that no other military commander would have been capable of, and then actively directing the campaign. When one searches the annals of that period of history for a person who would have been capable of such actions, the only one who comes to light is Akechi Mitsuhide.

When we press even further, in terms of those who harbored a grudge against Oda Nobunaga, surely Ieyasu's enmity was even deeper than Mitsuhide's. That Nobunaga had forced Ieyasu to kill with his own hands his own son Nobuyasu, widely seen as a genius, reveals just how deeply suspicious and jealous Nobunaga actually was. Surely Ieyasu must have been grateful to Mitsuhide for killing Nobunaga, and there would have been no reason for him to regard Mitsuhide with hostility. Further, Mitsuhide, who was hiding on Mt. Hiei, must have understood Ieyasu's mind extremely well. Might it not have been for that precise reason that Mitsuhide came down off the temple mountain to seek out Ieyasu?

"Setting that aside..."

Gensai did not so much as glance at the confused Seiichiro as he continued his tale.

"The Yagyu attack against Yoshiwara Gocho was fierce and desperate. They forced their way in, slaughtered people and set fires. They tried to confiscate the *gomenjo* through intimidation. A large number of Yoshiwara men died, as did a similar number of the Yagyu. Everyone said that if I died, everything would calm down, so I did, but that just seemed to escalate the attacks. In the end, it became necessary to kill the leader of both the Omote and the Ura branches of the Yagyu, Jubei."

"...!"

"I've made such a long introduction to the story because I don't want you to misunderstand. I don't want you to think that the people of Yoshiwara are simply a group of bloodthirsty murderers. The only reason we killed Jubei was that there was absolutely no other way. I hope you can understand that."

Seiichiro nodded assent.

"Jubei was a true genius in swordsmanship. In both technique and spirit, he was always thoroughly on guard. Especially when Jubei was in charge, the Yagyu band of ninja was positively invincible. So it was absolutely essential to get Jubei by himself. That is why we made desperate efforts to come up with a strategy for doing that. Finally, we discovered Jubei's one weakness."

"What was that?"

"Vengeful spirits."

"Vengeful spirits?"

"Yes, he was afflicted by the vindictive, vengeful spirits of all the people he had killed in his lifetime. That was why almost as soon as he succeeded his father as the personal swordsmanship instructor to the shogun, he returned to his home territory. We made use of that one weak point in his defense."

Gensai's tone turned gloomy.

Yagyu Jubei had run fast through the morning twilight. Shoji Jin'emon, who was supposed to have died, was still alive! That single thought had driven Jubei into a wild frenzy. What he had forced out of Gisen about the stature of the man who had been dancing so skillfully—it simply had to be Shoji Jin'emon.

What was more, the man was dancing with a white cloth across his face—it was customary in the Shoji clan.

It happened just as he approached the riverbank at Okawahara village.

"Yagyu Jubei!"

The voice sounded muffled. At that same instant, out of nowhere, nine shadows wearing white cloths over their faces arose from the river soaking wet.

Jubei's response was extraordinary.

"Aagh!" he shrieked. It was a sound entirely unworthy of an expert swordsman. In the same instant, he jumped backward six feet. The nine shadows appeared to him to be vengeful spirits.

"Yagyu Jubei."

This time the voice seemed to come from behind him. A shadow wearing a gray cloth came out between the boulders along the shore. It was Gensai. Jubei moaned again.

"Shoji Jin'emon!"

"You're mistaken. I am the coming together of the vengeful spirits of every person you have murdered. Come and fight!"

Swish! Two Chinese swords were drawn and held out to the side, like a bird with its wings spread—the *shicho-no-kamae!* Gensai hurried the battle. He had to strike down Jubei while Jubei was still agitated by the avenging spirits' sudden appearance, and that was why Gensai took such a daringly open offensive stance. He was inviting Jubei to attack. But Jubei was, after all, a genius in swordsmanship. In the instant that Gensai had drawn his swords, Jubei had drawn his own long sword, taking the *seigan no kamae*, the "aiming-at-the-eye" stance, and standing immobile. It was the ideal stance to take until his mind had calmed down.

The sun rose above the brow of the hill, shining a brilliant gold. Gensai's Chinese swords and Jubei's *katana* reflected the dazzling sunlight. But neither moved. Nor did the nine shadows encircling the two men. It seemed for all the world that along this one part of the riverbank, time had suddenly stopped.

Gensai had already abandoned the strategy of striking down Jubei while he was distracted by the vengeful spirits' sudden appearance. In a flash, it had come to Gensai that this was not an opponent who could be cut down through such a superficial strategy. He would have to wait for the right moment and gamble his life on a single blow... It was the only form of attack he could conceive of.

There was also a danger that at that very moment the Yagyu ninja were racing to the riverbank to join the battle. That would mean an attack by overwhelming numbers. This was, after all, Yagyu territory. If they arrived, Gensai and his group would have not one chance in a million of winning the battle. However, he cast aside all such fears too. All Gensai felt now was exultation. Through his entire life, he would never have another such chance—to take on an opponent of Jubei's ability. This was a once in a lifetime chance to pit his entire existence in single combat. That was a greater happiness than he knew how to handle. This was the extremity of playfulness for Gensai, a man of unusual ability who had lived half his life in the world of pleasure, and at the same time it expressed the spirit he had as a human being.

Oddly enough, it then became Jubei's turn to fret. As he began to calm down after his initial anxiety over the appearance of these vengeful spirits, he began to lose the patience required to maintain the defensive stance he had taken. By nature, the Yagyu school was one for attacking. To overwhelm the opponent by continuous attack was the Yagyu creed. That was their fundamental method, and Jubei was able to demonstrate his enormous talent precisely when his attack was extremely fearless and reckless. Whereas Gensai had spent a half-life in the world of pleasure, Jubei the assassin had spent a half-life murdering people, and his method was a manifestation of that spirit of butchery, and of his pride.

Slowly, a faint strength began to flow into the little finger of Jubei's left hand at the base of the sword hilt. Murderous intent by slow degrees flowed into the blade of the sword. The muscles of his left leg began to tighten imperceptibly in preparation for making a leap.

Then…

A small cabbage butterfly, as if half asleep, came flying lightly down, fluttering right between the two men, and as if struck by the men's spirit, it suddenly landed on the sharpened edge of Gensai's long sword. Almost imperceptibly the tip of the sword seemed to dip under its weight.

In that instant, Jubei's sword struck at Gensai's head, as if drawn to it. It was a purely natural movement, and it took place in the span of a single breath.

Gensai parried the blow with the short sword in his left hand. Astonishingly, the butterfly on the sword in his right hand didn't budge. It seemed as if Gensai's left hand had moved entirely of its own will, entirely separate from the rest of his body. In the next split second, the long sword moved with lightning speed, striking at the left side of Jubei's neck.

Jubei had drawn his sword in to his side in *wakigamae* to defend himself, and the two swords clanged together. That was when the dreadfulness of the Chinese sword made itself evident. Gensai's long sword used Jubei's as a fulcrum and bent in toward Jubei's side. At that moment, the sharp edge of the sword swiped precisely an inch-long incision across Jubei's carotid artery.

At that very last moment, the small butterfly rose into the air from Gensai's long sword. It was with just such speed that the match was decided.

In the eyes of the nine Yoshiwara warriors who had stood with bated breath awaiting the course of events, it had appeared that the butterfly had taken wing from Jubei's neck. From the small incision in Jubei's artery gushed a spray of blood which seemed to pursue the butterfly as it fluttered off. The butterfly was struck directly by the bloody fountain that rose into the air, and fell upon a rock on the riverbank.

His eyes wide open and his body drawn up to full height, Jubei lost all the blood coursing through his body and collapsed like a tree trunk to the ground. At that same instant, the butterfly with great effort moved its wings and took flight once more. It was stained crimson.

At that moment, Gensai believed that Jubei's soul had transformed itself into that deep crimson butterfly and had flown off into the void.

Cleansed by the previous day's rain, the skies were a perfectly clear, almost transparent blue.

The sky was high, and the pampas grass rustled in the wind.

There in the field, Seiichiro and Yagyu Munefuyu sat facing each other.

Seiichiro had just finished telling the story of Jubei's last moments, which he had heard from Gensai the previous evening in the falling rain.

His legs still crossed, Munefuyu placed his hands on the ground behind him and looked up into the sky. It was not a pose that the forty-five-year-old leader of the Yagyu clan would be expected to take. It was a pose that some twenty-year-old youth would take as he tried to hold back the tears that spilled from his eyes. One somehow wanted to put one's arm around him and cry along with him.

That was what a person's death was like, thought Seiichiro. To the person who is dying, what meaning does death have? No matter how one might hope to die, death in and of itself is empty and no more than the absence of existence. It is only to the living who grieve that death has meaning. Isn't it only then that the dead, as one might put it, return to life? Seiichiro thought that it was only at that moment, for the first time, that Yagyu Jubei had been restored to life.

"A butterfly of blood."

Munefuyu had spoken almost to himself, still in the same pose.

"That may have been appropriate for my brother. His life had certainly been stained with blood."

Slowly, he returned to his original seated pose. The tears that he might have shed were already dried. With eyes as clear as the skies above, he looked gently at Seiichiro.

"Thank you. Now, for me, my brother has at long last actually died. Until now, right here..." he said putting his hand over his heart. "It was as if I had a sharp bone stuck here. It was like living and dying at the same moment. It was intolerable. I am sincerely grateful."

Though still sitting cross-legged, he bowed formally.

Seiichiro bowed in return. He was glad that he had told Munefuyu. At the same time, he also knew that by informing Munefuyu, Gensai—as the one who had slain Yagyu Jubei—had consciously resigned himself to the probability of being pursued to the end of his days. The enormous dignity that Gensai had shown in serenely telling him the truth about what had taken place made Seiichiro bow his head anew.

"Thanks to my elder brother Jubei and younger brother Gisen, I myself have never killed anyone..."

It was a stunning confession for the leader of the Yagyu to make.

"I think that I was fortunate in not resembling my father but in being born a child of mediocre talent. In fact, if it is possible, I would prefer to live out my life in this state. You, however...you are different."

In Munefuyu's voice there was something entirely heartfelt.

"You have already killed a large number of men. And you will probably kill more in the future. It is likely that, like my brother, you will live out the life of a demonic *rakshasa*..."

Seiichiro felt a pain seize his chest. Munefuyu had put his finger squarely on the one thing that had pained him every single day since the night of his arrival in Edo.

"But...the blood that runs through your body is not that of an ordinary person of the world. You don't smell of spilt blood the way my brother did. To be able to cut down someone and yet maintain such a freshness—it is an entirely uncommon quality. Would that freshness of spirit continue in you for as long as you live."

The transmission of the Yagyu secret tradition of swordsmanship had come to an end that morning. In all likelihood this would be the very last time that Munefuyu and Seiichiro would meet. For that reason, these words seemed like a final parting blessing offered by Seiichiro's transitory master. For that, Seiichiro was grateful. But there was one thing that left Seiichiro dissatisfied.

"What exactly did you mean when you said that my blood is not that of 'an ordinary person'?"

Munefuyu seemed slightly perplexed.

"Do you mean that none of the Yoshiwara people have said anything to you?"

"About my lineage? No, nothing at all."

Momentarily there was silence.

"In that case, it seems even I have managed to blurt out something

I shouldn't have."

His tone indicated that he was embarrassed.

"At any rate, at some time or another you'll find out. There is no way to conceal the truth. You are the son of the retired-emperor Go-Mizuno-in."

Silence.

As was to be expected, Seiichiro was stunned. But Munefuyu's expression was totally serious.

"Your mother, for certain reasons, was murdered. You were to have been murdered as well, but it seems that you were rescued by Miyamoto Musashi. Had you been found as a child, you would have been killed. That is in all likelihood why Master Musashi prohibited you from leaving the mountains until you turned twenty-five. That was a wise move. And now that two successive imperial reigns have passed, you may rest assured that the necessity of having you killed has passed."

The silence continued.

When Seiichiro was born, the reigning *tenno* was Empress Meisho. Following her was Emperor Go-Komyo and the current ruler was Emperor Go-Sai. Even now, however, Seiichiro's father, the retired Emperor Go-Mizuno-o, was still living in an imperial villa.

"It is this sword only that proves who you are."

Munefuyu pointed to Seiichiro's long sword.

"The noted sword possessed by successive generations of the Minamoto clan, 'the Demon Cutter.' It is a sword Hidetada presented to the imperial court himself. But what really testifies to the truth of your lineage is blood. The blood that courses through your veins. I believe that."

Munefuyu suddenly fell silent.

Seiichiro abruptly spoke, almost in a shout, "So I wasn't abandoned!"

"What?"

"What that means is that I was not abandoned as a child!"

His voice was filled with elation. He appeared to be straining to suppress a jubilation which threatened to explode at any second.

"Of course you weren't. Why would anyone abandon the son of an emperor?"

"I wasn't a foundling!" Seiichiro repeated. Tears poured down his cheeks. Such emotion was beyond Munefuyu's powers of comprehension.

Abandoned child. How the young Seiichiro had been wounded by the cruelty such words possessed. His consciousness of having parents who would abandon their own child. His feelings of inferiority from having been cast aside as superfluous. This was at the core of what made him what he was at that very moment. An abandoned child—that was his origin, his birth.

"I was abandoned!" How many times in his life had he pounded the earth shouting that?

This sense of bitterness had given the youthful Seiichiro the strength to endure virtually anything, to quickly resign himself and to hold no hopes for anything.

And now....

"I was not abandoned!"

He was filled with a feeling of absolute jubilation that welled up from deep inside. At the same moment, a feeling of futility wafted through his heart as he wondered what he had been doing up to that point in his life. But the jubilation was far stronger than that sense of meaninglessness. He could feel that something in the depths of his heart which had frozen hard and stiff was somehow beginning to melt.

Compared to this, the fact that he was the child of an emperor meant hardly anything at all. The fact did not change who he was. Was it not a matter of little consequence? And in this conclusion could be seen what was unusual in the thinking of Seiichiro, who had become a man while living in solitude.

Munefuyu looked at Seiichiro with a baffled air.

(I shouldn't have told him after all)

He felt a faint sense of remorse, and yet what had happened had happened. Munefuyu looked once again at Seiichiro.

Nimbly he rose to his feet.

"This then is farewell," he said. He turned and walked off without a glance backward, straight out of the pampas field toward the gravel pit. It was a simple parting, highly appropriate to a warrior. A gentle breeze lightly fluttered his sleeves as he walked away.

Seiichiro formally placed his palms on the ground and lowered his head, watching the heaven-sent messenger—who had brought forth this momentous news—until he disappeared from sight.

In a thickly wooded area some two hundred yards away, a man lay with his stomach pressing the ground. He was a *mimisuke*, a ninja skilled in long-distance listening.

(Now I've really heard something!)

The *mimisuke* was barely able to keep himself from trembling with fear. That single phrase "emperor's son" was powerful enough to send a shudder through him. After all, it was a time when the water in which a member of the nobility—not to mention the emperor—had bathed could be sold as a secret medicine thought to heal all ailments, one that the purchaser would gratefully drink. It was only natural that it would be shocking to learn that a person one actually knew happened to be the son of an emperor.

(I'll be murdered!)

It may seem like a peculiar leap in logic, but to the *mimisuke* it was an entirely normal progression of thought. After all, he was not a man of such strong will that he could lock his lips and keep to himself the astonishing piece of information he had just overheard. Sometime, somewhere, without a doubt he would eventually divulge this secret. And once he spilled the secret, he would be killed. In an instant, his thoughts followed this path, reaching that frightening conclusion. For that reason, he virtually flew back to O-Miuraya, where he was employed as a night watchman.

As soon as he saw Shirozaemon, he wailed, "Please! Just kill me now yourself with your own hands!" Shirozaemon was flabbergasted at his man's outburst, but he had the room cleared immediately and then listened to the details of his story. When he had heard the entire tale, his face was pale.

"This is serious—very serious," he moaned, his voluminous body undulating like a quivering mass of gelatin. He immediately sent the *mimisuke* to the shops of Nomura Gen'i, Yamadaya Sannojo, and Namikiya Genzaemon to gather them for a sudden game of go.

"There isn't a person in this world who, if told, 'You're the child of an emperor,' wouldn't go head over heels."

The men had gathered in the large room on O-Miuraya's second floor. Two go boards had been set up for form's sake. Across these boards, Shirozaemon faced Gen'i and Sannojo faced Genzaemon. The stones moved mechanically on the boards, but the players' minds were elsewhere. Gensai alone, as was his custom, sat with his legs widely crossed, his back against a pillar, sipping sake.

"The man's entire world changes. At the very least, it would seem that way to him. That would only be natural. If all had gone normally, he would have grown up to become the emperor." Shirozaemon was garrulous today. He was as excited as if he himself had just been told that he was an imperial prince. "Now that this has happened, there's a possibility that he won't even speak to us Yoshiwara people. If the same thing happened to me, I might change like that, too. I might indeed."

"In that case, it's a good thing that Seiichiro isn't you," Gensai laughed loudly.

"There's nothing funny about this. For him, there is absolutely no reason to remain in Yoshiwara. He could just present himself in his own name and appear in the world. He could go to the capital, meet the shogunate's military governor who is stationed there, or go directly to the imperial palace, to the villa of the retired emperor. With the Demon Cutter sword and the accompanying letter from Master Musashi in his possession, it's obvious that he would be courteously received anywhere, and that he would be treated with the appropriate hospitality."

"*Go-inkyo*, what about the letter from Master Musashi?" Yamadaya Jinnojo's voice trembled as he spoke.

"I have that in my possession, but any time Seiichiro asks for it, I'll return it to him."

"This is no joking matter," Shirozaemon countered heatedly. "If you hand it back, he might not be so warmhearted…"

"Enough is enough!" Gensai spoke sharply. His face was unusually stern. Shirozaemon suddenly fell silent. The undulation of his flesh, however, suddenly increased, for no one knew better than he did how formidable Gensai could be when provoked.

"Do you think Seiichiro is such a worthless man? You forget that virtually from the moment he was born, Master Musashi nestled him in his bosom and raised him. Just because he has found out that he is the child of an emperor, he's not about to do anything strange. I've fought alongside him, and that's what I'm telling you!"

"I apologize. I lost my presence of mind. I was just suddenly afraid of losing something very precious."

"*Go-inkyo*, Shirozaemon's concerns are only natural. Whatever anyone says, Master Matsunaga is still young. Young men are apt to change suddenly," said Nomura Gen'i, coming to Shirozaemon's rescue.

"I'm telling you—he's not going to change just like that. I will vouch for that. And anyway, if he were the kind of person to change so abruptly, he certainly wouldn't be the kind of person who would support us in the first place."

"Indeed, that is true. From that point of view then, we should simply accept what happens," Genzaemon said in a somber tone. That was it. It was decided.

Gensai spoke next.

"We will set Seiichiro's *najimi* on the day of the Chrysanthemum Festival." He then added cryptically, "We will gather a large number of chrysanthemums to cover him with. It will be a most appropriate ceremony for the son of an emperor."

NAJIMI: THE THIRD VISIT

According to the lunar calendar, the ninth day of the ninth month was the Chrysanthemum Festival, one of the five main seasonal festivals.

On that day, in the imperial court a chrysanthemum blossom banquet was held, and the entire body of imperial retainers would gather to eat rice mixed with chestnuts and drink sake from cups upon which chrysanthemums were floated. It was from this tradition that the card representing the ninth month in the card game known as *hanafuda* included a chrysanthemum, a large sake cup and the character "*kotobuki*," or longevity.

That Gensai had set the day of the Chrysanthemum Festival as the day for Seiichiro's *najimi* with Takao could have been wittiness on his part, or it could have been an act of dead seriousness. In all likelihood, even Gensai didn't know which it was.

It is said that the chrysanthemum is the recluse of flowers, peony the wealthy nobleman. The chrysanthemum was the crest of Sento Gosho, the residence of the retired emperor, and later its usage was expanded to become the crest of the imperial house. It was in that sense that for

Seiichiro—who descended from the retired Emperor Go-Mizuno-o, and yet at present was a mere *ronin* with no recognized connection to the imperial family—there could be no more appropriate day for becoming a man. Surely it was impossible that such thinking would not underlie Gensai's decision to set that day as Seiichiro's third and decisive meeting with Takao.

In the Yoshiwara, to enter a *najimi* relationship—to become intimate—was in a manner of speaking to become a married couple. On the third meeting, for the first time, the customer and the *yujo* became bound together. Because they then became "married" to each other, they shared a bedchamber.

As an aphorism of the time put it, the third meeting was a time to know one another's feelings, to loosen the inner sash, to cast aside all forms of restraint. But that was not all that the new relationship meant.

When Seiichiro once again entered the second-floor room of the Owariya, a small raised lacquerware tray, gray on the outside and vermilion on the inside, with silver-inlay ivory chopsticks, was placed before him. On the paper envelope holding the chopsticks was inscribed the name "Seiichiro."

This was also a symbol of their becoming "wed." An on this occasion, for the first time, Takao called him by "Sei-sama." Until this evening, neither Takao nor her *kamuro* had uttered his name in any form at all. They had simply referred to him as "master" or "our guest." It was Yoshiwara custom to use the man's name for the first time on the third visit. In short, it was because on this visit the man became a member of the family.

Naturally enough, becoming a "regular partner" of a courtesan such as Takao required an enormous amount of money. In addition to the *agedaikin*, one also had to pay *najimikin*, a congratulatory gift of money. The latter was divided into *nikaibana* and *sobana*, the first of which was divided among the *oiran* and her accompanying *shinzo*, *kamuro* and *yarite*. It was a matter of custom that the *yarite* received one-tenth of the amount. The *sobana,* on the other hand, was divided among all of the employees of the house to which the courtesan belonged, and this became the custom after the Horeki era. It was also essential to slip an envelope of money called "pillow flowers" into the small drawer of the mirror stand in the *oiran*'s room. All of these amounts depended on the era, the status of the *oiran* and various other factors, but in the *Shobai Orai* manual published in the fifth year of the Kansei era (1793), the following was recorded: an *agedaikin* of one *ryo* one *bu*, a "pillow flower" gift amounting to three *ryo*, and a *sobana* amounting to five *ryo*. In *The Idle Essays of Morikawa* it was written, "Pillow flowers come after the *najimi*, there is no fixed amount, 57 *ryo* or more than 10 *ryo*, it depends on the customer's feelings." In the same book it was recorded that on one occasion the *agedai* fee was 3 *bun*, the *najimi* fee 2 *ryo* 2 *bun*, of which the *yujo* passed 2 *bun* to the *ageya*, 1 *bun* to the young people of the *ageya*, 1 more *bun* to the young peole of her own house. In effect, of the total amount that the *oiran* received, a full half of it was passed on to those who worked in the house of the assignation and in the house to which she belonged.

In Seiichiro's case, Gensai had paid all of the assorted expenses to Owariya Seiroku. Furthermore, *sobana* was not generally given at that time, Meireki 3 (1657). Naturally enough, the *shinzo, kamuro* and *yarite* as well as the employees of the Owariya came to Seiichiro to offer their congratulations. It was courteous treatment suitable for royalty. Seiichiro, however, interpreted all of the formal courtesies as a reflection of their esteem for Gensai, for he had no idea it was all on account of the power of money. Seiichiro had not yet learned the ways of the world. Yet no one could blame him for this, because until several months prior, he had lived in solitude deep in the mountains.

To Seiichiro, money was nothing more than a bother. When he departed from Kumamoto, he had received from Terao Magonojo a total of 200 *ryo*, and he had received cursory instruction concerning the price of various items he might need, but he rather quickly forgot all that he had been told. Along the way from Kumamoto to Edo, whenever he needed to pay for something, he handed the person his purse and requested that the person simply take whatever amount was appropriate. There had been plenty of opportunities for people to cheat him, and sure enough some did, but rarely did that happen. The fact that he had suffered no great loss was probably due to his own personal integrity. When he arrived in Edo, he still had 190 *ryo*, which he handed over to Jinnojo, master of Nishidaya. From that moment onward, Seiichiro never once carried money on his person. Had a townsman of Edo heard this, he would undoubtedly find it all too hard to believe. In this sense Seiichiro's lifestyle included a form of extravagance, one fitting the nobility.

On the night of *najimi*, says one tale, a certain *yujo* described to her new regular partner how she had been born in faraway Echigo province and had once woven cotton crepe. With Takao, however, there was no such innocence. She was a more mature, more sophisticated woman, one who maintained the dignity of a courtesan. Rather than being adorable, she possessed a gentle gaze and a soft way of behaving that gave others a feeling of serenity.

"Sei-sama, shall you continue to stay at the Nishidaya?" she asked.

Seiichiro looked at Gensai as if he were troubled as to how he should reply.

"Well, I've been told that I may, but I often feel guilty for taking advantage of their kindness."

"Don't be foolish," Gensai responded loudly. "It would be a problem if you didn't continue to stay right where you are. There's no lady of the house to help with the shop, so the master has to do everything that she would do, too, and that leaves no one to look after Oshabu. Things couldn't be any more insecure than that. If you weren't around and something happened, there's no telling what might happen to them."

What Gensai seemed to be intimating was the possibility of an assault by the Ura Yagyu. To be sure, as the current head of the family, Jinnojo was talented when it came to business, but he was an entirely temperate sort and lacked the qualities that would make him dependable as a man.

"So I'm Oshabu's bodyguard?" Seiichiro gave a wry smile. The actual situation seemed to him to be quite the reverse. Whether Seiichiro was at the Nishidaya or some place else, it appeared to make no difference at all to Jinnojo or any of his employees. His presence or absence seemed to matter only to Oshabu, and when he wasn't around for a short time, it was she who sent one of the younger employees around to try to locate him. As long as she knew where he was, she was reassured. He was the one who was constantly embraced in her concern, rather than the reverse. This constantly being concerned was the bodyguard's duty, so in that sense, Oshabu was serving as Seiichiro's personal protector.

But he had to admit that the job of being "Oshabu's protector" did have its appeal.

(To protect that child, I probably would do almost anything)

He really believed that. Oshabu was just that bewitching a creature.

"Oshabu-sama is certainly an enviable young woman," Takao said, leaning slightly against Seiichiro and twining her fingers around his. The strength in her fingers suggested that she actually meant what she said.

"We're speaking of a girl who is only nine years old, *Oiran*. She's far too young to merit any feelings of jealousy." Gensai laughed as he spoke, but Takao's serious expression remained unchanged.

"For a woman, age is unimportant. Some girls are splendid women at nine, while others who are twenty-eight have still not become full-fledged women. Oshabu-sama is already a splendid young lady."

Takao was recalling the day when Oshabu had called on her. "Please take good care of Sei-sama," Oshabu had said, lightly shedding a tear. To be honest, at that moment, Takao had felt she was already defeated. Oshabu's consideration had been far too deep, far too serious for mere childish yearning. That sense of consideration made even a woman of Takao's composure shudder. Takao had felt intimidated, as if the tip of a finely honed dagger had touched the nipple of her breast. And yet that fright could be said to have had the reverse effect because it intensified Takao's feelings all the more and made her that more determined. It had made her resolve that, for the sake of her dignity as a *tayu*, she must make the man Oshabu called Sei-sama powerless to resist her. But much to her misfortune, something else happened as well: she actually fell in love with Seiichiro.

Takao could not speak to either Seiichiro or to Gensai of her feelings toward Oshabu. Had she done so, they would have laughed. Having to keep silence made her all the more irritated and angry. But by one means or another, she had to pull Seiichiro away from Oshabu. She was serious. But Takao knew instinctively that to make a nine-year-old girl a rival in love was a virtually impossible task. Therefore she determined to make the battle one of endless attrition. To a courtesan, a war of attrition meant exhausting her entire body and soul on behalf of her man. For an *oiran*, to become absolutely enamored of one man and do her utmost for him left only one thing in her future: complete ruin. A woman of Takao's experience was certainly aware of that. In her clear awareness of what that meant, and in her decision to confront possible destruction, lay her fate and her radiance as a tragic woman.

A Comfortable Evening

Upon the cue provided by the wife of Owariya's proprietor, the banquet came to a conclusion.

"Tomorrow morning, I'll be waiting for you at the bath," teased Gensai, as Seiichiro stood up to leave the room. That the proprietress of the Owariya took it upon herself to conduct the evening's proceedings was due less to the power of money than to consideration for Seiichiro. Usually it was the *yarite* who took that role. Following this lady into the hallway was Seiichiro and then Takao. Takao's fingers were still entwined with Seiichiro's. Behind them followed two *kamuro*. After turning this way and that along the corridor, the lady of the house stopped in front of the door or a secluded room, knelt and slid the door open for those who had followed her.

"*Oshigerinanshi*, a very comfortable evening to you," she smiled and slid the door shut.

"*Oshigerinanshi*" was a graceful, elegant expression unique to Yoshiwara. It was a way of wishing them a quiet time as lovers. *Shikeru* referred to the natural warmth and moisture that would dampen both clothing and bedding as the night wore on. In the theater, this word was not used; rather "*chigiri*," and the phrase "*chigiriyanse*" on the stage, is roughly the equivalent of Yoshiwara's "*oshigerinanshi*."

Compared with the previous drawing room, this room was smaller and rather dark. The greater portion of the space was taken up by a large set of futon. There were three futon, two for underneath and one for cover. In winter, padded robes would be added. The futon was about the height of a low bed.

Takao sat facing Seiichiro before the bedding. During the entire time that it took the *kamuro* to prepare the traditional cups of sake for them to exchange, Takao gazed at Seiichiro, her eyes unmoving. To Seiichiro she was dazzling. When they had completed the customary exchange of cups, poured by the *kamuro*, Takao formally placed the fingertips of both hands on the tatami, bowed her head and said a single word.

"For a long time…"

An earnest expression on his face, Seiichiro nodded.

One of the *kamuro* brought forth a rather large lacquered box. Takao opened it herself. The fragrance of chrysanthemums suddenly filled the entire room. The box was filled with a large number of cotton floss covers. According to an ancient Chinese custom which held that the dew of chrysanthemum blossoms was an elixir that promoted longevity, cotton covers were used to collect the dew that accumulated on the flowers every day from the first day of the seventh month of the year and then, on the ninth day of the ninth month, the cotton were used to wipe the sacred body of the emperor. The custom was introduced to Japan during the Asuka period, from whence it spread among the high-ranking members of the imperial court. On the day of the Chrysanthemum Festival, the nobles would drink chrysanthemum sake and wipe their skin with the dew-infused cotton. It was a custom only within the imperial court, and could not have been a Yoshiwara tradition. That it was introduced on this occasion was entirely due to the arrangements of Gensai, who was aware of Seiichiro's lineage.

Takao took Seiichiro's hand and had him stand up. Then she knelt and untied the *obi* of his kimono. She removed each layer of his clothing and handed it one by one to one of the young girls. Finally, he stood before Takao in just his loincloth.

Takao then took the cotton and carefully used them to wipe his naked body. When the cotton touched his skin, it felt cool and somewhat ticklish. Gradually the ticklish sensation gave way to a pleasurable feeling, and by the time Takao had finished wiping his entire body, inside his loincloth Seiichiro's organ had swollen large. When at last she removed his loincloth, his hardened penis soared up and swayed back and forth before her. Takao tenderly pressed her cheek against it, then took cotton swabs and wiped it gently. She affectionately wiped his scrotum as well, and when she wiped from his anus toward his scrotum, he felt a strong feeling of pleasure run from the tips of his toes to the top of his head. Had Takao not at that precise moment tightly grasped the base of his scrotum, he might very well have ejaculated. As if to soothe it, she stroked his scrotum and then, as she caressed his member, she spoke.

"Why Sei-sama, you have a mole."

The two *kamuro* looked at his penis in surprise. Sure enough, midway along the shaft of his penis was a mole about the size of a small bean. From ancient times it was believed that such a mole was symbolic of a man of great virility, but of course Seiichiro had no idea of this. For his part, Seiichiro was simply embarrassed by the fact that the two young girls, who were almost the same age as Oshabu, were staring fixedly at his penis. It wilted under their gaze and the mole was no longer visible. This was rather sweet, and the two girls giggled.

"That is certainly not polite," Takao scolded them, but she herself was smiling. Even Seiichiro smiled wryly.

Takao took Seiichiro's hand and led him to the futon. Laying him down on his back, she turned her back to him and untied her *obi*. The *obi* of an *oiran* was always tied so that with the slightest tug, the bow would come undone. Underneath this one *obi* there was not a single string, not even on the waistcloth. This was not so that the clothing could be quickly removed in the bedchamber. Rather, it was done to make it easy to escape from a malicious customer who might try to carry out a murder-suicide or to commit some sort of violence.

For one brief moment, Takao sat without moving at all, still wearing her long lilac undergarment. Reading a clear coyness in the tips of her shoulders, Seiichiro's heart pounded. But he refrained from reaching out to her and waited patiently without moving, his standard of manners being high. Takao removed all of her ornamental hairpins, handed them to one of her young attendants and then shook her head once. Her abundant, long hair fell to her waist. This was not a traditional practice in Yoshiwara. An *oiran* usually retired with her hair still done up. Takao's letting down her hair was an emulation of the customs of the high-ranking ladies of the court. In the court, before retiring, a lady would gather her long hair and place it in the "*midarebako*" box by her pillow. This was the usage of the original *midarebako*, and it was only in much later eras that the removed clothing would be placed there. Just such a *midarebako* was placed by Takao's pillow as well. The two *kamuro* now picked up her clothing and hair ornaments and left the room.

Holding the lapels of her undergarment together, covering her breast, she lay down next to Seiichiro.

His breathing grew slightly irregular. And yet he had no idea what he should do.

Takao stayed absolutely still, making no movement at all. Seiichiro felt the entire room fill gradually with a feeling of energy.

"*Tayu...*" Seiichiro began to speak in a voice that had turned husky. By now, the room was filled with an almost unbearable sensuousness.

Takao smiled self-consciously, and when she did, the hand that held her undergarment released its hold. The front of her almost-purple, lilac robe fell open and her porcelain-white skin became visible. Light pink nipples stood out on her well-rounded breasts.

Her white skin seemed to shine. Seiichiro felt her skin seemed brighter now that she was lying on the futon than when she had sat on the tatami. This impression was carefully created by the Yoshiwara attention to detail, for the height of the candle stand was selected with that very purpose in mind. Seiichiro was of course oblivious of that strategy, but he was keenly aware of the brilliant beauty of the tone of her skin.

Takao lay on Seiichiro's left. It was said by a connoisseur of a later era that one could tell whether a woman of the quarter liked or disliked a customer by the side on which she lay down. In this case, her lying on his left was evidence that she was fond of him, because it allowed him the free use of his right hand.

Takao gently took Seiichiro's right hand in her own left and lightly guided his hand to her breast, in such a way that his hand delicately, very delicately, passed as light as a feather over her breast and then her nipple. Suddenly beneath his touch, he felt her pink nipple quiver. In response to that sensation, his finger also quivered. The nipple swelled slightly and became visibly pointed.

"Ah." A faint sound spilled from Takao's lips and her eyes closed halfway.

With the same gentleness, her hand slowly guided his fingertips downward. With this motion, the front of her robe slowly but surely fell open.

The smooth, ivory-like touch of her skin changed slightly, and the softness began to moisten. Seiichiro's fingertips gingerly reached her navel and then continued further downward. By then, the front of her robe was completely open and her private parts were completely in view. On the plump prominence between her legs was not a single hair. It was as smooth as that of a young girl, and running down the middle of her pudenda was a single pinkish line. The only difference from that of a young girl was that toward the top there was a plump glistening protuberance rising from the cleft, one of considerable size and length

All of this was beautiful, like a succulent white peach. In fact, it appeared so succulent that it seemed that if he were to bite into it, crystal-clear nectar would fill his mouth and dribble down his chin. It was his first time to look straight at a woman's body. To see such a beautiful living thing was enough to make him sigh.

Takao's hand did not cease its encouragement there. She now guided his fingers further down the warm, smooth slope to the protuberance within the cleft. His fingertips sensed greater moisture there than on her skin. When he tenderly touched the protuberance, her body shook strongly. The slightest of furrows appeared between her eyebrows, and her nipples grew even harder than before, soaring above her breasts. When his fingers reached the bottom of the protuberance, they were faintly pushed back upward. From within the cleft, a small, deep-pink core appeared, and when his fingers stroked across it, her whole body arched backwards.

"Aah."

This time her voice was clearer than before. Since Takao had arched back, Seiichiro's finger slipped straightaway from the protuberance all the way down to the moist part. The strength of her hand increased and his finger was slightly buried inside. It was hot. It felt as if his finger had slipped into a jar of heated honey. Seiichiro's fingers were guided into making a circular motion, round and round, deeper inside. It was different inside, hot and plump, with countless wrinkles, each and every one distended. And then these minute folds suddenly came to an end and there was a smooth open place. At the very moment his finger entered that space, his finger was squeezed strongly from midpoint to base.

"Aah!"

Just as this breath escaped her lips, he felt the wide place contract, and simultaneously detected a sudden fragrant smell, in fact, the same *jiyu* scent as from the second meeting, but now with another delicate fragrance combined.

Takao's right hand grasped Seiichiro's neck, and pulled it down toward her with unexpected strength. Their faces came together and his lips touched her moist lips. She first kissed his upper lip, then the lower one, and quickly her delicate tongue pushed its way into his mouth, entwining itself around his. Her mouth tasted sweet—even the saliva that seeped toward his tongue was sweet.

Then somehow Seiichiro was on top of Takao, lying between her modestly spread legs. Her left hand gently clasped his penis, which was about to burst forth. She touched it slightly against her moistness and gently bit by bit raised her buttocks. Once he was clearly buried inside, she pulled her buttocks back strongly. At the same time, she grasped the base of his penis. Although it was on the point of spilling forth, with this strong tension, it recovered. Her buttocks rose once again, and he was buried even further than a moment earlier. Then she pulled back hard. Next she rose up fast and even higher than before, and his penis went deep inside. From there she began to slowly move her hips round and round. He reached the wall deep inside. She retreated sharply several times then grasped his waist with both of her hands. Takao's fingers pulled down on his back as her own buttocks rose upward. His pelvis moved in rhythm with the movement of her hands. When her hands eventually released him, he maintained the same rhythmical strong-then-soft movements. Their lips remained pressed together, and her tongue pressed against his with the same rhythm as her buttocks. When her pelvis moved in a circular motion, her tongue did as well.

Suddenly, from deep within her body came a great shudder.

"Ah!"

She groaned as if taken suddenly by surprise, throwing her head back sharply. Seiichiro had the sensation that the tip of his penis was being pecked at by small birds. He realized it was accompanied by a hot gushing forth, and Takao embraced him strongly around the neck, pulling her upper body toward him. His penis was rubbing against something stiff.

"Ah, aah! Ah!"

When Takao's body quivered again, she held on fast to Seiichiro. His penis felt pressure in two places. Takao's vagina began to alternately contract and relax as if it were an entirely separate living thing.

Now Takao's legs were twined around his back, and she was sitting on his knees. His hands grasped Takao's buttocks and were helping the up-down rhythm. Both of her arms were wrapped tightly around his neck, and her firmly peaked breasts rubbed against his chest. Their rhythms were completely in sync. Like rippling waves, he penetrated her, then suddenly pulled away strongly. Like a surging wave, he penetrated deep inside and then powerfully pulled back. Seiichiro no longer knew whether he was Takao or whether Takao was him. The feeling of pleasure that she felt when he penetrated became his own feeling. The pleasure he felt became hers, too. It was altogether as if each was feeling the pleasure of two people, one a man and one a woman. In the end, there came a wave greater than any before. It penetrated deep inside, surged forth and collapsed into white, bubbling foam.

"I'm so happy," Takao whispered into his ear, still breathing hard.

Seiichiro silently embraced her, almost hard enough to crush her. The sweet fragrance he had detected earlier permeated the entire room now. He was still inside her. She still held him tightly inside and would not release him. Not only did he not wither—he gained a new burst of strength and began to swell once more.

"Goodness."

This time Takao seemed really surprised and her eyes opened. Before she knew what was happening, the same rhythms as before began and her body slowly began to rise up...

To prevent any misunderstanding, it should be said that Takao was not suffering from some illness that left her hairless between her legs. That beautiful peach-like place was the result of the long and careful grooming since she was a *kamuro* of twelve or thirteen. It is believed that the Yoshiwara *yujo* had arts unknown to lay women, and depilation was one of their arts of enchantment. Not every woman in Yoshiwara pulled out all her hair, of course. It was simply that each woman achieved what she felt was most beautiful. Some women left just one patch towards the top, some left a uniform shape, others soaked the hair in vinegar to soften it. There were all kinds of preferences. But in the quarter there was not a single woman who allowed her pubic hair to grow thick and luxuriant like a woman "on the outside."

Long afterwards, when there were no more *tayu* and no more *ageya*, and *yujo* had fallen from their rank to become mere prostitutes, this custom continued. Some patrons apparently thought that the hair was removed for hygienic reasons, such as to avoid lice, but we cannot but consider them to be ignorant men who knew nothing of the arts of enchantment.

In *Pillow Book*, Sei Shonagon listed in her chapter of "Things About Which To Be Thankful": "a silver hair-remover that works beautifully." The Chinese arts of the bedchamber became part of magician's lore, were studied by Daoists, incorporated into court custom, and furthermore passed down by doctors as part of medical learning. After that, through the Nara and Heian period, the arts were handed down amongst the intelligentsia of this country, to be researched and put into practice. Therefore it cannot be said for certain that Sei Shonagon's "thing for which to be grateful" was not used for the same purpose as that of the Yoshiwara *tayu*. There were various ideas of what constituted beauty in this part of the body, but women in the quarter shared the view that it was unconscionable to make great efforts to make up face, hands and feet and then remain totally unconcerned about the most important part of a woman's body. Only a base, haughty, ordinary woman from outside the quarter could possibly remain lackadaisical about allowing her pubic hair to bristle like brambles and remain complacent while emitting unpleasant odors that would turn a person's nose.

In fact, when it came to odors from the vagina, the elegant "castle topplers" used extreme caution. To avoid giving off any offensive odor, they refused to take so much as a bite of uncooked food or vegetables that produced a strong smell. These courtesans made impressive efforts, going so far as to bathe in perfumed water, burn incense to perfume their waist clothes and insert small sachets inside the vagina.

There was no facility within the Yoshiwara to teach these myriad ways of becoming more beautiful. Nor did the master of the houses, as popular sentiment assumed, give any instruction in this respect. The secret process of transmission was all done between one woman and another. That is, an "elder sister" taught the "younger sister" who attended her, or her *kamuro* attendants, by word of mouth.

From the "elder sister," the "younger sister" learned the arts of the bedchamber and the techniques of lovemaking. Telling a customer "I've lost my heart to you" was to be done gently, despite the lack of sincerity behind it all. A visitor to the quarter had of course to gently accept such untruths, if he expected to become a true connoisseur. And a refined *yujo* would feel and understand that visitor's gentleness, and respond again to that. Thus, sometimes from the hundred thousand falsehoods came one crystal-clear truth, like a beautiful lotus petal rising up out of the mud. Could that not be called the ultimate in pleasure, the ultimate in love?

The word *kinuginu* is said to have existed since the Nara period. *Kinu* here means not silk, but robe. In the *Kokinshu* imperial poem collection, there is the verse,

As dawn breaks brightly
How sad to put on our separate robes

And it can be seen from the above poem that the term *kinuginu* is a contraction of "our robes." During the Nara and Heian periods, lovers who spent the night together either lay on top of their garments or covered themselves with such garments. When morning came and they had to part, they retrieved their respective clothing. As the man left in early morning, remaining in his garments would be the warmth and the distinctive odor of his lover, but those reminders of the night before would gradually disappear, giving rise to the lament. *Kinuginu* therefore meant lovers' parting. It is said that during the Heian period, the Chinese characters for "after morning" were added to the term.

By the Edo period, the term came to be used to mean the farewells between a *yujo* and her customer. That was because it was otherwise no longer the usual practice for a man to visit a woman in her quarters, and it had become customary for a wife to move into her husband's home. Therefore the usage of the word changed, and *kinuginu* became seen as a word referring to the pleasure quarters. For a woman of the pleasure quarters, the *kinuginu*, or morning departure of a customer, was a crucial moment. If she did not succeed in capturing his heart, there was a possibility that he would never return. Because of that, the woman applied all of her skills in that single moment of truth. She had to be sure that there was nothing separating them, so that he would come back again.

Seiichiro had remained awake through the entire night. Pestered by Takao, he had spent the night telling of his life in the mountains from childhood on. In between these tales, they had made love five times. Indeed their clothes and bedding had been dampened by their *oshigeri*, their pleasurable night together. Surprisingly, each time, Takao's body had grown even more radiant and fragrant, but she clung to him like a mollusk, incessantly drawing him inside and wrapping herself around him, to the point that Seiichiro began to wonder whether he had completely melted within her.

Night fell on Yoshiwara and there was no sound at all, except for the occasional sound of a fulling block making Asakusa paper, coming from the direction of the Sanya Moat.

As dawn approached, a cuckoo cried piercingly. Normally

Seiichiro felt that particular bird's call ominous, but this morning it penetrated deep inside him. It was because he heard within its sound the heartbreaking grief of people who have to part from one another. Acutely sensing his feelings, Takao's eyes misted over. Seiichiro learned for the first time in his life that such a morning like this could exist in the world of humans.

One sleepy-eyed *kamuro* brought a *fusayoji*, a small dish of salt and a small tea bowl of water on a round tray for cleaning their teeth. The other brought a small pail for discarding the wastewater. The *fusayoji* was a toothpick made of willow with one end finely smashed and the handle slightly squared so that it could be used to remove the fur on the tongue.

Takao told Seiichiro that according to the customs of the quarter, with this single bowl of water, one was supposed to brush one's teeth, rinse one's mouth and wash one's face. Moreover, one was supposed to perform these ablutions without splattering water about. If one did not do this neatly, she added, one would be regarded contemptuously as a boor by the people of the quarter. Laughing, Seiichiro surprised the *kamuro* by carrying out the process quite neatly.

"Sei-sama already knows our customs," said one of the *kamuro*. But she was mistaken. Careful use of water was one of the rules of a swordsman. Splashing and dripping water here and there was a sign of an unprepared mind. The swordsman who worked at achieving a constant alertness in his everyday life naturally became efficient, wasted nothing, and performed everything in an orderly fashion.

Takao made no attempt at a beguiling "morning after" scene. She simply gazed at Seiichiro sadly—and said nothing. Her expression resembled that of a wife seeing her beloved husband going off to the battlefront. Grief oozed from every pore of her body. Seiichiro silently nodded his head.

After receiving his swords on the ground floor of the shop and inserting them in the *obi* that wrapped his waist, Seiichiro stepped out of the Owariya and instantly became the target of a powerfully shot arrow. Quickly pulling his short sword—scabbard and all—from his *obi*, he parried the arrow and it dropped to the ground. The arrowhead was moist with something blue—poison of the tiger beetle.

NAKA-TAMBO

In the early morning of the tenth day of the ninth month, the wind rustled and in the autumn sky clouds scudded across the sky.

Watching Seiichiro, on his way home from a night of lovemaking through the sparsely populated streets, dealing with a succession of poisoned arrows, was a woman feeling an intense thrill—Katsuyama. She watched through a thin crack in the *shoji* of a second floor drawing room of a nearby house of assignation.

Katsuyama had informed Gisen, leader of the Ura Yagyu, that the night of the day of the Chrysanthemum Festival had been set for the *najimi* of Seiichiro and Takao. She was informed of the full details of the attempt to assassinate Seiichiro on that morning.

From the rooftop of the shop directly across from the Owariya Seiiroku shop, five archers rained an incessant attack on Seiichiro with arrows tipped in the potent poison of the tiger beetle. If Seiichiro were to deflect those arrows with the blade of his sword, they would break and the arrowhead might strike him somewhere. It the head so much as grazed his skin, the poison would be absorbed through his skin into his bloodstream. That was precisely the aim in using the poison.

But...this was Seiichiro, no ordinary warrior. He did not hurriedly draw his sword. Instead, he pulled his short sword, still sheathed, and struck down each arrow without shattering it. To be more accurate, he struck the arrow tip and bounced it off. By doing this, he eliminated the slightest chance of being struck by an arrowhead, and therefore he virtually eliminated the efficacy of the poison. Moreover, immediately after striking down the first arrow of the volley, without turning around, he closed the door behind his back to be sure that Takao would be protected from the onslaught.

A deep jealousy gripped Katsuyama's heart. Seiichiro's face was just slightly pale, a sign of the sleepless night he had spent together with Takao. He must have held Takao's pure white body in his arms throughout the night.

Holding the short sword aloft, Seiichiro ran directly toward the shop the archers were firing from. The hem of his kimono split open with the rapid movement of this sturdy legs. Those long, powerful legs had divided Takao's white legs...

Her chest constricted at the mere thought.
"Die. Just go ahead and be killed."
Unconsciously she actually said the words aloud.

As he ran, Seiichiro raised his left hand high. He had launched one of the short knives attached to his sword sheath. It accurately pierced one of the archers in the right eye. Panicked, the remaining archers jumped to the other side of the roof. One of the drawbridges had been opened out over the Ohaguro ditch and the bowmen had planned to make their escape over it into the rice fields beyond the moat. However...

In fact, the archers were decoys. Having suffered the disastrous defeat at Saihoji, Gisen was not about to underestimate Seiichiro's skills as a warrior a second time. Gisen had not expected Seiichiro to be done in by a couple of poisoned arrows. The point was to entice Seiichiro out of the quarter. It would be virtually impossible to lure him out of the quarter into the town proper, but if Gisen could get him to come out just a few steps...into the fields where the rice plants were heavily weighed down with golden grain. It was this field that Gisen had chosen for a decisive showdown. Gisen had stationed two additional archers, hidden near one of the drawbridges to the quarter, but they were no more than pawns to be sacrificed. If Seiichiro were to kill these two, then as a matter of course, Seiichiro would have to step out into the rice paddies. The two archers would probably be cut down somewhere along the single path that transected the fields. That also fit within Gisen's calculations. Beyond that, Gisen even anticipated that the twenty some henchmen he had lying in wait in the field would also be cut down. What Gisen needed was for Seiichiro to take a certain amount of time slaying those twenty. Within that span, even a warrior of Seiichiro's ability would become drawn into the closing jaws of a trap from which there could be no escape.

Two carts filled with sheaves of harvested rice had been casually left along the path that ran along Ohaguro ditch. When Seiichiro was drawn into the interval between the two carts, his end would come. Both carts were loaded with powerful explosive compounds. At the exact moment he was passed between the two carts, the explosives would be simultaneously detonated. However superb a swordsman Seiichiro might be, he could not possibly escape the explosion. His body would be cut into minute shreds and scattered in every direction.

With an ecstasy that set her trembling, Katsuyama pictured the final scene in her mind. She had an intense desire to be there when it happened. She wanted to be there, to be showered with his blood when it sprayed in all directions. If she could not actually bury him within herself and show him all her tenderness, would this not at least be revenge? The more she thought of this, the harder she found it to restrain herself. She suddenly and agilely moved out into the hallway and almost dashed down the stairs.

Seiichiro ran. His speed was astonishing. He had strong, powerful legs, so strong that on occasion when he had chased wild animals in the mountains of Higo he had raced right past them. His was a speed that exceeded that of any ordinary ninja. In an instant, he ran around the building and came out to the riverfront, which was lined with *kirimise* shops. As he had suspected, a drawbridge was lowered and four archers were on the point of crossing over it carrying a seriously wounded companion. The group was entirely taken by surprise by his unbelievable speed, and when Seiichiro launched two more small knives at them, two of the men were struck in the neck and felled. They died instantly. The wounded man was quickly cast aside, as he had already breathed his last. The remaining two archers, with a look of desperation, managed to cross the bridge, and right on their heels was Seiichiro. But just as he was about to step onto the bridge, he was stopped in his tracks by the frail voice of a child.
"Sei-sama! Don't!"
It was Oshabu, barefoot, running frantically toward him.
"You mustn't cross that bridge!"
Her face was pale.

That morning, Oshabu had had a horrifying dream. Seiichiro's naked body, entangled with Takao's body, had suddenly swollen up and exploded with a deafening roar. Oshabu for a second saw his body scattered into fragments following a brilliant flash of light. She awakened at the sound of her own voice shouting "No!!" She was crying, and still crying, she sprang up from her bed. As if led by someone she headed straight for the riverfront, where she came upon Seiichiro just as was about to cross the bridge. She screamed at the top of her lungs, and that scream came out as words: "Sei-sama! Don't!"

"It's dangerous! Stay back!" He warned her not to come any closer, but she ignored him, continuing straight on, and threw her arms around him.

"Home...take me home."

Seiichiro was at a loss. Seizing that moment, two Yagyu who had concealed themselves at the foot of the bridge jumped out and thrust their spears at him. They were afraid that if they didn't attack him, he might step back into the safety of the quarter. Seiichiro instantly shoved Oshabu to one side as he drew both of his swords. Slashing upward he sliced off the necks of their spears, and with the return stroke he cut both men from the shoulder across the body. When he turned around, however, he was aghast. Doubled up, Oshabu was holding her inner thigh with both hands. From between her fingers oozed blood.

"What's wrong?"

"The spear..."

Seiichiro realized instantly that the head of one of the spears he had cut off had struck the ground, bounced up and grazed her thigh. Looking at the tip of the spear lying on the ground, he turned pale. It was shining bluish black: poison.

"Damn!"

Seiichiro pushed her to the ground, so that she was lying on her back, and without thinking twice, he turned up the hem of her kimono.

"What are you...?"

Oshabu turned red in embarrassment and tried to cover herself, but Seiichiro thrust her hands aside. The wound was near her crotch, and while the wound was a superficial one, it was already beginning to swell due to the poison. While pressing his thumb against the artery to stanch the bleeding, he pressed his mouth against the wound. Sucking with all his might, he then spat out the blood that had accumulated in his mouth. It had turned a darkish red, evidence that the poison had mixed with the blood. Again, he sucked with every ounce of energy he had. It was still a dark red.

"Stop it!"

Oshabu twisted her body to escape his hold.

"Stop moving! The more you move, the faster the poison will spread. Relax and breath slowly, okay?"

Still flushed pink, Oshabu nodded. Seiichiro once again put his mouth against the cut and sucked slowly and at length. When he finally spat out again, the blood was almost its natural color. But still, it was too early to rest easy. Once more, he changed his angle and placed his mouth against her thigh. Her not yet developed private parts were right in front of his eyes. Needless to say, there was no pubic hair yet. Still, despite her being a child, she was plump there and from within the luster protruded a charming pink core. It was beautiful. Seiichiro was slightly discomfited. Entirely separate from his own intention, he grew hard. The problem was, Takao had not had hair either. He had simply been unable to prevent making that sudden association.

"Stop that."

Oshabu's voice was a mere whisper.

"Please don't recall that."

Seiichiro felt a pang of guilt. He spit out, deliberately spitting with force. The blood was clear.

Sensing someone's approach, he raised his eyes. There stood Katsuyama, dressed in a long undergarment. She had a peculiar look in her eyes. It was clearly jealousy, but Seiichiro could not grasp that.

"Please bring a piece of clean cloth and some distilled spirits."

Katsuyama wavered for a second. The fierce jealousy and fear she felt for Oshabu caused her to spit out words that she had never thought to say.

"Give up the idea of crossing the bridge. If you cross it, you'll lose your life."

Startled at the words that she herself had spoken, she returned with hurried steps to her shop.

Seiichiro and Oshabu were not the only ones who had heard what she said. The wife of the owner of a *kirimise* next to the leaf bridge and the *tsubone joro* of that shop had also heard her. The wife was a ringleader who had lowered the bridge for the Yagyu, and who had, out of avarice, begun to work for Gisen. The *joro* was none other than the fifty-three-year-old Oren, the prostitute who was besotted with old man Gensai. What these two women overheard would later lead to the tragic series of events that befell Katsuyama.

While waiting for the distilled spirits, Seiichiro in the meantime took a plaster from his small medicine case and spread it on the wound and also gave Oshabu an antidote for the poison. The medicine was made to easily dissolve in the mouth.

Meanwhile a dozen or so Yoshiwara fighters, swords drawn and racing furiously, barreled across the drawbridge. They were met by the Yagyu men who had lain concealed in the rice fields, and a fierce battle ensued. Inside the quarter, a number of Yoshiwara warriors carrying small bows launched a shower of arrows on the enemy from the rooftops.

Katsuyama returned with the distilled spirits and clean cloth. Seiichiro wiped away the ointment he had applied and disinfected the wound with the spirits.

In that moment, a remarkable thing occurred.

From between Oshabu's legs there came forth a thin line of blood.

"Ah!" Seiichiro was startled. He thought that there was another wound, and reproached himself for his lack of awareness. The poison might already be working its way through her body. He hurriedly placed his mouth on the spot and began to suck the blood.

"Stop it!" With surprising strength, Oshabu pushed Seiichiro away.

"I have to draw out the blood. If there is poison left, it will spread throughout your body." Seiichiro's tone of voice was aimed at pacifying her, but she resolutely shook her head.

"That other place is the only wound."

"But..."

Unexpectedly, he was roughly pushed aside by Katsuyama.

"This is not something for a gentleman to see!"

Concealing Oshabu with her own body, and quickly tending to her with the cloth, she looked at him with unbridled animosity.

"How ridiculous! Hurry up and rinse your mouth out with spirits."

He still didn't understand. Someone shoved the earthen jar of spirits at him. It was Gensai.

"Do as you're told. You look like a man-eating demon."

Seiichiro's mouth was covered with blood.

"But Oshabu...."

"Don't worry. She's just become a woman, that's all. Seems a bit early, but it's nothing to squawk about."

Seiichiro still seemed unable to grasp the situation, and this caused Gensai to emit a deep sigh.

"It seems like there are just too many things in this world that you still have to learn about, Sei-san."

Boom!!

An enormous explosion occurred out in the *Naka-tambo*. Shocked, Seiichiro and Gensai ran toward the drawbridge, where they saw carts and men who had been blown to smithereens. The dead were half Yoshiwara and half Yagyu men.

"What was that?!"

"Planting damn explosives!" Gensai spat out. "If you had run out there, you would have fallen right into the midst of all that. What a rotten thing to do."

It was the first time Seiichiro had seen Gensai furious. Gensai's expression was as fierce as the wrathful look of the great Fudo, God of Fire.

Seiichiro, with the eye of a swordsman, judged the state of affairs and realized that he had just narrowly escaped certain death. A chill ran down his spine.

"It's thanks to Oshabu, and to Katsuyama…"

"Oshabu has the ability to read the future. That's something that occasionally a girl within our clan is born with. When Oshabu says something, you had better listen."

"Is that true for Katsuyama, too?"

"Katsuyama…" Gensai didn't finish what he was about to say.

"Anyway," Gensai changed the topic, "Gisen has really lost his mind to use gunpowder like this. It is absolutely unpardonable."

For some reason, he did not touch on Katsuyama, and that left in Seiichiro's mind a small shadow of concern.

SHIBAGAKI BUSHI

Three days passed, and for one reason or another Seiichiro's mood had not lifted. Since that momentous morning, Gensai was nowhere to be found, and there was no sign that his promise would be realized, that once the *najimi* was over he would tell Seiichiro the secret of the *Shinkun gomenjo* document. Oshabu was concealing herself in her own room and had not once appeared in front of Seiichiro. It was quite unusual for her. As to the result of the explosion out in the rice fields, neither Jinnojo nor anyone else would tell him anything at all.

Seiichiro was being kept entirely in the dark regarding everything that was happening. And then there was Takao... Seiichiro was confident that no one could comprehend how he felt about her. To be in love with a woman was an entirely new experience for him. He hadn't realized how helpless and how flustered loving a woman could make a man. If you wanted to meet, you should just meet, but something seemed to be preventing that from happening. Seiichiro couldn't tell whether it was self-restraint or a sense of embarrassment. But somehow he could feel a strong resistance checking his desire to indulge in seeing her. So all he could do was sit on the bench at *machiai-no-tsuji* in the early afternoon, alone and downhearted.

The words of a strange song floated through the air.

Brushwood hedge, through the brushwood hedge
I caught a glimpse of long sleeves
Sleeves of snow
By the brushwood hedge

The song was called *Shibagaki bushi*, and it had been popular since the end of the previous year. For a short time it had become such a fashionable song that everyone from feudal lords to townsmen sang it. There were even performers who specialized in it.

What was peculiar about the song was neither the tune or the lyrics but rather the movements that accompanied it. The dancer opened his eyes wide, screwed up his face, beat himself on the shoulders and chest and twisted his body constantly this way and that, as if experiencing a seizure. Contorting himself to the right, then to the left, the dancer gasped for air and made agonized faces. Altogether, the dancer appeared to be gasping and dying in anguish. People found the spectacle entertaining and stood round applauding and laughing. It is perhaps a truth that people find amusement in the portrayal of the suffering of others, but one could not but wonder what sort of nerves they possessed to perform their own suffering and discover enjoyment in the process.

On the eighteenth day of the first month of the new year, the Great Meireki Fire, which had originated in Hongo Maruyama Honmyoji, had literally reduced Edo to scorched earth. From the scorched ruins, it was said, some 100,000 incinerated bodies had been uncovered, lying in heaps. Strangely enough, almost all of them—eyes bulging, mouths contorted, joints akimbo—bore a close resemblance to those who danced to *Shibagaki bushi*. For that reason, those who had wandered the streets looking for the bodies of their kinfolk developed an abhorrence for the song and anything connected with it. That the song was now coming from the second-floor drawing room of a house of assignation within the new Yoshiwara was, therefore, entirely beyond belief.

Suddenly the song stopped. After a moment of total silence, there was a loud uproar. Amid the shouts, Seiichiro could hear Katsuyama's piercing voice. And through the green split-bamboo curtain he could see Katsuyama and Mizuno Jurozaemon. The shouting seemed to be directed at the two of them. Mizuno's hand searched for his sword, which of course he was not then wearing.

Seiichiro slowly stood up and walked away from the bench.

The ruckus was taking place on the second floor of the Owariya Seiroku. In the drawing room were Mizuno, four other samurai, five *tayu* and the attending *shinzo* and *kamuro*, all together a rather large party. The samurai were all members of the Jingi-gumi. The man energetically quarreling with Mizuno was Kageyama Sanjuro, a bannerman with a stipend of 500 *koku*. He was a direct shogunal vassal, and a newcomer to the Jingi-gumi. Given the amount of his stipend from the shogun, he was generous with his funds, and since he had become a member, three of the other men had become indebted to him. Kageyama was the one who had invited Mizuno, the leader of the band, to come along to a visit to Yoshiwara. This same Kageyama was the one who had suddenly begun to sing and dance to the much-disliked song. Unfortunately, one of the *kamuro* who accompanied Katsuyama had herself lost her parents and siblings in the great fire. As she watched Kageyama dance, this young girl turned visibly pale and in the end broke into uncontrollable sobs. Realizing the cause of this outbreak, Katsuyama, in an inadvertently strong tone of voice, told Kageyama to stop.

That was apparently the cause of the commotion. Katsuyama was said to have been extremely rude to a guest.

"Even if you are the boss's woman, such behavior is unpardonable!"

Katsuyama was Mizuno's partner that night. The *banto shinzo* accompanying the party skillfully launched forth on an explanation of the *kamuro*'s tragic experience and apologized for her behavior. But Kageyama remained obstinate in his indignation and Katsuyama maintained her own unbending self. Depending on Mizuno's next move, she was prepared to stand up and walk out at any moment, and there was no chance that she would apologize for her own role in creating the turmoil. Finally, Mizuno could no longer sit and watch the absurdity of the situation unfolding around him.

"Sanjuro! That's enough!" he finally shouted. Sanjuro's face changed color. To a samurai, one's honor was everything, and even though he was a newcomer to the Jingi-gumi, being treated like a manservant in front of others triggered the samurai within him to make a stand.

"Why don't you walk out!"

Mizuno was infamous for being short-tempered, and he slapped Kageyama on the side of the face, upon which he stood up. Reflexively, Katsuyama stood in front of Mizuno. It was because she felt Kageyama's strong bloodthirst. It was this scene that Seiichiro had observed from the bench at the crossroad.

Now, standing in the corridor of the Owariya, Seiichiro saw Kageyama being soothed and humored by three of her cohorts.

(What?)

There was something about Kageyama that he recognized. He had never seen the man's face before, but something about his plump, supple shape was stuck in Seiichiro's memory.

"Saihoji!" he exclaimed.

Kageyama, who had been trying to push aside the restraining hands of his cohorts and throw himself on Mizuno, jerked his head to see who had spoken. He saw Seiichiro and terror crossed his face. It was proof that he knew Seiichiro's skills with a sword. There was no mistake. Kageyama was one of the Yagyu who had attacked Gensai and Seiichiro that night at Saihoji.

Seiichiro smiled.

"So we meet again, gentleman of the Ura Yagyu."

This time, the one whose face turned pale was Katsuyama. She stared hard at Kageyama.

"How dare you be impudent! To a bannerman of the shogun!"

At that point he suddenly held his tongue. There was nothing more to say. A true bannerman would have no way of knowing anything about the existence of the Ura Yagyu.

"*Ura* Yagyu, you say? What's that, anyway?"

Mizuno's question was an honest one. The three Jingi-gumi samurai also looked on in puzzlement.

Kageyama Sanjuro realized in a flash that he had failed in his mission.

The man was in actual fact an Ura Yagyu plant. Normally a plant would remain concealed in enemy territory for years as a secret agent who adapted completely to the local community. There were even cases where such a plant would serve the local domain faithfully for two successive generations. However, to insert a plant not in an enemy camp but among the direct vassal bannermen of the shogun was a truly Ura Yagyu touch. Moreover, it indicated the complexity of the political administration of the bakufu's core leadership. Kageyama was one half of a successive-generation plant, but unfortunately, he was also a highly adroit swordsman. He could not bear to remain a passive agent so, having appealed directly to Gisen, he became an active operative. Hiding behind his status as a 500-*koku* shogunal vassal, he had mastered all of the secret techniques of the Yagyu school and used them freely. But his self-confidence had been destroyed by the swords of Seiichiro and Gensai. He had been made painfully aware that whatever he might do, there was a staggeringly powerful way of employing a sword that he could not defeat. Thus an emotion of painful bitterness rose up within him as a result of this entirely unanticipated appearance of Seiichiro. And it was this that led to the exposure of his true identity.

Kageyama's first mission that day was to initiate a fight with Mizuno Jurozaemon and assassinate him. Due to the simple fact that Mizuno knew the term *Shinkun gomenjo,* as far as the Ura Yagyu were concerned, Jurozaemon had to be killed. Kageyama's second mission was to kill Katsuyama. Through the report of the wife of the owner of the shop next to the drawbridge, Gisen had learned that Katsuyama had warned Seiichiro not to cross the bridge into the rice fields. That she had warned Seiichiro that certain death awaited him across the bridge made her instantly a traitor to the Ura Yagyu. An exemplary execution was to be carried out, and the sooner the better.

To carry out these two missions, Kageyama had brought a peculiar weapon at his side. It was a ten-centimeter-long needle with a sharp edge. It had a handle, and was usually carried along the side of his sword scabbard. Something like a pick, it was intended to be used in assassinations. The assassin hid it in his hand and in a flash stabbed the victim in the heart. The frightening aspect of the weapon was that it left hardly any trace and the person who was stabbed would not die immediately. The victim would feel a slight prick in the chest, and for a period of several minutes nothing at all would happen. The victim could still stand, move and talk. After the assassin had made good his escape, the victim would suddenly collapse dead. It would appear to be an entirely natural death, the result of a heart attack.

Kageyama reached inside his clothing and unobtrusively grasped the weapon. He debated whether to attack Kageyama, who was directly in front of him, or Seiichiro, who was behind him. That slight moment of indecision proved his downfall. Katsuyama realized that he had the weapon. As a fellow Ura Yagyu ninja, she of course knew the weapon and had on a number of occasions used it herself. So when his hand came out of his bosom, she instantly removed an ornamental hairpin from her coiffure and with all her strength stabbed it into the back of his right hand. The weapon dropped to the floor and Seiichiro swiftly picked it up.

"Well, well, this is unusual."

In the next second, Kageyama's body shot out through the window of the house like a ball. Still barefoot, and leaving behind the pair of swords he had checked on the first floor, he ran headlong toward the Great Gate. It was the last time that Seiichiro and the others would ever see him. Two days later, his body would be found floating in the Okawa River, cut from shoulder to hip. Since there was no heir, the Kageyama family ceased to exist.

And in even less time—within that very day Katsuyama Tayu disappeared from the new Yoshiwara.

Later, still unaware of the situation surrounding him, Seiichiro tried to find out about Katsuyama from Gensai.

"Katsuyama fell for you," Gensai responded nonchalantly.

Seiichiro and Katsuyama had only met face to face on three occasions—at *machiai no-tsuji*, on the road near the drawbridge and in the drawing room of the Owariya. None of these three occasions had lasted more than a few minutes. When Seiichiro protested that there had hardly been enough time for either to become enamored of the other, Gensai laughed.

"There are some who know each other for ten years and still don't fall in love. And then there are others who're struck with lightning at one look, falling in love at the risk of their very lives. That's the way it is between a man and a woman."

Gensai continued.

"I had a hunch that Katsuyama was an Ura Yagyu ninja. And, well, there's nothing as dangerous as a female ninja who has fallen in love with a man. You don't have to be Gisen to want to do away with her."

Without knowing precisely why, Seiichiro had grown sad. Where had she disappeared to in order to evade detection by the fierce ninja of the Ura Yagyu? Was it even possible for a woman to evade such a band forever all by herself? The thought left him feeling pity for her. Some way or other, he wished he could protect her. Gensai promptly read his feelings.

"Give it up."

For a change, Gensai was dead serious.

"Thoughtless sympathy ends up as mischief. We're all made up of deceit and cruelty, so night and day you had better apologize to the gods and buddhas. There's nothing more to do. You shouldn't attempt to do more than that."

There was no way that the young Seiichiro could comprehend the uncanny luster of Gensai's wisdom. In the end, his thoughtless sympathy would contribute to Katsuyama's demise. Only then would Seiichiro finally and painfully grasp just how true Gensai's words were.

Eight Hundred Priestess

Early afternoon of the seventeenth day of the ninth month.

An itinerant priest descended the three-curved slope heading toward the Great Gate. A self-important police aide named Isuke, who was killing time in a teahouse along the Fifty-Ken Road, felt something suspicious about the priest. In the first place, a priest, who was strongly prohibited from having relations with women, had no business entering Yoshiwara. That was the reason for the so-called *Doromachi Nakajuku*, along the Nihon Embankment. Priests would go there to exchange their religious habits for ordinary clothing and a hood and instantly transform themselves into physicians. It was a means of avoiding looking excessively religious as they passed through the Great Gate, a ruse that the officials at the gate found it convenient to overlook.

The gatekeeper's office on the right side of the Great Gate was enclosed with latticework, allowing a clear view of the area outside and inside the gate itself. Shifts of two police constables from the office of the city magistrate were on duty at all times, and if they noticed anyone suspicious, they would stop and interrogate the person. Isuke was a secret agent in the service of these constables. In order to make things easier for the actual constables on duty, Isuke would examine any suspicious character before he could reach the actual gate.

"You there, priest!"

It was Isuke's bad habit to be both arrogant and violent. One reason for this was his large build—large enough to be mistaken for a sumo wrestler—and his confidence in his own strength. This time, too, he had acted before he spoke, grabbing the shoulder of the diminutive priest with all of his strength.

"Oh!" the priest said painfully in a thin voice.

"Where are you from? Take off that *amigasa* so I can get a good look at you."

The priest did not move. It did not occur to Isuke that the priest might be immobilized due to excruciating pain.

"I said, take it off."

Isuke ripped the hat off. Underneath he saw the well-tanned face of a small priestess. Her facial features were well defined and she could even have been called good-looking. At first glance, she could have been twenty years old or so, but a further look showed that she was actually considerably older. Despite that, there was not a single wrinkle on her skin. Isuke felt a sense of anti-climax.

"What's this, just a priestess, eh?"

In that moment, a curious thing happened.

Isuke's face turned flaccid, making him look completely foolish. His eyes went blank, his mouth opened wide and drool fell from the corners of his mouth. It wasn't only his face that went limp. Every muscle in his body went slack. His right hand, which had grabbed the priestess's shoulder, fell limply to his side. His knees buckled and he collapsed with a thud on the bench outside the teahouse. In the coming days, this condition would continue, and he would no longer be able to speak. His eyes would no longer be able to see, and finally he would become bedridden and permanently disabled.

The priestess smiled, took her *amigasa* from Isuke's hand, placed it lightly on her head and calmly passed through the Great Gate.

When the man who was inside *Shirobei bansho*, which faced the *menbansho*, saw the figure of the priestess, he changed color and came running out. He placed both hands on the ground before her and in a trembling voice spoke to her.

"Obaba-sama! You...you haven't changed at all!"

Still wearing her woven-straw hat she looked tenderly upon the man.

"It's a relief to see that you are still in good health. But I sense that your wife is not doing very well."

In actual fact, the man's wife had suddenly developed a high fever, and for the past three days she had been confined to bed.

"It seems to be a problem of the liver."

She gave him the names of five or six medicinal herbs.

"Bring those to me later and I'll prepare a medicine for her."

"Thank you very much. You will...will you be staying as usual at Nishidaya?"

"Yes."

Responding cheerfully, she turned to look at the Nishidaya, just as Oshabu came stumbling out of the front door at a dead run.

"As usual, she's using her instincts. Very good."

"Obaba-sama!"

With a loud cry, Oshabu came running toward her at full speed. She leaped and embraced the priestess in tears.

"Obaba-sama! Obaba-sama!"

The priestess tenderly stroked her back.

"Well, well. It must have been hard for you, left alone all by yourself. When did you become a young woman?'

Oshabu rapidly blushed.

In the new Yoshiwara, there was not a single person who knew the name of this priestess. Not even Gensai—Shoji Jin'emon—knew her real name, so it was only natural that no one else knew it. Gensai and everyone else simply called her "Obaba-sama," grandmother. Of course, Gensai alone knew that she was one of the legendary priestesses known as the "Eight Hundred Bhiksuni." But that was not her name.

The Eight Hundred Bhiksuni were legendary figures, known to be itinerant mediums.

As to where the priestesses came from, there were various legends in the provinces of Iwashiro, Mino, Hida, Noto, Kii, Tosa and Echigo. According to the particularly detailed Echigo Teradomari legend, one of them was married 39 times but had the appearance of a sixteen or seventeen-year-old virgin, and when she became a priestess she lived to be 800 years old, hence the name. Becoming aware that she could not die a natural death, she entered nirvana.

Among the various other legends were some that claimed one such woman was married to a Yamabushi practitioner and traveled throughout the land carrying out aesthetic practices, eventually became an itinerant singer and later a bathhouse woman.

It would be most straightforward to say that such women were "sexual priestesses," and that by the mid-Tokugawa era, they were traveling prostitutes. However, one should not dismiss a "Kumano Bhiksuni" as just any ordinary prostitute. This is because they were first of all spiritual mediums and shamanesses. And this particular woman—the one known in the Yoshiwara as Obaba-sama—was actually the leader of all the Kumano priestesses.

"She's not a member of our clan," Gensai explained, introducing Obaba-sama to Seiichiro, "but you might say that she is related to us."

Obaba-sama bowed with her face pressed to the tatami and remained prostrate. It was a bow reserved for a person of high rank.

"Please rise," Seiichiro said, embarrassed. She raised her small face, surrounded in white silk, and smiled charmingly. Her expression was refreshingly beautiful; her tan face and white teeth gave an impression of absolute health. Seiichiro found it incomprehensible that this priestess, who seemed pure as a young girl, was called grandmother.

"Obaba-sama has come all the way from Kumano just for your sake, Sei-san."

"From Kumano? But…"

Seiichiro didn't understand. But when he thought of her frail body having come all the way from Kii province to Edo, he felt indebted to her.

"It was no trouble," she responded. "After all, it was for your sake."

Her voice was clear and devoid of any dialect.

"For my sake?"

He glanced at Gensai, his puzzlement growing deeper by the moment.

"I promised, didn't I? That I would tell you everything about the *Shinkun gomenjo*?"

"Well, yes."

Seiichiro had eagerly looked forward to hearing this word. But he could not for the life of him comprehend what the *Shinkun gomenjo* had to do with this priestess from Kumano.

"There is no connection," she said calmly.

Seiichiro was startled. This priestess was just like Oshabu—she could read other people's thoughts.

"That's right."

Somewhat shyly, she smiled again.

"You probably wonder why she came? Well, before you can comprehend the mystery of the *Shinkun gomenjo*, you have to learn something about our clan. And, it wouldn't have the same impact if we just told you some old tales from the past. The best way is for you to actually experience the past yourself. That is why we have asked Obaba-sama to come."

It was an entirely curious story. What could Gensai possibly mean by the need for him to experience the past himself? And what was Obaba-sama's role in all that?

"Dreams."

Once again Obaba-sama had read his thoughts and answered his doubts succinctly. In his mind, Seiichiro shouted with a sudden awareness. So that was it. He would experience the past through dreams. In that case, this priestess had the power to make a person have the dream she wanted.

"Kumano is the land of ghosts," she said serenely. "Upon dying, one brings the single blossom of anise that is placed at the pillow of the deathbed and sets out on what is called a Kumano pilgrimage. Therefore, when a living person makes a Kumano pilgrimage, along the path he may encounter a family member or friend who has died. The dark forest road through Kumano intersects the mountain road along which the dead pass. I have lived in this dark forest for many years and I know the dead very well. Their grief and sorrow, their joys, are all here in my heart. All I do is convey them to others."

Was such a thing at all possible? However, Obaba-sama spoke with absolute authority.

"You've heard the story of the dream of Handan? It is the story of a young man who had a dream of his entire life during the time it took to boil millet."

Long ago in the Zhao capital of Handan, an impoverished student encountered a hermit along the road. The student received from the hermit a miraculous pillow, and when he fell asleep on it, he saw his entire life, from his rise to prominence to his ultimate downfall. When he awoke, the millet the hermit had cooked was just ready to be eaten. The story of the pillow is one of the evanescence of earthly splendor.

"Naturally enough, there is no such splendid pillow. Instead, there is Obaba-sama's body…"

Seeming embarrassed, Gensai left off in mid-sentence. Obaba-sama smiled mischievously. For some reason, Seiichiro felt his heart pound. It was because Obaba-sama's smile was oddly captivating.

"Anyway…" Gensai cleared his throat several times. "All you have to do is go to sleep. Everything will be all right. Nothing frightening will happen. Just relax."

He spoke as if coaxing a child, and Seiichiro responded with a wry smile. He had already made up his mind. Even though it might be a dream, it would be wonderful to experience life in the past.

"Right here?"

They were in a back room of the Nishidaya. The sound of *Misesugagaki* and the bantering of customers with the lower-class prostitutes who could not set foot in any of the *ageya* came from the streets like the sound of waves.

"Won't you please lie down?"

Seiichiro docilely followed Obaba-sama's gentle suggestion. It was a warrior's custom to sleep on his right side. That way, even if he were attacked while asleep, his right arm would be safe. With just the right arm, he could still draw his sword and strike.

"It would be better if you lay on your back."

She helped him roll over onto his back. Feeling suddenly vulnerable to attack, his body reflexively stiffened, and she could feel it.

"Let yourself go limp… Please rest easy…"

Obaba-sama lightly touched his forehead and passed her hand over his eyelids. In the next moment, Seiichiro had fallen into a deep sleep.

"It's his lineage. So gentle and trusting."

Obaba-sama gazed fondly at Seiichiro as he slept.

"I leave everything to you now," Gensai said with a deep bow before leaving the room. After sliding the door closed behind him, he seated himself in the corridor in front of the door. From somewhere, Jinnojo appeared. He was carrying the Chinese swords. Gensai took them and placed them on the floor against his knees. While Seiichiro was sleeping, he intended to sit there on guard.

Jinnojo whispered, "Gen'i, Sannojo, and Genzaemon are all at their stations."

With the exception of Miuraya Shirozaemon, all the leaders of the new Yoshiwara contingent were now at their defense posts.

Gensai merely nodded.

The light inside the room went out.

From the darkened room came the rustling sound of clothing.

Obaba-sama was removing her vestments. When the final layer fluttered to the floor, her naked white body emerged in the darkness. Her body was magnificent. Any would say that she had the body of a young woman in her second decade. Her skin glowed with resilience, and though her breasts were small, they stood out firmly. Her buttocks were also small, but they too protruded outward. Every part of her body looked youthful and fresh.

Soon, Seiichiro too had been undressed. Obaba-sama edged close to him and reverently grasped his penis. Incredible as it may seem, there was nothing at all lascivious about this action. Any hint of salaciousness was exceeded by a great impression of reverence. In her hand, his maleness grew larger and larger. For a brief moment, she looked at it in amazement, and in the next moment she stood astride him.

"With your permission," she said, half sitting down on top of him.

Guiding him with her hand, she slowly lowered herself. Once she had entirely drawn him inside herself, her eyebrows contracted and she lightly breathed in. She stayed that way, not moving at all. Astride him, with her back straight as an arrow, she froze, absolutely motionless.

Seiichiro's expression began to change. His mouth opened and he began to pant.

THE KUGUTSU CLAN

Panting heavily, Seiichiro ran for his life along the riverbank. The dazzling mid-summer sun beat down mercilessly on the bare skin of his upper body. His entire body was soaked in sweat. He was bleeding from his wounds, but he had no time to think about the pain. He wiped · away the sweat that had gotten into his eyes. In his right hand he held a deeply curved naked sword. The blade was heavily smeared with blood. He thought it had dispatched eight so far.

Then came the vicious hum of an arrow. Instinctively he ducked. An arrow whistled right through where his head had been a split second before. He ran a zigzag course along the river's edge, slashing water as he sped along. He took a quick glance over his shoulder and saw there were still fourteen or fifteen chasing him. Each wore a *suikan* garment, carried a sword or a pole-arm with sword blade, and rushed furiously in his direction. Two or three also carried short bows.

Another arrow came at him. He dodged it. He couldn't remember what he had done. The only reason he had cut those other men down was because they had attacked him, and now their cohorts were after him. The men were all in the service of some provincial official.

(Provincial official?)

What the hell was a provincial official? And what period of history was this anyway?

(The year was Gen'ei 2, 1119, during the reign of the Emperor Toba.)

A woman's voice spoke in a mere whisper.

(The reign of Emperor Toba? That's 500 years ago!)

For an instant, confusion brought all of his thinking to a halt. But his legs continued to run.

He heard a great clamor ahead. In the distance he could see a large temple, and the tumult seemed to be coming from inside its gates.

(Just a little further! If I can just get that far! Somehow—just that far!)

Swish! From behind a sword struck at his neck. Seiichiro squatted to avoid the blow, and with all his might he struck behind him with his own sword. There was a scream of pain, and the tall man behind him who had been cut through fell as his intestines spilled from his abdomen.

(That's the ninth!)

The rest of the group was considerably behind. Seiichiro sprang up and began to run once more.

The moment he passed through the temple gate, his knees seemed to buckle from exhaustion and also a sense of relief.

(But this place is still dangerous)

He walked another five or six paces, then collapsed to the ground. He had reached his limit. He cast his sword aside.

A huge crowd was gathered within the temple precincts. A market was being held. There were blacksmiths and potters. Some people were selling salt and others were selling combs. They were exchanging products, and common people who seemed to be farmers were bartering for various goods with rice. In addition to the loud shouts of those buying and selling, there were various entertainments as well.

There was a magician, who was just at that moment pulling out a cow from a small cloth pouch. Seiichiro recognized the magician—it was none other than Miuraya Shirozaemon. As usual, he was obese and constantly wiping away sweat. Right next to him were Nomura Gen'i performing dangerous juggling tricks with sharp swords, and Gensai himself handling puppets. Behind them, beating a drum and singing, was Takao. He could also see Yamadaya Sannojo nearby, and Namikiya Genzaemon. Even Shoji Jinnojo and Oshabu were there. It was as if the entire Yoshiwara community had moved there.

(These people are the Kugutsu clan)

A woman's voice whispered to him.

(So that's it! The Yoshiwara people are all one big clan of puppeteers!)

All of a sudden, that realization flashed through his mind. The dance that Gensai had performed—that amazing dance at the Owariya Seiroku! Now it all made sense.

It was the same dance that the Kugutsu puppeteers danced in the mountains back in Higo province!

And then there was that dancing puppet that Takao had used. Both of these had shown that they were all members of the puppeteer clan.

(But just who are the Kugutsu?)

Before he could voice the question, loud voices of complaint sprang forth.

The subordinates of the provincial official had finally reached the temple precincts. Their voices were raised against those who were gathering around Seiichiro as if to protect him.

"Nine! He killed nine of our group. If you get in our way, you…"

"This is a *muenji*—a temple for those who have no relations in the outside world. No secular power or authority is allowed in here!"

From out of nowhere Gensai appeared, still holding his puppet, and spoke with great intensity.

"By regulation, all of those who take shelter here must cast aside all of their connections with the secular world. In exchange, even someone who has committed one of the three great crimes cannot be executed. You there! Have you forgotten that?" The three great crimes were theft, arson, and murder.

The official's men wavered momentarily. But perhaps their numbers and their weapons encouraged them to not back down so easily.

"The official we serve is a member of the same clan as the chancellor to the emperor! When the time comes, one or two temples of this sort wouldn't…"

"This isn't part of the territory of your lord. It is an unaffiliated temple, built in a wilderness that belongs to no one. Anyone who destroys one of these *muenji* will release a rampage of all the vengeful spirits of the rivers and the mountains. And all of us—we the 'companions of the way'—will avoid this province and in all probability no markets will ever be held here again. If you are fully aware of that, then just go ahead. But it goes without saying that we will not simply stand by and watch."

It was no mere bluff. All of the artisans, entertainers and traders who had gathered here to freely carry on their business now wore fierce expressions one and all. Each had some kind of weapon in his hand, and slowly they were encircling the men. They presented a direct menace even more frightening than the vengeful spirits that Gensai had evoked. The outsiders turned pale and escaped in all directions.

(Saved)

And then Seiichiro collapsed, unconscious.

When he awoke, he was deep in the mountains. Everything around him was pitch black, and Seiichiro and the clan of puppeteers were lit up by the large brightly burning watch fire.

"By the force of circumstances, we have brought you here…"

Gensai's tone was calm. There was no echo of the severity with which he had frightened off the official's men.

"You have no particular reason to feel indebted. Once your wounds have healed, you should feel free to go anywhere you want whenever you want. But…"

An intensity returned to Gensai's voice.

"You must not forget. You have become a person who has no connections with the outside world. You can no longer count on your immediate family, relatives, friends or acquaintances. From now on, you can only depend on your strength alone. Even if you are dying from hunger, there is no one to offer you a helping hand. Brace yourself for that."

"*Muen*—no relations."

Seiichiro tried saying the word.

He felt a chilly sensation, as if simultaneously feeling a sense of liberation and a coldness strong enough to deprive him of all the strength in his body. Both now and in the past, freedom was the flip side of starvation.

Gensai spoke.

"To live without relations requires that you have proficiency in some art. There is no other way to live than to possess and employ such a skill."

Seiichiro nodded. All he had was his skill with the sword. Was that actually an art too?

"As for those men who were after you. If you're worried that they might be hanging around somewhere, relax. We're in the mountains seventy-five miles from that temple."

"But how…?" Seiichiro couldn't believe it.

"You were unconscious for one full day. Our clan can walk some thirty miles through the mountains in a day."

Seiichiro had heard that such a clan existed, but he had thought that they were called *sanka*, or mountain nomads.

Was the puppeteer clan the mountain nomads?

"The mountain nomads are kinfolk. They wander the mountains, earning a livelihood by selling woven willow baskets. We wander from town to town earning our living performing with puppets and performing magic. That's the only way we're really different."

Up until World War II, the *sanka* were said to roam all around the land, living as people did in centuries past—with portable shelters and able to travel in large families through the mountains at incredible speeds. The men and women were both virtually naked above the waist; it was said that they used icy cold spring water for newborn babies' first baths and that they had intercourse standing, with great composure, on the top of sheer precipices. Their language was held to be archaic Japanese, and ordinary people couldn't understand what they said. They used heavy, sharp-bladed short swords with great skill. When for some reason one of them caused trouble in a settlement near the mountains, it was virtually impossible to pursue the culprit and capture him.

Members of the Kugutsu clan were brothers and sisters to these nomadic mountain people. If the mountain people were the shadow, the puppeteers were the daylight. Both the men and the women loved bright, colorful amusements and disliked labor. They walked between markets and post towns along the large roads making a living performing their various entertainments. The women—whether they had husbands or not—made their services available to other travelers. They were the beginning of the *yujo*.

The earliest records of the Kugutsu are from the Heian period. According to these records, the puppeteers originated as hunters, and the men were all adept at archery and riding horseback. They were also reported to be skilled at dancing with swords, manipulating puppets and performing magic. The women were skilled at singing, making themselves look beautiful and entertaining travelers through the night. They were, in short, a free-spirited people who, from deep down, loved amusement.

But one must not forget that in that day and age, to be free was extremely grueling as well. Those who followed that path lived literally face to face with starvation. It was hard to avoid starvation by performing shows and by prostitution, so they also sold whatever they could. It was recorded in the *Tadokoro Documents* that in Izumi province, the artisans who had an official monopoly on producing and selling combs complained that a group of puppeteers was selling combs without permission.

Alongside their cheerful vitality was a fierce will to survive. And this was particularly so for the women.

There are several theories regarding the ancestry of the Kugutsu clan. One is that in ancient society, their ancestors were shamans who wielded considerable authority. Such shamans forecast the future using such things as turtle shells, and most of those who performed such predictions of future events were consecrated shrine maidens. This is the most widely accepted theory, and according to it, these puppeteer clans were from the beginning dominated by females, and hence were matrilineal. From the contemporary point of view, it would be unthinkable for a man to watch while his own wife slept with a passing traveler. However, considered in the context of a matrilineal society where women took the leadership in providing for daily sustenance, and where women had the power to choose their men, this arrangement might seem less unusual. It follows that if the women of the puppeteer clan were the earliest *yujo*, then their real origin goes back to the shrine maidens who served as spiritual mediums.

A contrasting theory held that the *yujo* originated from people who immigrated to Japan. According to this view, the puppeteers themselves were also a naturalized clan.

In Korea during the Yi Dynasty, there was a clan of nomads who escaped into the mountains in order to evade military conscription. One group of these nomads made a living weaving willow baskets, hunting, raising horses and working leather, while another group made their living by singing, dancing and other kinds of performance, and whose women engaged in divination, exorcism and often prostitution as well. According to this theory, this nomadic clan settled in Japan and from them came the Kugutsu puppeteer clan. The evidence supporting this theory is that the varieties of arts performed by the puppeteers are almost identical with those of China and Korea, and the fact that their religious beliefs sprang originally from Taoism.

An extreme variation of this theory claims that these puppeteers were originally nomadic people who came from India. Those who drifted westward, says this theory, came to be known as gypsies, while those who migrated eastward ended up in Japan and gave birth to the puppeteer clan. True enough, in their innate lightheartedness and fondness for music and dance, the gypsies and the Kugutsu were strikingly similar.

In the twenty-eighth volume of the *Konjaku monogatari*, a late Heian period collection of tales, one of the narratives is called "the puppeteer account keeper." An official named Ono Itsutomo, who was appointed governor of Izu province, heard that there was a highly capable samurai in Suruga who was exceedingly proficient in keeping records. Itsutomo appointed the man as a local account keeper, and as had been reported, the man carried out his duties with integrity, was kind to the peasants, and was well thought of by all. One day in the provincial capital, as Itsutomo was having this man press an official seal on a certain document, a group of puppeteers suddenly barged in and began to perform (the Kugutsu were specially allowed to perform this sort of high-pressure salesmanship). The account keeper, upon hearing the music of the flute and drum, suddenly became excited and finally began to sing along. When Itsutomo rebuked him, the man stood up and said "It's hard to shake off the past" and cast the seal aside and ran off. In short, the account keeper was originally from the puppeteer clan. Itsutomo recalled the man to service, but the people from then on called him Kugutsu Mokudai.

The story illustrates just how deeply song and dance permeated the members of the puppeteer clan. That Gensai had suddenly stood up upon hearing Takao's drum and begun to dance despite himself was precisely because of this natural character—this karma—shared by the members of the clan.

In his dream, Seiichiro very naturally slept with Takao, on a mattress of moss. Takao sat astride Seiichiro, not moving her body at all. But by merely contracting the walls of her vagina, she brought Seiichiro to climax. A feeling of extreme pleasure penetrated his entire body, and his hands unconsciously grasped her buttocks.

Seiichiro's fingers were clawing Obaba-sama's buttocks. There were deep lines carved between her eyebrows—not due to pain but from enduring ecstatic pleasure. Her lips opened seductively, but as could be expected, she voiced no sound.

Along the mountain edge in the brilliant morning sunshine, Gensai led the group of puppeteers. Even the women and children moved along at an astonishing pace. But then Seiichiro too easily walked shoulder to shoulder with Gensai. He wanted to ask Gensai something. As they lay together and conversed the previous night, Seiichiro had discovered that Takao had a husband. Takao had made this comment without the slightest appearance of hesitation. Seiichiro was perplexed and troubled, out of a feeling that he had done something he shouldn't have by reaching for someone who belonged to someone else. On top of that, Takao was entirely open about it all, seeming not to hide at all the fact that they had slept together the night before. It occurred to him that since they had been outdoors, several people might have seen them. Seiichiro spoke to Gensai about how he wondered whether it had been wrong of him to do what he did, and he wondered whether he should apologize and somehow atone for it.

"Don't worry about it," Gensai answered lightly. "If it's okay with Takao, then it's okay with everyone else."

"But what would her husband think?"

"Nothing."

"But…how could a man not be jealous if he knows his wife is sleeping with another man?"

Gensai looked sharply at him.

"In our clan, wives and husbands are temporary. To stop one's wife from doing what she wants to do…well, there's not a man who could."

Seiichiro was dumbfounded.

"It's not just our clan, either. The situation is the same with the common people and with the nobility. To try to prevent a wife from doing what she wants is the height of folly. There's only one thing that distinguishes our clan from other people, and that is that we fully understand that fact. In other words, we revere women from the bottom of our hearts."

Gensai laughed loudly.

"Maybe it's just that our women are so outstandingly beautiful, and so strong. They're skilled in entertaining, they excel in the ancient arts and they know how to forecast the future. However good a man may be in feats of strength and military arts, he can't compete against a woman. Men in the outside world don't seem to be able to take that with good grace, and as a result, they are always frustrated. It's really foolish."

Everything Seiichiro heard seemed to go against common sense. And yet, there was a ring of truth to it all. That was what confused him even more. Seiichiro recalled Takao's porcelain skin from the night before. The treasure between her legs, like a succulent white peach, and the captivating, wondrous fragrance.

A captivating fragrance filled the room. Joy showed on Obaba-sama's face. Seiichiro recovered his strength once again. Obaba-sama's hips had stopped moving, but once again they moved, like dark swells on a pitch-dark ocean. And once again, his hands reached out and took a firm grasp of her buttocks, his hips moving in rhythm with hers...

THE KII OFFENSIVE

Riding on the dark swells, Seiichiro was swimming along the bottom of muddy waters. In his left hand, he carried a long bamboo tube. Around his waist he wore a stomach band and a loincloth. In his stomach band he carried a thick, sharp blade. Rain splashed on the surface of the water, and since no light reached the bottom of the water, it was darker than twilight. The water was cold.

(Where am I?)

Seiichiro had composed himself. He had grown accustomed to being suddenly thrown into a fantastic world by now. A woman's voice whispered softly.

(Tensei 13 (1585). The ninth day of the fourth month. Ota Castle, in Kii province.)

That meant: Toyotomi Hideyoshi's attack on the Kii region. Throughout the medieval period, the area had been known as a stronghold of independence. It warmly accepted people who served no lord and had no relatives. It was "a gathering of companions" who strongly defended themselves against worldly authority. When the period of warring states began, it was a thorn in the side of any military commander who had pretensions to supremacy over the entire land. The Catholic missionary Luis Frois, who had been taken in by Oda Nobunaga, wrote about the province in a letter to the head of the Society of Jesuits.

Kii province is dedicated to a religion that worships evil. There are four or five sects within the land, each forming a large republic of sorts, and because their doctrines are so ancient, they cannot be defeated by military force. Their names are Koyasan, Kokawadera, and Negorodera—which has cultivated troops of mercenaries—and Saika.

To strike at the root of interminable uprisings of Buddhist Ikko sect zealots, in the second month of Tensei 5 (1577), Oda Nobunaga had attacked Saika. After bitter fighting, by the end of the third month, the Saika group had exhausted its energies and submitted to Nobunaga's forces. Nevertheless, as soon as Nobunaga withdrew, the people reverted to allegiance with the Ikko sect. Their tenacity was such that one didn't have to be Nobunaga to desire that the whole lot of them be erased from the face of the earth.

When Hideyoshi succeeded Nobunaga as the supreme ruler of the land, this province of Kii, together with the autonomous merchant city of Sakai, continued to be a threat. To one who aspired to be an autocrat, any such people who aimed for a Pure Land Paradise in which everyone was truly free was—to quote Frois' description—a gathering of people who worshipped evil. It was this motivation that gave rise to Hideyoshi's offensive against Kii in the third month of Tensei 13 (1585). The campaign pitted Hideyoshi's 100,000 troops against the 20,000 adherents who defended Negorodera, Ota and Saika.

The offensive began with attacks on eleven fortresses—more accurately, bridgeheads—which the Kii contingent had fortified, followed by fighting at Negorodera. Easily routing the defenders of these defenses, Hideyoshi then turned to attack Ota Castle on the twenty-fourth day of the third month. The castle was a small one, measuring less than 300 yards square. It would be more accurate to say that this "castle" was a marketplace in where "people without ties" had gathered from all the various domains of the land. For that reason, the defending forces were composed not only of the forces belonging to Ota, Saika, and Negoro, but also included a contingent of the wandering "companions of the way" for whom the market was important enough that they stood to defend it. Besides the thousand Ota men commanded by Ota Sakon, the defending troops numbered about five thousand men and women, among whom it is unknown how many were the "companions of the way," including Kugutsu. To these people, the battle did not concern the territory around Ota. Rather their willingness to fight side-by-side with the local people arose from their desire to protect this assemblage of persons, this open market. In the language of a later era, it would be called a voluntary fight to protect freedom.

Hideyoshi launched his attack with a vanguard of 3,000 mounted warriors under Hori Kyutaro and a second troop also of 3,000 under Hasegawa Togoro. The castle was defended with a tenacity born of desperation. In addition, the defenders set an ambush along the shallows of the river that fronted the castle; these forces launched a fierce attack with bows and muskets just as the middle of the vanguard was crossing the shallows. It was said that among the casualties of this initial attack were 51 samurai who had made names for themselves in battle, not to mention the unnamed. Hideyoshi launched a second and third offensive, all coming to a similar result, while casualties mounted. Finally, he had to suspend his attack of naked force, and shift to an attack using water. The engineering work began on the twenty-sixth of the third month.

Hideyoshi's engineers gathered an enormous number of laborers to construct a four-mile-long levee, four to six yards high, surrounding the castle. Once the levee was completed, they dammed the Kii River ten or so miles upstream and directed river water inside the dike. They commenced filling the area around the castle on the first day of the fourth month and with heavy rains that continued from the third of the month the enclosed area was turned into a muddy sea.

Onto this sea of mud, Hideyoshi impatiently launched large boats carrying his troops. They ferociously attacked the castle with bows and muskets, but the defenders mounted a stiff defense. The defenders also sent out skilled swimmers to punch and bore holes in these boats, and countless attackers either fell to the musket fire or drowned, and eventually the attack was completely called off. Hideyoshi eventually decided to wait for the water to do its work.

Seiichiro, together with the puppeteers, had participated in the boring of holes in the attackers' boats, but on this particular day, he descended below the surface of the murky waters on a different sort of mission. Due to the continuing rain, the water level within the newly constructed levee had risen, and the impact was already being felt within the castle. Without the chance to fight and achieve some sort of victory, morale within the fortress would weaken. But unless the enemy attacked, they could not strike. Inside the castle, there were no boats, large or small, to carry troops against the enemy. And although their musketeers were highly skilled, there was no way to reach a target 300 yards away. Only one offensive option came to mind—turn the water, which was causing them grief, into a weapon in their own cause. In short, they would try to destroy the levee.

After investigating the various parts of the levee, the defenders decided that the inflow of water was putting the most pressure on the levee along the border between the villages of Kuroda and Idemizu. At that particular moment, Seiichiro and a dozen members of the puppeteer clan were swimming eastward toward that position, breathing through bamboo pipes with the nodes cut through. Could a group that small possibly manage to break a hole in such a substantial embankment? If they were spotted, that would be the end of them. They would perish in a hail of fire from the top of the levee. In order to remain out of sight they would have to swim submerged, breathing through bamboo pipes. How could they possibly carry out their mission under such conditions?

Even if by some miracle they were to succeed in their mission, it was doubtful that they would be able to return alive. They would be swallowed in the surging river water and pushed toward the enemy forces commanded by Ukita Hideie—their destruction certain. Each member of the submerged squad was well aware of that fact. Further, none of them held great hopes that their perilous mission could significantly extend the life of the castle. It might give another five to ten days at the most. However one looked at it, there was little chance of success. But there was meaning in fighting against force and authority so that the castle—whose occupants hoped for a truly free refuge, a sanctuary—might be able to fight one day longer. Each one of the men under water had firmly determined that for this cause they would die all covered in mud.

Seiichiro was finding it difficult to breath and had pushed off the bottom in order to reach the surface and take a breath. Another reason was to find out exactly where he was. The downpour struck the water's surface, sending up a spray.

(How can muddy water send up a clear spray?)

This worthless question flitted through the back of his mind. He shook his head in order to rid himself of the thought and then looked around. The embankment, black and silent, stood directly before him.

Two hours passed. Holding his breath under water, with a stirrup awl he cut the straw ropes that tied together the tightly piled sandbags and poked holes in the dirt packed behind it. When he could no longer hold his breath, he floated toward the surface, stuck the end of the hollow bamboo above the surface and breathed in. He first had to blow out the water inside the pipe, and frequently he did not have enough strength left to do it strongly enough, ending up with a mouthful of muddy water. Despite that, he would once again dive down and resume digging with his awl. Two hours of such harsh labor passed. He was rapidly becoming exhausted. After the strain caused by dozens of such dives, he misjudged when he kicked off the bottom and his head rose all the way out of the water. Stunned, Seiichiro looked up at the top of the levee. His eyes met those of a foot soldier on patrol who just happened to be looking at the foot of the embankment when Seiichiro surfaced.

For a second, both men were speechless, unable to believe what they were seeing. Seiichiro regained his senses a split second before the other man and threw his sharp awl with all his strength. Just before the man could call out an alarm, the awl pierced his throat. He staggered, tried to pull out the awl with one hand, then collapsed forward, spear still in his other hand. Seiichiro, grasping the spear, drew a deep breath and went under. There was no time to lose now. The soldier would not have been on duty alone, and Seiichiro had to assume that someone witnessed his death. It was only a matter of time before Seiichiro's work would be detected by the enemy forces.

Returning to the surface, Seiichiro used the spear to furiously tear at the levee. He had difficulty catching his breath, but there was no time to be concerned about that. Everything before him turned black and he saw sparks flitting about in front of him—a sign that he was suffocating. Nevertheless, he was still desperately thrusting his spear into the ground. The spear plunged into the embankment, all the way to the butt. He tried pulling it out, but he no longer had enough strength. To the contrary, it seemed as if his arms were being pulled forward. Just as he realized that his arms were being swallowed up, a sudden loud noise erupted and a large hole opened up in the levee. His whole body was sucked into the hole with enormous force. His arms, shoulders and head were drawn in. He couldn't breathe. He swallowed water and it caught in his throat. *It hurts!* He tried to extricate himself, but his body was stuck. *Air! Air!* Something inside his head exploded, and Seiichiro was enveloped in darkness.

The levee collapsed in a flash, and muddy water erupted in a fury, roaring as it swept down on the camp of Ukita Hideie's troops. The drowning casualties were innumerable, and Ukita's army was totally destroyed.

According to the records, it required 600,000 sandbags to repair the levee. On the twenty-fourth day of the fourth month, Ota Castle fell. It had withstood a month of inundation tactics. In the face of the autocrat, another truly free market was utterly destroyed.

Seiichiro was floundering. He couldn't breathe. Obaba-sama's breasts were pressing down on his face. Her pelvis was for the first time moving violently up and down as it rotated. Squirming, Seiichiro bit Obaba-sama's breast and ejaculated. Her buttocks, grasped firmly in his hands, twitched in repeated spasms. They ended at almost the same moment. For some time, she stayed as she was, covering him. Seiichiro slept as quietly as a dead man.

"Adorable," Obaba-sama whispered. She gently sucked Seiichiro's handsome lips. Again and again.

THE WORLD OF SUFFERING

The following day, early in the afternoon.

Seiichiro and Gensai were together on the second floor of Nishidaya, in the back room overlooking the inner garden.

The doors and paper screens were open, and a breeze blew through the room. The autumn wind left one feeling somewhat forlorn. On the tray were slices of sea bass and pickled autumn eggplant. With those side dishes, the two men silently drained cups of sake.

Obaba-sama was resting that entire day. The work of allowing people to see dreams consumed an enormous amount of stamina, Gensai explained. There would be one day's rest, and then Seiichiro would once again live in a dream the following day. That other day should be the end.

Seiichiro was still lost in thought. He still found it impossible to believe completely in the world of dreams. There was simply too large a gap between the world he had experienced in his dreams and the records of the past written in the books that his master Musashi had given to him in the mountains of Higo.

"Read books, but don't believe them."

That was what Musashi had in fact told him, and now Seiichiro was finally beginning to understand what Musashi meant. Yet he still could not rid himself of a sense of discomfort.

"How old is Obaba-sama?"

"Obaba-sama is one of the legendary Buddhist priestesses called Eight Hundred *Bhiksuni*. Because they fed on merpeople, they gained eternal youth and immortality. Might be 400, or even 800 years old."

"That can't be!"

It would not only be Seiichiro who'd find such tales beyond belief.

"Of course that's a lie. But then again, there is an element of truth to it."

There was no smile on Gensai's face—a sign that he was being serious.

"Because of her psychic powers and sexual skills, Obaba-sama has been chosen from among the Kumano *Bhiksuni* who are said to number in the thousands. The one who selected her was the previous generation Obaba-sama."

"…!"

"Just as you were last night, Sei, Obaba-sama was put to sleep by the previous Obaba-sama and had her dream. That went on for years. Over that period, the current Obaba-sama received all of the memories of her predecessor. And that means all the memories of every prior generation, too. All of it was passed on to the next generation and the next. So, in the Obaba-sama we know lies hundreds of years of memories."

It was an outrageous tale. Obaba-sama was a virtual compendium of past events.

"That's why some say she's 400 years old and why others claim she is 800, and why that may not be altogether a lie."

Seiichiro shuddered. If he himself were to have to bear such a burden, he was quite sure that he would go out of his mind.

"So…does that mean that everything in my dreams was real?"

"It does," Gensai replied unequivocally.

"That *muen* temple that was built in ungoverned territory in the wilderness. That free assembly of people who wouldn't give in to the authority of an autocratic general, was all of that real?"

"It all existed. A gathering of people subject to no secular authority at all. There was an era when all kinds of nomadic people—like our Kugutsu clan—were permitted to move about freely from one such place to another.

"Those who wandered about were seafarers and mountain folk. Artisans like blacksmiths, carpenters and casters. Entertainers like musicians, dancers, lion-dance performers, *sarugaku* performers, courtesans and prostitutes. Warriors who sold their military arts and companions who sold their knowledge, such as yin-yang diviners, physicians, poets, calligraphers and people who knew how to calculate numbers. There were professional gamblers and *go* players. Mediums, priests who solicited funds for temple construction, preachers and secular priests of different schools. These were all called *michimichi no tomogara*—companions of the way. And all of them were free to travel as they wished from province to province. Many of them took charge of tributes offered to the emperor, and others carried out rituals at shrines."

Seiichiro was astonished by the diversity and the large numbers of this group of companions. To think that at one time they all moved back and forth across the land with such freedom. The markets where these people congregated must have been full of life and enjoyment.

"And it wasn't all that long ago, you know. That world still existed in the Muromachi period and even in the Era of the Warring States. In those open communities there was a saying that servants of the unjust were barred from entering, neither powerful provincial officials nor warlords. Everyone was exempt from paying taxes and tribute, and the members of these communities were proud of the fact that they could enter and leave any province of their own free will. They had no relations with others, so the guilt-by-association regulations that held in the ordinary domains did not apply to them. Because they served no lord or master other than themselves, they were restricted by no one, either in body or mind. It was a kind of utopia, a perfect city..."

Gensai's eyes glistened. His strong longing for the free, open city which had been taken away struck Seiichiro's heart with painful acuteness.

(Master Musashi also had that look in his eyes from time to time)

He recalled distinctly the look he had occasionally seen in Musashi's eyes. Why did the Master get that distant look? When he was younger, Seiichiro had often wondered. And yet he had never managed to come right out and ask why. There had always been something in Musashi's eyes that prevented that.

(Could that have been because, like Gensai now, he was recalling the open cities and the open ports?)

Seiichiro couldn't tell, but he now knew that Musashi's life had been a succession of reversals.

Having devoted his life to the sword and having cut down a large number of opponents in more than 60 duels, Musashi's life had always been at risk. Musashi must have experienced a powerful longing to enter one of the "ungoverned territories," "open cities" or "free gatherings of people," where it was said one could separate oneself from all the love and hatred of the world. But in actual fact, Musashi had accepted a stipend from the Hosokawa domain in Higo, and spent the larger part of his final years in the remote Reigendo in the mountains of Kinpozan. Was this not evidence that such things as free and open cities and gatherings of the unconnected did not actually exist in this world?

"That is true," Gensai responded. "In this world of ours, there are *virtually* no truly free gatherings of people."

"Why is that? If such ungoverned territories are true utopias, then wouldn't it be perfectly natural for everyone to seek them?"

"It's just as you say. But there is another group of people in this world who don't need such a place. To be more accurate, they find such ungoverned territories to be *inconvenient*."

"But who...?"

"Administrators. People who run the government. The lords and masters of the common people. Or at least that's the way I see things. Doesn't it make sense that it's inconvenient, as far as they are concerned, for there to be a large number of people who have no relation to others and who are under no master?

"Any persons who are bound by no ties, who are free to move about as they please and who have cast aside all connections with the world— they are completely exempt from having to pay any tax whatsoever. And they have the right to pass back and forth across the boundaries that the feudal lords of the Warring States period suffered hard to create. Government doesn't work when there are people like that. People back then could move back and forth between being commoners and peasants. It was a period when the peasants' most effective means of protesting their lord's demands was to simply abandon the farmlands 'in concert.'

"And yet, the powerholders couldn't, out of the blue, use brute force

to crush the assemblies of free people. One reason was because they were
'ancient places,' and there was considerable difficulty involved when
it came to overthrowing traditional practices. In addition, there were
various forms of uprisings. Among them were the Ikko uprisings which
brought such grief to both Oda Nobunaga and Toyotomi Hideyoshi
when they were trying to grasp total control of the land. The ferocious
powers of resistance that those pockets of independence exerted had
a serious impact on those who wanted to gain power. The Tokugawa
bakufu—making full use of that lesson—employed considerable guile
when it launched its offensives against those ungoverned areas."

"And what was that?"

"A policy of discrimination," snapped Gensai. On his face was a
bitterness and anger that Seiichiro had never seen before.

Discrimination did not, of course, originate with the Tokugawa
bakufu. But the bakufu pushed that policy to an extreme, strengthening
its nuance to contempt, and institutionalizing it.

An example of this was the *hinin*—outcasts.

Until the medieval period, such people were called *hijiri-kojiki*,
wandering sage mendicants, and *hijiri hoshi*, mendicant priests, and
they made their living as "purifiers" who carried out funerals or as
sorcerers who removed the impurities of black magic. It is true that this
was a special kind of calling, but there was no pall of discrimination
over these people as there was once the Edo period began. For the most
part, they were indistinguishable from those who carried out funeral
ceremonies and belonged to the Ji sect of Buddhism, founded by Ippen,
and the Ritsu sect, which had included such eminent priests as Eison
and Ninsho. During the Era of the Northern and Southern Courts, a
group of Ji disciples, who took a position of neutrality and affiliated
themselves with no one, followed the various armies and, without
discriminating between enemy and ally, recited prayers for the casualties
of the battlefields and held memorial services for the repose of the souls
of the dead. It was said that in 1333, when the shogun's army attacked
Kusunoki Masashige's Chihaya Castle, there were some 200 of these Ji
adherents accompanying it. Further, it was eight of these believers who
carried the remains of Nitta Yoshisada, leaving their names to history as
"the Eight Ji Adherents."

Further, because these gatherings of priests were recognized for not taking sides in a conflict, they were frequently called upon to serve as messengers in negotiations, traveling freely from one side to another. They were, in reality, envoys of peace. During the constant fighting of the Era of Warring States, this role became even more conspicuous. When these envoys of peace were so indispensable to the feudal lords in wartime, how could anyone possibly show contempt for the *kiyome*, those "outcasts" who worked together with them?

Therefore, those who did not belong to any of the four classes of society were forced into separate *hinin buraku* villages, the entertainers were categorized as itinerant beggars, and all of the so-called "unrelated people" were isolated from the rest of society. One could definitely say that it was the Tokugawa bakufu policy that segregated these people, a policy which not simply forebade them from marrying commoners but banned them from even sharing fire with a commoner. Under Tokugawa edict, these outcasts and beggars were not allowed to warm themselves by the open-air fires built by commoners, or even to borrow a light for smoking tobacco. They were only allowed to light a fire from embers left by commoners.

The changing of the open society to a dark world of suffering, and the change of the meaning of the "free unrelated" to "those who died with no one to tend their graves" was a conspiracy laid out by the Tokugawa bakufu. Those who had once been free to move about were denied their freedom; they became sealed up in a shell of prejudice and discrimination. Since such prejudice is still active even in the present day, it can be seen that the Tokugawa policy was a grand success.

"Since my father's generation, we have been vassals of the Hojo clan. My older sister was a concubine of Hojo Ujimasa named Oshabu. I have to say—even though I am her brother—she was a fine woman. Proud, talented in all the arts, so remarkable that she put Ujimasa's actual wife to shame."

Ise Shinkuro, progenitor of the Hojo family, was originally one of those who were free to move about at will. Probably because of that connection, Shoji Jin'emon's father, Matazaemon, entered the service of Shinkuro. After Hideyoshi crushed the Hojo at Odawara, Shoji Jinnai went to live with his clan at the post station of Tokaido Yoshiwara. They returned to being puppeteers. At the time, Jinnai was fifteen.

"But there was no real future at the Yoshiwara post town, and it just wasn't developed enough to support our clan. So, in order to check things out before making any decisions, I set off for Edo all by myself. It changed my life."

Edo at that time was a town of men. Even the bannermen—the hereditary vassals of the Tokugawa—who had moved to Edo from Mikawa left their wives and children behind in their home domain and lived in Edo on their own. Servants and attendants were all single men. The townsmen, merchants who opened branch stores of the large merchant businesses of Kyoto and Osaka, and the bannermen were either single or had to leave their family behind when they set up residence in Edo to fulfill their duties. The same was true for the enormous throngs of artisans and craftsmen who flooded into the city to meet the needs of a rapidly expanding population. This was a frontier town, no different in character from America's Wild West. It had an atmosphere of violence, with peace and public order by no means established. Rough, lawless, a city that knew neither gods nor buddhas.

But to Shoji Jinnai, that made it all the more intriguing.

(This town is alive)

Edo was living and growing, and for a young person, it seemed like a place where one could grow freely. In every sense, it was a town of hope and ambition. Day and night, Jinnai wandered the streets, taking it in with all his senses. He wondered which part of the future city was most likely to prosper. No matter what he would attempt, smelling out the likeliest location would be crucial.

One wintry evening.

As always, Jinnai was walking through the streets. He wore a stylish short-sleeved kimono and a short sword, with his long sword tied across his back. Both swords were straight-bladed Chinese swords mounted as Japanese swords. Jinnai had learned Chinese swordsmanship from his father, and he had reached a level of considerable finesse. At the fall of Odawara Castle, at the tender age of fifteen, his skill with two swords had inspired fear in those who were attacking. Handling his mount with just his legs, he wielded his two swords at will like an *Ashura*, charging through the enemy ranks and earning the accolades of friends and enemies alike. Yet Jinnai had not the slightest intention of earning his living as a warrior. What was most important to him was that his clan be allowed to live happily. He was, in short, a born leader of the puppeteer clan.

(What's this?)

Jinnai looked up into the sky. Snow was falling from the sky. A feeling of sadness gripped his heart.

(It's about time to return to the Yoshiwara post station)

Just as he was absentmindedly considering his return, a woman's scream pierced the darkness.

GREAT CROW

The snow began to fall thick and fast.

Heading in the direction from which the scream came, Jinnai found a group of men on the riverbank. There were six, all street ruffians wearing ostentatiously long swords at the waist. And there was a woman, who looked to be a prostitute, with her arms pinioned and her legs pulled wide apart by two of the men. The boss of the gang sat cross-legged between her thighs with a dagger in his hand. Another two men stood by watching and laughing. A cotton towel had been stuffed in the woman's mouth so that she couldn't scream, but her entire body convulsed as she tried to pull free. Her kimono was so torn that she was almost naked. Then Jinnai noticed a young man, dressed as a merchant, tied to a nearby tree.

"What are you doing?"

Jinnai spoke calmly, and since he had approached without making a sound, the ruffians noticed his presence for the first time. They started, peering into the darkness. The two men standing nearby promptly drew their swords. But the boss remained calm, apparently because Jinnai was alone. Furthermore, Jinnai's stylish outfit signaled that he was not an official.

"Don't worry. She's just a prostitute."

It was as if he had said she were a stray dog.

"I asked you: What are you doing?"

"Banging her. Six of us, three times each. Hold it right there!" The man raised his hand to stop Jinnai from doing anything rash. "Don't get things wrong. This is punishment. Actually, you see, this woman was trying to cheat the young master over there. Trying to get him to redeem her, set up house with her. The old master asked us to put her back in her place."

"What are you doing with the dagger?"

Jinnai's voice had sunk deeper.

"This woman here, she's a Kugutsu. They say that Kugutsu women have their cracks sideways, instead of up and down. But this one, well, hers is up and down, just like a regular woman. It's disappointing, so we thought we'd give her one that is cross-shaped."

Jinnai's eyes narrowed. It was a sign that Jinnai's wrath had reached a peak, but the men had no way of guessing that. They were making light of the young man standing before them like a wooden puppet.

"It'll give her a unique tool, make her more popular than before. Ha! Ha! Ha! If you want to look, come closer."

The boss turned his back to Jinnai and got a firmer grip on his dagger. With his left hand, he spread her vagina open. Just as his right hand was about to move forward, a sword slashed through the air, and his right arm came off at the shoulder.

"Aaagh!" he screamed.

Seeing their boss rolling on the ground in agony, the five suddenly pale henchmen drew their blades. Jinnai sniffed. They showed no proper stance, no swordsmanship. Nonetheless, he had no interest in letting the fiends live.

Drawing his short sword with his right hand, he leaped. He cut two of the men from head to throat and they died immediately. As soon as he landed, the heads of the other three danced in the air—*denshun*, an attack of lightning speed. As he returned his long sword to its sheath on his back, with a shake of the short sword in his left hand he cut the ropes that had tied the young master.

"Shin-san!"

The woman had removed the gag from her mouth, and tried to clutch the young man's waist. But the man shrank back, evading her clasp.

"Shin-san!"

Once again she reached out, but cruelly he brushed her hand aside.

"Why didn't you tell me you were Kugutsu?"

His voice was icy, cold enough to send shivers down one's spine.

The woman was speechless. She stared at him in disbelief. The life drained from her eyes and she lowered her head. In her expression, Jinnai read the woman's resignation. His heart felt a stabbing pain. Wanting to strike down the frivolous young master, his hand trembled, but at that moment, he saw the woman pick up the dagger. The gang leader's severed hand still grasped it.

"Shin-san."

The woman grasped him with all the strength she could muster, and the sharp point of the dagger plunged with precision into the left side of the man's chest. He died without a sound. Vigorously ripping out the dagger, she then placed the point under her own left breast and fell upon the fallen man as if embracing him.

Her profile as she lay with her cheek upon the man's chest seemed beautiful to Jinnai. Snow fell lightly upon their bodies. Her face was beautifully sorrowful. Had she not been a prostitute, and had she not been Kugutsu, she would not have died thus. Together with the man she loved, she might have lived happily. Jinnai was beside himself with anger. How could such a thing be allowed to happen? How could someone of the puppeteer clan—those who were free to move about wherever they wished, like a bird uses flight, and above whom no one was superior— how could such a person be treated with such contempt and end up dying so miserably?

"Kugutsu women have their cracks sideways."

More than anything else, that single comment pierced Jinnai. A woman of the puppeteer clan whose attractiveness and sensuality were the ultimate in beauty. How could anyone disparage that beauty as monstrous? In that moment, Jinnai realized that he had confronted something that was not merely a problem involving the handful of puppeteers under his protection. Rather, he faced something that was a life and death matter to the entire clan. In the heavily falling snow, Jinnai wept. Leaning against the tree where the young master had been tied, he cried tears of anger and despair, for there seemed no solution to the problem.

With the coming of dawn, a large flock of crows assembled. The ominously plump crows swarmed first upon the corpses of the men. The birds savagely plucked out the eyeballs and tore off the testicles. When the first crow landed on the woman, Jinnai moved for the first time. His long sword struck the pitch-black bird. Probably thinking that their prey was going to be stolen from them, the others flew up, turned and launched a concerted attack on Jinnai. It was a straightforward, voracious, concentrated attack. As he attacked with both swords, he was pecked violently by the birds' sharp beaks. Amid the corpses of its black companions, which lay like so many blotches on the snow covering the human dead, one significantly larger crow leisurely set about feeding on the woman's flesh. It pulled out the oozing eyeball and pulled at the tender wrinkled flesh between her legs. Apparently the latter was the most delectable. In Jinnai's eyes, this great black crow symbolized the Tokugawa clan. With rage, he hurled his short sword at the bird. The sword pierced it, but the great crow flew briefly upward before crashing to the ground. Its beak red with blood, it managed to caw menacingly at Jinnai. What uncanny power of survival! Jinnai lunged and cut off its head. It was in that moment that Jinnai felt the irresistible strength of the discriminatory policies of the shogunate. The head of the crow tumbled across the snow, its red mouth open in ridicule.

"The only thing to do was to build a castle. It had to be built."
Gensai threw back the cold sake.
"A castle, you say?"
Seiichiro parroted the phrase. It seemed a funny thing to say, something out of the period when the warlords were battling each other throughout the land.
"Yes, a castle. A castle to protect our women from those crows, and where the women can 'rinse themselves clean.'"
"Rinse?"
Seiichiro hadn't a clue about what Gensai meant.
"A place where women can 'rinse away' their origins, shed all traces of their background. Exactly what is going on here in Yoshiwara at this moment."
Seiichiro looked at Gensai in open-mouthed amazement.
"I don't understand."
"Don't you see how it is that these *oiran* get to Yoshiwara?"

Zegen were people who traveled around the country procuring good-looking girls. They were despised by the citizenry at large, and almost all of them had been in and out of prison. They wandered around the country looking for attractive young girls, buying them if they could and abducting them when they couldn't. These procurers would straightaway sell a girl to the pleasure quarter of some town. Then another procurer would sell her to another town, and before one knew it, no one was quite sure where the girl came from. This process was called *kuragae*, "change of quarter," or *tama korogashi*, "tumbling gems." Eventually the "gems" tumbled into the Yoshiwara quarter and became *kamuro*. Not all of them came that way. Some girls arrived with proper proof of their families—parents and siblings. It was only the Kugutsu girls who tumbled along in this way from place to place. The procurers gathered these girls from all over the country, very carefully erasing all traces of their background and purposely mixing them with the other girls. These Kugutsu girls would gradually rise from *kamuro* to *shinzo*, and on to *oiran*, and without exception, at the age of twenty-eight they were released from their term of service and given their freedom.

"At twenty-eight, the castle-toppler at last wears *tabi*" went one saying, a reference to the fact that even in the depth of winter a woman of the pleasure quarters always went barefoot. "At twenty-seven, the end of having to tell lies" went another.

At the end of her term of service, a *yujo* was completely free. She could return to her family, go off with a man she loved or simply remain within the quarter. The puppeteer women had two choices, either marry or stay in the quarter. Some fell down a few ranks into the employ of a *kirimise*, but the period of service in such places was short, and while they were working, they were able to keep a portion of their *agedai*. A superior *oiran* could be redeemed without waiting till the end of her term of employment. Some of these *oiran* became mistresses of feudal lords or rich merchants, and some even became the legal wives of merchants. Others even became the wives of immediate retainers of the shogun. An *oiran* of the Matsubaya named Mihozaki became the beloved wife Oshizu of a well-known composer of satirical poetry. For a daughter of the Kugutsu puppeteer clan who had faced starvation and who had not been allowed to share as much as a warming fire with ordinary commoners, such a destiny could only be called true happiness. It was this that Gensai meant when he said that a woman could "rinse away" her past.

The procurers were, to a man, members of the Kugutsu clan. They were neither avaricious nor villainous, and were, to the contrary, deliverers of happiness. Resigning themselves to notoriety and enduring the disdain of others, they silently served as unnamed soldiers in the service of the women of the clan. As Gensai described the fate of these men, he choked up and there was something shining faintly in his eyes.

"But it was pretty difficult to build such a castle. We made repeated earnest appeals to the government, but permission to build a licensed pleasure quarter wasn't issued to us. Finally, in the fifth year of Keicho (1600), I made one last gamble..."

The year 1600 was the year of the decisive battle at Sekigahara. Shoji Jinnai was 25. On the first day of the ninth month of that year, Tokugawa Ieyasu led a great army westward to a showdown with Ishida Mitsunari. On that very day, Jinnai opened a new teahouse in front of Suzugamori Hachiman Shrine. In front of the shop, he had eight carefully selected beauties line up wearing red cotton towels over their coiffures and wearing identical vermillion *obi* at their waists. He had them serve tea to the troops who passed by on their way to the battlefront. A palanquin stopped near the shop, and from it alighted none other than Ieyasu himself.

"Who is that young man in the *hakama* at that teahouse formally greeting our men? And who are those young women lined up serving tea?"

According to *Dobo Verbal Garden*, which records this encounter, Jinnai replied that he was the master of a house of women of pleasure, using a particular word that also indicated that he was the head of a group of puppeteers. Jinnai made it very clear to Ieyasu—the source of the political strategy of discrimination against the nomadic peoples— exactly who he was. It was an audacious thing to do. This group of people who were not allowed to share fire with the common people was here, serving tea on the auspicious day of the march to battle. It would have been only natural for the whole lot to be butchered on the spot. Whether Ieyasu realized this or not, he did not find fault with them. The records simply comment that Ieyasu found the group's offering of tea to his men "laudable." At any rate, Jinnai believed that he had been successful in that he had made both his name and his face known to the great Ieyasu. He had only one step more to take.

The Battle of Sekigahara ended in a great victory for Ieyasu. When Ieyasu was returning in triumph toward Edo with his army, Jinnai once again set up a tea shop at Suzugamori Hachiman Shrine, and he joined the same beautiful women in the same outfits in expressing their gratitude and congratulations to the passing troops.

A palanquin protected by a large escort of guards stopped outside the tea shop. Once again, the great Ieyasu stepped out. His head reverently bowed, Jinnai waited to be spoken to.

But the expected voice did not come.

"Aaah!" came a loud, hoarse voice.

Jinnai couldn't help raising his head to stare. Right in front of him stood Ieyasu, his arms raised high, stretching himself. He paid no attention to Jinnai at all. But...Jinnai could hardly believe what he was seeing. The man before him was not Ieyasu. His appearance was identical, but this man was an entirely different person. What was even more astounding was that the man in front of him was someone with whom he was well acquainted.

"How...?"

Seiichiro was on the point of adding "...could such a ridiculous thing be possible?" But Gensai had to this point never told him a lie. Even when it was inconvenient for Gensai—as had been the case with his honest answer regarding the assassination of Yagyu Jubei. Gensai would surely not lie to him now. What was more, what came next was too incredible to be a lie.

"Well, who was it then?"

"Sarada Jirosaburo Motonobu. Of course that won't mean a thing to you."

Gensai was perfectly right, for Seiichiro had never heard the name.

"His childhood name was Kunimatsu, and he was a storyteller who lived in Miyanosaki in Sumpu, Ieyasu's home province."

Storytellers like him were called *sasaramono*, after the bamboo whisks, called *sasara*, which were used to accompany the stories they told. Such storytellers often gathered outside temples and shrines on festival days to tell their stories. Like the puppeteer clan, these *sasaramono* were public performers who had absolute freedom to move freely about the country—nomadic "companions of the way."

Seiichiro was incredulous. Despite the fact that the words were coming directly from Gensai, it was impossible to simply swallow the story whole.

"Hard to believe, isn't it?" Gensai teased.

"I'll have to admit, it is a bit beyond reason."

Gensai laughed loudly. For a moment, Seiichiro thought Gensai had been joking all along.

"And that's why my simply telling you isn't sufficient. We have to depend on Obaba-sama."

There was one more thing about which Seiichiro had doubts.

"What am I going to dream about the next time?"

"You're going to dream that you have become Sarada Jirosaburo Motonobu."

Gensai now grinned with a certain measure of malice. "I should remind you that Jirosaburo was a short, unattractive man. He wasn't a handsome young man like you, Sei-san. That's part of the reason why Obaba-sama is going to have a hard time of it."

Seiichiro let out a deep sigh.

The following day at midday.

Seiichiro was sleeping. They were again in the back room of the Nishidaya. And as before, Obaba-sama was naked above Seiichiro. Not moving at all. And yet, she seemed to be in distress. Her eyebrows tightly knit, she seemed to be mumbling something, a kind of chant. Abruptly her buttocks rose high and with great force she collapsed. It seemed as if his penis had penetrated straight through her uterus. Seiichiro's face contorted with pain.

In his dream, Seiichiro was looking out over the choppy surface of a lake.

The waves gradually calmed and a man of rather peculiar appearance was reflected on the surface of the water.

He was almost abnormally short. Above the waist, he was solid, with thick, well-defined muscles. From a distance, he seemed to stand almost square. Furthermore, his face was muscular and strongly featured. If he had been of normal height, he would have the majestic appearance of a military commander, but unfortunately, his legs were extremely short. One could even call them miniscule. As a result, the more impressive his head and upper body, the stranger was the overall effect. Many concluded at first sight that he was a dwarf. And since no man is ever entirely indifferent to his own physical appearance, he who lived in such a body since childhood was bound to have a warped character.

He was an extreme misanthrope. He didn't talk much, and when he did speak, he stammered. He was obstinate, and kept his feelings to himself, but when his emotions did rise to the surface, they gushed forth with frightening explosiveness.

As a child, he was known as Kunimatsu. Sent to live in a temple, he received the Buddhist name Jokei. Later in life he came to be known as Sarada Jirosaburo Motonobu.

During the Tenbun era, a man claiming to be the descendant of Nitta Yoshishige drifted into the Sumpu domain and began to earn a living by offering prayers and incantations. His name was Edo Matsumotobo. Kunimatsu was born to this man and the daughter of a local storyteller. The year was Tenmon 11 (1542) and Matsumotobo was a member of the so-called "companions of the way," a man who simply could not settle in one place. Around the time Kunimatsu was born, Matsumotobo deserted the mother and child and returned to his wandering ways. The mother had to marry into another family and left Kunimatsu to be raised by her own mother. Kunimatsu and his grandmother lived in a rowhouse on the premises of Kayoin Temple in Miyanomae-machi.

At the age of six, Kunimatsu was given into the care of a priest named Chitan, who presided over Chigenin Temple, a small branch temple within the execution grounds at Kitsunegasaki. The head temple of this subordinate temple was Toshozan Enkoin, a Jodo sect temple which held ceremonies for those with no relatives to mourn for them. Kunimatsu had his head shaved and was given the name Jokei. When he was nine, he was caught by a priest catching small birds with birdlime in the mountains where the Imakawa clan's Bodaiji Zozenji was located. It was a sacred place, where the taking of life was absolutely forbidden. There could be no special forgiveness on account of the fact that he was still a child. Chitan expelled him from his temple, barely saving the boy from punishment. Unable to return to his grandmother, who would be implicated in his crime were she to harbor him, he wandered the streets briefly, until a certain man captured him and sold him for five *kan* to another family. The evil man who had captured him was a slave trader named Mataemon. The boy was eventually purchased by a mountain ascetic named Sakai Jokobo.

Mountain ascetics, unlike their strictly Buddhist counterparts, not only married but also ate meat. As "companions of the way," such itinerant priests wandered the provinces practicing faith healing and selling paper talismans, amulets, and secret charms.

For ten years, until he turned nineteen, Jokei was forced to undergo ascetic discipline. Even on the coldest days of winter, he would walk the streets of towns barefoot and naked, pouring buckets of water over his head. Whenever Jokei performed these austerities, the local people would gather. When he was naked, his short legs became even more conspicuous. Between the cold, shame and anger, his face would turn a bright purple, making him look like a fearsome demon. But that seemed to be what attracted people. They would gather to gawk and laugh. This pleased Jokobo greatly because those who gathered would buy talismans from him. Whenever the pair entered a new town, Jokobo would have Jokei repeat this demeaning performance, and Jokei found it unbearable.

In fact, however, Jokei's true aim was not to simply take in a few small coins from this exhibition. He used Jokei as a kind of camouflage for another purpose. In the days when the feudal lords were constantly battling with one another, information became extremely valuable. Itinerant priests like Jokei found behind-the-scenes employment as gatherers of information. The austere ascetic practices of this strange-looking child provided the perfect front, and as a result, Jokobo garnered an enormous quantity of information. When he sold it to a hostile feudal lord, it would bring him good money.

As Jokei lived his life of public humiliation, he also became adept in the arts of gathering information. As he did this, he wandered time and again through the provinces of Sumpu, Totomi, Kai, Shinano, Izu and Sagami. Somehow or other he also learned how to use a sword and a spear.

In the third year of the Eiroku period (1560), Jokei turned nineteen. Casting aside the decrepit Jokobo, he became a *yabushi*—a wandering samurai—and took the new name Sarada Jirosaburo Motonobu. It was the same year that Oda Nobunaga defeated Imagawa Yoshimoto at Okehazama.

During this period, the term *yabushi* had two meanings: "robber" and "mercenary." In their attitude toward life and consciousness, they were vastly different from later bandits who were constantly pursued by the authorities and had to live in hiding. *Yabushi* had almost no sense that they were leading a shady life. They lived free and easy. From the perspective of a subordinate of a daimyo or a member of a major merchant family, who were forced to endure being treated like a slave, these men lived in a world that was almost dreamlike. They lived in circumstances a young man would consider ideal.

Sarada Jirosaburo gloried in his youth. He got hold of money. He had his way with women. But there was one thing he lacked—honor for valorous deeds. He was the ultimate coward, to the point of being pathologically cautious. It wasn't that his skills with a sword or spear were that much poorer than those of others. In a critical moment, he would fight with abandon and had the strength to come through a fight alive every time. But Jirosaburo made every possible effort to avoid a situation where carnage was likely. He always schemed to find a way to easily and safely come out on the winning side. He would always work out two or three alternatives for retreat if worse came to worst. Despite being slow in resolving to fight, he was extremely quick and precise when it came to resolving to retreat.

Jirosaburo's character, had it been possessed by a military commander in charge of a domain, would hardly have been anything to be ashamed of. Among the active military commanders who survived the period when the domains were constantly at war with one another, there were many who fought their way to power through such strategies. But among the group of wandering samurai who had no responsibility beyond themselves, it was only natural that he was mocked. So no matter how much of a display he might make of himself, he achieved no success. Nonetheless, he was able to earn some sort of living for himself through the skills he had mastered for gathering information during his days as an itinerant priest. He never again wore the robes of a beggar priest, but by clothing himself in the garb of various types of "companions of the way," he was able to obtain valuable bits of information. Just as when he was a child, his physical peculiarities could be used to advantage. In physical appearance he was virtually square, and he was no taller than the average woman, so when a man, woman or even a child saw him for the first time, they could not help grinning. They seemed to find it all the more amusing that the face that stood atop that body was peculiarly prudent-looking. He always had the face of one deep in thought, and sometimes he pulled a sorrowful face. He must have had the character of a born clown. At such times, virtually anything Jirosaburo did brought laughter from those around him. Due to this, whatever he did, he was safe. He was the reverse of a ninja, who made every effort to remain inconspicuous during a mission. In his case, he performed his duties with far greater ease by making himself extremely conspicuous, and moreover, he did so with great safety.

The era shifted from Eiroku to Genki, to Tensei. Military supremacy fell to Oda Nobunaga, then to Toyotomi Hideyoshi.

Summer of Tensei 17 (1589). Jirosaburo was employed by the Hojo clan and was sent to the capital city of Kyoto. His mission was to reconnoiter and gather detailed information regarding the encampment of Hideyoshi's troops prior to their decisive confrontation. Among the Hojo clan, the man who was charged with this probe was Shoji Jinnai's father, Matazaemon. It was likely that Matazaemon was placed in charge of this reconnaissance because as a member of the Kugutsu clan he had influence among the various "companions of the way."

Matazaemon and Jirosaburo got along extremely well. The natural cheerfulness of the puppeteer found great value in the clown. The two men drank together at Matazaemon's residence on a number of occasions. In emulation of Matazaemon, who began to dance whenever he became intoxicated, Jirosaburo also danced, but in his own peculiar way. The members of the Shoji family who had gathered would all burst into laughter. Among them was the fourteen-year-old heir to the leadership, Jinnai. In the family's laughter, there was no contempt but only warmth and empathy. It was the first time that Jirosaburo was not angered when people laughed at him. He exerted his utmost ability to make the good-spirited people laugh. When Jinnai joined in, rolling about on the tatami as if he were insane, even Matazaemon noticed. This was when Jirosaburo's features became engraved in Jinnai's memory.

Receiving a large advance allowance, Jirosaburo headed off to the capital. It was there that he made the biggest blunder of this life—he fell in love. Jirosaburo was forty-eight that year, which in those days made him an old man. But he fell in love, and with all the ardor of a boy. The object of his affections was a woman working in the house of a court noble. She was not what one would call beautiful, but her plumpness exuded a succulent sexual appeal, and, most important of all, she was so fair-skinned that her entire body seemed almost translucent.

In fact, Jirosaburo had seen her through a crack in the mud wall while she bathed in a tub of water in the open air. In the middle of her white nakedness was an abundance of jet-black pubic hair. It was wet from the hot water of the tub and it stuck flat against her body. It was abnormally long, hanging more than a foot below. He had never seen such prolific hair, and it made his whole body tremble. Whatever it took, he decided, he wanted her. For a forty-eight-year-old wandering samurai of odd appearance, however, there was only one way to accomplish that—he would simply have to take her. That night, Jirosaburo stole his way into the nobleman's residence. He was an expert at sneaking into such places. He then waited until four in the morning, when people are in their deepest sleep. No one detected him and once he was inside the premises, he immediately began trying to locate the room where the woman was sleeping. Incredibly, the lady was sleeping with the courtier! He was clinging to her fast asleep. Jirosaburo succeeded in replacing the woman with rolled up clothing and leaving that in the courtier's embrace. Then he succeeded in carrying off the woman, who remained completely naked. Naturally he stunned her unconscious with a light blow to a vital point.

To Jirosaburo's misfortune, however, there was a guest staying in the residence that night who possessed abnormally acute senses. This guest was a Buddhist monk, and his name was Tenkai. One day he would be known as a prominent priest. The sixth sense that he had possessed as a military commander when he went by the name Akechi Mitsuhide was still keen. Jirosaburo's intrusion was detected by this sixth sense, and Tenkai silently crept out into the garden and hid among the shadows of the trees along the outer wall. It was a natural precaution for a warrior who had experienced being on the run. Jirosaburo emerged from the building carrying the completely naked woman over his shoulder, heading at full speed for the tree behind which Tenkai was hidden. To get back over the wall, climbing the tree was the easiest route. Just as Jirosaburo was about to reach the tree, Tenkai unleashed a succession of stones at him. Each was a superb throw. The first struck him in the shin; the second struck the center of his forehead; and the third hit him in the testicles. Without a sound, Jirosaburo fell unconscious.

Tenkai stepped close and first inspected the woman, whom he discovered was unconscious but all right. He then pulled Jirosaburo to one side, and peered into his face. A small cry of surprise escaped Tenkai. For some time he gazed at Jirosaburo, then for some reason covered him with a hood and tied him up. Tenkai reported the affair to the courtier in whose residence they were staying and asked the nobleman to allow him to take custody of the intruder. The nobleman, assuming that his unfortunate affair had been discovered, immediately acquiesced to the request. As a result, Tenkai took possession of Jirosaburo. After taking Jirosaburo with him back to Mt. Hiei, Tenkai gave him a mask and ordered him to do something most unusual.

"From now on, you are never to take off that mask. If you can obey this command, I promise to provide you with security for the rest of your life."

At the age of forty-eight, Jirosaburo was completely worn out from the life of a wandering samurai. True enough, it was an ideal life and occupation for a young man, but for a man of forty-eight, it was a hard way to make a living. There were no advancements or promotions of any kind. However great a feat he might accomplish on the battlefield, his compensation rose only slightly and he never received credit for what he did. The rewards, monetary and otherwise, decreased as he grew older, if only because his body wasn't as strong as it used to be. That was why, at his age, Jirosaburo had begun to hope, for the very first time in his life, to find a position in the service of some samurai household. Even if the stipend were minimal, it would be nice to have a regular income of some kind. Tenkai's offer found ready reception in Jirosaburo's mind, and Jirosaburo quite willingly agreed to follow his orders.

Tenkai sent Jirosaburo to Mikawa with an accompanying letter. Tenkai instructed him to go straight to the residence of one of Tokugawa Ieyasu's "Four Devas"—Honda Tadakatsu—and ordered Jirosaburo not to remove the mask unless he was directly ordered to do so by Tadakatsu himself.

"Only two things stand above Ieyasu: a war helmet and Honda Tadakatsu." So went the caustic comment offered by the samurai who supported Ieyasu's adversary, Takeda Shingen. At the age of forty-three, Honda Heihachiro Tadakatsu was at that time Ieyasu's most trusted military commander. When Jirosaburo arrived at the Honda residence, he was immediately led to one of the rooms in the back. Tenkai had already sent an express messenger to alert Tadakatsu concerning Jirosaburo's arrival, and Tadakatsu had arranged for everyone to leave the room so that the two men were alone.

"Take off the mask and let me see your face."

Jirosaburo removed the mask, and a gasp of astonishment escaped Tadakatsu's lips. Jirosaburo was beginning to realize that he must bear a striking resemblance to someone.

"How old are you?" Tadakatsu asked.

"I am forty-eight years old, sir."

Jirosaburo answered respectfully, aware that a potential stipend was at stake. His intuition told him that if he could somehow clear this one hurdle, his hoped-for stipend—whatever the amount might be—would be within his grasp.

Tadakatsu was once again astonished.

"Even the age is the same."

His voice was almost a groan. Jirosaburo was virtually certain that he would be successful.

Once again he was ordered to put on the mask and never to show his face to anyone.

Little by little, Jirosaburo grew uneasy, and a bit unhappy with the situation.

He knew that he resembled someone, but what left an unpleasant taste in this mouth was the fact that his usefulness in this situation appeared to be due not to his abilities but only to his physical features.

He was also displeased by the fact that he was being constantly ordered around. But what bothered him the most was that he had to wear the mask. It was made of copper and was quite heavy. He wasn't supposed to remove the mask even when he took a bath. And even though he was wearing the mask, he was warned to avoid appearing before Tadakatsu's vassals as much as possible.

For ten days, Jirosaburo was left to his own devices. Each day he was served sumptuous meals and an abundance of sake, but he could not step foot outside. On top of that, his only companions were three burly samurai; there was no female presence in the entire residence. It was insufferably dull, more than he could endure.

He recklessly decided to escape from the Honda residence. But on that very day, for the first time in ten days, Honda appeared.

"Tomorrow, early in the morning, we'll go to the castle. Make your preparations. Your clothes will be brought later. Keep the mask on. But first shave carefully."

That was all Honda said. Going to the castle probably meant that he was about to be introduced to Lord Ieyasu. He would finally find out whether he would receive the long-sought stipend. Jirosaburo immediately postponed his plan to escape.

The following day, at an ungodly early hour, he was shaken awake and made to change clothes. The clothes he was handed were unobtrusive but elegant—so fine, in fact, that for a moment he thought there had been some mistake. In outward appearance, the two swords he was given were of superb workmanship, but when he pulled out the blades, he discovered that they were not at all special. Ironically, the fact that only the external appearance of the swords was splendid was of some relief. And yet, when he finished dressing and stood in front of a mirror, Jirosaburo simply could not keep from laughing. It was said that the tailor makes the man, but his laughter came from the fact that his attire was so obviously a façade. Were they going to make a laughingstock out of him once again in his life? Half sullenly, he accompanied Tadakatsu to the castle.

Perhaps because it was still so early in the morning, the perimeter of the castle was heavily guarded but the inside was virtually deserted. Tadakatsu walked briskly along the corridor. If Jirosaburo fell even slightly behind, Tadakatsu paused and waited with irritation for him to catch up. Something abnormal was in the air, and Jirosaburo became anxious. They were led not to a large room, but rather to a small study.

"His Excellency," Tadakatsu announced with an awesome tone of voice.

Jirosaburo prostrated himself flat against the floor. Perhaps it was his imagination, but the next voice he heard sounded very much like his own.

"Rise, and take off the mask."

Jirosaburo raised his head. Right in front of him stood a man wearing the exact same clothes and carrying the exact same swords that he himself had been given. His face was quite similar, too. The man grinned broadly and stood up. His legs were extremely short, and the contours of his body were virtually square. He looked exactly like Jirosaburo.

Finally, Tadakatsu spoke.

"This is your lord."

The man before Jirosaburo was none other than Tokugawa Ieyasu.

KAGEMUSHA: SHADOW WARRIOR

Sarada Jirosaburo was enlisted into the service of the Tokugawa clan, which did not yet rule Japan, with a behind-the-scenes stipend of 200 *koku*. He was not given a place to live, but rather was ordered to live within the castle itself, where he was taken care of by an aged priest named Fukuami.

Every morning started with a visit from Fukuami. Jirosaburo would wash his face and brush his teeth with water brought by Fukuami. The priest would then shave Jirosaburo's face and the center of his forehead, and arrange his topknot. Fukuami dressed him as well. The clothes and swords changed from day to day. Jirosaburo was dressed exactly the same as Ieyasu. After eating a light breakfast, he was led by Fukuami to a room directly behind the room where Ieyasu attended to administrative matters. He would stay in that room virtually the entire day.

At night, his circumstances were roughly identical. Jirosaburo's room was adjacent to the room where Ieyasu slept, and Jirosaburo would wear the same nightwear and sleep on identical bedding as Ieyasu used. The only difference was that each night Ieyasu would sleep with a woman, while Jirosaburo usually spent the entire night alone. On occasion—out of sympathy for him—a lady-in-waiting would be sent to his room to keep him company for the night. But the woman would be selected to accord with Ieyasu's own preferences, which were for robust, plain-looking types. Jirosaburo earnestly wished that he would be allotted an attractive woman to sleep with at least from time to time.

Needless to say, Jirosaburo had been taken on to serve as a *kagemusha*—a double for Ieyasu. Attired precisely as Ieyasu was, Jirosaburo followed Ieyasu about, as a shadow follows a form. In the event that an incident should occur—if a spy should sneak into the castle—he was to immediately rush to Ieyasu's side. In this sense, he was also a bodyguard, for if an assassin snuck into the castle to kill Ieyasu and succeeded in locating the room of his intended victim, he would be confronted by *two* Ieyasus. These two Ieyasus had slightly different facial features, but in terms of clothing and physique, they were two versions of the same person.

The assassin would naturally be confounded and decide that to carry out his mission he had to kill both men. For an assassin, however, there was great danger in a moment of indecision. A second's delay could be fatal. In passing, it should also be mentioned that Ieyasu was a master swordsman. Over a period of seven years, he had been initiated into Okuyama-ryu swordsmanship under Master Okuyama Kyugasai Kimishige. This training was not of the watered-down type that later generations of feudal lords would acquire. The skill that Ieyasu possessed was the willful murderousness of the battlefield. Jirosaburo's own skills were the practical skills he had gained through his long career as a samurai for hire. Any ordinary assassin who confronted these two men would find that he had taken on more than he could handle. Further, if they could gain even an extra moment's advantage, numerous samurai on watch duty would come running at full tilt. The assassin's chance of carrying out his mission was virtually nil.

Whenever they left the castle, Jirosaburo wore the mask. This was the only change in the routine; everything else was the same. In the event of an emergency, Jirosaburo was to throw off his mask and stand in front of Ieyasu. On the battlefield, their positions were reversed. In battle, as a rule, the general who was commander in chief did not wear a helmet. If anything, he wore a mere hood. If a melee ensued and there was danger that the headquarters would be overrun, then and only then would the commander put on a helmet and a mask. When that happened, Ieyasu and Jirosaburo became identical. Not even allied generals were able to tell which was the real Ieyasu, so naturally the enemy had no way of knowing. Under such circumstances, Jirosaburo stood before Ieyasu, serving as a shield to protect Ieyasu from attack by archers.

The first time Jirosaburo entered battle as a "shadow warrior" was at the attack on Odawara. Standing behind Ieyasu with his mask on, Jirosaburo felt sick at heart because he pictured in his mind the faces of Shoji Matazaemon and his family. In the service of the Hojo, Matazaemon had been sent to smuggle himself into the capital city, and now he was at the front of the enemy forces, while he himself was the attacking commander's *kagemusha*. The irony of this destiny produced an inexpressible sadness that pained Jirosaburo.

Be that as it may, the attack on Odawara was a peculiar engagement. The attacking force took two forward castles in the hills of Nirayama and then laid siege to Odawara Castle. While conquering more than 50 subsidiary castles one after another, the main forces kept their sights on

Odawara Castle. The Taiko, Toyotomi Hideyoshi, whom Ieyasu served at that time, brought his beloved concubine Yodogimi and an enormous number of prostitutes were gathered together. They all participated in boisterous merrymaking night and day. While this boosted the morale of the attacking forces, it naturally left the defenders of the besieged castle in low spirits. After a four-month siege—and with little in the way of significant military combat—Odawara Castle fell. In a sense, one could say the offensive was a glorious one. But it was also the beginning of another phenomenon—the grand spectacle of the decline of the heroic Taiko Hideyoshi—which would reach a denouement eight years later at the Daigo no Hanami, a spectacular flower-viewing party where the Taiko's vassals jostled for power. Be that as it may, this campaign proved to be one that Jirosaburo would remember to the end of his life.

After that, Jirosaburo traveled with Ieyasu from the Hizen Nagoya headquarters of the invasion of the Korean peninsula on to Fushimi Castle. During this period, Ieyasu, whose domain had formerly been Mikawa, took over the six provinces of the Kanto region which had formerly been governed by the Hojo clan. His residence was also transferred from Hamamatsu Castle to Edo.

Ten years passed, and both Jirosaburo and Ieyasu had turned fifty-eight.

On the one hand, Jirosaburo had reason to be satisfied with his circumstances during those ten years. He had had no reason to fear starvation and had sake to drink and women to sleep with. On the other hand, it had been an extremely boring ten years. His freedom was severely limited. His earlier unfettered life as a wandering samurai, accompanied as it had been by unease, came to seem a time worthy of nostalgic remembrance. And yet, escape was entirely beyond the realm of the possible. Without a doubt, he would be hunted down within three days' time and mercilessly executed. And even if by some miracle he were able to succeed in escaping, Jirosaburo hadn't the faintest idea how he would earn a living. In all likelihood, he would collapse on a street somewhere and die of starvation.

Jirosaburo found one single diversion in his monotonous daily routine. Oddly enough, that diversion was politics. As a result of being constantly in a room adjoining the one where Ieyasu administered political affairs, he observed the totality of ten years' worth of decision-making: analyzing current circumstances, predicting changes five or even ten years into the future, exerting immeasurable perseverance and implementing cold-hearted, Machiavellian realist policies. Jirosaburo found all of this of great interest. Whenever there was something he failed to comprehend, he could always get help from the priest Fukuami (who, surprisingly, was still alive). Fukuami also informed him in great detail about the background and personality of each of Ieyasu's vassals and the behind-the-scenes maneuvering that took place between them. On such subjects, Fukuami was a great reservoir of knowledge. Ten years was an enormous length of time, and Jirosaburo came to realize that he had mastered not only Ieyasu's smallest quirks, but also his way of thinking. Whenever a vassal came to ask Ieyasu's advice on a matter, Jirosaburo, in the next room, would come up with a recommendation in his own mind. In the ensuing interview, what he had come up with would turn out to be exactly what Ieyasu conveyed to the vassal. Not once did Jirosaburo's intuition miss the target. He would smile complacently to himself. But he felt utterly lonely having nobody to whom he might boast about this skill. He wasn't even able to tell his constant companion Fukuami.

(If Lord Ieyasu ever heard about it, I would undoubtedly be killed on the spot)

Knowing how Ieyasu's thought processes operated, Jirosaburo knew that he had to remain completely silent. And so, he simply studied Ieyasu's distinctive way of dealing with issues, put up with his own situation and kept his accomplishment to himself.

THE BATTLE OF SEKIGAHARA

Then came the fateful day.

The fifteenth day of the ninth month of Keicho 5 (1600). The day that Tokugawa Ieyasu would gamble the fate of his clan in the Battle of Sekigahara.

The respective armies of Ishida Mitsunari, Konishi Yukinaga, Ukita Hideie and Shimazu Yoshihiro, which had been holed up in Ogaki Castle until the previous day, turned pale when they learned that Ieyasu had ignored Ogaki Castle and instead had marched westward on the Nakasendo to attack Ishida's residence castle at Sawayama and appeared to be moving on to take Osaka Castle. It had been the strategy of the allied forces of western Japan to tie up Ieyasu's main forces at Ogaki, to await the arrival of Mori Terumoto, who was to come from Osaka in the west, and then to attack Ieyasu from both east and west. The source of the news was none other than Ieyasu himself, who was plotting to avoid the time-consuming siege of the castle and to bring things to a head in an encounter on an open battlefield, the kind that he excelled at. The opposing forces instantly fell into the trap.

Late on the night of the fourteenth, Ishida and his allies left Ogaki Castle in a torrential rain. Early on the morning of the fifteenth, they took up positions on the northwest side of the Sekigahara valley, commanding a view of the plain upon which the Nakasendo road intersected with the Hokkoku Kaido, the road leading to Echizen province.

When he heard that the allied western forces had left Ogaki Castle, Ieyasu danced for joy and immediately directed his entire army toward Sekigahara.

Daybreak on the fifteenth. A drizzle remained from the previous night's heavy rain, and the Sekigahara plain, locked in between mountains, was shrouded in dense fog.

Ieyasu's forces numbered 76,000; Mitsunari's numbered 100,000. However, when it came to the number of troops who would actually participate in combat, all 76,000 of Ieyasu's saw action, whereas only 35,000 of Mitsunari's actually fought. It seems that many of the units from Mitsunari's side betrayed him or fell prey to indecision.

The march continued through thick mud and fog so heavy that it seemed to cling to the body. Due to the weight of their armor, the soldiers' legs sank into the mud and the going was rough. Each step forward was exhausting. Along the march, even Ieyasu grumbled to himself. According to the *Tokugawa Jikki* (Chronicles of the Tokugawa Shogun), Ieyasu's words were:

"Now the years begin to weigh on me, and this work is hard. How much better if my son were here."

It wasn't entirely clear, to those who overheard him, which son he had in mind. Could it have been Hidetada, who was supposed to be coming up the Nakasendo road but had been blocked by Sanada Masayuki and had still not arrived? Or, could he have been referring to his intrepid, renowned eldest son Nobuyasu, whom he had been forced to kill in the seventh year of Tensei? It is unknown. But all things being equal, we would like to think it was the latter, all the more if these words were Ieyasu's last.

Ieyasu had settled on establishing his headquarters on Momokubari-yama, and just as he was doing so, a minor incident occurred.

As it was recorded in the *Tokugawa Jikki*, that morning the area was covered in dense fog, penetrated only by the loud reports of muskets firing. Everyone in the headquarters was tense and mounted warriors were coming and going in great turmoil. In this tumult, an ally named Nonomura Shirouemon came rushing toward Ieyasu on horseback. Already tense due to the anticipated battle, Ieyasu drew his sword and struck out at the man. Stunned, Shirouemon turned his horse around and took off unscathed. Irritated that his strike had missed, Ieyasu vented his anger on the sheath of another man at his side named Sukezaemon Munekatsu. According to the record, Nonomura was not subsequently censured for his inopportune appearance in front of Ieyasu.

There is nothing momentous in the incident as recorded. In the moments leading up to the commencement of a battle, it would only be natural for everyone involved to be highly strung, and it is rather charming that even a hard-bitten veteran like Ieyasu would have been worked up. Some people would find it all even easier to understand in light of the fact that Ieyasu was about to enter a battle that would determine the fate of the Tokugawa clan.

But would such pent-up emotion be sufficient cause for Ieyasu to draw his battle sword and attempt to cut down one of his own retainers, whose only fault was to ride up suddenly on horseback? Moreover, would Ieyasu really have randomly vented his frustration by striking the weapon of one of those gathered around him? Such behavior seems entirely unlike the prudent Ieyasu.

In actuality, an absolutely astonishing fact lies hidden behind the curious but seemingly insignificant events of the records.

That day, as usual, Sarada Jirosaburo, wearing mask and war helmet, was riding immediately behind Ieyasu. Also as reported in the *Tokugawa Jikki*, Ieyasu was wearing a brown crepe hood. The wind was blowing the fog around in swirls, and just at the moment the fog grew suddenly dense, a horse and rider suddenly came through the fog on Ieyasu's left side. First, the horse's head came into sight, and then an armored warrior, wearing a mask. The armor and the identifying personal banner affixed behind his armor were indisputably those of Ieyasu's old friend and ally Nonomura Shirouemon. Realizing who it was, Jirosaburo was just about to breathe a sigh of relief, when he noticed the weapon Shirouemon carried in his right hand, a long spear blade mounted on a shaft. He could tell it was a spearhead because the blade was unsheathed. Shirouemon did not possess such a peculiar short sword, to say nothing of the fact that no one would be foolish enough to draw a mere short sword just as a battle was about to begin. Suddenly aware of the danger, Jirosaburo slapped the hind quarters of Ieyasu's horse just as the spearhead flashed and slipped beneath the left side of Ieyasu's armor. Shirouemon turned his horse to escape. Sukezaemon, the loyal attendant who was on Ieyasu's left side, realized in an instant something had happened.

"My Lord!" he shouted as he attempted to grab Shirouemon. Shirouemon swung the hilt-mounted spearhead. Sukezaemon just barely parried the blow, and instead, his own battle banner was sliced off. Recovering from momentary astonishment, Jirosaburo drew his sword and slashed Shirouemon. It was a powerful, telling blow, and the right arm which had held the spear was sliced off. But Shirouemon nevertheless spurred his horse and attempted to make good his escape. Sukezaemon's spear pierced his side, and Shirouemon fell from his horse. Sukezaemon jumped off his horse and yanked off the battle mask. He saw the face of a completely unfamiliar man, an assassin sent by Mitsunari. At the same moment, Jirosaburo jumped from his own horse, ran to Ieyasu's side and raised his lord in his arms. Ieyasu was dead. The assassin's spearhead had skillfully struck just below the left side of Ieyasu's armor and pierced his heart.

Jirosaburo immediately took off his own battle surcoat, covered Ieyasu's face with it and roared:

"Sarada Jirosaburo has been killed on the battlefield! Hurry! Be likewise courageous!"

From the depths of the fog, from all sides of the headquarters, there arose a vigorous war cry. Sukezaemon stood rooted to the spot, looking at Jirosaburo in amazement.

It is hard to know what would have happened next if Honda

Heihachiro Tadakatsu had not arrived at the headquarters of the main forces. Honda's forces composed the left flank. He came rushing in, impatient since the main forces were not moving into action. Hearing that Ieyasu had been assassinated, Tadakatsu turned gloomy. Yet he was himself a well-seasoned military commander, worthy of his reputation as second to none—including Ieyasu. He recovered himself immediately. That day's battle was a crucial one. If they did not claim victory on the field that day it would spell the end of the Tokugawa alliance. If the enemy learned that Ieyasu was dead, defeat was certain. To the bitter end, they would have to keep Ieyasu's death a secret and fight with a *kagemusha*—a shadow warrior—at the front. On Ishida's side were troops who had secret promises with Ieyasu's side. Kitsukawa Hioie had promised not to fight, and Kobayakawa Hideaki had promised actually to fight on the Tokugawa side. If either of these parties learned about Ieyasu's assassination, it was highly unlikely that they would fulfill their pledges. If they reneged, the outcome of the conflict would be uncertain. Tadakatsu ordered that anyone who breathed a word about Ieyasu's demise was to be killed on the spot. He had Ieyasu's body covered with a battle banner and laid to rest in the back of the battle headquarters, and he had Jirosaburo placed in a conspicuous place within the headquarters. It was at that moment that the fog finally dissipated.

The battle commenced at around eight in the morning. Heavy fighting continued until about noon, with little obvious advantage to either side. Honda Tadakatsu remained at Jirosaburo's side. Tadakatsu was prepared to command the army. Yet he intended to have his orders delivered by Jirosaburo.

But Tadakatsu's expectations were entirely upset when Jirosaburo himself began issuing orders on his own. Jirosaburo's commands were absolutely stunning. They were efficient and appropriate—as if they were coming from Ieyasu himself. Tadakatsu particularly marveled when Jirosaburo fiercely ordered that warning shots be fired in the direction of Kobayakawa Hideaki, who had promised to switch sides but had remained stationary on Matsuon-yama. It was a truly daring move. The attack could very well have brought a counterattack from Kobayakawa, but Jirosaburo's intuition was accurate. Kobayakawa was stunned by the fusillade, but as the shots echoed, he launched his forces against the encampment of Otani Gyobu Yoshitsugu, who had allied with Ishida. With this, the course of events of the battle was set. By two in the afternoon, the Tokugawa victory was indisputable. The battle had lasted six hours, and it was said that on the Ishida side alone there were some 8,000 casualties, of which 4,000 were deaths. During the battle, there had been no time to eat, and in the evening, when it came time for the Tokugawa forces to cook their rice, it was stained cinnabar red. The battle had been a literal bloodbath.

It is recorded that on the twentieth day of the ninth month Ieyasu entered Otsu Castle and remained there until the morning of the twenty-sixth.

At the urgent entreaty of Honda Tadakatsu, Tenkai, who was at Mt. Hiei, proceeded to Otsu on the twenty-first. Tadakatsu was among the very few who knew that Tenkai in his earlier incarnation was Akechi Mitsuhide. That was precisely why, ten years earlier, Tenkai had sent Jirosaburo, wearing a mask and bearing a letter, directly to Tadakatsu, and why now again Tenkai, at great personal risk, came down from the religious sanctuary of Mt. Hiei and headed for Otsu Castle.

Upon arriving, he was kept waiting by himself in a small room for an hour. Finally a man entered. It was Ieyasu. But what happened next astonished Tenkai. Ieyasu took a lower seat, and prostrated himself before Tenkai.

"Has your Lordship forgotten my face?" asked *Ieyasu*, as he raised himself upright and looked intently at Tenkai.

"I Im...?"

Tenkai looked back at him. From the time when he went by the name Akechi Mitsuhide and served under Oda Nobunaga, Tenkai had been on intimate terms with Ieyasu. But that had been some eighteen years earlier. Both of them had grown older. But...the longer he looked, the more peculiar the sensation he had. Where could it be coming from? Tenkai abruptly closed his eyes—the better to peer deep into his own memory.

"Hm."

When he opened his eyes once more and looked again at the man before him, he understood why he had experienced that peculiar sensation. The man before him was *virtually* a stranger, but not a complete stranger. This time, he did not need to close his eyes. In a flash, a long-forgotten face came from the depths of his mind: the face of a wandering samurai running toward him carrying on his shoulder a woman servant with large white buttocks!

"Well, well." Tenkai laughed softly.

"Yes. I am that wandering bandit you encountered, sir." *Ieyasu* responded with no trace of a smile, his expression a brooding one. "I would like to ask you to honor the promise that you made on that occasion." His tone was one of desperation.

"Eh?"

"'I promise you security for as long as you live'—that is what Your Reverence promised me."

Tenkai said nothing. There was no doubt that something abnormal had occurred. No warrior with the status of Honda Tadakatsu would destroy a long-lasting friendship and call Tenkai all the way to this highly dangerous castle in Otsu merely to ensure the safety of a *kagemusha*.

"How can a *kagemusha* who has lost his master go on living?"

This time Tenkai was rocked from the depths of his being. And at that very moment, Honda Tadakatsu entered the room.

It was Tadakatsu who explained to Tenkai the facts of Ieyasu's untimely death. Tenkai gradually began to grasp how the single small pebble he had cast upon the waters ten years earlier had given rise to enormous unforeseen ripples in human affairs. Fortunately, victory had been snatched from the enemy at Sekigahara. To that extent, Sarada Jirosaburo Motonobu had played a crucial role. Under normal circumstances, the death of Ieyasu would be announced; he would be mourned in an elaborate funeral; Jirosaburo would be retired after being given an appropriate allowance for services rendered. But there were circumstances that did not allow such a natural procedure.

What prevented that was the presence of Hideyori in Osaka Castle. The remaining warlords who received patronage from the Taiko—Hideyori, the heir to Toyotomi Hideyoshi—made Hideyori's continued existence an even more imposing hindrance. It was precisely because Ieyasu was alive that Sekigahara had been such a decisive battle. It would be precisely because Ieyasu had survived the long period of successive battles to extend control over the land, and because he was alive and strong, that the military lords who enjoyed the patronage of the Taiko refrained from fighting and remained submissive. If Ieyasu were dead, that would leave only Ieyasu's second son, Yuki Hideyasu, who was twenty-six; his third son, Hidetada, who was twenty-two; and his fourth son Tadayoshi, who was twenty-one, as successors.

Regardless of which of these three succeeded to the Tokugawa leadership, he would be nothing more than a sniveling child in the eyes of those hardened military commanders. The country would once again fall into turmoil, the battle for hegemony more than likely becoming a struggle between Hideyori at Osaka Castle, with the support of the illustrious commander Kato Kiyomasa, Date Masamune to the east, Mori Terumoto in the west and possibly the Shimazu in Kyushu. The Tokugawa clan would drop out of the contest completely.

In order to exploit the victory at Sekigahara to forge indisputable control over the country, Ieyasu had to be kept alive. In other words, the only choice was to make the shadow warrior, Sarada Jirosaburo, the real Ieyasu. For ten full years, Jirosaburo had been serving as Ieyasu's double, and both Jirosaburo and Tadakatsu were confident that Jirosaburo could pass for the real thing in public. They were even confident of internal success as well. Immediately after the Battle of Sekigahara, Jirosaburo had dared to show his face in public, in hooded attire, to his military commanders to commend them for their meritorious service. On that occasion, Ieyasu's fourth son Tadayoshi and Tadayoshi's father-in-law Ii Naomasa had been present, and neither of the two realized that he was actually Jirosaburo. Both Tadayoshi and Naomasa had sustained wounds in the fighting, and Jirosaburo, with his own hands, placed ointment on their wounds. It was a considerable gamble, and Jirosaburo felt as if he were treading on thin ice, but his performance was a brilliant success. The reason was simple: with the exception of Honda Tadakatsu, none of the Four Tokugawa Devas—much less the hereditary bannermen below them—had ever seen Jirosaburo's face before. Whenever Jirosaburo had been present with Ieyasu, he had worn the mask. The same had been true when he was present with Ieyasu's own sons.

The only exceptions were those who knew Jirosaburo's face quite well: the women he had slept with, and Ieyasu's third son, Hidetada.

The historical appraisal of Hidetada is for the most part firmly established. The general view of him: considering that he was Ieyasu's son, he was surprisingly conscientious, remarkably filial, and henpecked. But that appraisal is entirely one-sided, and mistaken. In reality, Hidetada was the most ferocious of all of Ieyasu's offspring. The source of this ferocity was simple: Hidetada was not a genius. He knew that he wasn't, and he absolutely detested anyone who was.

Ieyasu's oldest son, Nobuyasu, and second son, Yuki Hideyasu, were both brilliant military commanders. Resolute and undaunted in courage, they were men born with all the markings of superior leaders. However, because they were men of genius, Nobuyasu aroused fear in Oda Nobunaga and Hideyasu aroused fear in Toyotomi Hideyoshi. Nobuyasu was killed, and Hideyasu was sent off to become the adopted son of the Taiko. Because Hidetada was a man of mediocre ability, he was left at Ieyasu's side and became first in the line of succession. Hidetada was clearly aware of why he had been left where he was. To put it bluntly, in the very marrow of his bones he knew that the Taiko, as well as the warlords and even his own father, Ieyasu, disdained him and held him in low esteem. Surrounded by such opinions, no man could possibly remain normal. In his innermost heart, Hidetada was constantly enraged. At his core, he seethed with hatred. Several times a day, in his mind, he brutally killed these men who looked upon him with scorn. How many times had he, similarly, flayed his own father alive and hacked him to pieces? Yet he knew his father's ferocity very well. Ieyasu had killed his own son to save his own skin. Hidetada's extraordinary conscientiousness, his remarkable filial piety and his allowing himself to be bossed around by his wife were all a cover, a mask that he wore in order to survive.

As one would expect, Ieyasu saw through Hidetada's subterfuges. Ieyasu's own hardships and the stoicism bred during his own early years as a political hostage resembled Hidetada's situation. Curiously enough, because of this, Ieyasu actually felt esteem for his son. Like Hidetada, Ieyasu also detested geniuses.

"He's a fearsome man," Ieyasu said to Tadakatsu one day. "When I die, Heihachiro, you will probably be murdered, poisoned."

Tadakatsu remembered Ieyasu's words distinctly—as did Jirosaburo in the adjacent room. The two men also remembered that Ieyasu would never take medicine prescribed by any physician that Hidetada had sent around. Ieyasu's caution was that of a man who had managed to live through extremely turbulent times.

How would this Hidetada take the news of the death of Ieyasu? That was the issue. Taking everything else into consideration, even if one had to use a stand-in, keeping Ieyasu alive was to the advantage of the Tokugawa clan as a whole. But there was a significant risk that all of the grudges and hatred that Hidetada had suppressed over the years might suddenly on this occasion come bursting forth. If that happened, Jirosaburo would be killed. That was what Jirosaburo was referring to when he reminded Tenkai of the latter's promise of protection. That is, Jirosaburo was asking Tenkai to talk Hidetada into going along with the ruse.

"Why me?"

It was a natural question for Tenkai to ask, because he had never met Hidetada face to face. It was preposterous to think that Hidetada would listen to anything a priest from Mt. Hiei would tell him, especially a priest who was a complete stranger.

"There's nothing imprudent at all about the idea."

The words were Tadakatsu's. Tadakatsu then told him the astonishing facts of what had occurred.

Hidetada had always liked Akechi Mitsuhide. He admired Mitsuhide as the ill-fated, ordinary general who had stood in contrast to the genius commander Nobunaga. Born in an illustrious house, Mitsuhide managed to become the lord of a castle but only after wandering through the provinces and enduring enormous hardships. And then he was disgraced as a traitor because of a certain man of genius. Mitsuhide's perceived innermost feelings were ones that Hidetada could understand with great empathy, almost as if they were his very own. Only to those closest to him did Hidetada ever disclose these thoughts. What was frightening was that every single one of those words, spoken in strictest confidence, reached Ieyasu. So Jirosaburo knew about this, and that was why he had immediately thought of summoning Tenkai. Hidetada had been late in arriving at the momentous battle at Sekigahara. It was a full five days after the opening battle that he had finally reached Otsu and requested an audience with Ieyasu. Jirosaburo had consulted with Tadakatsu and refused the initial request. It was an entirely appropriate punishment for Hidetada's having arrived late for an important battle, but to Jirosaburo, it was an extremely dangerous gamble. There was no doubt about it— Tenkai was the only one to whom Jirosaburo could turn.

After a long silence, Tenkai gave his assent. He did so not for Jirosaburo—or for that matter, for the future of the Tokugawa clan. One reason was that he had grown weary of seclusion after eighteen years at the religious center on Mt. Hiei. A second reason was that, as a result of the death of his third daughter, Hosokawa Gracia, his hatred of the Toyotomi clan had grown only the more fierce.

That evening, led by Tadakatsu, Tenkai visited Hidetada's camp. It is said that Hidetada went into raptures when he learned that the man before him was actually Mitsuhide. Tadakatsu urged Tenkai-Mitsuhide to join his retinue, but the priest declined. Tenkai then explained the matter of Jirosaburo. If they maintained the momentum that Ieyasu had built up with the advantages achieved at Sekigahara, the Tokugawa could prune and then transplant the various provincial lords like so many potted plants. There would be no one left to oppose the Tokugawa, other than the master of Osaka Castle, Hideyori. The imperial court would have no option other than to appoint Ieyasu as *Seiitai shogun*. He would accept the appointment, set up headquarters in Edo, and establish a bakufu-domain system. And finally, he would destroy Hideyori at Osaka Castle. Once he had let *Ieyasu* complete these objectives, Hidetada would succeed as the second-generation shogun. By that time, among all the daimyo of the country, there would be not a single one who could stand against the Tokugawa bakufu. This, said Tenkai, was the path that Hidetada should take—the most ingenious strategy for gaining power.

Tenkai was astonished at how readily Hidetada accepted the proposed strategy. The only condition that Hidetada set was that the shogunate be handed over to him within a period of two years. Hidetada added, with a creepy smile on his face, that three years of being shogun would whet any man's appetite. Tenkai realized that Jirosaburo and Tadakatsu's estimation of Hidetada had been right on target. They had correctly intuited Hidetada's underlying ferocity. However, it would be extremely difficult to defeat the Toyotomi clan within a mere two years. Moreover, toppling the Toyotomi was something that only Ieyasu could do. Even if Hidetada were to accept the imperial appointment as shogun, he lacked the ability to do the job. Hidetada and Tenkai entered lengthy negotiations on this point. Because of that, the records indicate that Ieyasu refused Hidetada's request for an audience for three full days.

In the end, it was Tenkai who came up with a solution. There would be a two-tier administration, one in which the retired shogun would still control affairs of state, in effect acting as shogun. The system emulated the *insei* system, cloistered rule, in which a retired emperor exercised real power behind the actual throne.

THE NORTHWEST PASSAGE

On the twenty-first day of the first month of Keicho 8 (1603), ensconced at Fushimi Castle, Ieyasu received the unofficial notification that he was to be appointed *Seiitai shogun*. The formal ceremony for his appointment was the twelfth day of the second month. On that occasion, Ieyasu, at the age of sixty-two, became the head of all the military houses in the country. It was three years after Sekigahara.

In actual fact, on the twentieth of the second month of the previous year, the imperial court had discreetly intimated that it was prepared to make Ieyasu shogun, but he had declined the appointment. Historians generally explain this by pointing out that Ieyasu had not yet settled scores with the Shimazu clan in the southwest, but could that really have been the case?

Following his victory at Sekigahara, Ieyasu distributed generous rewards to those who had sided with him, moving warlords about and arranging their holdings just as a cultivator trims his bonsai to suit his own designs. In the process, he made the Tokugawa position unshakable. He divided up the 6,000,000 *koku* fiefs that he had taken away from the daimyo who had joined the western alliance that fought against him. As a result, the Toyotomi clan's domains had been reduced from 2,000,000 *koku* to a mere 650,000 *koku*. In contrast, the directly-ruled lands of the Tokugawa clan swelled from somewhat over 1,000,000 to 2,500,000 *koku*. Further, the affiliated Tokugawa families as well as the *fudai* daimyo—the hereditary vassals of the Tokugawa—numbered sixty-eight. Now that things had come to such a pass, regardless of what the single domain of the Shimazu did, it would make hardly any difference. Might Ieyasu's declining the appointment simply been a diversionary tactic, one that Ieyasu-Jirosaburo used in dealing with Hidetada? To decline the long-awaited appointment to head the shogunate no doubt must have stunned Hidetada and kept him in suspense.

Ieyasu-Jirosaburo also restrained and nettled Hidetada in other ways. One example was the fact that he sought counsel with his senior vassals regarding his successor.

According to the *Tokugawa Jikki*, shortly after the Battle of Sekigahara, Ieyasu-Jirosaburo assembled his key retainers—Okubo Tadachika, Honda Masanobu, Ii Naomasa, Honda Tadakatsu and Hiraiwa Chikayoshi—and in all seriousness asked them which of his children they felt was most suitable to follow him as head of the Tokugawa clan. It is said that one after another named either Yuki Hideyasu or Ieyasu's fourth son, Tadanobu, but that only Okubo Tadachika pulled for Hidetada. Ieyasu-Jirosaburo waited two days before announcing his decision. Hidetada must have been scared stiff.

Moreover, even after Ieyasu-Jirosaburo had become shogun and the expected two-year period was coming to an end, he seemed in no hurry to pass the reins of government to Hidetada. It was the seventh day of the fourth month of Keicho 10 (1605) before he reluctantly yielded the position of shogun—under threat from Hidetada. Two months earlier, in the second month, Hidetada had led a large army, of 100,000 troops, out of Edo and into the capital at Kyoto. In Osaka, Toyotomi Hideyori immediately went on the alert, and the residents of Kyoto shuddered with the premonition that another battle was about to ensue. But in actual fact, this was nothing more than Hidetada's way of intimidating Ieyasu-Jirosaburo. On the sixteenth of the fourth month, the title of shogun passed without incident into the hands of Hidetada.

As Tenkai had proposed, Ieyasu-Jirosaburo became the retired shogun and moved to Sumpu. A two-tiered administration was established between Edo and Sumpu, but this was primarily a façade, as virtually all of the decisions were made by Hidetada. However, because Ieyasu's name was used, later historians mistakenly assume that it was actually Ieyasu who was in charge. Hidetada was the one who encouraged this view, and he did so out of cunning. The strategy employed to annihilate the Toyotomi clan also sprang from his covert methods. He began by having the Toyotomi vassal daimyo killed off with poison, one after another. Four of them—Akino Nagamasa, Horio Yoshiharu, Kato Kiyomasa and Sanada Masayuki—all died within a three-month period in Keicho 16. The last three died in a single month. No matter how one sees it, all three deaths could not have been the result of natural causes.

Ieyasu-Jirosaburo knew, naturally enough, that this was Hidetada's doing. Realizing the accuracy of the deceased Ieyasu's perceptions of Hidetada, Jirosaburo was left feeling an unpleasant chill in the air. When the Toyotomi met their doom, he was convinced that he would be next, probably done in with poison.

Unfortunately, around this time, Ieyasu-Jirosaburo began to feel an attachment to the world around him. The reason was a woman. During his days as a *kagemusha*, Jirosaburo had shared his bedchamber with a number of ladies in waiting, but none of those relations blossomed into true affection, and falling in love would not have been allowed in any case. But things had changed, and he now fell in love—with Oman, Okatsu, Oume, Onatsu and Oroku. Oman gave birth to Chofukumaru (later Kishu Yorinobu) and Tsuruchiyo (later Mito Yorifusa). Okatsu gave birth to Ichihime. They were all born after he reached the age of sixty. It was truly as if all that he had held inside during his years as a double for Ieyasu had suddenly burst forth all at once. As one might expect, Hidetada was incensed by these actions, but there was nothing he could do to prevent them. However, it was because of this that once it was formally established that the lord of Mito domain could not succeed to the position of shogun, Hidetada strongly opposed allowing the lord of Kishu domain to take the position, either.

Ieyasu-Jirosaburo vigorously pursued means of staying alive. In Keicho 5 (1600), after the Battle of Sekigahara, among those he met for the first time was the English pilot William Adams. Adams was aboard the Dutch ship *Liefde* when it was shipwrecked, and he drifted ashore in Bungo province. It was amazing how well Ieyasu-Jirosaburo and Adams seemed to get along with one another. They had something in common that transcended the language barrier. Adams had boarded the *Liefde* in order to explore and develop the Northwest Passage. This was the sea route believed to connect England to the Pacific Ocean via the northern extremity of the American continent. The sea route from Europe eastward around the southern tip of Africa to India was monopolized by the Portuguese. The route westward via the Strait of Magellan to the Pacific and Indian oceans was monopolized by Spain.

For England, therefore, the only remaining route was to the northwest. Adams described his dream of finding the Northwest Passage with great enthusiasm, and his passion kindled a fire within Ieyasu-Jirosaburo's heart as well.

Ieyasu is known as a merchant-shogun, but that appellation was applied to him only after Jirosaburo became the new Ieyasu. His goal was the accumulation of wealth. His employing Okubo Nagayasu, placing mining in every province under direct shogunal control and digging for gold and silver everywhere conceivable was all to the same purpose. Why would money be so important for someone who had moved to Sumpu and become a political puppet? When Ieyasu died, it was said that some 6,000,000 *ryo* of gold was stashed away inside his castle at Sumpu.

Formerly the Hojo clan had owned a warship called *Ataka Maru*. When the Hojo were annihilated, this vessel came into the possession of the Taiko, Hideyoshi. Following the Osaka Summer Campaign, the first thing Ieyasu-Jirosaburo did was to take possession of the vessel. He ordered Adams to overhaul it and make it seaworthy, just like the *Liefde*. On the fifteenth of the twelfth month of the first year of Genna (1615), seven months after the Toyotomi clan was obliterated, Ieyasu-Jirosaburo ordered built a retreat for his old age at Izumigashira near Izu Mishima. It was built secretly, and he specifically ordered that day laborers be employed in its construction. Once the work on the *Ataka Maru* was completed, he intended to use the villa as a base for exploration of the Northwest Passage. Hidetada discovered the scheme, and a month later, early in Genna 2, construction was halted. And on the twenty-first of that same month, on Ieyasu-Jirosaburo's return home from a hawking expedition, he fell ill. He doggedly hung on for almost three more months, but finally died on the seventeenth of the fourth month. He was seventy-five years old, and it was almost certain that he died from poisoning.

A LESSER CUCKOO

The wind was whistling.

With the cold air blowing on his skin, Seiichiro woke up. He was completely naked, with only a deep-blue lined kimono thrown across him. The room was still submerged in the half-light of early morning.

He could hear the faint breathing of someone sleeping, and when he looked beside him, he saw Obaba-sama lying fast asleep. She too was completely naked, with only a white vestment covering her.

On her noble face, he saw signs of complete exhaustion. She seemed to have expended all of her sexual energies, but somehow she exuded all the more a mysterious seductiveness that one could call enchantingly beautiful.

Seiichiro too was languorous from exhaustion. His dreams had worn him out completely. He had been dreaming all the way from noon the previous day to dawn, and in his dreams he had lived through the life of a peculiar man named Sarada Jirosaburo Motonobu. It was only natural that he would be exhausted. The fatigue of Obaba-sama, who had caused him to have such dreams, must have been several times worse.

Noticing that perspiration glistened on Obaba-sama's white forehead, Seiichiro gently wiped it with his finger. Her face was as cool and smooth as white porcelain. His finger slipped down along the side of her nose and traced the shape of her lips. From there it followed the tip of her chin and down her throat. Slowly, it lifted the robe that covered her.

A fragrant, fresh perfume made him numb. Her breasts were small, but even when she was lying down, they were pointed. Gently his finger traced the areola of her nipple. He touched her nipple and felt a ripple pass through her body.

Her lips parted slightly.

His finger descended further, down toward a shadowy verge. Once more a tremor passed over her body, while her legs rose up and slowly spread to left and right. His finger slipped naturally into the valley between them and sank within her.

A thick, musky fragrance rose up.

Seiichiro languidly raised himself and entered her. He was drawn inside, enveloped in the rhythm of folds of flesh tensing and relaxing.

His mind was blank. How had all this happened to him? He had no idea. Things had simply happened. He heard a voice somewhere saying that it was all right.

The wind whistled, the trees blew, and the grasses rustled. He was somewhere deep in the Kumano mountain range. Far away, the sea also sounded. When people are frightened of the sea, the forest, and the gods, and when they feel weak, as if they were so many minute poppy seeds, the only thing for them to do is to embrace one another. As the gentle rhythm repeated itself over and over, Seiichiro's mind filled with fear, and his cheeks grew wet.

"Thank you."

He heard Obaba-sama speak faintly. Her legs were lifted high, and she was desperately grasping his back.

A cuckoo cried once, as if it were coughing up blood.

The leaves of the *mikaeri* willow fluttered in the strong wind.

It was said that in autumn, when a strong wind blew in Edo, it was either from the west or the northwest. That day, it was a westerly wind, and it lashed directly against the face of anyone climbing the Fifty-Ken Road.

Holding Obaba-sama's hand tightly, Oshabu with her other hand brushed aside the willow leaves that struck her face. She was unutterably sad. Obaba-sama's departures were always unforeseen.

When Obaba-sama had appeared at breakfast that morning, she was packed and ready to leave. Her worn, pale face, with its subdued seductiveness, was so beautiful that it made one shudder.

"I've performed my role here, so I'll be returning to Kumano."

She added that she would be returning by boat. Gensai attempted to convince her to stay longer, but she would not.

"This time, my duties have really worn me out, and if I stay any longer, I may no longer wish to return home."

Deep in her eyes, Gensai saw something helpless and not altogether in jest, and for a moment he stopped breathing. But when he spoke, his voice was one of laughter.

"It seems that this old heart of mine can still burn with jealousy."

Obaba-sama laughed like a girl, and then she quickly pressed the corners of her eyes with her sleeve.

Without understanding what it was all about, Oshabu felt an unexpected turmoil within her.

(Somehow, this involves Sei-sama)

Oshabu was alert to the fact that what Obaba-sama and Gensai were talking about was an extremely important secret involving Seiichiro.

"Oshabu, you're a fortunate young woman. Hold tight to Sei-sama with everything you have in you and don't ever let him go."

Oshabu nodded.

"When you turn fifteen…"

Obaba-sama's pronouncement was startling.

"…become Sei-sama's woman. Here…"

In a flash, Obaba-sama's hand spread Oshabu's knees and nestled against her mound. Her finger lovingly caressed her, then penetrated.

"Take Sei-sama in, but…"

After a moment of pain, Oshabu's knees were back as they had been. Obaba-sama smiled radiantly.

"You mustn't be jealous."

Oshabu nodded once more. Gensai swallowed hard. He had been assaulted by a wave of sexual excitement.

To the right along Nihon Embankment, past the gravel pit, on the other side of Imado Bridge at the foot of Matsuchiyama, there was a boat landing. A plank landing pier jutted out into the river, and several boats were moored there. Most of them were broad boats or roofed boats, but among them was a single "boar's tooth" boat with a sharp, narrow prow. Obaba-sama said she was going to take this swift boat out to a cargo vessel off the coast.

After being bid farewell by Seiichiro, Oshabu, Gensai, Jinnojo, Miuraya Shirozeaemon, Nomura Gen'i and the others, Obaba-sama boarded the unstable narrow boat, without the least bit of difficulty. Gen'i nimbly climbed in after her. He was to serve as her bodyguard.

Obaba-sama looked straight into Seiichiro's eyes.

"Do not forget that thoughtfulness at the first light of dawn. That—is the ultimate love."

Seiichiro's face blushed slightly. Without saying a word, he bowed his head to her.

"Fifteen years from now, we will probably meet again. On that occasion, you will come to Kumano. Next time, it will be on the top of a mountain where the sea will glisten, the leaves of the trees will flicker and the grasses will shine…"

All of a sudden, with eyes half-closed, Obaba-sama smiled.

(So, fifteen years from now I'm going to Kumano)

Seiichiro took her announcement as truth, as if their meeting were predestined.

Miuraya Shirozaemon bent his enormous body and with great effort untied the mooring line. For someone of his enormous girth, that act was one of great service on her behalf. Immediately sweat began to pour down his face. With both hands, he pushed off the boat. His thrust and the boatman's push on the pole were in perfect sync, and the boat immediately moved away from the Sanya embankment and into the Okawa River.

"Oshabu, go on home with your father. I have some things to talk over with Sei-san," Gensai said.

Upon hearing this, Oshabu was close to tears, but she bravely held them back, turned around and rushed off. Jinnojo hurried off after her.

"Poor thing. She's turned into quite a young woman," Gensai muttered to himself.

Seiichiro was silent, but he understood well what Gensai meant. True enough, during Obaba-sama's stay, Oshabu had suddenly begun to look more mature. Moreover, she had become surprisingly beautiful. Without any definite reason, Seiichiro understood what Gensai was trying to say. Come to think of it, Seiichiro himself had changed considerably during the month or so since he arrived in Yoshiwara.

Gensai slapped him on the back.

"Let's climb up Matsuchiyama. From there, we should be able to see Obaba-sama's boat all the way."

Miuraya Shirozaemon quickly broke in:

"You'll have to forgive me, but there's no way that I can climb up there. It would kill me, it really would."

He wagged his head, which was already covered with sweat, as if he were trembling from fear at the mere prospect of having to climb the hill.

At the top of the long stone staircase was a shrine to worship Shoten, or more properly Daishokanki Jizaiten.

The head of the object of worship was that of an elephant, the body that of a human being, and it was sometimes a single figure or a pair of figures. Where the figure was a pair, they were a male deity and a female deity embracing.

Walking around behind the shrine, they had a panoramic view over the entire Okawa River.

Off in the distance, they could see the boat Obaba-sama had boarded poling along hurriedly. She tilted her woven-straw hat to one side and waved her hand.

A surge of emotion filled Seiichiro's breast. Even if she reached Osaka safely, she then had to face the long mountain trail leading to Kumano. She had made that long, long journey all for the purpose of letting him have those dreams, and now, she was retracing her path back to Kumano. What was there about him that made him worthy of all that effort, expended by the leader of all the Kumano priestesses? He could find no rationale for it at all.

He felt immersed in sadness. Fifteen years was too far into the future. He wanted to follow her immediately. If he could just go, he would do anything at all to be of service to her.

Gensai seemed to read the feelings conveyed by Seiichiro's sad expression.

"Kindheartedness is a bad thing, you know."

"Yes?"

"Sei-san, every time you have an encounter with a woman, you think about throwing away anything and everything for her. Right?"

"I suppose that's true."

"You're not wrong to feel like that. I suppose that's what it means for a man to be kindhearted. But if it happens each and every time, do you really think you'll last very long? No, and I'm not just talking about you. The woman involved wouldn't last long, either."

Seiichiro remained silent.

"That's why I say that being kindhearted is a bad thing. I'm in no position to blame you for it, because I used to be exactly the same. That's why I'm telling you this. You can call me brutal, but I'm telling you the truth."

Gensai's voice had a crushing impact, the kind that only truth can generate.

Seiichiro simply stood dazed, looking into Gensai's eyes.

KOSAKA JINNAI

It was the sixteenth year of the Keicho era (1611). Gensai—Shoji Jinnai—had turned thirty-six. Eleven years had passed since he first arrived in Edo.

During those years, he had in effect risen to the position of boss of the gay quarter facing Motoseiganji Temple.

The quarter had originally been in Kyobashi Yanagimachi, but in preparation for the restoration of Edo Castle in Keicho 10, that area was taken over by the government. The quarter was ordered to relocate to Nihonbashi Muromachi. In the sixth month of 1604, it was decided to rebuild Edo Castle, and after a year and nine months of preparation, the actual work began in the third month of Keicho 11. By the following year, the work on the castle had been completed. It was at this time that Jinnai submitted his first petition to the government, the gist of which was that he requested permission to consolidate all of the pleasure quarters in Edo in one location as a licensed quarter. The bakufu rejected his petition point-blank. One reason it did so was that it saw at a glance that the opinions of the three pleasure quarters in Edo—Kojimachi, Kamakura Quay and Yanagimachi—did not necessarily agree.

Jinnai became painfully aware of his powerlessness. He was still too young, a mere 30 years old. He therefore made efforts to become more influential. In this world, power meant money, women and military might. Jinnai made an appeal to all the Kugutsu of various provinces, gathered together the most beautiful women and looked for men of exceptional talent. Already in the Yanagimachi quarter was a man named Yamamoto Hojun, who became his aide. All the men and women hid their Kugutsu origins and disguised themselves as commoners. Among those who assembled were the Rokuji-ryu swordsmanship master Nomura Gen'i, the Niten'ichi-ryu masters Namiki Genzaemon and Yamada Sannojo, and the business genius Miuraya Shirozaemon.

Little by little, the pleasure quarter at the entrance to Motoseiganji came to be filled with people from the Kugutsu puppeteer clan. At the same time, Kugutsu who were trusted confidantes of Jinnai nonchalantly began establishing positions of influence in the quarters in Kojimachi and Kamakura Quay as well. There was no one in the world of pleasure who could compete with men or women of the puppeteer clans, who were natural-born appreciators of life. Even in terms of military talent, aside from the professional samurai, virtually no bands of fighting men were a match for the Kugutsu, who were originally a hunting people. Even the ninja bands of Iga and Koga went out of their way to avoid fighting against the Kugutsu.

Five years after the move to Motoseiganji, the pleasure quarter there was thriving, to the detriment of the other two quarters, and Jinnai had gathered considerable influence.

During that time, within the core leadership of the bakufu, Honda Heihachiro Tadakatsu—Ieyasu-Jirosaburo's chief supporter—had died, in Keicho 15 (1610), and Tenkai finally left Mt. Hiei to take a role in the headquarters of the government in Tadakatsu's stead.

Jinnai had been the first to realize that Ieyasu had been replaced by someone else after the Battle of Sekigahara, but he had remained uncertain as to how to employ that information. He recognized immediately that if the current Ieyasu was simply a stand-in, the real political power was being exercised by the second-generation shogun, that is, Hidetada, and that if Jinnai were to carelessly mention to anyone that he knew about Ieyasu's double, he and his entire clan would stand in danger of extermination.

Jinnai had therefore simply stood by and waited. He watched the movements of Ieyasu-Jirosaburo, the movements of Hidetada, just speculating and calculating. Finally in Keicho 16, he came to a conclusion. He decided that there was no point at all in submitting a petition for a licensed pleasure quarter to the bakufu controlled by Hidetada. Despite all the obstacles, the petition should be submitted directly to Ieyasu-Jirosaburo.

Jinnai's observations over those eleven years hit the mark. At the time, the bakufu was rapidly falling into the hands of young bureaucrats. The older retainers who had survived the civil wars that had ravaged the nation—the Era of Warring States—and who were tolerant in various matters were being replaced by a younger group of men who were close to Hidetada. They came from the hereditary vassals of the Tokugawa and were far less flexible. Though Hideyori was still in good health and occupying Osaka Castle and presentiments of a battle with him still lingered, the eleven years of peace indicated that a period of public order and government control was at hand.

In comparison with what was going on in Edo, what was happening among those close to the retired shogun Ieyasu-Jirosaburo at Sumpu? Things there were different in every way from what the Tokugawa had experienced to date. Gathered there were Konji'in Suiden, Nankobo Tenkai, the Confucian scholar Hayashi Razan, Goto Shozaburo of the gold mint, the wealthy Kyoto merchant Chaya Shirojiro, the master carpenter Nakai Yamato, the Englishman Will Adams. True enough, there was also Honda Masazumi—clearly a bureaucratic type—but he was the son of the former falconer Honda Masanobu, who had turned his back on the Tokugawa at the Mikawa uprising. In other words, these were all people who could understand the value of *muen*—exemption from conventional social norms—and *kukai*—sanctuaries and refuges where freedom and protection were assured. And they could empathize with the *michimichi no tomogara*, the "companions of the way." The puppeteer clan could hope for no more favorable assemblage of powerful figures to approach.

It was time. Jinnai had made his decision. He had decided that he had to meet Ieyasu and submit his petition directly to him. Of course, it would be impossible to gain entrance to Sumpu Castle. The only option was to watch for an opportune moment while Ieyasu was out hawking. In actual fact, whenever Ieyasu-Jirosaburo went hawking, he received an enormous number of petitions from farmers near the hawking grounds, and in each case, he took measures that proved advantageous to the farmers. This was nothing less than a means of harassing Hidetada's autocratic rule, but the public had no way of realizing that. Jinnai himself was unaware of that part. At any rate, the knowledge that at the hawking grounds Ieyasu-Jirosaburo would casually meet with farmers and listen to their pleas was of enormous import to Jinnai. He then secretly investigated where Ieyasu was planning to go and when. Once he had learned of the planned hawking expeditions, Jinnai selected Shimosa Togane.

Having learned from his painful experience of the previous petition, this time he devoted more than enough energy to behind-the-scenes consensus-building with those who operated the Kojimachi and Kamakura Quay pleasure quarters. Still there was opposition from one man in Kamakura Quay: Okada Kurouemon, a man inordinately fearful of the government, a single-minded pragmatist and a brothel master from the bottom of his heart. One day, this very same Kurouemon suddenly died from blowfish poisoning, and that was the end of the opposition. After Jinnai had discovered when Ieyasu intended to hunt at Shimosa Togane and made plans to take action in one month's time, another man blocked Jinnai's path.

The man's name was Kosaka Jinnai. He was the son of the ferocious general Kosaka Danjo, who had made a name for himself within the Takeda clan as "Danjo of the Spear."

As a child, Kosaka Jinnai was known as Jintaro. After the downfall of the Takeda clan, he had been taken in by his grandfather and had lived in Akugawa in Settsu province. As a young man, he had become a disciple of the master swordsman Miyamoto Musashi and had come with Musashi to Edo at the age of twenty-one. In Edo, he had tried out his skills on a passerby and robbed the man of fifty *ryo*. Legend has it that this event was the beginning of his fall from grace. He was expelled by Musashi, and he eventually went into hiding at Soshu Hiratsuka, becoming the boss of a gang of bandits. However, the name Jinnai does not appear in any of the records of Musashi, so the story that he was once a disciple of the master must be taken with a grain of salt. There was no doubt, however, that he was a wandering samurai and an exceptional swordsman. He was said to have a following of fifty, or even a hundred. They made their living by robbing people, but such men also took employment as mercenaries, also carrying out the work of foragers and spies. In this sense, they were auxiliary troops for the battling warlords. Consequently, as long as there were no highly reliable witnesses to a crime, it was very difficult to inflict punishment on them. Kosaka Jinnai's robberies were distinguished by the fact that he slaughtered everyone present. His ruthlessness in not leaving so much as a three-year-old child alive resulted in no one being able to prove that he was the perpetrator of these crimes. Rumors arose, of course, but it was not possible to execute someone on the basis of a mere rumor.

That Shoji Jinnai became entangled with Kosaka Jinnai was due to a peculiar woman named Osei. At the time she suddenly appeared at Jinnai's shop in Motoseiganji, she was nineteen. It was in the early afternoon of the twelfth day of the last month of Keicho 16 (1611).

Shoji Jinnai had not shown his face in the shop that day because he had spent the whole day in his private quarters at the back, contemplating a method of approaching Ieyasu. The hawking expedition to Shimosa Togane was to take place in the middle of the first month of the new year. That was less than a month away. He had polished and refined the text of the petition, but the content was rather mild. What was crucial was the verbal presentation, and that was the subject of his contemplations that day. He decided not to criticize the bakufu's extremely discriminatory policies. He concluded it would be more effective to appeal on behalf of the puppeteer clan and others exempt from conventional social ties who found themselves in desperate straits. He would appeal to emotion rather than to intellect. Moreover, whatever he said would have to be concise. No man would listen to a long-winded plea in the middle of a hawking expedition. He would have to be brief, and effective. He shook his head furiously, as if to shake off all the superfluous things that he really wanted to say. Just then, his chief clerk Yashichi called to him from the corridor.

Yashichi said that a curious woman was at the entrance of the shop insisting that she had to speak with the master and that she would not budge until she did.

"Is she good-looking?"

"Well..."

Yashichi stumbled over a reply. For his head clerk, who had long experience in dealing with women, it was a peculiar response.

"To be honest, I really don't know."

He spoke as if he were despairing of forming an answer. If he didn't know whether she was good-looking or not, it could only mean that she was either quite idiosyncratic, or that she was tremendously alluring.

"She's that appealing?"

Poking fun at the clerk elicited a shaking of the head.

"No...it's not really that. It's just...looking at her makes me feel warm..."

Jinnai gasped. Yashichi was blushing, all the way to the nape of his neck. Jinnai's curiosity was aroused.

"Okay, then, show her in."

That he was willing to meet a complete stranger, just as he was preparing this crucial plan, meant that he had already surrendered to the woman—but Jinnai was as yet unaware of the fact.

The woman introduced herself as Osei.

At first glance she didn't seem particularly beautiful. But her skin was as white as snow, and the whites of her eyes almost seemed tinged with blue, and clear enough to make one gasp. She sat down comfortably without the slightest shyness and looked straight at Jinnai. It wasn't as if she were staring at him, but rather as if she were gazing at a flower. From this languor, there came on the other hand a vague sense of freshness, like a rustling breeze.

"Are you a Kugutsu woman?"

His inquiry was straight to the point. Osei nodded and told him the name of a clan head whom Jinnai knew. The man had died some time earlier, so the members of the clan must have scattered.

"Did you come to see me because you want to become a *yujo*?"

"If that's what you want me to do."

Her response was noncommittal to say the least.

"What do you mean?"

"I was told that everything would be fine if I were at your side."

As before, she seemed completely detached.

"Who told you that?"

"I don't know."

She seemed to be making fun of him.

"Stop talking nonsense."

"Someone in my head told me. Go to *another* Jinnai—that's what I was told. So, I came."

"Another Jinnai?"

"Kosaka Jinnai. He's a big, strong man. But it's useless now. In another two years he'll be dead."

If someone else had heard this conversation, he would undoubtedly have concluded that Osei was crazy. But Jinnai's expression was rigid with strain. The women of the Kugutsu clan were originally shrine maidens, and among them were women born with what might now be called extrasensory powers. They were born with one or more spiritual talents that included telekinesis, spirit possession, mind-reading, prediction, and thinking oneself to another location. Osei possessed the ability to see into the future. Jinnai had known one other woman with that ability—his sister Oshabu.

"The Hojo will be destroyed, next year, in the seventh month."

These were the first words Oshabu had said to him when she ordered him to follow her on a long ride and they had finally reached the top of a mountain overlooking the sea. That was in the autumn of Tensei 17 (1589). Jinnai was fourteen. His sister Oshabu, eight years older, had reached the pinnacle of authority as the favorite concubine of Hojo Ujimasa.

"I will die, and so will Father. How disappointing—to die at twenty-three!" Oshabu shouted with irritation, as she slid down from her horse. Jinnai quickly dismounted and grabbed the horse's reins.

"Leave the horse! Come here."

Jinnai offered no resistance at all. Everyone close to Oshabu knew that if they stood up to her when she was like this, there was no telling what might happen.

"Take off your clothes! Oh, this is so irritating! I am going to die and you are the only one who will survive!"

Jinnai protested.

"That can't be true. If you and Father die, I…"

"Hold your tongue. You don't understand anything about this. Come on, take your clothes off. How ridiculous! You'll be wounded, but you won't die. And take that off, too. Everything!"

She shouted, hopping mad, pointing at the loincloth Jinnai still wore. He surrendered to her demand and took that off as well. He should have been fine in front of his own sister, but he still felt a sense of embarrassment. He was squirming.

"How disgraceful! Stick out your chest! A man should throw out his chest, no matter what. That's the way a man is supposed to be. Yes, now that's the way!"

As she yelled, she deftly removed her own clothing. Her thin robe floated in the wind and her translucent naked body stood before him. The thick shadows beneath her arms and between her thighs trembled lightly in the breeze.

"Sister!"

Jinnai was in a dither. The chest that he had thrust forward suddenly collapsed.

"Hush! Lie down in the grass! Hurry!"

"But…"

"Hush. This is the only thing I can leave to you. Savor what it's like to be with a real woman. And don't forget as long as you live!"

Shouting loudly, she gently stroked Jinnai, and then took him into herself. From then until the sun set, without so much as an hour's respite, Oshabu continued going at Jinnai. He could not have counted the number of times that the slowly darkening blue sky fell down upon him. But forever etched in his memory was the way in which the faraway, brilliant gold ocean sparkled before it changed any number of hues and finally turned silvery gray.

In the seventh month of the year that followed, Odawara Castle fell and the Hojo clan was destroyed. Jinnai's father, Shoji Matazaemon, was killed in battle. The jealous Hojo Ujimasa, fearful that Oshabu might be seized by the Taiko, killed her with his own hands. Jinnai suffered severe wounds in the fighting, but aided by subordinates, he managed to reach safety in the post town of Yoshiwara on the Tokaido road. Everything came about just as Oshabu had foreseen.

Twenty-one years later, Jinnai had slept with a large number of women, but in all those years he had never come across a woman who surpassed his sister in sensuality.

By the time Jinnai had finally returned to his senses, she was in his arms. He had no idea when or how it had happened. She rested there gently, as if it were the most natural thing in the world. Abruptly, Jinnai felt the blue sky falling down on him. Ecstasy, as the deep blue dashed to pieces. This was it. This for certain was what Oshabu had shown him. His brain grew numb. He felt keenly to himself that although it had taken a full twenty-one years, this was it.

"Stay with me the rest of your life. I mean—please stay with me."

Their bare bodies still pressed together, Jinnai whispered into her ear, and she nodded her willingness. Relieved, Jinnai once again lost himself in her soft nakedness.

As she had promised on this occasion, Osei stayed at his side until she died on the eighteenth day of the tenth month of Keian 2 (1649). Their only child was a daughter named Nabe. The Oshabu who currently lived at Nishidaya was the child of this Nabe and Jinnojo. Jinnai had given her the name of his own elder sister, and because the name originally meant "woman who excels in the arts," it would be the perfect name for a top-ranking *yujo*.

Three days later, Kosaka Jinnai appeared at the door of the shop. He was a large man with thick hair like a bear, and the air of a wild beast.

He was blunt. "Osei."

"Is she your wife?"

Unconsciously Shoji Jinnai had begun to use the manner and language of his earlier days as a warrior. He looked Kosaka Jinnai over closely.

"No."

"Is she a slave?"

At that time, slavery had become illegal, but in fact there were still quite a number of slaves.

"No."

Kosaka Jinnai shook his head. At least he was not a liar. He wouldn't go to the trouble to lie.

"In that case, you can't take her back."

Without a word, Kosaka Jinnai reached into his sleeve, took out a stack of shiny, oval gold coins and slid it in front of Shoji Jinnai. There were 100 *ryo*.

"Osei is not a *yujo*. She can't be ransomed with money."

"In that case, how can I get her back?!"

Kosaka shouted with rage, but the next moment, he completely recovered, suppressed his anger and placed both hands on the tatami in entreaty.

"I'm begging you. Return her to me...please. Without her, I'm no good at all. Please understand. I'm begging you."

Jinnai understood Kosaka's feelings painfully well. Once could even say that he empathized with Kosaka, because after living with Osei for a mere several days, Jinnai was filled with the same feelings. Infatuation was not quite what he felt. Just the thought of her possibly going away brought a sense of uneasiness. The idea of losing her sent a chill through his body. It left him with the precise feeling that Kosaka had expressed: "Without her, I'm no good at all."

And therefore, all the more, the man's entreaties were pointless. There was no way that he could return Osei.

"Tomorrow, before dawn..."

Jinnai spoke almost without being aware of what he was saying. He listened to his own voice as if it belonged to someone else.

"We'll fight. If you win, you can take Osei with you."

Kosaka looked at Jinnai as if he couldn't quite believe his ears.

"Are you serious?"

"I'll leave the time and the place to you."

Kosaka shook his head a number of times out of pity.

That was why Yamamoto Hojun was livid with rage. In preparation for the following morning's duel, Jinnai had communicated to Hojun the plan he had come up with for approaching Ieyasu and the words he had so carefully worked out for that occasion, and then he had asked his assistant, Hojun, to take care of this momentous petition requesting a license for the pleasure quarter. Of course, these were precautionary measures in case Jinnai fell in the duel.

"I seriously misjudged you!" Hojun shouted. "Five years! We've been waiting for this kind of opportunity for five years. And now...after all that...are you planning to throw all that away for one woman?"

"What can a man ever accomplish if he can't protect one woman? And moreover, a woman of our clan?"

"What a worthless excuse. You're just infatuated with that woman. You're mad over her and abandoning your important duties as a man. That's all you're doing."

"I've fought many times until now and I've never lost. I'll win this time, too. But I've told you about this just in case something goes wrong. That's all."

"Kosaka Jinnai is a scoundrel. He's not about to come after you one-on-one. Tell me the time and place he sets, and we'll take care of things somehow. But when it comes to approaching the retired shogun, there is no one who can do that except you. In this entire quarter, the only one who knows Sarada Jirosaburo Motonobu is you."

Reason was on Hojun's side. And yet, Jinnai was still not disposed to abandon his duel with Kosaka. In the first place, Jinnai himself had been the one to issue the challenge, and if he called on the services of Hojun, it was clear that a large number of men would show up and kill Kosaka. Jinnai could not allow that to happen. There was meaning in two men who where in love with the same woman meeting face to face and fighting it out. He simply could not allow that to degenerate into a shabby assassination of a rival. Jinnai remained tight-lipped. However much Hojun implored him, Jinnai refused to tell him when and where the duel was to be fought. And then, taking advantage of a brief moment when Hojun ran off to ask for help from Miuraya Shirozaemon, Nomura Gen'i and the others, Jinnai left the house with just his long and short

Chinese swords. He sat up all night in a drinking place on the outskirts of town, and at six the next morning, he was at the appointed riverbank.

Jinnai realized how idealistic he had been the moment he descended from the embankment to the river's edge. Still enveloped in darkness, the riverbank was infused with a heavy air of murderous intent. Kosaka had brought twenty of his henchmen along with him.

"You've no right to take Osei into your arms ever again."

Jinnai called out in a tone of deep vexation. Kosaka laughed mockingly. In terms of the strategy employed by brigands, nothing could have been more natural than what he was doing. To the contrary, Jinnai seemed like an absolute lunatic to appear all by himself. Jinnai was angrier at his own foolishness than at Kosaka's dirty tactics. He awoke to exactly how much he was risking just to carry out a shabby duel with this small-time crook. This aggravation redoubled his strength. In a flash, he had cut down eight men. But when he killed five more, he suddenly felt his head swim. He was unaware of just how badly he was injured and yet, with supreme self-control, he managed to dispatch four more. It had become difficult for him to stand up. His body swayed back and forth. To someone who didn't know better, it would appear that he was intoxicated. His eyes began to blur. All the same, he killed two more.

"What kind of man are you? Some kind of goblin?"

Kosaka's voice was loud with combined terror and anger. Jinnai's knife flew at Kosaka, sticking into his thigh. Jinnai had aimed at the chest, but he no longer had enough energy. The moment he released the knife, he pitched forward onto the ground. But when the last standing Kosaka minion closed in on him, Jinnai raised himself halfway up and cut the man in the side. Then he sat there cross-legged. Kosaka, too, sat on the ground with his legs thrown out, unable to move but loudly venting abuse at him. The sun rose, and when the authorities who had been out on the lookout for arsonists and night thieves descended to the river's edge, Kosaka was still cursing in a raspy voice.

Once the two men had received medical attention, they were questioned immediately. Kosaka said that his woman had been stolen, and Jinnai said that twenty men had arrived for a duel. The head official became irritated. They were Shoji Jinnai and Kosaka Jinnai, and it was confusing to have two Jinnai to deal with, he said. In a fit of pique the official shouted that one of the two should change his name right then and there. Shoji Jinnai responded immediately.

"I am reborn this moment. I now take the name Shoji Jin'emon."

Shoji Jin'emon was immediately set free, while Kosaka Jinnai was thrown into prison. Three days later, however, with the help of another group of his henchmen, Kosaka broke out of prison and escaped. Kosaka was recaptured and two years later he was crucified at the Asakusa Torigoe execution grounds—exactly as Osei had foreseen. He had become afflicted with fits of ague and was in such a state that he couldn't move. As he was passed over the bridge in front of Torigoe Myojin shrine, on the way to the execution grounds, Kosaka shouted out:

"If I hadn't been suffering from the shakes, no one would have been able to take me! Detestable!"

People would name the bridge "Jinnai Bridge" in honor of his passing over it.

SANSHU KIRA

The seventh day of the new year, Keicho 17 (1612). The retired shogun Ieyasu departed from Sumpu Castle in order to go hawking at Sanshu Kira.

The report that he would be hawking at Shimosa Togane during the first month had been false. That such a story was circulated indicated Ieyasu-Jirosaburo's great caution. His enemy was neither Toyotomi Hideyori, heir to Hideyoshi, nor any of the daimyo who had long enjoyed the support of the Toyotomi clan. It was none other than the second-generation shogun, Hidetada.

On the twenty-eighth day of the third month of the previous year, Keicho 16, Ieyasu-Jirosaburo, who was in the capital city to supervise the enthronement of Emperor Go-Mizuno-o, met with Toyotomi Hideyori at Nijo Castle. Their meeting was the result of an insistent request from Ieyasu-Jirosaburo. The daimyo Kato Kiyomasa escorted Hideyori to the meeting, a dagger hidden in his shirt, with the intention of dispatching Ieyasu if anything untoward befell Hideyori. He took an enormous risk in doing so. Another man who accompanied them was Asano Yoshinaga, who kept a constant watch in every direction. When the meeting between the two men came to an uneventful end, they both expressed their gratitude to the myriad gods and deities.

However, Ieyasu-Jirosaburo had absolutely no malicious intent in wanting to meet with Hideyori. To the contrary, he sincerely hoped to peacefully enlist Hideyori in his own camp. The eleven-year peace that had followed the Battle of Sekigahara had made the gap in military capability between the Tokugawa clan and the Toyotomi clan definitive. If they were to fight, the Tokugawa side was certain to prevail. However, if the Tokugawa won, Ieyasu-Jirosaburo would no longer be of use. It was obvious that Hidetada would have him murdered. For that reason, Ieyasu-Jirosaburo wanted to avoid a conflict and to peacefully bring the Toyotomi clan and its followers under his control. The conference between the two at Nijo Castle ended without incident, and the people of Kyoto and Osaka were said to have breathed a collective sigh of relief at the apparent arrival of peace.

Hidetada was infuriated. Even if it were a mere formality, he found it impossible to continue to respectfully bow to this low-born *kagemusha* who was a stand-in for his father. The only people Hidetada feared were a handful of military commanders including Kato Kiyomasa. This was the first time that Hidetada employed the services of the Yagyu ninja led by Yagyu Munenori. These Yagyu secret agents lived up to Hidetada's expectations remarkably well. During the sixth month of Keicho 16, they assassinated in quick succession Kato Kiyomasa, Horio Yoshiharu and Sanada Masayuki. The person most horrified by these three deaths was Ieyasu-Jirosaburo. He saw through Hidetada's intentions. The way things were going, if Ikeda Terumasa, Asano Yoshinaga, Fukushima Masanori and Maeda Toshinaga were assassinated, all of the Taiko's vassals would be eliminated—and the next to go would be Ieyasu-Jirosaburo. He would undoubtedly be murdered in a fashion that was "obviously" an assassination, and the blame would be pinned on agents of the Toyotomi clan. That would serve as an excuse for engaging in hostilities.

What rationale could be more powerful than that?

Ieyasu-Jirosaburo's faintheartedness caused him to take swift measures. To protect himself, at Tenkai's recommendation he secretly put into action a group of Takeda ninja, to whom he had been covertly paying a stipend, and at the same time, dispatched secret messengers with warnings to Ikeda Terumasa and the other three warlords. Because of this, the Yagyu agents were headed off and killed. It took two years for the Yagyu assassins finally to succeed in eliminating the four daimyo. Ikeda Terumasa escaped death until the twenty-fifth day of the first month of Keicho 18. Asano Yoshinaga lived until the twenty-fifth of the eighth month, dying at the age of thirty-eight. Maeda Toshinaga survived until Keicho 19, when he succumbed on the twentieth day of the fifth month. For the Yagyu, this was a severe setback, and to Hidetada it was so infuriating that in a pique of anger he had ordered Yagyu Muneyori to assassinate Ieyasu-Jirosaburo immediately.

The *Tokugawa Jikki*, in the entry for the first month of Keicho 19, simply records that on the sixteenth, Aoyama Narishige headed a delegation to call on Ieyasu at Kira to inquire about his health. Accompanying him were Kyogoku Wakasa-no-kami Tadataka and Kyogoku Tango-no-kami Tadatomo, who presented gifts of clothing and food to Ieyasu. It also records that Ieyasu went hawking that day. The entry conceals a shocking truth.

Needless to say, it was Hidetada who dispatched the three. Their role was to serve as witnesses—to the assassination of the retired shogun Ieyasu.

Seven carefully selected Ura Yagyu assassins had concealed themselves in the hawking grounds at Kira that day. These ninja had been summoned from Yagyu Village in Yamato province, and therefore, no one would recognize them. On top of that, in the small medicine case that one of the men carried was concealed a farewell letter written to his *father*. The father was a senior vassal of Toyotomi Hideyori and this old man, faced with having to decide whether to follow the Toyotomi or not, was under pressure to commit suicide. Needless to say, this was all staged by the Yagyu. Four of the seven were highly skilled in the use of muskets, while the other three were expert with long-shot bows. It was an almost perfect assassination plot. If Shoji Jinnai—now Jin'emon— had not strayed into the hawking grounds, the retired shogun, Ieyasu-Jirosaburo, would have met an untimely death that day, and a great battle between the Tokugawa and the Toyotomi would have ensued.

That Shoji Jin'emon realized the report of the hawking expedition to Shimosa Togane was false was due to Osei's ability to see the future.

It was the second day of the new year, *hime hajime*. They were lying together when Osei, with her usual abstract air, suddenly blurted out an astounding pronouncement.

"Something important will happen, on the sixteenth of this month. At Mikawa. You have to be there."

"Mikawa? Not Shimosa?"

"Mikawa," she replied vacantly.

Jin'emon immediately sent five swift-footed men to Sumpu to report on the movements of Ieyasu-Jirosaburo. On the seventh, Ieyasu-Jirosaburo set out from Sumpu and stayed the night at Tanaka. On the eighth, Sagara. On the ninth, Yokosuka. On the tenth, Nakaizumi. There was a blizzard, and some twenty centimeters of snow accumulated. On the eleventh, there was a day of hawking. On the twelfth, Hamamatsu. On the thirteenth, Yoshida. On the fourteenth, he arrived at Kira, where he stayed for several nights and went hawking. Apparently the hunting was good at Kira. Jin'emon joined his men at Nakaizumi on the tenth. Beginning on the fifteenth, he snuck into the hunting grounds alone, seeking an opportune moment to approach Ieyasu-Jirosaburo. Jin'emon discovered the seven concealed Ura Yagyu assassins on the following day.

Dressed as *ashigaru*, foot soldiers, the seven men were armed with muskets and bows. To the casual observer, there was nothing suspicious about them. But Jin'emon felt an extraordinary bloodthirst exuding from each of the men. Such intensity would have been entirely unnecessary if the men were merely hunting birds and wild animals. Close to the ground like a snake, Jin'emon entered the underbrush covered with lingering snow and followed the seven men. Presently the men removed their *ashigaru* attire. Underneath it was the persimmon-colored garb of the ninja. Dressed like this, they would be able to conceal themselves in the desolate hunting fields and remain invisible even at a short distance. They went into the field, and Jin'emon followed them, by slow degrees closing the gap between them and himself. Ieyasu's hunting camp was set up nearby. When Jin'emon raised his head slightly above the grass, he saw, for the first time in eleven years, Ieyasu-Jirosaburo as he slowly lowered himself onto a campstool. To one side, lowering himself onto another stool, was Tenkai. Then there were the three would-be witnesses—Aoyama Narishige, Kyogoku Tadataka and Kyogoku Tadatomo. The only others in the camp were a few members of the entourage and the falconers. The Takeda ninja were spread out on guard in a wide ring around the camp just out of eyesight. Having concealed himself in this hawking ground since the previous day, Jin'emon had full knowledge of the defense pattern that had been set up. No doubt the seven attackers had already, by sheer force, broken through the defensive ring at one point or another. The moment must be at hand. It was certain that the Takeda ninja would detect the invaders and at any moment would gather around Ieyasu-Jirosaburo as human shields.

The smell of the fuse of a musket drifted through the air. Four Yagyu aimed their weapons. Jin'emon leaped. Landing on the back of the second man from the right, he slashed the man's throat with his short blade. At the same instant, with his left hand he drew the straight sword attached to that man's back and with it sliced the right arm of the sniper to his left. Rolling to the right, he dispatched a third musketeer just as the man was aiming his musket. A deafening roar echoed, and a falconer standing in front of Tenkai grabbed his abdomen and fell to the ground. Shortly after, Jin'emon was engaging the three Yagyu with bows. Their weak point was that they had laid so much emphasis on sharpshooting that their skills with the sword were inferior. In no time, the three men were cut down. Two died immediately; one was seriously wounded. As Jin'emon was drawing a deep breath to recover, he was surrounded by the Takeda ninja.

Ieyasu-Jirosaburo remembered Jin'emon. With his aides at a distance—with the exception of Tenkai—he met with Jin'emon.

"Eleven years ago, on the way back from the Battle of Sekigahara. You're the head of that group of *yujo* we came across at Suzugamori," Ieyasu-Jirosaburo said, as if testing him.

"And before that as well. It was the summer of Tensho 17 (1589)..."

Ieyasu-Jirosaburo laughed. He neither affirmed nor refuted Jin'emon's claim.

"So then, tell me. What has brought you to this hawking ground?"

Jin'emon handed his petition to Tenkai to pass on.

"A licensed pleasure quarter? For such a trifling matter you've risked your very life?" Ieyasu-Jirosaburo said with some surprise. Without question, to the person who stood at the apex of the government, such issues as a gay quarter seemed trivial.

"I do not believe the hope expressed in this petition is of such small consequence. Upon it rests the survival of the Kugutsu clan and by extension all of those who are unbound by social conventions, all the companions of the way."

Unbound. Companions of the way. Hearing these terms for the first time in many years, Ieyasu-Jirosaburo must have felt a degree of nostalgia. His expression momentarily softened. Jin'emon passionately described their current circumstances and their predicament.

It was Tenkai who spoke next. "So, is it your proposal to create a place that has the outward appearance of a licensed pleasure quarter but is in actuality a sanctuary for the Kugutsu?"

"It is as you say, sir." Jin'emon's reply was straightforward. After so much thought, this was the daring plan he had come up with. Jin'emon had infiltrated the hunting grounds with the full determination that even if he were to be cut down on the spot, he would declare his intention clearly. Wasn't the person he would address also originally a member of the unaffiliated, a member of the companions of the way? Since the other party had experienced the freedom of the nomadic life, there should be no necessity for makeshift falsehoods or temporary expedients. If you don't like the idea, kill me. That was precisely the kind of determination that filled his entire being at that moment.

"What is your opinion, Master Mitsuhide?"

Ieyasu-Jirosaburo had not spoken inadvertently. There was a discernible intention in his not addressing the priest as "Reverence" or "Master Tenkai," but rather as "Master Mitsuhide." In doing so, he divulged Tenkai's true identity to Jin'emon, indicating that Mitsuhide was on the same side as Jin'emon, and at the same time conveying to Tenkai that he wanted to go along with Jin'emon's plan.

"Well," Tenkai smiled, gathering Ieyasu-Jirosaburo's intent, "when I wandered the world under the name Akechi Jubei, I incurred immense moral obligations to the 'companions of the way.'"

Thunderstruck, Jin'emon gazed at Tenkai. The incredible thought that had crossed his mind upon hearing the name Mitsuhide was confirmed by Tenkai's words. Nankobo Tenkai was in reality the traitor under heaven Akechi Mitsuhide!

"And permitting a modest sanctuary for women in Edo could hardly be of any harm."

Ieyasu-Jirosaburo nodded assent. This was the two men's answer to Jin'emon's bold proposal. Approached by someone who exposed his mind to full view, they had responded in kind. This was the code of the *muen no to*, those who were considered exempt from social norms and secular government, and the *michimichi no tomogara*, the companions of the way. One could go so far as to say that this was a conversation between three companions of the way. Here, there was no government, no authority, no wealth. There were just three unadorned, stalwart men. Jin'emon was genuinely moved. He shed tears in spite of himself.

"A man who cries will certainly have a hard time keeping women under control." It was Ieyasu-Jirosaburo who laughed.

Tenkai, too, laughed softly, then made a suggestion. "Let us pass this petition to Master Kozuke-nosuke—together with Your Lordship's personal instructions as to what should be done."

"Please do so. However..." Ieyasu-Jirosaburo looked at Jin'emon. "You will have to wait a year or two. Until relations with Osaka are brought to a conclusion, Hidetada will not be properly disposed."

"You are planning to launch an offensive against Osaka?"

It was Tenkai who had asked. His piercing gaze explored Ieyasu-Jirosaburo's face.

"It cannot be avoided. If I do not attack, I will be killed. I couldn't stand being cut off like that."

Ieyasu-Jirosaburo's loud laugh rang hollow in the Kira hunting fields.

A powdery snow had begun to fall across the hunting fields.

Two years passed. On the eleventh day of the tenth month or Keicho 19 (1614), Ieyasu-Jirosaburo departed Sumpu and moved toward Osaka. It was the beginning of the Osaka Winter Campaign. The following year, in the Osaka Summer Campaign, the Toyotomi clan was destroyed. The year after that, on the seventeenth day of the fourth month of Genwa 2, Ieyasu-Jirosaburo died at the age of seventy-five. He had been poisoned. On his deathbed, he entrusted to Tenkai and Honda Masazumi the document giving Shoji Jin'emon permission to establish a licensed pleasure quarter within the city of Edo. Before writing his signature and pressing his seal on the document, he took up a brush and in his own hand added something to the formal permission. The three characters which he inscribed right above Jin'emon's name read *waga do-bo*, "to my kinsman." As a result, the document read, "Herein permission for the above is granted *to my kinsman* Shoji Jin'emon." The addition of a mere three characters turned this permit into a bombshell.

Shoji Jin'emon was a member of the Kugutsu clan. To refer to Jin'emon as "kinsman" meant clearly that Ieyasu was either a member of the same clan, or at least a member of the so-called *muen no to*, those who stood outside the four classes of society. Unless Ieyasu were admitted to be a fake, Hidetada and all future shogun would be seen as having *muen* blood in their veins. From the point of view of the bakufu, which was suppressing any form of sanctuary which attempted to escape rule by any military government, and which confined any "unaffiliated" who did not fit within the class system of the Tokugawa within walls of discrimination and prejudice, this wording was explosive. It would rock the bakufu off its very foundations, and Honda Masazumi was naturally overwhelmed.

Masazumi, however, was a highly capable official, as well as being completely loyal to Ieyasu. He masterfully negotiated opinions among bakufu leaders, and in the year Genwa 3, Shoji Jin'emon was summoned to the court of the shogunate and, under five provisions, granted permission to establish a licensed pleasure quarter. In addition, Jin'emon was appointed overall headman of the quarter. The permit, inscribed with the three characters *waga dobo* in Ieyasu-Jirosaburo's own hand, was passed directly by Tenkai into Jin'emon's hands.

The skies were far away.

The winds had swept the skies clear of any sign of a cloud, and clear blue spread as far as the eye could see.

Seiichiro lay in the grass looking up at the sky, his arms crossed under his head.

Gensai sat beside him, arms wrapped around his knees. His eyes looked out on the sparkling waters of the Okawa River.

Neither spoke.

And then, still gazing up at the sky, Seiichiro asked a question.

"So that document of permission is the *Shinkun gomenjo*?"

"That's it," Gensai replied languidly.

"And the whole reason why the Yagyu are out to get Yoshiwara is those three extra characters?"

"Right."

Seiichiro nimbly pulled himself up to sit beside Gensai.

"It seems ridiculous to me."

"Why's that?"

"Well... After all, it's just a note jotted down. For such a simple reason, a lot of people are murdering one another. That's nonsense."

"So, what are we supposed to do?"

"Give it back. Either to the Yagyu or the shogunate. Even without it, Yoshiwara wouldn't be destroyed."

"You think so?"

"Of course. As long as there are men and women in this world, Yoshiwara will survive."

"You're too easygoing."

"...?"

"Yoshiwara as a place dealing in sex might never disappear. But do you really think that the shogun would leave Yoshiwara untouched as a place where the Kugutsu can live in freedom and with protection?"

"Well..."

"The shogunate won't do that. The Kugutsu would be completely driven out, the men killed and the women and children would become outcasts."

"But if you demanded as a bargaining point..."

"Do you really think that the government would negotiate over anything? Just like the Toyotomi clan, no matter what we negotiate, our clan would be wiped out, annihilated."

Once again they fell silent.

Finally, Seiichiro broke the silence.

"So, what could be done?"

"Sei-san. I want you to take over Nishidaya."

Gensai's tone deepened.

"You're the child of the retired emperor Go-Mizuno-o. You're of noble birth. I'd like you to take over as the overall headman of the Yoshiwara. That's the only way to put a complete stop to this endless bloodshed. All of us believe that's the only way."

Seiichiro said nothing.

Plovers flitted over the surface of the river. The pure white birds seemed to fly about anxiously between the blue of the sky and the blue reflected on the surface of the river. They seemed to Seiichiro just like himself.

The Sound of Trees

Shoji Jinnojo, the second-generation master of Nishidaya, was a peculiar sort. By nature, he was pudgy and of affable manner, but all day long as he sat at the clerk's desk at the foot of the stairs, handling the business of the shop, with his left hand he constantly stroked a small metal statue of a calf, called "the rubbing calf," which was enshrined on top of a futon. It was said that rubbing the small statue was a charm to pull in customers. For the first two months since Seiichiro's arrival, Jinnojo had not once dropped by the detached room where Seiichiro was staying. On the occasions when they did by chance come face to face, Jinnojo would smile cheerfully, but never once did he say more than a greeting. Once Obaba-sama departed for Kumano, however, Jinnojo began visiting the detached room with excessive frequency. It wasn't because he had any particular business with Seiichiro. He just seemed to be happy if he could sit with Seiichiro. The previous day Jinnojo had visited, telling about trivial affairs such as how at O-Miuraya a fox had eaten a hen, and today he told about a pair of twins who had been born in the dormitory at Minowa. It was always such triflings which he would chat about before taking his leave. Then, a few hours later, he would return with some new trivial tale. It was fine for other people to enjoy such chatting, but this sort of friendliness was the kind that Seiichiro was worst at. At length, his expression would go stiff with the strain.

That morning, too, as soon as Seiichiro woke up, Jinnojo had come calling, and Seiichiro was left feeling depressed. Therefore, immediately after breakfast he had gone out. When he thought about it, he had no real destination in mind, but he casually headed out the Great Gate. He walked up to Nihon Embankment, but still he had no real idea where to go. When he reached the pier at the foot of Matsuchiyama, from which they had watched Obaba-sama depart, a boar's-tusk boat which had carried off patrons returning home early in the morning was just coming back in.

"Is it all right?" he asked.

The boatman smiled foolishly and welcomed him to board. With one thrust of the pole, the boat entered the stream.

"Where shall I take you?"

"Anywhere."

Once he responded, Seiichiro realized that he had no money at all on him.

"I'm not carrying any money with me, but could I ask you to drop by Nishidaya later for it? If you'd rather not do that, you can just take me back and drop me off again."

"Don't mind at all."

The boatman shook his head as he worked his scull. The man's face was surprisingly wiry and tough. He was thirty years old or thereabouts. His body was muscular and nimble.

"There's no one in Gocho-machi who doesn't know Matsunaga-sama."

With a broad, cheerful smile, the boatman introduced himself as Kichiji.

"Looks like there's a commotion back there."

Turning around to look at the dock, he saw a group of men pointing in his direction and yelling about something. Perhaps they were the men who were secretly providing protection for him. For some reason or other, he became lighthearted.

"Don't mind them."

"They'll come after you."

Kichiji's eyes sparkled as he spoke.

The men were racing along the riverside path at a furious pace.

"Could you drop me off at some promising place? I'd rather not be overtaken."

"You really don't have a destination in mind?"

"No, I just set out on a whim."

Kichiji's eyes gave off a momentary flash. What he said next was entirely unanticipated.

"In that case, would you kindly help me pick up a little money?"

"What do you mean?"

Kichiji explained that a certain customer of his had heard rumors of Seiichiro and expressed a strong desire to meet Seiichiro if possible. The customer, who appeared to be a retired bannerman, had promised to pay him five gold *ryo* if Kichiji would fulfill his request. If Seiichiro would just wait at the bathhouse called Gohei at Yanagi Bridge, he would make the arrangements for them to meet.

Seiichiro looked fixedly at Kichiji. The proposal smelled of a trap, but for a trap, everything was too much based on coincidence. Even

Seiichiro himself had only decided to board this boat by sheer chance. In addition, if it were a trap, the other party would undoubtedly be the Yagyu. At that moment, Seiichiro was entirely willing to get into a fight that would bring physical fatigue. That would be far more refreshing than to grow weary as a result of thinking too much.

"I'll leave the arrangements to you," he replied emphatically, then lay down in the bottom of the boat.

He rested his cheek on one hand and looked out over the waves that glistened in the morning sun. He was in a good mood, feeling free for the first time in a long while.

More than ten days had passed since Gensai had implored him to take over Nishidaya. Due to the fact that he was related to the imperial family by blood, if Seiichiro became the overall headman of the Yoshiwara, not even the shogun would make a move against them. Moreover, even if the *Shinkun gomenjo* were to be made public, the mere fact of his imperial lineage would eliminate the potency of those three characters inscribed by Ieyasu-Jirosaburo. Gensai had stressed that this was the one and only way. Seiichiro felt it was a hard path to set out on, but he could understand Gensai's point. The purpose in doing so was none other than to protect the free, ungoverned society of the Kugutsu. There was ample significance in doing that, and he himself felt that he would do whatever was necessary.

But something left him feeling dissatisfied. Something in his heart wasn't clear yet. Somehow the political struggle involved in all of it left him uncomfortable. If he were being called upon to take up his sword to defend the threatened fortress of the Kugutsu puppeteer clan, Seiichiro would rally to their cause with pleasure. But when it came to the business of the imperial blood that coursed in his veins, he found it hard to go along. To begin with, was there any real meaning in lineage? What significance could there be in being descended from an emperor? Making a big deal out of something that had no meaning and, moreover, using it to gain something, left him feeling as if he were covered with grime. There was an innate scrupulousness about Seiichiro which came from growing up in the wild.

With all his heart, Seiichiro wanted to return to his mountains. He longed for the forests, the mountain streams and the wild animals there. He wanted to hear the wind blowing through the trees. Why in heaven's name had he come to Edo?

The second night Seiichiro slept with Takao, he had on impulse divulged his thoughts to her.

"How about coming with me to the mountains?"

Just talking about it, he felt as if he were enveloped in the scents of the wild.

The scent of soil. The scent of trees. The scent of the wind. The scent of nameless flowers. The thought made him quiver. In the mountains, even sunlight had a scent. A forest without a single human being. Swimming with nothing on in a deep pool in the river on a summer day. On a wintry day, by the warmth of a sunken fireplace, listening to the sound of snow falling suddenly off the roof. Step outside and see various kinds of tracks crisscrossing the snow. Rabbits, foxes, tanuki, wolves, bears, wild boars. All these different creatures coming in search of warmth and light. But not a single human footprint. Just their own mountain. Their own snow. Their own freezing wind. Just the two of them, together, beating the drum and plucking the shamisen. They could sing and dance. In spring, the young leaves of the trees would be delicate and blurred; in autumn, the foliage would set the mountains aflame. They could compose poems, write, make tea from the waters of the stream. They could drink sake with the fruits of the mountains as a side dish. They could cook rice over a fire of fallen leaves. They could grill fowl over a fire of pine needles.

As he talked on, like a man possessed, Seiichiro's cheeks glistened with tears. With a finger, Takao caught one and placed it in her mouth.

"I'm envious."

Her whisper was so soft that he barely heard her.

"What are you envious of? You would be with me."

She shook her head faintly.

"It's a dream, the dream of a dream."

"That's not true. The people of Gocho-machi would understand. Surely they would."

Growing passionate, his voice grew louder. As if she were soothing a fretful child, she embraced him. As she held him, it seemed as if she wept.

With the thud, Seiichiro unconsciously pulled himself up. He had dozed off. The boat had reached Yanagi Bridge, and Kichiji, naked above the waist, was covered with sweat.

"Go straight ahead, and just after you turn left, there's the Goe Bathhouse on the right. Tell them that Kichiji sent you, and just wait there. There's no danger. I stake my life on that."

The group of men who had pursued them had fallen five or six blocks behind. Seiichiro leaped onto the shore and took off running. He briefly considered running all the way back to Higo. The very thought made him happy.

The *furoya* was different from a *yuya* bathhouse in that it was entirely a steam bath. The bath there was closeted; the bath itself was sealed off like a cabinet and the inside was thick with steam. Once inside, Seiichiro stretched out comfortably. As a precaution, he placed his swords just outside the compartment door. There was no way that a ninja could possibly escape detection by his five senses and make off with his weapons. Seiichiro was that confident. Ordinarily swords were placed in the rack provided inside the changing room, but there were no other patrons when he entered, and the bathhouse keeper had indulged him.

The pores of his entire body opened, and oil, grime and sweat oozed out. Just as he was becoming comfortable and mellow, he heard the faint rustle of clothing. Hardly half an hour had passed since he had parted from Kichiji. It seemed far too soon for the expected retired bannerman to be showing up. In one movement, Seiichiro opened the door of the compartment, grasped both swords and stood up in the washing area. He gaped in astonishment. There, standing completely still at the entrance to the washing area, with her straight posture, was Katsuyama.

"It has been a long time," she said with a smile, as if she were truly glad to see him. She showed not a modicum of hesitation.

The signature Katsuyama hairstyle was gone, and her long black hair hung straight down her back. She wore a pure white cotton yukata with a narrow obi. The color of her well-proportioned body showed faintly through the material of the yukata. Her beauty was enough to take one's breath away.

"Sei-sama, how have you been?"

Her words were no longer in the *arinsu* dialect of the courtesans of the quarter.

"So, you are still alive."

Seiichiro's voice conveyed a depth of emotion. When Katsuyama had disappeared, dropping out forever from the ranks of the Ura Yagyu, for some time thereafter he had painfully imagined Katsuyama's figure, her corpse showing signs of having been tortured to death. That image had tormented him, because he felt at least partially to blame for what had happened. To see her safe and sound was no less than salvation.

"So, Kichiji…"

"I took care of him when I was *inside*. If it had become known, he couldn't have stayed for a single day. So he has to do anything I tell him to do."

Katsuyama smiled. In comparison with Takao, she was shameless, but as a result, there was something down-to-earth about her, something that gave her a somewhat masculine gallantry.

"Anytime is fine, I told him. If he ever had a chance to run into you, I told him to tell you I was here."

"I heard it wasn't allowed for women to work in the bathhouses anymore."

In the previous year, Meireki 2, when the government ordered the Yoshiwara quarter to move to a new location, as compensation, the government closed down all the bathhouses in Edo which employed women. All of the women who had lost a place to go were taken in by the houses of the new Yoshiwara. And it was not only the women. The owners of the bathhouses were also taken in, so that when the new Yoshiwara opened, there were an enormous number of new shops in business there.

"I'm not a *yuna*. I'm Goemon. I'm the owner of this bathhouse. We met a short while ago, remember?"

She chuckled.

Seiichiro had no idea how she could have disguised herself, but he had indeed seen the proprietor of the bath, an ugly character somewhere around fifty and moreover a hunchback. There was probably not a person on earth who could have imagined that the bathhouse owner was actually Katsuyama in disguise. That was precisely how she had survived. But in order to stay alive, she had had to spend the majority of each and every day in that dreadful disguise. It was painful to contemplate.

"Well, let's not talk of such dull matters. Let me wash your back."

"No, that's all right."

Seiichiro was flustered.

"I've already been in the bath, so how about if we have something to drink instead?"

"No. Sei-sama, you obviously don't know about the skills that a *yuna* has to offer. Soon nobody will remember why the bathhouse girls who scraped off the grime that builds up in skin were once so popular. So today, I'll show you."

Seiichiro was once again trapped within the steam cabinet. Katsuyama securely placed his swords outside the door.

"I won't attack you by surprise," she said. Seiichiro was beyond worrying.

In the dizziness produced by the steam, he realized that anyone who wanted to could try to kill him and he would be powerless to defend himself. If Katsuyama wanted to do him in, well, let her do it. Life itself was not so precious to him. The faces of Oshabu and Takao flitted across the back of his mind.

(It can't be helped. It's just the natural course of things)

Thinking this, his heart grew lighter.

Following the course of things, he had come to Edo. The same was true of his visiting the Yoshiwara quarter. His cutting down the Yagyu and being able to have dreams thanks to Obaba-sama. All of this was part of the natural turn of events. Becoming the headman of the Yoshiwara Gocho-machi, too, might well be part of that natural flow. If someone wanted to make use of his lineage, well so be it. It had nothing really to do with him. He was simply riding the drift of the tide.

He became drowsy. He was being drawn into sleep, a deep, serene sleep.

The door clattered open.

Katsuyama stood there. With the escaping steam, her white yukata immediately dampened and the shadow between her legs showed through dimly.

"You can't fall asleep."

A harsh hand grabbed Seiichiro, pulled him up and dragged him to the washing area. After she wiped the sweat from his face with a cool towel, his drowsiness finally dissipated. In due course, he was seated on a bench, and Katsuyama moved around behind him.

Her slender fingers delicately scratched his back. Instantly a shiver shot through his body. It was a feeling of such pleasure that his brain grew numb. All of his pores opened and it felt as if each and every one of them heaved a deep sigh. Her fingers moved little by little. Careful not to scratch him with her nails, she adeptly rubbed off the embedded grime that came oozing out. It was miraculous. Shivers passed constantly through his body and he groaned unconsciously. The state of rapture continued endlessly. It was as if he were afloat on a sea of ecstasy, but this sea had swells. The billows rose and retreated, until finally he thought his entire body would shatter into waves of foam. The swells moved from his bottom up his spine and finally into his arms. Eventually her body came directly in front of him. And the swells moved from his chest to his abdomen. Her back stretched to reach a small bucket of hot water. She splashed the hot water over him. A pleasant shock passed instantly through his body. The shadow between her legs turned even darker. His lips moved toward it and he sucked with all the strength he possessed.

"Ah!"

After her faint gasp, her body collapsed. Catching her as she fell, Seiichiro lay down face upward on the floor of the bath. Her white yukata spread open and the dark shadow emerged distinctly. Seiichiro sucked on it. The surges continued. Within the rises and falls, he came to his senses, then lost himself once more.

It is said that the grime removing art of enticement was handed down from the bathhouse women of Arima. This art is thought to have disappeared from Edo around this time, but in the onsen of the provinces it continued to exist. It is written in Dr. Fujinami Goichi's *Tozai mokuyoku shiwa* (Essays on the History of Bathing, East and West) that when the Meiji period novelist Ozaki Koyo visited Ogi on Sado Island, he was carried by this very art of enticement to the very edge of ecstasy.

KATSUYAMA'S END

When the tenth month—the month of the frost—finally came round, the number of days when snowflakes fluttered down from the skies began to increase. Jinnojo commented that given the sudden arrival of bitter cold that year, it seemed there would be no softly falling snow to accumulate. When it is too cold the snow freezes and dances in the air.

The first snow came on the twentieth, and sure enough, it didn't stick, and turned to ice. People rumored, shivering at the thought, that at this rate the Ogawa River would freeze early. In all the castle-toppler houses, wooden braziers were brought out, and in some houses, the proprietors crawled into warm *kotatsu* and stayed there all day long.

"I'm thinking of going to talk to Lord Munefuyu."

Seiichiro said this to Katsuyama as they lay in bed. It was after the steam bath, so they were both glowing with warmth. On this occasion they had gone into the steam compartment together and there in the steam they had made love, so Katsuyama's body, too, was so soft and hot that it seemed she would melt if he embraced her.

During the tenth month, Seiichiro had secretly visited Katsuyama's place on three occasions. This was the fourth. He could be described as harboring an extraordinary attachment. But it was neither because he was wallowing in the pleasures of her body nor because he could not forget the ecstasy of the scraping she gave him in the bath. More than anything else, he pitied Katsuyama. That a beautiful woman like Katsuyama, who could compete with Takao Tayu in her heyday, should have to disguise herself as a hunchbacked old man in order to stay alive was simply too sad for words. It was her face when she said good-bye to him—emptied of expression, as if all her feelings had been suppressed— that struck him most deeply. It wrung his heart, particularly when he was alone and thinking of her.

It was always the dead of night when he stealthily left the Nishidaya. He would sneak across the rooftops to the western edge of the quarter and from the Enomoto Inari Shrine he would jump over Ohaguro ditch and enter the Yoshiwara rice fields. Then all he had to do was to run along the Okawa riverbanks past the Asakusa Great Gate to Yanagi Bridge. On several occasions he had made a long detour, purposely going by Kan'eiji and from there crossing an alley down to Yanagi Bridge. He never took the same route twice, and he had only gone by boat that first time. He took the greatest precautions to avoid being followed. If the Ura Yagyu got wind of where she was, she would be dead. He had to be wary. He was certain that until now neither the Ura Yagyu nor the Yoshiwara men had followed him.

He had gone out in the middle of the night and returned before the break of day, but it seemed that the Nishidaya were aware that he had been out. Jinnojo came to his room one morning and seemed on the point of saying something, but finally left after offering another piece of local gossip. Seiichiro assumed that at some point, word of his nighttime escapades would reach Gensai, but he was convinced that no one would ever figure out that the woman was Katsuyama. Seiichiro was sure.

"Why would you go to see him?"

Katsuyama's expression was one of terror.

"I want to ask him something."

"What?"

"If I become the headman of Gocho-machi, would that really bring an end to all the fighting?"

Katsuyama looked fixedly at Seiichiro for a moment, but then as if in resignation, but also with resolution, she shook her head.

"I believe that Lord Munefuyu is not a man to fight when it is unnecessary," Seiichiro said.

"But now the Ura Yagyu no longer obey the Omote Yagyu. Master Gisen has nothing but contempt for his brother, Lord Munefuyu."

"Because his skills as a swordsman are inferior?"

"In swordsmanship and in the ways of stealth, Lord Munefuyu is several rungs below Master Gisen. Everyone back in the Yagyu homeland finds it hard to comprehend why Lord Munefuyu is the one who succeeded to the leadership of the Yagyu clan."

The reason was that Munefuyu had been the "safe" choice, but the majority of the Yagyu, starting with Gisen, were unable to comprehend that. Munenori had a sharp eye when it came to perceiving the character of each of his children. Munenori's own father Sesshu Sai had promoted Munenori within the shogunate, and had instead passed on the leadership of the Shinkage-ryu to Yagyu Hyogo Toshitoshi of Owari province. This was because he feared that the dark blood in Munenori's veins would defile and destroy the genuine Yagyu-ryu swordsmanship. Munenori had then applied the same principle as his father when he determined who would succeed him. Munenori's own sinister blood flowed thickest in Gisen.

In battle, use every cowardly, despicable means available, but win every time. This inordinate obsession permeated the sinister, dark blood within the family. All of the fearsome hidden techniques of the Ura Yagyu sprang from this tenaciously held belief. This kind of swordsmanship was not justifiable for single combat or for use in protecting oneself. It was entirely aimed at assassination and massacre. Had Gisen become overall head of the Yagyu, it would have led inevitably to the demise of the Yagyu clan and, by extension, to Yagyu-ryu swordsmanship. Regardless of how powerful it was, if it were detested by the public, denounced and hated, as a form of swordsmanship it would not spread. It would thrive on the dark side of life, but it would not survive on the side of the world in which the sun shines. The only one among them who had not once taken the life of another, Munefuyu was the only one who possessed the brightness of spirit suitable for becoming the head of a school of swordsmanship.

It is not easy to comprehend such an ironical logic, but that is precisely how the Yagyu family was composed. In order for the clan leader Munefuyu never to kill, Gisen and those under him had to continue their butchery. In order to maintain Munefuyu's brightness, Gisen lived his life covered with blood. That was what Munenori was demanding of them. Gisen's misfortune was that he did not have the ability to understand his father's intent, nor, ultimately, the ability to accept it.

"You think it's a waste of time? I really would like to hear how Lord Munefuyu judges the situation."

It seemed that Seiichiro was unable to give up on the idea.

Suddenly Katsuyama threw her warm body on top of his.

"What's wrong?"

Seiichiro spoke as if he were taken aback, but Katsuyama was silently engrossed in that movement. She moved recklessly as if she had suddenly foreseen their impending separation.

Outside the Goe Bathhouse, in the darkness, snowflakes fluttered down from the skies.

Wearing an unusually severe expression, Gensai took Seiichiro out of Nishidaya for a walk. Even though Jinnojo had dithered about, playing the fool in hopes of lightening the mood, Gensai didn't break a smile.

"Let's go out," he said brusquely, before falling into a moody silence. Under the cheerless, leaden sky, they passed through the Great Gate, along the embankment and down into the precincts of Saihoji. That was where Seiichiro had first crossed swords with Gisen.

Dotetsu's chanting of the sacred name of Amitabha flowed so

constantly as to make one drowsy.

Leaving Seiichiro waiting outside, Gensai entered the prayer hall without asking permission, and quickly returned carrying his short and long swords. Measuring his footing, he unsheathed the swords with a swish, and like a sacred phoenix spreading its wings, he raised the swords to left and right in readiness.

"This is called *Shichiseiken*, Sword of the Seven Stars."

It was an ancient form transmitted from Shandong, and there were eight forms, including *Shichiken teiboho, Jusanken* and *Nijuyonken*. Gensai-Shoji Ji'emon had learned the Sword of the Seven Stars from his father, Matazaemon.

Seiichiro braced himself, his eyes riveted on Gensai. In the next second, a tremendous murderousness attacked Seiichiro. By mere inches, he parried a blow just over his head, barely escaping Gensai's ferocious attack. His lack of alertness came from his careless expectation that Gensai was simply showing him a stroke form. But without the slightest interval, Gensai attacked him again with both swords. With difficulty, Seiichiro manage to evade the blows. He had still not drawn his own weapons. He was afraid that if he inadvertently blocked strikes with his own sword, the thrust of the pliant Chinese blade might very well bend inward. Seiichiro believed that in this unceasing attack from Gensai he was seeing every single one of the twenty-four strikes of the Sword of the Seven Stars. It was an exuberant form of swordsmanship, but underneath it lay an unsparing cold-bloodedness. The strikes bespoke absolutely no emotion, but were determinedly calculated. As evidence of this, Gensai's eyes were absolutely calm, as if he were incessantly calculating how his opponent might draw, how he would move, how much strength he would exert, and, in response, how he himself would press forward or draw back with maximum effectiveness. Seiichiro awakened to the fact that as long as that expression showed a total lack of emotion, he had no chance of winning. If at all possible, he wanted to draw forth a look of astonishment from Gensai.

After displaying all the twenty-four strokes, Gensai returned to the beginning once more. In that instant, Seiichiro, with lightning speed, moved inside the gap between the two swords.

"Aaah!"

Gensai instantly abandoned his intended jump backward. Gensai had seen that Seiichiro's right hand was grasping the hilt of his sword.

If Gensai launched himself backward, in all likelihood he would be cut down with an upward stroke of his own sword. All the strength drained from Gensai's body.

"That's the problem," Gensai spit out, as he picked up his sheaths and put away his swords.

"What is?" Seiichiro asked.

"You're too strong, Sei-san. That's why you think that no matter what happens, you'll somehow manage."

"That's not so."

"No, it's true. That's why you're strolling around at night by yourself."

So that's it, Seiichiro thought to himself. He knew after all. That was why he was in such an unpleasant mood. But in the next moment Gensai said something that stunned him.

"It's true that Katsuyama is a good woman. But your life is too high a ransom to pay to redeem her."

"How did you know?" Seiichiro asked, with a gulp.

"You don't have any other women. Besides, Oshabu was saying that you return in the morning smelling of Katsuyama."

Seiichiro blushed. Now he knew why Oshabu, who had watched out for him so attentively, had not been dropping by to check up on him at all.

"Apparently Kichiji the boatman is Katsuyama's guide, but Gen'i is Sei-san's bodyguard. Recently the old man's eyes have become fixed, and he keeps saying that if anything happens to Sei-san, he'll have to cut his stomach open. And if that happened, young men would die, too. All told, there would be about fifty dead."

Seiichiro gave up.

"Tell old man Gen'i that I'll be going out today, too, so please guard me to his heart's content."

"In the middle of the night, as usual?"

"No, in the early afternoon. I'm going to the Yagyu main residence."

Gensai's eyes widened.

Upon hearing Seiichiro's question, Munefuyu fell silent. He closed his eyes, and with his hands still resting on his knees, he almost seemed to have fallen asleep. That he was not asleep, however, was evidenced by the faint twitching of his left eyelid.

Seiichiro did not repeat his question, but sat composedly waiting for Munefuyu to speak.

Munefuyu suddenly broke the silence.

"Something happened the other day."

He had gone up to the castle, and after speaking with the family of the shogun, he had completed his responsibilities and was stepping out into a corridor when a priest came up to him and said that someone named Sakai was asking to see him. These days, the name Sakai had to mean a senior councilor of the shogunate: Sakai Tadakiyo. The former chief councilor, Sakai Tadakatsu, had retired from his position the previous year.

Sakai Tadakiyo was born in the first year of the Kan'ei era (1624) as the heir of the illustrious hereditary vassal Sakai Utanokami family. His grandfather Tadayo had exercised considerable influence as the closest adviser to Hidetada. But during the rule of the third shogun, Iemitsu, he had fallen from favor as a result of the Nishi-no-maru Fire Incident and had died in despondence. The fire had occurred on the twenty-third day of the seventh month of Kan'ei 11, while Iemitsu was away from Edo at the capital in Kyoto. Tadayo had been left with the responsibility for the castle in the shogun's absence, and he took responsibility for the fire by secluding himself in Kan'eiji. It was this latter action that infuriated Iemitsu, who felt that the fire itself was a variety of natural calamity and not Tadayo's fault. He rebuked Tadayo saying it was absolutely outrageous for him to abandon the castle in his lord's absence and seclude himself in a temple. A castle without a commander in charge could easily be taken by someone who decided to attack. By the end of that year, Iemitsu's displeasure with him had subsided, but his influence had immediately declined, and within two years he died. His son Tadayuki succeeded to the fief of 102,500 *koku*, but a mere eight months after his father's death, Tadayuki died at a youthful thirty-eight years old. Responsibility for restoring the fortunes of the Sakai clan then fell on the shoulders of Tadayuki's son, Tadakiyo.

At a mere fourteen years of age, Tadakiyo became the lord of a hereditary fief of some 10,000 *koku*. Following Iemitsu's death, he became responsible for the disposition of top-secret shogunate documents, and two years later in Jo'o 2 (1653), that is to say four years before the present moment, he rose to the position of senior councilor within the shogunate. At that time he was only thirty, youngest of all the senior councilors.

It was this Sakai Tadakiyo who was summoning Munefuyu.

"I wish to hear about the *Shinkun gomenjo.*"

Munefuyu was aghast.

The recovery of the *Shinkun gomenjo* was a personal order from Hidetada, and the bakufu itself was not involved at all. There were only five men who knew of the license's existence: Hidetada, Honda Masazumi, Tenkai, Yagyu Munefuyu and Jubei Mitsuyoshi. Hidetada had been deeply afraid that the secret of the *Shinkun gomenjo* might be discovered by others. On his deathbed, Hidetada had told Iemitsu alone about the existence of the document and its contents and had enjoined him to retrieve it with great secrecy by whatever behind-the-scenes strategy was necessary. Iemitsu had promised to do so, but he was not zealous in implementing this inherited duty. In fact, Iemitsu had liked Ieyasu more than Hidetada, his own father. And the Ieyasu he liked was in fact Ieyasu-Jirosaburo.

That Iemitsu had become the third-generation Tokugawa shogun was due to this Ieyasu-Jirosaburo, Tenkai and the wet-nurse Kasuga no Tsubone. And the latter two were half-hearted about pursuing this particular matter. Iemitsu had not passed word of the matter to anyone prior to his own death. The fourth-generation, Ietsuna, was only eleven years old when he rose to become shogun. By that time, there could only be two people who knew about the *Shinkun gomenjo,* Yagyu Munefuyu and Gisen. And yet—this youthful senior councilor also knew!

Tadakiyo wore a somewhat sinister smile.

"You are of course aware that before I became a senior councilor I was in charge of the confidential documents of the shogun. At that time I found a document concerning the conflict between the Yagyu and the Yoshiwara over the *Shinkun gomenjo.*"

It's a lie! That was Munefuyu's intuitive response.

The expression *Shinkun gomenjo* was not something that would appear even in ultra-secret documents. He had to have heard about it from Gisen. Gisen must have been trying to draw closer to this young successor in whom he had detected ambitions for power. If Hidetada's deathbed injunction became null and void, in this peaceful era, the very existence of the Yagyu clan—particularly the Ura Yagyu—would become meaningless. That had to be the reason why Gisen had used the *Shinkun gomenjo* as bait—to get Tadakiyo to issue another directive to retrieve the document. Tadakiyo's avaricious expression indicated that he had swallowed Gisen's bait in one gulp.

"I responded that the Yagyu clan had no knowledge of such a document, and managed to deny everything," Munefuyu muttered somberly.

Seiichiro said nothing.

None of the Yoshiwara people were aware of how abruptly circumstances were evolving. Munefuyu's disavowal was meaningless to Sakai Tadakiyo. Rather, it was easier to cut off the Omote Yagyu altogether and make use of the Ura Yagyu alone. That was far more expedient for his own ambitions. But if Munefuyu had real ability as head of the Yagyu clan, that would not be possible. The Ura Yagyu had been forbidden to move without the permission of the Omote Yagyu. But Gisen thought nothing of such a prohibition. To the contrary, he might become intoxicated with being the leader of the Ura Yagyu if it were completely cut off from the Omote side of the clan. There was only one path left for the Yagyu clan to take—kill Gisen. And yet...

"I myself cannot kill Gisen as he is now. It is a regrettable thing to admit, but it's true."

A lonely smile crossed Munefuyu's face.

"Now that things have come to this pass, all I can do is to ask you. I'd like to ask you to kill him—for the Yoshiwara, and for the Yagyu clan, too."

And then the commander-in-chief of the Yagyu clan, still seated formally, bowed deeply to Seiichiro.

When Seiichiro emerged from the gate of the Yagyu residence this time, the entire landscape was mantled in silvery snow. It had begun to fall during his long discussion with Munefuyu.

There was no sign of any of the men who had supposedly been protecting him. The men were all ingeniously concealed, to the point that it was astonishing. The only one who was supposed to be waiting for him in front of the Yagyu residence was Nomura Gen'i. But now suddenly there were two men. Gensai had appeared.

Under other circumstances, Seiichiro would have laughed and

thought to himself that he was being treated like a child, but in this case, he did not have the leeway to respond so casually. He was troubled by how to convey what he had learned from Munefuyu—and what to do about it. But when he saw the expression on Gensai's face as it turned towards him, Seiichiro instantly realized that Gensai had not come to act as another bodyguard.

"Kichiji's been murdered. There are indications that he was tortured."

No sooner had Seiichiro heard this than he broke into a run. Katsuyama was in danger! If Gensai had been able to make the assumption that Seiichiro had been seeing Katsuyama, then why couldn't Gisen? It would be foolish to imagine that Kichiji would not have revealed Katsuyama's location under Ura Yagyu torture.

(Let her be alive!)

Praying to no one in particular, Seiichiro ran through the snow that floated down upon him. He didn't notice that Gensai, Gen'i and some fifty other men were also running through the snow behind him.

The snow grew heavier, and night was beginning to fall in the town.

The Goe Bathhouse at Yanagi Bridge stood dark in the thick snow. Not a person was to be seen along the embankment in the dusk and the shop was shrouded in silence. The Ura Yagyu must have carried Katsuyama off somewhere. As Seiichiro reached to slide open the door, Gensai grabbed his hand. Gensai held a finger to his lips. Sure enough, as he calmed himself, he too could hear the faint sound of someone breathing. But there was something abnormal about it. It was the breathing of someone on the verge of death. Seiichiro pushed Gensai's hand aside and opened the door with a clatter. Nothing happened. He entered roughly. Gensai and Nomura Gen'i followed. Gen'i turned back and silently signaled to the fifty men outside to search the surrounding area. They scattered. In that instant, a cry like that of a wild beast arose.

"Ohhh!"

It was Seiichiro. He stood petrified in the entrance to the washing area.

In the center of the floor was Katsuyama. Completely naked. Both arms and even her legs spread wide. After a closer look, one could see long nails holding the palms of her hands and the insteps of her feet to the wooden floor. It was an absolutely gruesome sight. There was not a single wound on her face, but her breasts had been cut out and her ribs showed through. The place between her thighs had been cut out with some kind of razor-sharp blade and it was a mass of bleeding flesh. And ominously thrust inside her was a thick, dark metal rod. The flesh surrounding her vagina was hideously burned, evidence that the bar had been red hot when it was rammed in. It was quite likely that the top of the rod had pierced the uterus and entered the abdominal cavity. That blood continued to flow from the corner of her mouth was proof. There were no other wounds on her entire body, not even a drop of splattered blood. It was white as porcelain, as if it had purposely been wiped clean. That made the sight all the more blood-curdling.

But the most inhuman part was that Katsuyama had been left alive. What sent shivers down Seiichiro's spine was the fact that she had been left in a condition from which she absolutely could not recover, her most important part as a woman completely ravaged, and yet she had been left without a finishing blow. The only conceivable reason for this was to seal her heart up with despair. He could clearly visualize Gisen's expression as he with relish slowly but steadily shoved the burning iron rod into her. The expression on Gisen's face, as Seiichiro pictured it, said he'd be damned if he let her die at once, that a quick death was far too easy.

This was no simple execution, Seiichiro thought. It was an act of evil that went far beyond the conditions that allowed one to be called human. It was the vomiting up of all the vile, black blood that had built up in the vital organs of the heathen demon called Gisen.

(Unforgivable, Gisen!)

To allow such a vile act to go unpunished would make Seiichiro an inhuman fiend as well. At that moment and for the first time, Seiichiro determined to kill Gisen, and the Ura Yagyu as well. It was not for the Yoshiwara, for Munefuyu or even for the way of the sword. Seiichiro had to kill Gisen to prove that he himself was a human being.

Katsuyama murmured something. He bent down and leaned close to her. He could hear clearly, one word at a time, as she forced them out.

"Gunpowder. Hurry. Compartment. Wall. Move. Riverbank. Gisen…"

"Gunpowder?!"

Thunderstruck, Nomura Gen'i looked around.

"The compartment wall is an exit!"

Gensai was already opening the door to the bath. The trapped steam floated softly out.

"Matsunaga-sama!"

Gen'i tried to hurry him up, but Seiichiro didn't rise to his feet. With tremendous strength, his fingers were pulling out the nails that pierced her hands and feet. He intended to carry her out. But Katsuyama shook her head.

"Kill me. Quickly."

"Katsuyama! Forgive me!"

She shook her head once more. And astonishingly, a smile passed faintly across her face.

"Hold me."

Seiichiro lifted her, embraced her, and kissed her mouth. She tasted of blood. Without hesitation he swallowed it. Katsuyama stretched her arm around his neck and whispered.

"Kill me. Don't let…anyone…see me."

Seiichiro nodded. All he could do was nod. Still embracing her tightly, he unsheathed his short sword.

"I fell in love…with you."

For the first time in a long while, she reverted to the language of the women of the quarter. Seiichiro was overcome with heartrending sorrow. Various images of Katsuyama during her time in the quarter flitted across the back of his mind. Katsuyama when she slowly and softly stroked his hand on the bench at *machiai-no-tsuji*. Katsuyama with the hems of her kimono flying as she raced toward him to warn him in the alleyway.

And then. Swallowing his tears, with perfect accuracy, Seiichiro thrust his sword into her heart. When her head fell back, for a brief moment, she smiled.

"Sei-san!"

Gensai's tense voice called out to him. The wall of the bath swiveled around, and snow immediately blew in.

Seiichiro gently lay Katsuyama down and in a single breath leaped out into the snow. Gensai and Gen'i were right behind him. The instant they landed like three cats in the snow, the Goe Bathhouse exploded in a ball of fire with a deafening roar.

That day Gisen had mobilized fifty Ura Yagyu. Twenty Yagyu ninja were ordered to deal with the Yoshiwara fighters and the other thirty were to handle Seiichiro and Gensai. The moment the explosion went off, the twenty ninja attacked the Yoshiwara troops. The remaining thirty lay flat on the ground on the riverbank, observing Seiichiro's movements.

Gisen's misfortune was in the falling of the snow and the fact that his own men were attired in black. The Yagyu had reversed their clothing at the Goe Bathhouse and were wearing black ninja attire, anticipating that the battle and flight would occur at night. But in the dim light that remained and the falling snow, they stuck out like a flock of large crows. In terms of sword technique, the Yagyu were superior to the Yoshiwara fighters, but the latter had a special weapon: blowguns that shot darts. The Yoshiwara men fought in groups of three, and one in every three used a blowpipe. The black clothing that the Yagyu wore made them easy targets for darts. The darts didn't have to strike a vital point. All they had to do was strike some point of the body, because the tip of each was dipped in deadly poison. Darts came at the ninja from everywhere, from blowguns invisible in the falling snow. The Yagyu fell, their expressions that of men betrayed.

The black-clad ninja lying beside Gisen looked at him inquiringly. It was Sagawa Shinzaemon and he was pressing for sending in reinforcements. Gisen paused a moment, then nodded. It was a fatal mistake that Gisen would forever gnash his teeth over. In the instant that Sagawa and ten new men on the riverbank stood up, white shadows appeared from behind them on the right, blasting at them like a blizzard. There were three shadows—Seiichiro, Gensai and Gen'i. Crouching in the snow, they had been trying to detect Gisen's location. It all came about because Gisen and his men had overlooked the trapdoor inside the compartment bath. They were by now halfway certain that the three men had fallen in the explosion.

A snow of blood fell. The ten Yagyu were immediately cut down. That day, Seiichiro's sword was murderous. He himself had been transformed into a killing machine. He entrusted defense to his unconscious instincts and devoted his entire conscious awareness to cutting men down. There, too, the black-clothed men were at a disadvantage, because Seiichiro did not have to worry about accidentally cutting down one of his own men. Immediately sending the remaining twenty men against the three,

Gisen regretted bitterly having enjoyed so greatly what he had done to
Katsuyama. It was obvious that the atrocity committed on Katsuyama
was what had transformed Seiichiro into this raging *Ashura* spirit. But
that was not the end of it. Gensai's Sword of the Seven Stars and Gen'i's
Rokuji-ryu swordsmanship were so ferocious that they were virtually
unassailable.   Seiichiro's own wrath had possessed them, too. What
was worse, Gisen felt that all of the Yagyu men found their opponents'
rage to be only natural. Not all of the Yagyu warriors felt their leader's
brutality had been justified. Some of them had averted their eyes from
start to finish, while others had grown nauseous. In a way, one could
say that they all felt some guilt for what had been done to Katsuyama.
And every single one of them could *understand* the white-hot sharpness
of the three men's swords. In battle, one who understands his assailant
dies. It is self-explanatory. Sagawa Shinzaemon rushed up to Gisen. One
cheek had been deeply slashed by Gensai's Chinese blade.

"Boss!"

He shook his head sideways, a signal that the battle was lost. It was
not an Ura Yagyu strategy to fight a losing battle. If they were losing, they
would immediately turn tail and run. There was no disgrace in escaping,
as they would win another day. Gisen blew the bamboo whistle that hung
from his neck, a signal for retreat. Just as he was about to board a boat he
had arranged for himself in case of a retreat, he came to an abrupt halt.
A man stood blocking his escape route. It was Seiichiro. The swords that
hung down from his hands were dripping with blood.

"Yagyu Gisen!"

Seiichiro's voice was low, but it penetrated the air.

"No mercy today."

Seiichiro's words were distinct. Sagawa launched a furious rapid
attack, but was easily repulsed. When Yagyu men tried to come to the
aid of their leader, Gensai and Gen'i held them in check. The Yoshiwara
warriors closed in.

"No aid required!"

As he shouted, Gisen drew his sword. What he said wasn't directed
toward his own men. It was intended, rather, to call off Gensai's group,
especially the blowgun men. One on one, Gisen still had a chance of
winning. At the very least, there was a significant chance that he would
be able to flee. Just as he had thought, Gensai and Gen'i held off their
own men. The surviving Yagyu rapidly jumped into boats and pushed

off into the current of the river. They did so believing in Gisen's prowess. A leader with the soul of a demon would certainly not be bested by a swordsman possessing an ordinary human soul, no matter how expert he might be.

Gisen lowered the tip of his sword—the *jizuri-no-seigan* position. It was a posture for defense. For the first time in his life, Gisen was frightened. Seiichiro was the man who had artlessly defeated the supposedly undefeatable *Koran no jin*, and the one who himself made use of one of the Yagyu-ryu hidden techniques—*gyakufu no ken*. One could only assume that Seiichiro was considerably accomplished in the other techniques of the Yagyu-ryu. Gisen couldn't use any of the deceptive techniques that the Ura Yagyu had developed on their own against this particular opponent. In the instant such a deceptive strategy was penetrated, he might suffer a mortal wound. During the past two months, Gisen had been frantically mastering the Niten'ichi-ryu style. After all, a swordsman who has mastered one school's techniques found it comparatively easy to master the techniques of other schools. The fundamentals were the same. At this point Gisen had mastered the two-sword technique so that not even Sagawa Shinzaemon could defeat him. That was something Seiichiro did not know, and it was the one element that could possibly lead to a victory for Gisen.

Seiichiro had cast aside all techniques. He stood with one sword in each hand, allowing them to hang loosely at his sides. It would be the flashing speed of the attack that would determine the victor. And the speed of the attack would come from innate ability combined with persistent training. Seiichiro knew that the only other necessity was an imperturbable state of mind, one that would allow that inborn talent and constant training to go into action. As always, he consciously relaxed every part of his body, naturally assuming the *yoroboshi-no-kamae*.

The *jizuri no kamae* slowly rose up, becoming a *chudan-no-seigan* posture. Then it rose further, not stopping until the sword was in a full *daijodan-no-kamae*—the sword held high over his head in a posture of threat. Gisen was measuring his breathing. The direction of the wind was to Gisen's advantage; the driving snow was striking Seiichiro straight on. Seiichiro's body was wavering. At first, it was only a faint movement, but it gradually grew more noticeable. Gisen was still unable to grasp the *yoroboshi* stance. He saw the wavering as a method of measuring breathing.

Suddenly, the wind stopped. The snow stopped hitting Seiichiro's face and, instead, fell straight down. Seiichiro's wavering, however, had not stopped. Gisen felt he had lost something with the change of the wind.

Now!

Leaving his long sword overhead in just his right hand, Gisen drew his short sword with his left. It was a two-sword stance.

Unconsciously Gensai let out a yell. Gisen's move was entirely unexpected.

That was precisely Gisen's intention. But it was Seiichiro who had to be shocked. In that instant, Gisen's long sword had to come crashing down and slice open Seiichiro's skull.

However…

In that instant, completely unconsciously, Seiichiro drove in his long sword. Without raising it aloft, he had attacked with just a twist of his wrist in a move faster than the eye could catch. Completely betraying Gisen's expectation, Seiichiro's long sword struck at the elbow of Gisen's right arm, which held the long sword overhead. Gisen's forearm, still gripping the sword, flew off into the snow. From Gisen's throat came a cry like that of some eerie bird. The body of that eerie creature soared up high into the air as if in pursuit of its lost arm and fell with a great splash into the waters of the river. A great one-winged crow sank into the icy river.

He did find it painful. After all, he shared flesh and blood with his younger brother. But he could not disguise a stronger feeling, one of enormous relief.

With cold eyes from which emotion had been extinguished, Munefuyu looked down at the recumbent figure of his brother. A night had passed since his brother, missing an arm, had been brought into the Yagyu main residence. Gisen had lost a lot of blood, and the physician who looked after him seemed doubtful about his survival, but Munefuyu was sanguine. He knew it would take more than the loss of an arm to kill Gisen. In fact, it was unfortunate that he hadn't died. This brother of his had constantly exposed him to danger. In particular the recent episode in which Gisen had approached the head of the senior councilors, Sakai Tadakiyo, and attempted to make the Ura Yagyu independent was to Munefuyu, as commander and head of the Yagyu clan, quite impossible to forgive. But now, that was over.

In the Ura Yagyu swordsmanship, which uses the group to suppress the individual, there was one fatal flaw. If a superior leader was lost, the others immediately scattered. Matsunaga Seiichiro had taken precise aim at that chink in their armor. Without Gisen, the Ura Yagyu were, in the final analysis, no more than a disorderly mob, not enemies of the Omote Yagyu. In terms of swordsmanship, Sagawa Shinzaemon, who sat at the foot of Gisen's cot, was the best of the Ura Yagyu. But Sagawa, a country samurai from the neighboring Itahara Village, hardly had the makings of a leader.

Gisen opened his eyes. He gazed blankly in the direction of Munefuyu and spoke bluntly.

"Brother, are you going to kill me?"

Munefuyu smiled faintly. It was a callous smile, one that would send a chill up the spine of anyone who saw it.

"That won't be necessary. Not with that arm."

Gisen's expression contorted. He attempted to move his right arm, which was thickly wrapped in white cotton cloth. It was cut off cleanly, just above the elbow.

"Where's my arm?"

He addressed the question to Sagawa.

"At the bottom of the Ogawa River. Someone said they saw that old man fling it in there."

"Shall we dredge the river bottom, Rokuro? Even if it won't do you much good now, it's yours."

Upon hearing Munefuyu's sarcastic comment, Gisen turned away and stared fiercely at the ceiling.

"Once your wound heals, go back to Yagyu Village. And don't leave there as long as you live. Stay there and devote yourself to maintaining the graveyard at Hotokuji."

Gisen did not respond. In effect, there was nothing he could say. If he muttered so much as a single word of defiance, his older brother would kill him. As he was then, he had no strength to escape a blow from Munefuyu, and even if Sagawa Shinzaemon were to defend him briefly, it was obvious that he would be immediately surrounded and slaughtered. The moment he had opened his eyes, Gisen had detected a murderous air filling the entire room.

"Munefuyu now commands the Ura Yagyu," the older brother

announced. "I expect you have no objection."

Gisen remained silent. That meant that Munefuyu now commanded both the Ura and the Omote, making him true commander-in-chief of the entire Yagyu clan. Under his leadership, the Ura Yagyu would simply die out gradually. The secret agreement with Sakai Tadakiyo would come to nothing. In an age of tranquility and peace, there would be no role for the Ura Yagyu to fill. Complete hopelessness crashed down upon Gisen's heart. Just one single strike of a sword! All because of that stroke, much had been lost and he had fallen into dire straits. He thought with hate of Matsunaga Seiichiro. Rather, he thought with hate of Seiichiro's swordsmanship.

(No matter how many years, how many decades it takes, I'll vanquish that sword. Even if I have to call forth every demon in the hells of the universe, some day, some day…)

Gisen did not realize that his own face had changed into that of a ferocious demon.

(*Ashura!* Rokuro remains an *Ashura* forever. And his target, Matsunaga Seiichiro…)

Munefuyu stood looking darkly at the fiendish expression on his brother's face. Then his eyes turned toward Sagawa. The man was intently awaiting some form of counterargument from Gisen. In Sagawa's mind, there was no thought other than himself becoming the new leader of the Ura Yagyu.

He waited for Gisen to tell him to do just that.

"Sagawa."

Munefuyu's tone was harsh.

"You have permission to found a new school of swordsmanship."

"Huh?"

Sagawa wore the slow-witted, brazen expression of an ignorant peasant. It was an expression Munefuyu detested.

"From now on, you are prohibited from calling yourself a member of the Yagyu."

Unless he came right out and said this clearly, the thick-headed man would not catch on. Sure enough, a look of astonishment appeared on Sagawa's face.

Gisen intuited the crisis that Sagawa faced. If Sagawa resisted, he would be cut down. Gisen also knew that Sagawa was incapable of grasping that. The only way to save Sagawa from the crisis was for Gisen to say something himself, and he did so without delay.

"Name it the Kokage-ryu. Make it the 'old' shadow school to contrast it with the Shinkage-ryu."

Munefuyu looked at Gisen with a wry smile. It was the first time he had observed this brother of his standing up for a subordinate.

ITEZURU: FROZEN CRANE

"Matsunaga-sama has become a puppeteer's doll."

That was what the people of Nishidaya were whispering among themselves. It was only natural, because, since Katsuyama's violent death, there had been a drastic transformation in Seiichiro's countenance and behavior. He had lost all emotion, and more ominously, all vitality. He seemed like a mere shell of his former self.

He never went out. He sat alone in his detached room within the Nishidaya, gazing at the small inner garden. Despite the cold, he refused a brazier, instead sitting in a room cold enough to serve as an icehouse. If a meal was brought to him, he would eat it, but it seemed as if he might not eat for days if left on his own. He drank no tea at all. He didn't bathe or shave. The stubble that grew on his face further concealed his expression and he became evermore puppet-like.

But if someone had told Seiichiro that he seemed devoid of emotion, he would surely have been taken aback. It was just the opposite. He felt as if he were nothing but emotion. Absolutely helpless, he was held hostage by emotion. What he felt was remorse. Strong feelings of contrition had formed an enormous lump of ice that completely filled his heart. Nothing would melt it.

Seiichiro had not been consumed with love for Katsuyama. In terms of feeling charmed, he was more charmed by Takao. But Katsuyama had been different from Takao in one respect: she had faced unimaginably harsh circumstances, having to disguise herself as a hunchbacked old man simply to remain alive. More than anything else, Seiichiro was moved by pity for the situation she found herself in. He simply could not cast her aside. That was why he continued to see her. And by going back and forth to see her, the feeling that Katsuyama relied on him grew, as did the pain of parting from her each time. It became necessary to visit her more and more frequently. It seemed almost as if he were being drawn deeper and deeper into a morass. In the end, Katsuyama had been brutally murdered.

On one occasion, Gensai had made a comment to him.

"Thoughtless sympathy is mischievous. Night and day, we have to pray to the gods and the buddhas for forgiveness because we are made of nothing but cruelty and heartlessness. That's all we can do. And we shouldn't do anything more than that."

And Gensai had said something more.

"It's wrong to be kind. Every time you have an encounter with a woman, Sei, you think about casting everything aside for her. Well, I guess, after all, that's a man's gentleness coming through. But if you do that over and over again, will there be anything left? It's not just a matter of there being nothing left of you, Sei-san, but of the woman either."

Gensai had been right. The woman couldn't hold up either. More than anything else, Katsuyama's violent end had been proof of that.

Seiichiro faulted his own self-indulgence. It was a self-indulgence that could not be forgiven in a swordsman. As a result, he had lost Katsuyama. It was like losing an arm. Like Gisen. But, no, if it had been his own arm or leg, it would be endurable. When it was someone else's life that was lost, what was there to do?

Some would say that it was too late to feel remorse. But it was precisely because it was too late, that he felt regret. Precisely because what he had done could not be undone, he was so tormented, that his face could reveal no emotion at all.

Actually, remorse was not the only thing that was eating away at his heart. There was also an intense loathing of the unsightly ruthlessness that lurked behind the gentleness and beauty of the human world. The slimy hands of power maneuvering in the shadows. Its strength and cruelty, which no ordinary person had a chance of opposing. It was absolutely unbearable. Katsuyama, Takao and Oshabu—they were infinitely gentle and beautiful—and so sadly fragile. One who wanted to protect such delicate, fragile beauty had to throw off his own gentleness and become as cruel and vicious as his opponent. In order to triumph over a barbarous enemy, one had to transform oneself into exactly the same sort of *Ashura*. But didn't that mean degenerating into depravity?

Aspiring to a beautiful, graceful eternal paradise, and to degenerate into a fierce *Ashura*. Could such a contradiction be possible?

He wanted to throw it all off. Just discard everything and go back to the mountains. But something powerful was standing in the way of his doing that. It was that stubborn lump of remorse inside him. Seiichiro was unable to move at all. He simply sat there in his room at the back of Nishidaya nursing that lump of regret.

Shoji Jinnojo came rushing into the drawing room.

"Today he's like a crane that has frozen!"

The usual group of five was assembled in the second-floor drawing room of O-Miuraya: Gensai, Shirozaemon, Gen'i, Sannojo and Genzaemon.

Jinnojo had been given strict orders to come every evening to report on Seiichiro's condition that day.

"A frozen crane? What does that mean?"

It was the corpulent Miuraya Shirozaemon, wearing heavy layers of clothing and sweating profusely, who had asked.

"Like this," said Jinnojo, standing on one leg and crossing it with the other. "He's just like this—for two hours. Doesn't that seem a bit strange?"

Jinnojo seemed on the verge of tears.

Shirozaemon looked at Gensai.

"It's just a variety of seated meditation—nothing to worry about."

With Gensai's reply, the others seemed relieved.

Jinnojo, however, still seemed unconvinced.

"So, you think it's okay to just leave him alone like that?"

"Yes. That's the only thing we can do."

Gensai's tone and expression were glum.

"But it's been nearly ten days now."

Shirozaemon's voice was filled with apprehension.

"Just let him be. What's ten days or a month? For that matter, it may even take a year, or two years. One way or another, he'll recover. He's that kind of man."

Shirozaemon shook his head as is in disbelief.

"But all that...over just one woman..."

"He's made of different stuff than all of you. Sei-san has a tender heart."

"In that case, he certainly wouldn't be suitable for a *keiseiya* proprietor."

It was true that if he were too tender of heart he would make a poor proprietor of a house of castle-topplers.

"Of course not! Do you really think that a man with the character of a proprietor could become the chief headman of Gocho-machi?"

Gensai had exploded in irritation.

"To be truly tenderhearted is to taste your own emotions down to the last drop. When you're happy you're so happy that others start to feel happy. When you grieve it's so deep that the people around feel like crying. Suffering means falling to the very bottom, and moaning and groaning. Only one man in a hundred, or even a thousand, can go that far. In most cases, a man will compromise halfway and fake his way through. But Sei-san isn't half-hearted."

In the end, Gensai himself was in tears, but even so, he was complaining out loud. Tears flowed endlessly down his cheeks.

Everyone had become hushed.

"It's all right to cry. Go ahead and cry. If you just let it all out, things will be a bit better. But, that man—he can't do it. It's so hard. It's unbearable. If I could, I'd change places with him."

It was such an emotional outburst, it was hard to believe that it had come from a man who was past eighty.

Far away at *machiai-no-tsuji*, there was someone who saw Gensai arguing vehemently in her mind's eye, just as clearly as if Gensai had been right in front of her. It was Oshabu. In addition to the arts of forecasting the future and reading the minds of others, this peculiar young girl had also mastered the art of seeing through physical obstacles. She had discovered this ability only after her first period had arrived, and she had learned how to use it.

She may have looked like any other sweet young girl, sitting quietly on the bench at the intersection and dangling her legs, but her eyes reflected more level-headed intelligence than that possessed by most half-hearted adults.

It was this Oshabu who sighed.

"Five years... Even if it were just three years..."

She heaved a deep sigh.

Suddenly her eyes changed color. What appeared so abruptly in her eyes was an astonishingly mature expression of jealousy.

"The only thing to do is to ask Takao-sama. It's frustrating, but it won't do to be jealous. That's what Obaba-sama said."

She was trying to convince herself of this, but she couldn't quite carry it off. She shook her head violently. Her black hair swayed back and forth.

The following day, Seiichiro went to see Takao. It was the result of Oshabu's persistence, the sense that she had set her heart on it. By nature, the young girl had curious powers, but when she pestered and begged him, her hands placed on his knees, Seiichiro hadn't a chance of refusing.

For the first time in a long while, he went to the bathhouse. He went to a barber, had his beard shaved and his hair tied up properly. It was Oshabu who pulled him along by the hand from place to place. Seiichiro was like a puppet on a string. It didn't take much to return him to his usual clean-cut appearance, but even then, there was something lacking. More than anything else, he lacked vitality. There was no animation. His expression was stiff, and even a bit edgy. Finally, still dragged along by Oshabu, he went to the *ageya* Owariya Seiroku. At the doorway, Oshabu grasped Seiichiro's fingers tightly, and in the effort to conceal her tears, she rushed off with her sandals flopping.

Takao was dazzlingly beautiful as always. Just by her presence, the dimly-lit reception room became bathed in resplendent brilliance, like that of the sun. For Seiichiro that night, Takao's radiance was hard to bear.

"As usual, you're absolutely radiant."

To Takao, his words seemed to contain a reproach. Katsuyama had died so wretchedly, but you... That was the way he had seemed to say it. But Takao said nothing.

"Sei-sama, you've become thinner."

That was all she said. Sake was poured, and the party proceeded at an unusually fast pace to a conclusion, whereupon she led Seiichiro to the bed chamber. In the Yoshiwara quarter, such a rush to the bed chamber was called *tokoisogi suru*, and it was something only the most boorish would do. In this case, it was Takao who brought it off.

Seiichiro had no desire to go to bed. From the beginning, he had intended to stay up drinking all night. Takao said nothing, simply pouring sake for him with a gentle, soft manner. Seiichiro said not a word, either, simply emptying one cup of sake after another.

He had no idea how much time had passed, or how much sake he had drunk. His upper body wavered slightly. He felt as if the lump of ice that had settled in his chest had risen upward into his throat. The effort it was taking to swallow it was shaking his body.

"Rest your head..."

Takao's voice was filled with unbounded tenderness.

"Let it all out, here in my lap."

With thorough gentleness Takao drew his head onto her thighs.

"Let it out, just as you would in your mother's lap."

Her hand slowly and softly stroked his back.

All of a sudden, that icy lump gushed forth in the form of bitter weeping. Seiichiro contorted himself in her lap and wept uncontrollably. As he cried, he felt the lump within his chest begin to melt little by little.

"Go ahead. Cry. Cry until you don't feel like crying anymore."

With an expression like Kanzeon Bosatsu, the Bodhisattva of Compassion, she continued caressing his back.

It is said that for every man, the lap of a prostitute transforms itself into the lap of his mother. It is also said that when a man takes himself off to a prostitute, he is searching for the figure of his mother. Seiichiro did not know his own mother, but even so, at that moment the warmth of Takao's lap was as he imagined his mother's would be. For the first time since he had stabbed Katsuyama's breast with his own hand, the frozen lump within his chest partially melted.

As the gray light of dawn began to lighten the translucent paper of the sliding *shoji* of the bedroom of the Nishidaya, Oshabu smiled sweetly.

DANCE OF THE PUPPETEERS

The wind was crying.

There was still time before sunset, but the area was already in twilight. An icy wind whistled through Nakanocho.

It was *shiwasu*, the twelfth month, and that morning the employees of Nishidaya were clamoring over the fact that the Ogawa River had finally frozen over.

In the early afternoon, Seiichiro went out to take a look at the river himself, and had just returned. For some reason he had not felt like heading toward the Nishidaya, and instead he sat down on the wind-swept bench at *machiai-no-tsuji* and absentmindedly let time pass.

As a result of crying to his heart's content upon Takao's lap, the icy lump of remorse had for the most part melted. Regret was gradually turning into resignation. But at the same time that the ice was melting, another feeling was beginning to eat away at him. It was a strong feeling of abhorrence toward plunging himself into the cold-blooded, inhumane world of the *Ashura*, Lord Buddha's demonic protector against demons. With a loud, crunching sound, its jaws gripped his heart with unbearable force. Whether he was awake or asleep, it continued to grip his heart like starvation itself. Run away, run away from it, his instincts shouted, but something prevented him from doing so. What prevented it, Seiichiro could not comprehend. In his frozen heart, there was now a passionate irritation. He wanted to know, by whatever means necessary, exactly what it was that was holding him back against his will. There seemed to be any number of clues, but whenever he reached out to grasp one, it disappeared. The effort was endless and wasted.

"Recently, he's begun to have the look of a wolf..."

Just as Jinnojo had reported to the group of five, Seiichiro's features had grown increasingly gaunt, his jaws had become sharply pointed, and his eyes were piercing. It truly seemed as if he were on the point of attacking some quarry.

The wind whistled again.

Seiichiro casually stood up and walked aimlessly away from the bench. His irritability simply would not allow him to stay in one place for very long. He walked along Nakanocho, where the lights were gradually being lit, and turned off to the left making his way into a back alley. Somehow the back alleys seemed to suit him at that moment. As he meandered, he came out onto a narrow path covered in planking. There were wooden doors with a red paper lantern hanging in front of each of them. On each lantern in a virtually indecipherable scrawl was the character *tsubone*. If he had stood in the middle of the path and held his arms out, his fingertips would have touched the wainscoting on either side. That's how narrow it was. The planks creaked under his feet. These were *kirimise*, cheap markets of human flesh, where for a low charge—and in a short time—one could settle the matter. It was the particularly notorious section of the *kirimise* area known as Rashomon Riverfront. On his first night in the Yoshiwara quarter, this was where Gensai had brought him. They had gone round from one place to another, drinking and listening to the endless complaints of women past their prime. Since that first night, he had not set foot in the neighborhood.

"Oh."

He heard a woman, and when he turned around, he saw it was chubby Oren. Seiichiro remembered how she had twisted her body like a young girl when Gensai had pressed her to divulge her actual age. She was a fifty-three-year-old apparition of a woman. Seiichiro came to a halt.

"You're Oren, aren't you?"

"Ah...yes."

The cheeks of the woman blushed brightly at his unexpected recognition of her.

"Could you serve me a few drinks?"

"Why...of course!"

She came toward him with unconcealed excitement. A pink blush spread from her neck down to her breast.

"With just you would be fine too, but I'm feeling really gloomy, and if it's all right, I'd prefer to drink with many people. Of course, I'll pay for everyone."

Oren was momentarily disappointed, but she quickly recovered and hurried off to summon the women.

It was a curious drinking party. The partition in Oren's small shop having been removed, a dozen or so women of a certain age piled in, as well as five hard-up *kirimise* proprietors. They all sat around in a circle under a paper-covered lamp, with a few small side dishes, drinking sake. Sake bottles were constantly passing from person to person, as were plates of things to nibble on. From start to finish, Seiichiro was silent, but those who had gathered paid him no attention at all as they talked loudly with one another.

In the beginning, he thought that he was being ignored as a glum patron, but eventually he came to realize that the circumstances were completely different. Their drinking, eating and chatting away, leaving Seiichiro to himself, was their way of showing sympathy for him. Each person in the room understood his pain. They understood it not simply as knowledge but they felt it with their hearts, their skin and their bones. Women who had had only bad luck with men—but who could not live without men. Brothel owners at the very bottom of the ladder trying to support those women's feelings and help them earn a little money, while they themselves eked out a meager living for themselves. Each and every one of them in the shop had been hurt time and time again, and each had endured suffering so bitter that they could not share their feelings with anyone. That was why these men and women possessed hearts that understood Seiichiro's pain as their own. They had the tenderness to just let him be and not bother him. Seiichiro was on the verge of tears. He remembered being wrapped up in this sort of gentleness several times before.

Suddenly within his heart he let out a cry of astonishment. The beasts! The wild animals in the mountains of Higo. He couldn't remember how many times as a child he had been saved by their gentle eyes. Their unspeakable gentleness was of the same nature as the tenderness hidden within the boisterousness of these people surrounding him. The darkness of this *kirimise* was exactly like the dark cave on Mt. Kinbo in Higo. Just like the cave, before the snow came, when the freezing wind outside was howling. Again, tomorrow, he would have to break through the ice before he could draw water... There was a feeling of serenity, the same kind of peace of mind he had felt in the mountains. Why did he have to return to Higo? Now that he thought about it, where he was right then was not so different from the mountains. Now that he listened, he might be able to hear the sound of the wind blowing the trees against one another. Right then, Seiichiro cried. Wrapped in gentleness, he was crying with deep emotion.

"Let me join you."

It was Gensai. A large gourd filled with sake hung from his hand.

"Of course."

Seiichiro smiled with tears still pouring down his face. Gensai scratched his head self-consciously.

"Actually, I've brought someone with me—if you don't mind, of course."

"You've brought a woman? Damn you!"

Oren shouted at him jovially.

"Yes, but she's not my woman. I swear. I promise you!"

"In that case, we'll let you off. But something's suspicious about this."

The women all laughed uproariously.

"Come on. They say it's okay for you to come in."

The moment Gensai turned around to speak to his companion, she came straight in. The one who stood in the narrow doorway was Takao. Now every woman in the room was speechless. It couldn't, shouldn't be the glorious Tayu Takao appearing in a low-class *kirimise*. With a small drum in her hand, she made a slight bow.

"Excuse me for intruding."

She spoke easily and entered the small shop. Immediately sake cups were passed and filled. The gathering grew even more lively. They began to sing, and one of the proprietors began tapping a bowl in rhythm.

All of a sudden, the sound of the shamisen playing *Misesugagaki* broke out. It was time for Yoshiwara to open for business. Seiichiro listened to the sound of the music with a feeling of excitement.

"Sei-san."

Gensai's voice was low.

"When we Kugutsu are sad, or when we're heartbroken, we dance. A lively place befits sadness more than a quiet one."

Seiichiro nodded unconsciously.

"How about it? Want to try it? Why not dance, all through the night, until the crack of dawn?"

"Let's do it."

Seiichiro stood up. He had no idea of any dance forms, but it didn't matter a whit. Something welled up within his breast. It was an impulse, an urge, that made him feel like he would go out of his mind if he didn't do something.

"'That's what I wanted to hear!"

With a yell, Gensai jumped up and right out the door, still barefoot. Gensai danced, and Seiichiro followed behind, imitating him. Takao joined in, and all the kirimise women did, too. They became one long procession of dancers. Moving to the music of *Misesugagaki*, they danced from Kyomachi Nichome to Suidojiri, then reversed course toward Nakanocho and the Great Gate. As they progressed, the number of dancers grew. The *tayu, koshi, yarite* and *kamuro*, and even proprietors, night watchmen, fighters and clerks—a huge number of dancers was caught up in the throng. And in the middle of them, shoved and pushed along, Seiichiro danced with abandon.

(What could be wrong with falling into the world of the *Ashura*?)

As he danced, he reached a resolution.

(I shall gladly fall into the *Ashura* and cut down demons—if it is for such wonderful creatures)

Large drums, small drums and flutes joined with the shamisen of the *Misesugagaki*, and the timeless dance of the puppeteers raged on and on, throughout Gocho-machi.

TOSHI NO ICHI: THE YEAR-END FAIR

On the seventh day of the last month of the year, the Ogawa River froze over once again.

"Why on earth is it necessary to set out on a day like this?"

Sitting on the bench at *machiai-no-tsuji*, with a scarf wrapped around his neck and even his nose, Miuraya Shirozaemon complained to Gensai.

"You're absolutely right. Going off like this, just when the long-awaited Kannon Year-end Fair has come round."

It was Nishidaya Jinnojo who complained with a snivel.

Gensai replied wryly, "No point in telling me. If you have a problem tell Sei."

"That's out of the question! How can we complain to the chief headman?"

In a great flurry, Shirozaemon shook his head repeatedly at the very idea. With each movement, even covered with thick clothing, his massive body could be seen shaking back and forth. Dressed for travel, Seiichiro emerged from the Nishidaya holding Oshabu's hand.

The *Toshi no Ichi*—the Year-end Fair—at Sensoji was, long ago, held on the third and eighth, or on the ninth and tenth, of the last month of the year. By the time of the new Yoshiwara, it was always the seventeenth and eighteenth. Held at the end of each year, the merchants who gathered dealt in the essential items for greeting the new year. In the beginning of the Edo period, the market at Sensoji was the only one in the entire city. Needless to say, people came from all over the city of Edo, and there also gathered at the market farmers from all over the surrounding plain, hoping to buy things that they would need in the coming year.

On those days, it was customary for the various daimyo, bannermen and large merchants to dress several of their household servants in leather half-coats, and have them carry large woven baskets and large oblong chests to the shops they regularly patronized to buy necessities for celebrating the new year. In the new Yoshiwara, the headman gathered those around him and sent them off in great style. They packed new year's goods into the large woven baskets decorated with masks of plump-faced women, all in hopes of bringing good business in the coming year. They would make the rounds of the same shops every time, Namiki Mannenya, Ueno Hirokoji for duck noodle hotpot, Komagata for river trout, Bakurocho for noodles in soup with duck meat. The grand banquet was both a festive custom and a display.

Among the items for sale at the fair itself were everything from sacred straw festoons to wooden pestles, flint and steel, pairs of long metal fire tongs. Then there were the phallic symbols that were displayed in the small offices of the bordello owners and the large stylish battledores that the women wanted.

Needless to say, the fair filled the precincts of Sensoji, but stalls also spilled out over Senso Bridge with stalls lining both sides of the road in Kuramae and Komagata, continuing all the way along Namiki boulevard to Kaminari Gate. The shops and stalls also extended from this gate to Hirokoji, Taharamachi and Inarimachi, all to the way to Yamashita in Ueno. The market flourished in all directions.

The day was also a red-letter day for the new Yoshiwara. In contrast to the usual days, it was expected that a large number of patrons would pack the shops from midday onward. That day only, the *Misesugagaki* would not wait until the evening but would commence at one in the afternoon, as was agreed on by the community leaders.

It was two o'clock on that busy day that Seiichiro set out. His destination was none other than the capital, Kyoto.

The day following the wildness of the puppeteers dance, Seiichiro had announced to Gensai that he had decided to succeed to the Nishidaya, and hence to the headmanship of Yoshiwara Gocho-machi. Gensai and the other leaders were ecstatic. To the Kugutsu puppeteer clan, the son of an emperor was incomparably more significant than a shogun. Throughout the Middle Ages, the "companions of the way" had invariably held some position in the service of the imperial court. Because they performed this service, they had been granted the privilege of permits to move around at will throughout the provinces. Furthermore, the *muen no chi*—the mountains, plains, rivers and seashores—were places of safety and refuge for them because these lands were originally recognized as belonging to the emperor. They could not be violated by local power figures. The Kugutsu clan were members of these "companions of the way," and the imperial presence stood in the absolute center of them. Seiichiro, who carried in his veins blood of the imperial family, had agreed to become the head of the entire Yoshiwara, that is, he was head of all the Kugutsu. It was only natural that they should cry with joy.

But before becoming the chief headman, there was something he needed to do. It was to get the imperial court to explicitly recognize his lineage. To do that, he had to go to the capital. Through the auspices of some intermediary, he would have to call on the retired-emperor Go-Mizuno-o and offer the evidence of Miyamoto Musashi's testimony and the "Demon Cutter" blade. Seiichiro's purpose was not to have the retired emperor recognize him as an imperial prince at this late date. It would suffice if the emperor simply said, "You seem like my dead son." It would open old wounds and surely the bakufu would be dismayed, but there would be little it could do. The bakufu would simply have to be satisfied with keeping matters from becoming public. Even if it were to be treated extremely confidentially, every member of the bakufu leadership would learn about it. Even though Sakai Tadakiyo was head of the senior councilors of the shogunate, he would hesitate to put pressure on the new Yoshiwara with the "dead son of the retired emperor" serving as its headman.

Purposely selecting the day of the fair for Seiichiro's departure was actually Gensai's idea. He had decided that such a crowded day would help to conceal Ṣeiichiro's departure from the men of both the Ura Yagyu and Sakai Tadakiyo. To detect Seiichiro, wearing one of the concealing hats, in the midst of the festival throngs would be like trying to locate a single grain of gold among the sands of a seashore. To protect him, Gen'i and Yoshiwara men had already gone ahead dressed in everyday attire. Once they reached Kawasaki, the plan was for them to change into a variety of traveling outfits and unobtrusively protect him from front and rear as he made his journey.

"Well then."

With these brief words, Seiichiro parted from them. Gensai, Shirozaemon, Jinnojo and Oshabu all bowed slightly.

It had been arranged that they would go no further than *machiai-no-tsuji* to send him off. That way they avoided attracting the attention of the secret shogunate police agent at the *menbansho* at the Great Gate. With a senior councilor as their enemy, it was necessary to take every precaution with any and all vassals of the shogun.

At a leisurely pace, Seiichiro walked under the Great Gate and started up the gentle slope of the Fifty-ken Road.

Suddenly from all the houses in the entire Yoshiwara there arose the sounds of shamisen playing *Misesugagaki*.

Seiichiro stopped and turned around. The new Yoshiwara spread out beneath him. The buoyant sound of *Misesugagaki*—concealing a boundless loneliness—stirred his heart. Takao's face flitted across the back of his mind. The night before, he had slept with her for the last time. It was agreed among the leaders of Yoshiwara that the chief headman of Gocho-machi did not sleep with *oiran*. Takao cried and clung to him the entire night.

"I've fallen in love with you."

Katsuyama's voice came back to him. The sound of *Misesugagaki* resounded as if with forlorn sadness and sorrow.

(What have I been doing until now?)

Seiichiro's cheeks were wet. He recalled clearly how he had wept in exactly that same way on that first day, exactly four months earlier, when he had stood on that slope and heard that music for the first time.

THE END

ABOUT THE AUTHOR ·

Nominated for a Naoki Award, *The Blade of the Courtesans*, late-blooming novelist Keiichiro Ryu (1923-89)'s debut work, instantly made him a doyen of historical fiction. Prior to his debut, he had been first an editor and later an acclaimed screenplay writer. Although his meteoric five-year career as a novelist ended with his untimely and much-lamented death, with just a handful of works he won a firm place in the pantheon of a highly competitive industry teeming with storied luminaries. An influential voice, Ryu is especially credited for bringing unprecedented numbers of younger readers into the rich folds of the samurai drama.